VICTIM
2117

ALSO BY JUSSI ADLER-OLSEN

Stand-Alone Novels

The Washington Decree

The Alphabet House

The Department Q Series

The Keeper of Lost Causes

The Absent One

A Conspiracy of Faith

The Purity of Vengeance

The Marco Effect

The Hanging Girl

The Scarred Woman

VICTIM 2117

A Department Q Novel

Jussi Adler-Olsen

Translated by William Frost

DUTTON

DUTTON

An imprint of Penguin Random House LLC
penguinrandomhouse.com

LIBRARY OF CONGRESS CATALOGING-IN-PUBLICATION DATA
has been applied for.

9781524742553 (hardcover)
9781524742577 (ebook)

Printed in the United States of America
10   9   8   7   6   5   4   3   2   1

Dedicated to Sandra

The Fingers of the Drowned

The life
of the hands
of the drowned
is
longer than our history
far away
and so close
we see the drowned
see their longing
for life and peace

every day
we see the tips
of their fingers
disappear into the ocean
but our eyes
have not learned to see

their fingers emerge
from the ocean
stretch
toward the sky
they are no longer wet
the fingers of the drowned
are forever dried up.

—Falah Alsufi, poet and
quota refugee from Iraq

VICTIM
2117

PROLOGUE

A week before Assad's family left Sab Abar, his father took him to the Saturday market with its bustling throng of stalls with chickpeas, pomegranates, bulgur, brightly colored spices, and cackling poultry awaiting the ax. He laid his hands on Assad's slender shoulders and looked at him with deep, intelligent eyes.

"Listen well, my son," he said. "You will soon dream of what you experience today, and there will be many nights like those before the hope of reliving these sounds and smells dissipates. Take a good look around you while you can; keep what you see in your heart and you will never lose it completely. This is my advice to you, my son. Do you understand?"

Assad squeezed his father's hand and nodded as if he understood. But he never understood it.

1

Joan

Joan Aiguader wasn't religious. Quite the opposite, in fact; he left town when the Easter processions with their black-robed Catholics invaded the Rambla, and he was also someone who collected irreverent statues of popes and the three wise men defecating. But despite this blasphemous tendency, he had nevertheless crossed himself numerous times over the last few days, because if God did exist after all, then he had to be absolutely sure to be in his good books due to the unfortunate turn things had taken.

When the morning mail finally arrived with the long-awaited envelope, Joan crossed himself again, because the contents would come to shape his destiny. He was sure of it.

Now, three hours after reading the letter, he was sitting at a café in the Barceloneta district, shivering in the heat, devastated and devoid of his spark. For thirty-three years he had lived with the ridiculous hope that luck would favor him at some point or other; after this, however, he didn't have the energy to wait any longer. Eight years ago, his father had tied an electric cable around his neck and hanged himself from a water pipe in the building where he worked as the administrator. His small family was devastated, and even though his father had never been a carefree man, they didn't understand why. From one second to the next, Joan and his sister, who was five years younger, were suddenly left alone with a mother who was never quite herself again. Joan tried his best to be there for them. Back then, he was just twenty-five and working himself to death studying journalism and holding down numerous small jobs to try to make ends meet. But the following year was the final turning point in his life, when his mother took an overdose of sleeping pills, followed by his sister a few days later.

It was only now, in hindsight, that it made sense that he couldn't deal with any more. Somewhere along the way, the Aiguader family had slowly lost its perspective on life. Darkness had claimed them all. It would soon be his turn. So apart from short-lived moments of happiness and minor victories, it was a life of damnation. And in the space of just a month, his girlfriend had left him and his career had been flushed down the toilet.

Fuck it. Why torment yourself when everything was so meaningless?

Joan put his hand in his pocket and glanced over at the waiter behind the bar.

Would it be too much to ask to end my life with an iota of self-respect intact and pay for my coffee? he thought, staring at the dregs. But his pocket was empty, and the failed projects and ambitions of his life came back to him in an endless loop. All his bad relationships and constantly dwindling low standards had suddenly become too difficult to ignore.

He had reached rock bottom.

Two years ago, when another deep depression had taken root, a fortune-teller from Tarragona had told him that he would shortly find himself with one foot in the grave but that a light in the middle of the day would save him. She had seemed very convincing, and Joan had clung to her prediction—but where the hell was the light? He couldn't even leave the café with dignity. He couldn't even pay the couple of euros for his cortado. Even the filthy beggars sitting on the pavement with outstretched hands at El Corte Inglés could scrape together the cash for an espresso; hell, even the homeless dressed in rags and sleeping rough in bank doorways accompanied by a dog could manage that.

So even though the fortune-teller's intense gaze had seduced him and given him hope for the future, she had been terribly wrong. And now the day of reckoning had arrived. That was a certainty.

He sighed as he looked down at the café table and the pile of envelopes lying there—testimony to the corner in which he irrevocably found himself. He could, of course, ignore the reminder letters at home, because while he hadn't paid his rent in months, the insane Catalonian tenancy laws meant he couldn't be thrown onto the street. And why should he worry about the gas bill when he hadn't cooked a warm meal since Christmas? No, it was the four envelopes in front of him that had pushed him over the edge.

As far as his relationship with his ex was concerned, Joan had repeatedly repented, promised stability and improvement, but his earnings had never materialized, and in the end, she had had enough of supporting him and told him to take a hike. In the weeks that followed, he had kept the aggressive creditors at bay with assurances that when he had received payment for his four latest essays, he could easily pay them all. Wasn't he in the process of writing a collection of brilliant texts? Why shouldn't he believe it?

And here on the table were the rejections, which weren't hesitant, vague, elusive, or indirect but heartless and to the point, like when the matador in "Tercio de Muerte" thrusts his *estoc* into the bull's heart.

Joan raised his cup to his face to enjoy the faded aroma of his coffee while looking out over the beach with its palms and the throng of colors exhibited by the bathers. It wasn't long ago that Barcelona had been paralyzed by a madman's crazy driving on the Rambla and the central government's slaughter of normal citizens in front of the voting stations, but this all seemed to have been pushed to one side now, because the sight that greeted him through the shimmering heat was a throng of happy people. Their heads were filled with their own chatter and shouts, sweaty skin and sensuous looks. For the moment, the city seemed to be reborn—almost scornful—while he sat in vain looking for the fortune-teller's glowing star.

The distance from the café where Joan was sitting to where the children were playing on the edge of the beach was tantalizingly short. In less than a minute, he would be able to run past the sunbathers and into the water, dive under the foamy waves, and inhale quickly and definitively. With the buzz of activity on the beach, no one would take notice of a crazy guy throwing himself fully clothed into the water. And in less than one hundred seconds from now, he would be able to leave his life behind him.

Despite his heart's beating ten to the dozen, Joan laughed bittersweetly at the thought. Those who knew him would find it unfathomable. A weakling like Joan Aiguader committing suicide? The dull, anemic journalist who didn't have the balls to speak up during a discussion?

Joan weighed the envelopes in his hand. Just a few hundred grams' extra humiliation added to the rest of the shit life had thrown at him, so why cry about it? He had made his decision. In a second, he would tell the waiter that he couldn't pay and make a run for it toward the beach, ignoring the protests behind him, and execute his plan.

He had tensed his calf muscles and was preparing to make his move when a couple of guests dressed in swimwear stood up so abruptly that they toppled their barstools. Joan turned to face them. One of them was staring blankly at the TV screen hanging on the wall while the other one scanned the beach.

"Turn it up!" the first guy shouted at the screen.

"Hey, look! They're right down there on the promenade," the other one shouted, pointing at a mass of people gathering outside.

Joan followed his gaze and spotted the TV crew that had positioned themselves in front of the three-meter-high pillar the municipality had erected a few years ago. The lower part of the pillar was metal but at the top, four numbers were lit up on a digital counter. Joan had long since read the text on the pillar that explained that its purpose was to keep count of the refugees who had drowned in the Mediterranean since the start of the year.

People from the beach in swim trunks and bathing suits were drawn like magnets to the TV crew, and a few local lads strode out from Carrer del Baluard toward the scene. Maybe they had seen it on TV.

Joan turned his attention to the waiter, who was polishing glasses like a robot while staring at the TV. Text on the screen declared, BREAKING NEWS, so Joan took his chance and slowly made his getaway down to the promenade.

He was still alive in spite of everything—and he was still a journalist, after all.

Hell could wait a little longer.

2

Joan

Unaffected by the runners, roller skaters, and general commotion all around her, the female reporter stood in front of the large pillar, fully aware of the effect she was having. She tossed her hair, licked her lips, and brought the microphone up to them while the men and boys from earlier stood openmouthed, staring at her breasts. It wasn't exactly what she had to say that had attracted them.

"We don't know exactly how many have drowned escaping to Europe, which represents paradise and freedom for these unfortunate souls," she said. "But the number in recent years has reached the thousands, with more than two thousand casualties this year alone."

She turned slightly while pointing up at the digital counter on top of the pillar.

"Here we can see the number that tells us how many refugees have drowned in the Mediterranean this year right up until this very moment. This time last year, the number was even higher, and we can expect next year to be just as bad. It's thought-provoking that even though it's an unfathomable and terrifying number, the world—you and I—can look the other way without a second thought as long as these dead people remain anonymous."

She looked directly into the camera with dramatic painted eyes. "Isn't that what we—and the rest of the world in particular—do? We simply ignore it. As a counterreaction to this—you could even call it a protest—TV11 has decided to focus our upcoming reports on one of the deceased, more precisely the man whose body very recently washed ashore on a beach in Cyprus in the Eastern Mediterranean. We will show that this refugee was a real man of flesh and blood."

She glanced down at her flashy watch. "Less than an hour ago, this poor man's body was splashing around in the surf toward the beach among contented summer beachgoers, not unlike those here at Platja de Sant Miquel." She gestured with her arm at the sun worshippers to illustrate to whom she was referring.

"Dear viewers, this young man I'm talking about was the first whose body was washed up on the popular beach Ayia Napa in Cyprus this morning, and he brings the number on our counter on the beach here to two thousand and eighty. That's how many have died this year alone." She paused for dramatic effect and looked up at the counter. "It's just a matter of time before the number increases. But the first victim this morning was a dark-skinned boyish man wearing an Adidas sweatshirt and worn-out shoes. Why should he have lost his life in the Mediterranean? When we look out over the tranquil azure waves here in Barcelona, is it possible to imagine that at this very moment the same sea thousands of miles from here is crushing hopeful refugees' dreams of a better life?"

She took a pause from her speech as her producer cut to images from Cyprus. The beachgoers were able to follow on the monitor erected next to the cameraman. The sight put an immediate end to the buzz. Frightful images of the body of a young man on his stomach in the swash and then a couple of Good Samaritans dragging him onto the shore and flipping him on his back. Cut, and the monitor once again showed the reporter in Barcelona. She was standing a few meters away, ready to wrap up the report.

"We will know more about this man in a few hours. Who he was, where he came from, and what his story is. We will return after the break. In the meantime, the number behind me continues to rise." She ended by pointing at the counter while looking earnestly into the camera until the cameraman said, "Cut."

Joan looked around and smiled. This could be big! But could there really be no other representatives from the media among the hundreds of people gathered here except himself and the TV crew? Was he in the right place for once? Did he really have a big scoop?

He had never had such a strong gut feeling before.

Who could let an opportunity like this pass them by?

Joan looked up at the digital counter.

Moments ago, the death toll had been 2080, and now it stood at 2081. And like the boys staring at the reporter's breasts while she lit a cigarette and spoke with the cameraman, Joan also hung around.

Ten minutes ago, he had been determined to contribute to the statistic of people who had drowned in the Mediterranean, but now he was glued to the counter instead. The devastating number was so present and real that it made him feel faint and uneasy. He had been standing here with a childish focus on himself, filled with self-pity and defeat, while at the same time people were fighting for their lives out at sea. Fighting! The word hit him, and suddenly he understood what he had experienced and repressed. The relief brought him almost to tears. He had been so close to death, and then the light had come that had saved him. Just like the fortune-teller had predicted. The light that would give him his raison d'être; the light from the digital counter in front of him bearing witness to the misfortune of others and that now offered an unwritten and fantastic story. He saw it all clearly now.

As predicted, his foot had been pulled from the grave at the very last minute.

The next few hours were hectic for Joan now that he had hatched a plan to save his career and thereby his very livelihood and future.

He checked departures for Cyprus and ascertained that if he took the 16:46 flight to Athens, he could catch a connecting flight to Larnaca airport in Cyprus and be on Ayia Napa beach around midnight.

He stared at the ticket price. Almost five hundred euros each way, which was money he didn't have. So, half an hour after making his decision, he was forcing entry into his ex-girlfriend's grocery store. He opened the back door with the key she had been begging him to return for the last few weeks and walked determinedly behind the counter where she hid the cash in a small box under a couple of vegetable boxes.

In twenty minutes, she would return from her siesta to find the IOU he had left in the box, while at the same time, he would be at the airport with almost sixteen hundred euros in his pocket.

The screams from the beach in Ayia Napa cut through the sound of the ocean, and the foam of the otherwise dark waves was illuminated by the floodlights shining over the scene. On the sand a few meters in front of a group of uniformed rescue workers, bodies had been laid out, their faces covered by gray woolen blankets. It was an awful—but journalistically fascinating—sight.

Heavily guarded by police fifteen meters farther up, a group of twenty to thirty people stood despondent and in shock, shivering from the cold although covered with blankets—the same style as those covering the faces of the deceased. Silent tears of despair at reality's lack of mercy spread among them.

"Those standing over there are the lucky ones," someone said in response to Joan's scrutinizing gaze. "They were wearing life jackets and were fished out by the boats farther out at sea. Our crew found them just half an hour ago huddled together like a shoal so they didn't get separated from one another."

Joan nodded and took a few cautious steps forward toward the bodies. A couple of police officers made to motion him away, but when he flashed his press pass, they turned their authority and admonitions to the horde of nosy tourists and party animals who were trying to record the scene on their smartphones.

Heartless people, thought Joan as he pulled out his camera.

He didn't understand Greek, but there was no mistaking the rescue team's body language. Just now, they were gesticulating furiously, pointing at the slowly approaching waves while one of them directed a floodlight toward an object floating to shore.

When the body was twenty meters from the shore, one of the rescue workers waded into the water and pulled at it as if it were a pile of rags. As the lifeless body was pulled up onto the sand, some of the survivors began wailing.

Joan turned to face the group. The cries of anguish were coming from two women who, bent over and with their hands raised toward their faces, tried with all their might to take in what they were witnessing. It was a sorrowful sight. A man with an unkempt black beard tried ardently to stop their reaction, but his efforts did nothing to alleviate their audible despair, which only worsened when a young man with a shaved head and wearing a blue uniform jacket sprang forward to photograph the body at close quarters. He looked official and was probably there to document every rescue, so Joan photographed him and nodded to him as a precaution, hoping to give the impression that he had special permission to be there. Fortunately, there were no other journalists at the scene.

Then he turned around and shot a series of photos of the wailing women in the group; from a journalistic perspective, it always worked when you captured raw human grief—even though that wasn't his only purpose. He would do exactly the same as the TV crew in Barcelona. Uncover, detail, shock, and share.

This drowned man, regardless of how unfortunate it might have seemed, was his personal trophy; he would attempt to bring a dead man back to life—and not only for a small Catalonian readership. It would be for the whole world, just like when the three-year-old Syrian-Kurdish boy drowned and was plastered all over the world's media a few years back. Regardless of how terrible the situation was, he would shine a light on a single person's fate—and make himself rich and respected in the process. That was his plan.

He hesitated for a moment. The screams in the background were very real. There hadn't been that strength of emotion when TV11 in Barcelona had shown images from Ayia Napa. It gave that extra something, a sense of realness, everything you needed to ensure your story triumphed over the others. But confusingly, it also added something else. He knew the feeling from other situations, but he didn't think it befitted the current context. Why should he feel a pang of guilt about what he was doing? Wasn't he engaged in something very special?

The camera suddenly felt heavier. He had thought he was onto something special, but hadn't he actually just stolen the concept from TV11? Because regardless of the fact that he was researching on the scene, what made it stand out? He was just a copycat; why not just admit it to himself?

Joan shook off the doubt. Copycat, and so what? As long as he did it authentically enough, who could complain?

In a moment, when he had documented the rescue of the man's body, he would turn his attention to the crying women to try to find out why this hit them so hard in particular and whether they knew the drowned man personally: something to put the details to his identity and why he had fled. Where did those people know him from? Why had he died and not them? Was he weak? Was he a decent man? Did he have children?

Joan stepped toward the body and readied himself to photograph the man as he lay there with his head facing away from him in the swell. The man's clothes were nondescript and twisted around his body. And then one of the rescue team pulled the body out from the swash.

Joan was close to the corpse when the body was turned slightly, and what he saw made him stop abruptly. With a final jerk of the arm, the head turned to reveal that it was the body not of a man but rather that of an older woman.

He flinched. Never before had he been confronted with so present a death; it was really unpleasant. He had seen the victims of car crashes, bloodstained tarmac and flashing blue lights from ambulances arriving on the scene in vain, and in his short time as a reporter, he had also seen his share of the city's morgues. But in relation to those deaths, the fate of this defenseless woman hit him much harder. That such a long journey filled with hope had ended so tragically . . . It would surely make for an especially impressive story.

He inhaled the sea air deep into his lungs and held his breath as he looked out over the darkness of the sea to keep his emotions in check. Because in the midst of the obvious tragedy, it was without doubt a scoop that the deceased wasn't a man, young woman, or child. His intuition told him that the story was suddenly much more marketable with an elderly woman as the victim. Who could fail to see the meaninglessness and grotesqueness in this unfortunate fate? Such a long life and such a terrible end.

After a brief moment, Joan nevertheless came to terms with the situation. He turned the camera on the body and took a series of shots before turning on the video function and moving around the corpse to ensure he captured every detail before the rescue team put a stop to what he was doing.

Despite the time the corpse had been in the sea and the hardships endured on the sea voyage, it was easy to see that the woman came from an affluent home, which would definitely add to the sales and interest in the pictures. How often had people seen images of brutally exposed people in rags as testimony to the suffering of a long journey? This woman, on the other hand, was well dressed, though her fur jacket was torn and her shoes were missing. Her pale red lipstick was still visible and her eye shadow somewhat intact. Around seventy, she had been beautiful. However, one couldn't overlook the furrows that ran the length of her face and undoubtedly bore testimony of some of the trials that had led her to this desperate escape, and yet she seemed strikingly dignified. "Do we know where these people came from?" he inquired in English of an authoritative man in civilian clothes kneeling by the body.

"I imagine they're from Syria, like the flood of refugees have all been over the last few days," he replied.

Joan turned toward the survivors. Dark skinned, but only slightly darker than the Greeks, so Syria seemed like a good bet. He looked at the row of bodies in the sand and counted them. Thirty-seven. Men, women, and possibly a single child. Joan thought about the beach in Barcelona on the other side of the Mediterranean, where the figure 2117 shone in the night sky. What a senseless waste of life.

He pulled out his notebook and jotted down the date and time to at least give a sense of having started with the task that would pull him from the abyss and give him new meaning. It would be an article about the dead who were overlooked, not about a healthy adult in their prime or a defenseless child but about an old woman who had drowned moments ago. About a woman who, like the 2116 other casualties, hadn't made it across the Mediterranean alive this year.

He scribbled down his headline, *"Victim number 2117,"* and looked over at the group of survivors and the women who had screamed. There were still a lot of tormented faces and shivering bodies standing clinging to each other up there, but the two women and the man with the beard were gone. In their place stood the man in the blue uniform jacket who just moments before had been taking photos next to Joan.

Joan put the notebook in his pocket and was about to take a couple of close-ups of the woman's face when the clear, open gaze of her eyes hit him.

Why did this happen? the eyes asked.

Joan fell backward. In his world, occult phenomena were laughable, but in that moment, his body was shaking. It was as if the woman wanted to contact him. Make him understand that he knew nothing and that it wasn't good enough.

Joan couldn't tear his eyes away because these beautiful, living eyes had yet more questions.

Who am I, Joan?

Where do I come from?

What's my name?

Joan knelt down in front of her.

"I'll find out," he said, and closed her eyes. "I promise."

3

Joan

"No, you can't have your travel expenses covered as a freelancer if it isn't agreed on beforehand. How often do we need to tell you, Joan?"

"But I have the receipts here. Look, I have a complete travel budget!"

He pushed the folder with the tickets to Cyprus and evidence for all his other sundry expenses across the desk and flashed his best smile. He was more than familiar with Marta Torras's authority as an office assistant, so what right did she have to refuse him, especially now?

"Didn't you see my article on the front page yesterday, Marta? It wasn't just some column in the supplement; it was no less than the top story at *Hores del dia*—and the best I've ever written. I know for a fact that accounts will approve my sixteen hundred euros. Have a heart, Marta; I can't afford to pay the travel expenses myself. I borrowed the money from my ex."

And Joan's imploring expression wasn't just for effect. His ex had smacked him one and threatened to report him to the police. She'd called him a thief and cried because she knew that she would never see the sixteen hundred euros again. Then she had put out her hand and demanded that he return the key to her shop. And with that the relationship was no longer just finished, it was well and truly over.

"And accounts will approve this for a fact, you reckon? Ha! Well, I *am* accounts, Joan," she snorted. "And your ex must be a total idiot if she thinks you can just swan in here and demand money from the paper whenever you feel like it."

Joan was still regaining his composure as she walked back behind her desk.

"Well, at least refund my flights, Marta. The paper can deduct it anyway."

"Complain to your editor. See if that helps," she said tersely. She didn't even bother to look up.

He had perhaps expected a little applause from the editorial office. Well-deserved acknowledgment that his reporting had finally given *Hores del dia* a scoop for which they had won the recognition of the world press. The international media had even used his photos. A drowned old woman in a fur coat bathed in floodlight, the bodies on the beach, the screaming women. *Hores del dia* had probably earned a fortune from it. But apart from a young foreign correspondent who visibly shook her head as Joan walked through the cubicles of the permanently employed staff, there was no reaction from anyone. Not even a nod or a faint smile. What the hell? In films, your colleagues always stood up and clapped for something like this. What was wrong?

"I've only got five minutes, so keep it brief, Joan." His editor closed the office door and seemingly forgot to invite Joan to take a seat, which he did anyway.

"Marta from accounts has just called to tell me you want your travel expenses covered." She looked at him sternly from over her glasses. "You can forget that, Joan. You'll receive the eleven hundred euros for the Ayia Napa article that I was stupid enough to promise you when you submitted it. Not a cent more. And you should be grateful for that." Joan didn't understand. He had assumed the story about the drowned woman would result in a bonus and the prospect of a permanent job. So why was Montse Vigo, the editor in charge of freelancers, staring at him like he had spat on her?

"You've made a laughingstock out of us, Joan."

Joan shook his head. What on earth did she mean?

"Right, well then, let me fill you in about how the story of victim number twenty-one seventeen has developed. It certainly seemed like a good story yesterday. However, this morning, this was printed in at least fifty international newspapers—not to mention that every paper in Barcelona except us has the same story. The bottom line is that you didn't do your job properly, Joan. You don't even come close to your colleagues. You should've done your research when you were in the thick of it, my fine friend."

She slammed a few of the Spanish dailies on the table in front of him, and the headline nearly made him gasp.

VICTIM NUMBER 2117 MURDERED!

Then his editor pointed to a line a little farther down. "Information in *Hores del dia* about victim 2117 is incorrect. The woman did not drown; she was murdered. Brutally stabbed to death."

"You are aware that such a poorly researched story reflects badly on me," she said, brushing the humiliating pile to one side on the table. "But the fault is mine, of course. I should've seen it coming after the uninspiring features you tried to fob off on us."

"I don't get it," he implored, and he really didn't. "I watched her wash ashore. I was there when it happened. You've seen my photos."

"Then you should've waited to take your photographs until they'd turned the woman over. She was stabbed straight in the back of the neck between the third and fourth neck bones with something this long." She demonstrated the length with her hands. "Death was immediate. Thank God we aren't the only ones who've made fools of ourselves. TV11 has certainly changed its glorified images of the young man who washed ashore in Ayia Napa the day you were there. Turns out he was the leader of a terror cell."

Joan was shaken. Murdered? Was that what her eyes had told him? Should he . . . Should he have seen it?

Joan turned toward his editor. He wanted to explain the experience he'd had with the woman. Why he hadn't done his job better. That he had allowed himself to be affected and that he knew all too well that journalists shouldn't allow that to happen.

There was a knock at the door, and Marta from accounts entered the room. She handed two envelopes to Montse Vigo and left without so much as glancing at Joan.

The editor handed one of them to Joan. "Here's your eleven hundred euros, although you don't deserve it."

Joan took the envelope without saying a word. Bullying came with Montse Vigo's job, so what could he do? Nothing! He bowed a little and turned to sneak out the door. The question was how long this envelope could sustain him. He was already beginning to sweat.

"Where do you think you're going?" he heard from behind him. "You aren't getting off so lightly."

Shortly after, he was standing on the street, staring up at the building. Another demonstration was heading toward town from Diagonal with the accompanying sound of whistles, slogans, shouts, and aggressive-sounding car horns, and yet the only sound resounding in his head was what his editor had just said.

"Here is five thousand euros. You have exactly fourteen days to get to the bottom of this story, and you're on your own, got it? You're an emergency solution because none of your colleagues will touch this case. Too many leads have gone cold already. But you're going to warm them up; you owe the paper that much. Find some of the survivors who can tell you who the woman was and what actually happened to her. Understood? You know from your interviews with some of the survivors that she was with two women, one younger and one older, and that a man with a full beard was speaking with them during the voyage—right up until the inflatable raft sank. Find them. You know who they are because you have photos of them. I want daily updates about your whereabouts and what you're up to. In the meantime, the editorial office will spin the story to keep it hot. The five thousand euros will have to cover everything you do; do you understand? I couldn't care less who you bribe or where you live. If you don't have enough money for somewhere to stay, sleep on the street; if you don't have enough money to eat, starve. Do not turn up here asking for more money until the job is done, understood? This isn't *El País*."

He had nodded and felt the weight of the envelope. What else could he do but see the job through?

The five thousand euros was answer enough.

4

Alexander

Over the last few months, his fingers had become so flexible that it almost felt as if he and the control had become one flesh. For the best part of the day, his PC and the Kill Sublime universe became his only reality; the distance between him and the soldiers on the screen—and the people they killed—became all and nothing at the same time.

Alexander had surrendered body and soul to the game for more than one reason. While his high school classmates threw their graduation caps in the closet and attempted to put their exam ordeals behind them by jetting off on voyages of discovery to far-flung places such as Vietnam, New Zealand, and Australia, Alexander sought out the darkest recesses of his contempt for the world. How on earth could his idiotic classmates go globe-trotting and ignore that humans were like dirty rats whose sole aim was to dominate and eat one another? He certainly couldn't, not even if he tried with all his might. In fact, he hated everyone. If they got too close to him, he exposed their worst attributes mercilessly; this made him an obvious target for bullying and resulted in anything but contact or friendship.

No, Alexander had chosen a different path. He would live in a virtual reality and refuse to leave his room if there was a risk of meeting other people. And when the day came that he chose to leave his room, it would be the last day of his life.

It had to be that way.

For a large part of the day, he could hear sporadic noise from the other side of his bedroom door. From four in the afternoon until midnight and the following morning from six fifteen until quarter to eight, he could hear his parents moving around the house. When they finally slammed the door behind them on their way to work and all was quiet, he unlocked the door and crept out of his bedroom. Once outside, he emptied his pot in the toilet, made enough sandwiches for the rest of the day, and filled a couple of thermoses with coffee before creeping back, locking the door, and sleeping until one in the afternoon. When he woke up, he played Kill Sublime on his computer for twelve hours and slept again for a couple of hours to rest his eyes before sitting in front of the screen for another hour or two.

And so he passed his days and nights. Fire, fire, fire, while his kill count rose steadily and his win rate, which increased when he exterminated all his enemies in the game, improved day by day. If anyone could be deemed an elite player of this game, it was him.

Alexander prepared especially well for the weekends. Every Friday morning, he stocked up with plenty of oatmeal, milk, and bread and butter, and as week passed into week, he grew accustomed to the heightened rank smell from his pot until he could empty it on Monday. When his weekday routine was ruined by the bloody weekend, it meant that he could normally hear his parents outside his bedroom. Their increased fighting didn't perturb him—he almost delighted in it—but when it suddenly went quiet, he was on his guard. They would soon be outside his bedroom threatening to kick in the door and have him committed. Next was the threat to disconnect the Internet, which didn't fluster him in the least as they were equally addicted to it. Besides, they knew he had a powerful wireless modem and was capable of hacking into the neighbors' Wi-Fi if it came to it. Then the threat would come that they would stop drawing on his inheritance from his grandmother and so would no longer buy food for him. And finally, that they would bring someone to talk to him: a psychologist, a social worker, a family therapist, even his former schoolteacher.

But Alexander knew better. The way his parents' minds worked, they wouldn't want anyone to know what was going on in their quaint little yellow house in the Copenhagen suburbs. When they stood in front of his door pleading for all they were worth, fighting to regain the illusion of their normal bourgeois family life, he spat on the floor or laughed like a madman until they shut up.

He didn't give a damn how it made them feel. They had brought it on themselves. Was he supposed to cave in when his mother implored him so pathetically? What did she expect? That it would be enough to break him? That her hideous traits would simply drift away or that her desperation would eradicate all her shit? That he would forget how little she and his laughable parody of a father concerned themselves with the rest of the world?

He detested them. And when the day finally came for him to leave his room, they would rue the day they had wished him to open the door.

For at least the twentieth time that day, he gazed with a sense of plea-sure at the paused screen with its landscape of color and violence, and then at the front page of the newspaper that had been hanging on the wall for a couple of days now and had unequivocally given him the answer to how he could react to the indifference and cynicism his par-ents and their peers displayed. Because it was people like them who were the guilty ones in this world. They were the reason that there would continue to be victims like the woman on the wall.

While his parents were at work, the paper had lain unopened in the hallway, as if world events were of no concern to them, and the headline had caught his attention. The resemblance of the woman to his grand-mother hit a raw nerve, and painful memories of the closeness and care only she had given him came back with a vengeance.

When he read the newspaper article about the woman's fate from among thousands, he was overcome by an intense anger that he had observed growing inside him month by month and on which he now had to act.

Alexander stared at her for a long time. Even though death radiated from her eyes, and despite her being from a world far removed from his, it would be in her memory that he would sacrifice himself. His message would be devastating and clear. Every abuse against humanity should be severely punished.

First, he would inform the police about his mission, and when he finally made his move, it would hit the headlines.

He pursed his lips and nodded. He currently had 1970 wins. He had killed more than 20,000 opponents, and even if it took all the hours in the day, he would reach his goal of 2117 wins in a relatively short space of time. All this in solidarity with the anonymous victim on the wall, number 2117.

And when he finally reached that unimaginable number of wins, he would leave his room and avenge the old woman and all the insults to which he had been subjected, and there would be no mistaking it.

He looked over at the opposite wall where he had hung the samurai sword inherited from his grandfather, which he had honed back when he used to play Onimusha on PlayStation 2.

He would shortly have occasion to use it.

5

Carl

It was one of those paradoxical rainy days when Carl thought that the pale light through the blinds made Mona's naked flesh and the white walls glow. This morning his eyes were again caressing the grooves that gently formed between the tendons on her throat. She had slept heavily that night, as she always did when he was with her. The first months after the death of her youngest daughter, Samantha, she had sobbed constantly, begging him for daily companionship and desperately reaching out for him when he lay in her bed. Even when they made love, she cried—usually all night long. And Carl gave in to her needs.

Naturally, that period had been strenuous for them, but had it not been for him and the sense of responsibility Mona felt for Samantha's fourteen-year-old son, Ludwig, it would probably have been too difficult for her to carry on living. It certainly wasn't due to Mona's eldest daughter, Mathilde, that a more tolerable situation had begun to materialize; in fact, Mona never spoke with her.

Carl reached out for his watch. It was time to call Morten at home to make sure he was getting Hardy ready.

"Are you leaving?" said the sleepy voice next to him.

He placed his hand on her short hair, which had now all but grayed. "I need to be at HQ in forty-five minutes. Go back to sleep; I'll make sure Ludwig is up and out the door."

He got up and allowed his gaze to linger on the contour of her body under the duvet and had the same thought as every morning.

The women in his life had it really hard.

Dark clouds hung over HQ like a woolen blanket and had been there for almost a week. It was a wretched autumn that slowly but surely weighed him down on the path to the dark winter months. He loathed that time of year. Sleet, snow, and crazy people tearing about like lunatics, buying presents nobody really wanted. As early as October, the Christmas music was already blaring out, and the sea of lights and amount of plastic and glitter that was supposed to remind humanity of Jesus's holy birth were terrifying in their scale. And as if all this weren't enough, behind these gray walls a pile of folders lay on his desk as testimony to how many killers unaffected by the fir trees and Christmas decorations were on the loose in Denmark at this very moment without anyone around them knowing what they had done. It was obviously down to him alone to find the bastards.

Piece of cake, one might think. But since the case two years ago where a social worker had killed her clients in cold blood, the world had grown more twisted. Gun violence in broad daylight, lockout threats against civil servants, the burka ban, the circumcision ban, and no end of other measures that were impossible to try to administer or uphold. Colleagues who would rather enter local politics than go after tax evaders, maladjusted immigrants, and criminal moneymen. The new administrative regions that were finally starting to work and were now about to face their demise. It was time and energy spent in vain. Carl had almost reached his limit with this shit.

But who on earth would investigate the serious crimes that the people on the second floor couldn't solve if Carl suddenly threw in the towel? And the idea of stopping had already been planted. Maybe he could find work as a babysitter or a dog walker and decide for himself when to work and for whom. But then who would take care of all the bastards out there in society if everyone thought like him?

Carl wasn't sure how much longer he would have the energy to answer that question and sighed audibly when he nodded to the security guards. Everyone at HQ knew that sigh from Carl was a signal to keep their mouth shut and keep their distance, but strangely enough, it seemed like they noticed neither him nor the sigh today.

He was already aware that things weren't quite as they should be as he walked toward the basement. People were staring into space, and except for an almost nonexistent crack of light emanating from Gordon's office at the end of the basement corridor, it was totally dark. All the lights in Department Q were turned off.

Carl huffed. What now? Where the hell was the light switch? There were normally people to do this sort of thing.

He fumbled to find a switch at the bottom of the stairs, but there wasn't one. But there was a big heavy block against which he stubbed his toe and banged his knee. Carl swore and took a step to the side and then forward, stumbling over yet another large boxlike object, resulting in his slamming his head against the wall, hitting his shoulder against a vertical pipe, and falling flat on the floor.

Lying there, he let out a tirade of expletives that he hadn't even known existed.

"Gordon!" he bellowed with all his might, as he stood up and felt his way along the wall. No answer.

In his office, he finally managed to turn on a desk lamp and the PC, sitting down to rub his aches and pains.

Was he really the only one here in the department? It would be the first time that had happened in a long time.

He reached for his thermos, where on rare occasions there was a drop of coffee left over from the day before.

It'll do, he thought after shaking it and deciding there was enough for half a cup, cold or not.

From the drawer, he took out a purple cup given to him by his stepson that should never have seen the light of day due to its extraordinary hideousness. He poured his coffee.

"What the . . . ?" he said to himself when he saw the note on his desk.

> *Dear Carl,*
>
> *The archival material you requested in connection with your current case is in the hallway because the boxes were too heavy for little me to carry so far.*
>
> > *Love,*
> > *Lis*

Carl frowned. It was a bloody stupid place to leave them, but to whom could he give a piece of his mind when the culprit was the hottest woman at HQ?

Then he placed his mobile on the desk and looked at it for a moment.

Why didn't you use it when you needed some light! he thought, punching his fist on the table in frustration and causing the cup to jump and land on its side, spilling coffee not only over Lis's note but also over all the papers that he shortly had to go through, leaving them resembling something that had been dragged up through the toilet.

He sat for ten minutes staring at the soiled case files and thinking about cigarettes. Mona had asked him to stop and that was that, but the desire to fill his lungs and nostrils with smoke was uncontrollable. The withdrawal symptoms made him cranky, which Assad and Gordon knew all too well, but he had to take it out on someone over the course of the day so he was ready to meet Mona with a hint of natural positivity.

Shit! was his mantra when the urge to smoke became too much. As if that would help.

The telephone rang, taking him by surprise.

"Can you come up here, Carl?" It was a question that wasn't up for discussion. The chief constable had a voice that was unusually squeaky even for a petite woman and that, consciously or not, had the ability to make anyone feel uncomfortable.

But why was *she* ringing? Had the department been closed down? Is that why it was so dark in the basement? Or was he up for the chop? Had the decision been taken out of his hands? If that was the case, he wasn't especially happy about it.

He immediately noticed a somber atmosphere on the second floor. Even Lis seemed conspicuously gloomy, and the corridor of the chief constable's office was full of silent investigators.

"What the hell's going on?" he asked Lis.

She shook her head. "I don't know exactly, but it isn't good. Something to do with Lars Bjørn."

Carl was surprised. Had they finally dug up some dirt on the chief of homicide? It would bloody well make his day if they had.

A minute later, he was standing in the parole hall with his colleagues, who were all surprisingly expressionless. Was their budget being slashed again by the politicians? And was it Lars Bjørn's fault? It wouldn't surprise him. He certainly wasn't here as far as Carl could see.

The chief constable pushed her shoulders forward as she was wont to do in the vain hope that it could help in the struggle between the slightly-too-tight uniform blazer and her chest.

"It is my sad duty to inform you, as some of you already know, that we received a call forty-five minutes ago from Gentofte Hospital with confirmation that Lars Bjørn has passed away." She lowered her head for a moment, and Carl tried to fathom what she had just said.

Lars Bjørn dead? He might have been an arrogant bastard and always in your face, and it was also true that Carl's sympathy for the man was minimal, but he'd never wished him dead.

"Lars went for his usual early-morning run in Bernstorff's Park today and was apparently in good form when he returned home. Just five minutes later, however, he experienced breathing difficulties followed by a heart attack, which . . ." She composed herself for a moment. "His wife, Susanne, whom many of you know, attempted CPR, but despite the ambulance coming immediately and the best efforts of the cardiology department, they were unable to save him."

Carl looked around. A few of his colleagues seemed genuinely affected, but he interpreted the reactions of the majority as one of speculation: Who would be his successor?

We've had it if they choose someone like Sigurd Harms, he thought with trepidation. On the other hand, it would work out nicely if it was Terje Ploug or, even better, Bente Hansen.

Fingers crossed.

He searched in vain for Assad's face in the crowd. He was probably already visiting Rose or following up on a case somewhere. He did, however, see Gordon standing head and shoulders above everyone else at the back, his face ashen and his eyes red like Mona's when things were at their worst.

Carl beckoned him over as their eyes met.

"Naturally, we should take it easy today," continued the chief constable. "I am aware that some of you will have taken this hard because Lars was a respected leader and an asset to the force."

Carl had to bite his tongue to stop himself from an inappropriate coughing fit.

"We will have to let time heal, but over the coming days we also need to continue working at our usual pace. I will, of course, inform you as to Lars's successor as soon as possible, which will also be an opportunity to rethink procedures at HQ in the future."

Head of Communications Janus Staal was standing nodding by her side. Of course he was. Wasn't the greatest weakness of any manager the temptation to turn everything on its head at the smallest of opportunities? How else could management, and especially in the civil service, justify their existence?

He heard Gordon sigh behind him and turned to face him. It would be a stretch to say he looked well. Carl knew that it was Lars Bjørn who had eased Gordon's way into HQ, so his reaction was understandable. But since then, hadn't Bjørn made it difficult for Gordon to keep his position?

"Where's Assad?" asked Gordon. "Is he with Rose?"

Carl frowned. Gordon was right to think about Assad in connection with Lars Bjørn. Strangely, there had always been a sort of brotherly bond between Lars Bjørn and Assad. Shared experiences in the past to which Carl was not privy had seemingly created a strong connection between them, and when it came to it, it was also Bjørn who had recruited Assad to Department Q. So, Carl had something for which to thank Bjørn.

And now he was dead.

"Shall I call Assad?" asked Gordon, fully expecting Carl to step up to the task.

"Maybe we should wait until he's back here. It might also agitate Rose if she's with him just now. You never know with her."

Gordon shrugged. "You could send him a text to call you when Rose is out of earshot."

Good plan. Carl gave him the thumbs-up.

"I had another call from that weird guy again this morning," said Gordon, when he was finished sniffling and they were on their way down the stairs.

"Okay." That must have been the tenth time in two days that Gordon had mentioned it. "Have you asked why he calls you specifically? Has he told you?"

"No."

"And you still haven't been able to trace the call?"

"No. I've tried, but he uses a phone card."

"Well, if it bothers you, hang up next time."

"I've tried that. It doesn't help. He just calls back five seconds later and keeps at it until I've heard him out."

"Remind me again what it's about."

"That he will kill when he reaches the number twenty-one seventeen."

"Quite a few years until then." Carl laughed. It was the sort of come-back he might have expected from Rose back in the day.

"I've asked him what twenty-one seventeen means, but his answer was really cryptic. He said it was obviously when his game reached twenty-one seventeen, and then he burst out laughing. And it was a really eerie laugh, I can tell you."

"Shall we just put him down as a disturbed idiot for the time being? How old would you guess he is?"

"Not so old. He almost sounded like a teenager, but a little older, I reckon."

The morning dragged on, and Assad didn't call or answer Carl's texts.

Someone or other must have informed him by now.

What Carl really wanted was just to go home. He hadn't touched a case file since they had been called up to homicide, and his sense that everything was about to collapse had become overwhelming, much like his desperation for a cigarette.

If Assad hasn't turned up within half an hour, I'm off, he thought, and surfed the Internet looking at job ads. Oddly enough, there was nothing specifically directed at a fifty-three-year-old detective inspector with a BMI approaching twenty-eight.

That really only left local politics, but what the hell would he do on Allerød city council? And for which party?

Then he heard the distinctive sound of Assad's footsteps in the corridor.

"You've heard?" said Carl, referring to the two deep furrows be-tween Assad's eyes when he appeared in the doorway.

"Yes, I have. I went straight over to Susanne for a few hours. It wasn't pretty."

Carl nodded. Assad had comforted the widow. That was how close he was to the Bjørn family.

"She was furious, Carl."

"Well, that's understandable. It was very unexpected."

"No, not that. She was angry that he ran himself out."

"'Wore,' Assad. It's 'wore himself out.'"

"I don't get it, he was running. Anyway, she was also angry about all the hostage negotiations he worked on when he came home. Angry about his lover. That he spent money like it was going out of fashion."

"Hold on, back up a minute. Lars Bjørn had a lover?"

Assad looked at him, puzzled. "Lars Bjørn would do anything on two legs if he could get away with it; you knew that."

Carl looked shocked. That wretched bore? What on earth did women see in that jerk?

"Why didn't she just kick him out?"

Assad shrugged. "Camels don't like new watering holes, Carl."

Carl tried to picture Bjørn's wife. For once, the camel metaphor wasn't totally misplaced.

"What do you mean by 'hostage negotiations'?"

"Detained businessmen, journalists, stupid tourists, aid workers . . ."

"Yes, yes, I do know what type of people are susceptible, but why Bjørn?"

"Because he knew the pitfalls better than anyone when those on the other side kill because of the slightest wrong move."

"Is that how you and Bjørn knew each other? Did he help you in a hostage situation?"

Assad's face stiffened. "More the other way around. And it wasn't a hostage case. It was imprisonment in one of Iraq's worst jails."

"Abu Ghraib?"

He nodded and shook his head simultaneously. "Yes and no. Let's call it the annex. There were several, but let's just call this Annex One."

"What do you mean by that?"

"I didn't understand it either to begin with. I later found out that that building complex was much smaller than Abu Ghraib. It was isolated from the main prison, and the inmates were prisoners who required special attention."

"Like who?"

"Captured foreigners, high-ranking officials, politicians, spies, and wealthy people. Sometimes entire families who had defied Saddam's regime. People who knew too much and who they wanted to speak. People like that."

Bloody hell, thought Carl.

"Lars Bjørn was in there?"

"No, not him." Assad stood for some time shaking his head slowly and staring at the floor.

"Okay," said Carl. This was the sort of topic that Assad preferred to avoid. "That's what I heard from Tomas Laursen. I also thought you confirmed it when I asked you. But listen, I know this is a difficult subject for you, Assad. Just forget I asked."

Assad closed his eyes and took a deep breath before looking Carl straight in the eyes.

"No, Lars wasn't in prison and he wasn't a hostage. The inmate was his brother, Jess." He frowned and looked like he might clam up again. Did he regret revealing something that shouldn't have been spoken?

"Jess? Jess Bjørn?" Something about the name rang a bell. "Have I met him?"

Assad shrugged. "I don't think so. Maybe you did, but he's in a care home now." He pulled his phone from his pocket. Carl hadn't heard it, so it must have been on silent.

Assad stood nodding with his phone at his ear while the furrows between his eyes grew deeper. He sounded dissatisfied when he answered. As if what he heard wasn't the deal, whatever that might be.

"I need to head off, Carl," he said, and put his mobile back in his pocket. "That was Susanne Bjørn. We'd agreed that I would inform Lars's brother, but she called him all the same and told him."

"And he didn't take it well, is that it?"

"He took it really badly, so I need to go again, Carl. I would've waited until later today, but it can't wait now."

It had been almost a week since Carl had last been in the house in Allerød. Since he had begun commuting between there and Mona's flat, his tenant, Morten, had slowly but steadily made his mark on the place with his highly alternative talent for interior design. The entrance alone, flanked by two gold-painted statues of naked athletic men, would have rattled any care assistant, not to mention the living room, which was now transformed from its practical seventies style with plain furniture to a veritable orgy of color in saffron yellow and bright green. Actually, the overall impression was almost one of moldy Emmental if he were to try to describe it. All it needed now was for Morten to bring up the rest of his precious Playmobil toy collection from the basement and cover the living room with it.

"Hello," shouted Carl by way of warning that normality was entering.

No answer.

Carl frowned and tried to catch sight of Hardy's wheelchair van through the kitchen window. His old friend and colleague was obviously out.

He collapsed in the armchair next to Hardy's empty bed in the living room and laid his hand on it. Maybe it was time to change Morten's rental contract and give him tenancy of the whole house. With the understanding, of course, that if he and Mona couldn't make things work, they would revert back to the former agreement that Morten had the basement.

Carl smiled. If Morten Holland had the run of the house, his boyfriend, Mika, might also move in. They were both old boys now, so they were probably ready for something more formal.

There was a rattle from the door, and the sound of Hardy's electric wheelchair and Morten's laughter filled the room with life.

"Hi, Carl. I'm glad you're here; you'll never guess what happened today," said Morten when he saw him.

Nothing bad at any rate, he thought when he saw Hardy's gleaming eyes and Mika's muscular body dancing in behind them.

Morten sat in front of him without taking off his jacket.

"We're going to Switzerland, Carl. The three of us: Mika, Hardy, and me," he said, beaming.

Switzerland? The country of cheese with holes in it and heavy-duty bank safes? How exciting could that be? There were lots of other places where Carl could better think of being bored than in Switzerland.

"Yup," continued Mika. "We've arranged an appointment with a Swiss clinic who've promised to assess whether Hardy is ready to have a brain–computer interface implanted." Carl looked at Hardy. He had no idea what the guy was talking about.

"Yeah, sorry you don't know about it, Carl," whispered Hardy. "It's taken so long to scrape the money together. We didn't know if we'd manage it."

"A German fund is paying for the accommodation and part of the operation. It's crazy," added Mika.

"What are you all babbling on about? What's this interface thing?"

Now Morten went into overdrive. Strange that he hadn't blurted it out long ago.

"The University of Pittsburgh has developed a method where they implant microelectrodes in the part of a paralyzed patient's brain that controls hand mobility. They've had success with the method in enabling a paralyzed body to regain feeling in the fingers, for example. That's what we want to try with Hardy."

"It sounds dangerous."

"Yes, but it isn't," continued Mika. "And even though Hardy can already move one finger and has some shoulder movement, it isn't enough to enable him to use an exoskeleton."

Carl couldn't follow. "Exoskeleton?! What's that?"

"A lightweight robotic skeleton attached to the body. Small electric motors in the frame help those who can't walk independently to be able to move, almost as if it's the patient walking alone."

Carl tried to imagine how Hardy could stand and walk again after all these years. Six foot eight in an iron frame. He would end up looking like Frankenstein's monster, or worse. It was almost laughable, but Carl felt no urge to laugh. Would it ever be a reality? Weren't they just giving him false hope?

"Carl!" Hardy drove his electric wheelchair a few centimeters closer.

"I know what you're thinking. You're thinking I'll be disappointed, that it might get me down. That it will take months and months and still prove futile. Am I right?"

Carl nodded.

"But, Carl, since that day when I lay paralyzed at the spinal injuries center in Hornbæk and asked you to kill me twelve years ago, right up until today, I haven't had any goal for my future that would go any way to making me feel normal. I can certainly drive around in my wheelchair more or less as I want, and I'm extremely grateful for that. But the idea that there might be something else to fight for gives me so much energy. So, don't you think we should just deal with it if and when it doesn't work out?"

Carl nodded again.

"I hope that the operation will allow me to feel my arms and maybe even my legs, using my mind. They've conducted experiments on paralyzed apes who have regained the ability to walk. The question is whether I have enough muscle power."

"And that's where the exoskeleton comes into the picture, I imagine."

If Hardy could have nodded, he would have.

6

Assad

A sinister blue flashing light danced over the wisteria on the facade of the care home.

Allah hafiz. *Please don't let it be Jess,* thought Assad when he saw the empty ambulance with its rear doors flung open wide.

He took the stairs to the entrance in four strides and stormed into the reception. There were no staff there, only curious elderly residents who whispered and turned their heads away when he rushed past them and down toward his friend's room.

The three healthcare assistants on duty stood in the doorway with ashen faces, their eyes fixed on the room in front of them. There was a sound of muffled voices from inside the room; Assad stopped and took a deep breath. For almost thirty years, his fate had been inextricably linked to Jess, and he had cursed the day they'd met for many of those years. But despite that, Jess had become the person closest to him in this life and who knew more about him than anyone else, so the feeling that came over him was one of the worst he had experienced over the last ten years.

"Is he dead?" he asked.

The assistant closest to him turned toward him. "Oh, Zaid, is that you?" She held up a hand toward him. "Don't come in here."

No further explanation, although none was needed, because in the next moment a stretcher was wheeled out; the feet were placed peacefully next to each other under the white cloth. It was only when the rest of the body came into view that Assad's worst fears were confirmed. The paramedics had attempted to cover the face with an extra sheet but the blood had still seeped through.

Assad held up his hand and asked them to stop when the stretcher was next to him. He had to be sure that it was really Jess. As expected, the paramedics protested when he lifted the sheet, but they fell silent when they caught his eye.

Jess's eyes were half-closed, and one corner of his mouth was sagging down toward the place where he had stabbed himself in his carotid artery.

"What happened?" he whispered as he closed the eyelids on the lifeless face.

"Someone or other called him," said the eldest of the healthcare assistants while the stretcher was wheeled down to the front steps.

"We heard him scream, but when we came running down to see what was wrong, he told us to leave him in peace. He just wanted a moment alone and said he would call us when he wanted to be wheeled out to be with the others."

"When was that?" asked Assad.

"It's only thirty minutes since we found him with a pen cartridge stabbed into his carotid artery. He was still breathing, and—" She stopped short with the sentence stuck in her throat. Even for a seasoned healthcare worker, this must have been a shocking sight.

"The duty doctor had by chance just arrived to complete the death certificate for one of the other residents, who passed away last night. I think he's still sitting in my office going through Jess's medical journal," said the other one.

Assad steadied himself with the doorframe and tried to swallow the saliva at the back of his throat. Lars Bjørn and his brother on the same day; how was that possible? Was Allah standing right now with a heavy hand on his shoulder? Was it God's will that he should suddenly feel as if his arm had been cut off? That his link to the past had been severed and thrown into the fire in which all memories end? It felt devastating.

"I can't grasp it; it's too hard," he said. "Jess and his brother were fighting fit this morning, and now they're both gone."

Assad shook his head. If Lars and Jess had lost their lives in the countries that had bound the three together, they would have been laid in the ground before rigor mortis had a chance to set in.

"No, it's uncanny," answered the healthcare assistant. "'Blissful, blissful, every soul that finds peace. Still, no one knows the day before the sun sets,' as the hymn says. We need to make the most of life while we can."

Assad stared into the room. Judging by the blood under the wheel-chair and the dark stripe on the floor, Jess had done this while sitting down, and then after his death, he had been lifted to the left and up onto the stretcher. The Parker pen he had unscrewed the pointy car-tridge out of was still disassembled on his coffee table. It was the pen that Assad had gifted him many years ago.

"Where's the cartridge he stabbed himself with?" he asked out of habit.

"In a plastic bag in the office with the doctor. I heard him call to arrange to have some people sent down here. He also took some photos. He always does."

Assad looked around the room. Who would inherit the things in here now that his brother, Lars Bjørn, was also dead? Jess had no chil-dren and no other siblings. Were these greatly condensed remnants of eighty-three years of life to end up with Susanne? Brass-framed photos of a man who had once been almost six foot two and adorned with an array of medals on his uniform? And his cheap furniture and flat-screen that was long ago outdated?

Assad walked into the office where the doctor was sitting typing with half-framed glasses perched on the end of his nose.

Assad and the doctor had politely nodded to each other quite a few times in the years Jess had lived at the care home since his transfer from the home for retired servicemen. He was a taciturn and somewhat weary sort, but who wouldn't be with his job.

Now they acknowledged each other once again.

"It was suicide," he said tersely from behind the computer screen. "His fingers were still gripping the pen when I entered, and the position his head was in stopped him from letting go."

"It doesn't surprise me," said Assad. "He'd just received the terrible news that his brother was dead. Probably the worst news he could possibly receive."

"I see. That's tragic," said the doctor, devoid of empathy. "I'm in the middle of writing up my report, so I'll note that down as the assumed reason for his actions. I'm given to understand that you've known each other for many years."

"Yes, since the 1990s. He was my mentor."

"Had he talked before about committing suicide?"

Had Jess talked about committing suicide? Assad smiled unintentionally. What soldier who had taken as many lives as he had didn't talk incessantly about it?

"No, not while he's been a resident here. Not to me, at any rate. Never."

Assad called Jess's sister-in-law, Susanne, calming her down from the shock and bringing her somewhat back to her senses when she began saying that it was her fault. He reassured her that it would probably have happened no matter what.

He was lying about that too.

Assad stood in front of the care home and stared up at the gray sky drifting by. What a fitting backdrop for the terrible events of the day. His myriad thoughts about these two men made him feel physically weak. His legs were unsteady and limp, and the rest of his body felt exhausted in a way reminiscent of having influenza. He took a couple of steps backward and reached out for the bench beside the steps where he and Jess had so often said a quiet good-bye. He sat down and took out his mobile.

"Carl, I won't be back in today," he said, after giving him a short rundown of what had happened.

It went quiet for a moment on the other end of the phone.

"I don't know what this Jess Bjørn meant to you, Assad, but I think that two deaths in one day—and people so close to you—are two deaths too many," he finally said. "How long do you think you need?"

Assad thought for a moment. How could he know that?

"You don't need to answer just now. Shall we just call it a week, Assad?"

"Er, I don't know. Maybe just a few days. Is that all right?"

7

Assad

On the walkway under the dirty windows of Rose's flat, a new pile of newspapers had already accumulated. If you took into account that the residents in the block donated around six kilos of magazines and newspapers on the average day, it amounted to over two tons a year, and the walk down to the recycling bin wasn't exactly Assad's favorite. But what the hell, the neighbors were being friendly and Rose lived and breathed for her newspaper clippings, so why not. At least people weren't leaving all their papers in front of her kitchen window like they had a year ago. And the variety was good, he had to give them that. She didn't only cover Danish publications; the diversity of news was considerably added to by magazines and newspapers in German, English, Spanish, and Italian from the foreign residents of the building.

In the living room, Rose was sitting with her back to the windows facing out onto the grass area outside and with a pile of clippings in front of her as usual. This was her universe; since her ordeal of being cuffed to her neighbor's toilet and held hostage by two brutal young women, she hadn't really returned to reality. That was two years ago now. Back then, Rose had been thirty-six, but today she resembled a woman of forty-five, a good twenty kilos heavier and unsteady on her feet. The blood clots in her calves and not least the comfort-eating and antidepressants had taken their toll.

Assad dropped the shopping bag and pile of publications at the end of the dining table and put the keys in his pocket, only saying hi when

Rose looked at him. Her reactions were delayed, but otherwise the old, gruff Rose was still intact somewhere in there. And that was just the kind of stability he needed right now.

"So, have you been out for a wander today?" he asked with an ironic smile, because she definitely had not. The world outside was no longer Rose's world.

"Did you remember the trash bags?" she asked.

"Yup," said Assad, unpacking the goods. Four rolls of transparent trash bags, enough for four to five weeks. "I've bought canned food for you, so you'll be fine for the next few days, Rose. That's why I'm here for the second time today."

"Is it a case?"

"No. It's indirectly related to Lars Bjørn. I take it you've heard?" he said, walking over to the radio to turn it down.

"Yes, I heard it on the radio," she said without seeming particularly affected.

"Okay. I also heard it on the car radio just before."

"You said 'indirectly'?" She put down her scissors for a moment, more as a formality than out of genuine interest.

Assad took a deep breath; time to get to the point. "Yeah, it's really tragic, for me too. His brother committed suicide after Lars Bjørn's wife called and told him that Lars was dead."

"Called him?" Rose put her finger to her head and rotated it. "She's never been the brightest spark. What a stupid bitch. He committed suicide? I didn't know anyone could care that much about Lars Bjørn." Her hollow laughter normally lifted Assad's spirits, but not just now. Rose's empathy for most people was hidden away somewhere remote.

She noticed his reaction and looked away. "I've made some changes in here, can you tell?"

Assad looked along the walls. Two of them were still covered from floor to ceiling with brown archive boxes filled with systematized clippings, while the third wall around the TV was covered with a large collage of clippings stuck up with tape. No subject was apparently devoid of interest or outside Rose's sphere of curiosity, but her indignation was consistent and unmistakable. The topics varied from traffic safety during Copenhagen's never-ending building projects and complex road-works to animal welfare and a little splash of royal coverage, which as usual was overshadowed by journalistic attacks against bad political management, corruption, and politicians' exemption of liability. For a contemporary historian, weekly photos of this variable and constantly changing selection could reveal the current status of Denmark and the rest of the world. But at this moment, Assad couldn't pinpoint what was new.

"I can, Rose," he said anyway. "It looks good."

She looked annoyed. "It isn't good, Assad. Denmark has been mur-dered, killed. Doesn't it get to you?"

He stroked his face; he had to get it out in the open. Maybe then she would understand.

"Lars's brother was called Jess, Rose. I knew him for almost thirty years. We had so many good memories and awful experiences together. And now I'm the only one who remembers them. I just need a few days to process everything, you know? Jess's death has brought back so many memories."

"Memories come and go, Assad. You can't control them, especially the bad ones; I should know."

He looked at her and sighed. Two years ago, these walls had been covered in distraught sentences from Rose's diary. So painful that she had once drunkenly confessed to Assad that she would have committed suicide if she hadn't been hindered by her captors. Of course, Rose knew only too well about the memories the mind stores that you would rather forget.

Assad stood for a moment staring into thin air. Jess had taken his own life: the life Assad had once risked his own to save. And now both he and his brother were dead. All that was left was the memory of the life that ended on that fateful day many years ago when Lars Bjørn called, begging him to save his brother. Were it not for that phone call, he would still have his family, and that was so difficult to think about. Sixteen years had gone by since then. Sixteen years of hoping and fighting and doing everything in his power to keep the pain and tears at bay.

He couldn't take it anymore.

He reached his hand back, and when he felt the chair, he collapsed in it and let the tears come.

"What on earth's the matter, Assad?" he heard Rose say. Without looking up, he could sense her struggling to stand, walk over, and squat in front of him. "You're crying. What is it?"

He looked into her eyes and observed a presence she hadn't exuded for over two years.

"It's too long and sad an account, Rose. But I feel like the ending caught up with me today. I'm crying to let it out and be done with it, Rose, because I can't do anything about it anyway. Ten minutes. Just give me ten minutes and I'll be fine."

She took his hands in hers. "Assad, what would I have done if you hadn't opened the book that I was hiding my past in? I would've killed myself; you know that."

"That's also what the camel said when all the water was gone, but it kept standing by the trough, Rose."

"What do you mean?"

"Look around you. Aren't you slowly killing yourself? You've stopped working, and you're just living off your pension. You never go out. You get kids and me to buy your groceries. You're scared of the world. You'd rather sit behind these filthy windows so you aren't overwhelmed by impressions from outside. You don't talk with your sisters; you almost never call HQ. You forget the positives that Gordon, Carl, me, and being part of a fantastic team can give you. It seems like you don't want any more from life. And if that's the case, what's the point?"

"There is something I want, Assad, and you can give it to me right here and now."

He looked at her pensively. Probably not something he could or would give her.

She started breathing heavily, as if what she wanted to say was stuck in her throat. For a moment, he almost recognized the former Rose from the intense sense of purpose in her eyes.

"Right," she said finally. "What I really want is for you to be the one to open *your* book this time, Assad. I've known you for eleven years and you're my best friend, but I know nothing about you. Not about your background and not about who you actually are. I'd really like you to tell me about it, Assad."

He knew it.

"Come with me to the bedroom and lie down beside me. Just close your eyes and tell me what you want to. Don't think about anything else."

Assad tried to frown but couldn't. The feeling of reluctance and mistrust simply couldn't survive in the mire of sorrow he was experiencing.

She tugged at him, and it was the first time in a long time that Rose had taken the initiative for something that wasn't about herself.

Assad had not been in Rose's bedroom since her collapse. But where it had once been a despondent and lifeless room, it was now transformed into a sanctuary where flowers on the bedspread and a sea of golden pillows dominated. Only the walls served to remind him that the situation here was also unstable, as even in this room they were covered in newspaper clippings accusing the world of being broken.

Assad lay down on the bedspread and closed his eyes as she had requested.

He felt the warmth from her body when she lay down next to him.

"Come on, Assad, tell me what comes to mind," she said, and placed her arm across his chest. "Just remember that I know nothing, so nothing is a given."

For a few minutes he fought his doubts: Was he ready? Was this the right time? But when she was lying perfectly still and no longer insisting or pressuring him, he slowly began.

"I was born in Iraq, Rose."

He sensed her nodding beside him. Maybe she knew that.

"My name is not Assad, even though today I don't want to be called anything else. It's Zaid al-Asadi."

"Said?" It sounded almost like she was tasting the name.

He squinted. "My parents are dead, and I have no siblings. I now perceive myself as having absolutely no family even though that's probably not true."

"So, you don't want me to call you Said. Are you sure?"

"You need to voice the first letter as 'S,' but it's Zaid with a 'Z.' But no, for you and the other people I care about and know in Denmark, I'm still Assad."

She moved in closer to him. He could feel how bringing her into his confidence was making her heart race. "You've said that you were from Syria."

"I've said a lot of things in recent years that you should take with a granary of salt, Rose."

He felt her beginning to chuckle. It had been a long time and felt almost liberating. "It's 'with a grain of salt,' Assad, not 'a granary,'" she said.

"I don't get it."

"They sound a bit similar, but a granary would be a hell of a lot of salt in comparison with a grain. And salt isn't kept in a granary."

"Then this time I'm right, Rose. A granary couldn't possibly be too much in this case. And never mind if it should be kept there or not."

He opened his eyes and was about to laugh with her when he saw a clipping on the wall above her head that made him freeze.

Victim number 2117, he read.

Assad jumped up. He had to take a closer look. The grainy photos in newspapers often tricked the eye. It was probably just someone who looked like her. It had to be. It just had to!

But from half a meter away he already knew that his doubt was in vain. It *was* her.

He covered his eyes as he felt his throat constricting. He almost couldn't hear his own whimpering. He felt his warm breath on his face and the drool running down his wrists.

"Please, don't touch me just now, Rose," he gasped as he felt her hand on his shoulder.

He tilted his head back, took in a deep breath, and slowly opened his eyes a fraction to allow the picture to slowly come more into focus. When he finally opened his eyes fully, it was painfully clear. The drenched body was positioned on its back, limp and all too obviously lifeless. The woman's eyes were still vibrant despite staring up at nothing. The hands, which had so often caressed Assad's cheek, seemed to be symbolically clutching the sand.

"Lely, Lely . . . ," he whispered over and over as his finger caressed her forehead and hair on the photo. "What happened? What happened?"

Assad's head fell down toward his chest. The years of uncertainty, longing, and sorrow grew stronger, paralyzing his senses. Lely was no more.

He felt Rose's hand again. It carefully linked with his, and with the other hand she gently turned his head so their eyes could meet.

They looked at each other for some time without saying a word before she ventured to ask her question.

"I change the clippings almost every day, and this one is very recent. You recognize her?"

He nodded.

"Who was she, Assad?"

For many, many years, Lely's fate had been unknown to him, but in his heart, Assad had always fooled himself that she would live forever. Even when the war in Syria was at its worst and no one cared who was killed or by whom, he knew inside that Lely would find a way out of the Ragnarök, because if anyone could, it was Lely. And yet there she lay, and Rose was asking who she was. Not who she is but who she was.

He moved his hand from the newspaper clipping and struggled to find the breath he needed to speak.

"Lely Kababi was the woman who took care of my family when we fled from Iraq. My father was an engineer and an official who had come too close to Saddam Hussein through the Ba'ath Party, and one day he inadvertently criticized him. Had it not been for my father's ethnic background as a Shia Muslim, it might have been all right, but at that time, any criticism or wrong move could easily mean death for a Shia like him. My father received no more than an hour's warning that Saddam's guard had orders to arrest him, so my mother and father made the decision to flee from one second to the next. They took nothing with them except some jewelry and me. I was just one year old when Lely Kababi welcomed us into her home in Sab Abar in southwest Syria. We lived with her even though we weren't family and remained there until my father finally secured an opportunity to work in Denmark. I was just five at the time and a very happy little boy when we arrived here."

He looked up again at the newspaper clipping in the vain hope of catching the slightest hint of a message in her unseeing eyes.

"You have to understand, Lely Kababi was our savior. And now . . ."

He tried to read the text under the photo, but everything was blurry for him. God, what a terrible, terrible day. He had taken almost as much as he could bear.

"I'm so sorry, Assad," whispered Rose. "I don't know what to say."

He shook his head. What *could* she say?

"When you want to know more about what happened, I have some clippings from foreign newspapers that are more detailed than this one. I know exactly where they are because it only happened a few days ago. Do you want me to fetch them?"

He nodded, and Rose left the bedroom.

When she returned, she placed a brown archive box next to him on the edge of the bed and opened it.

"This one is from *The Times*. They made a big deal out of it because the victim was so unusual. Look at the date. The article was published the day after a Spanish newspaper broke the story. It doesn't make for pleasant reading, Assad. Shall I read it for you? Then you can tell me when to stop."

He shook his head. He preferred to do it himself; that way he might be able to control his reaction.

Assad read. Like cautiously tiptoeing across an unsafe suspension bridge, his eyes moved tentatively over the words. The article was very detailed, as Rose had said it was, and it was all too real. The mucus in the victim's mouth, the long row of bodies lying in the sand. The article stated that a holy warrior had been the first to wash ashore. The skin was still full of nicks after the necessary shaving off of the full beard that was a trademark of the militia.

Assad struggled with the images and questions the article prompted. Why had Lely chosen to flee? What had happened?

Rose passed him another newspaper. "The following day, *The Times* printed this. I'm telling you now, Assad, because it's really awful. The old woman didn't drown. She was murdered. That's why I taped her photo on the wall. I wanted to tell her that I felt deeply sorry for her."

Assad's shoulders gave way.

"She was stabbed in the back of the neck with a sharp object. The autopsy details were made public yesterday. She didn't have much seawater in her lungs, Assad. So she was more than likely already dead or dying when they threw her into the sea."

Assad didn't understand. This warm, affectionate person without an evil bone in her body had been murdered. What vile pig would do that? And why?

He picked up the newspaper. The photo was different from the one they had used the previous day. The angle was slightly different, but the stare and the position of the body were the same. He observed her again for a moment. She looked so trusting, just like he remembered her. And the hands lying flat on the wet sand. The hands that had caressed him, the mouth that had sung for him, the eyes that had inspired in him a belief that everything would one day be good.

Just not for you, Lely, he thought as anger and a thirst for revenge began to take shape.

Assad let his eyes wander over the grainy photo of corpses on the sand. It was terrible, almost unbearable. The outline of powerless bodies, rows of feet sticking out from the sheets. Women, children, men, and then Lely, who moments after this photo was taken would have been lined up with the others. Now this warm and soulful woman, to whom his family owed everything, had become a statistical testimony to the cynical and disgraceful errors of the world.

Was this the sort of world he wanted to live in?

He turned his attention to a photo of a group of people a little farther up from the beach whose faces were etched with terror.

Did one of you do this? he thought.

He screwed his eyes shut. If it cost him everything, he would get the people who had done this. He promised himself that.

The photo was slightly unclear due to the poor light, and yet something caught his eye. A painful sense of recognition. Among the other survivors, there was a man standing in the background staring directly at the camera, almost as if he wanted it to capture him. His beard reached halfway down his chest, a reminder of the fanatical reign of terror from which he had fled, and his eyes were stern like the rest of his demeanor. Next to him stood a young woman with a distorted face. And next to her another woman who . . .

And then the darkness consumed him while a voice far away shouted, "Assad!"

8

Joan

Joan took an immediate dislike to the man sitting like a king on his throne behind the counter at Larnaca airport, a glowering man who stank of sweat and the reek of domestic defeat.

He finally turned to face Joan. Two hours Joan had spent gawking at this unshaven, questionably put-together immigration officer before he deigned to answer Joan's questions. It took him no more than ten seconds, and all the uniformed staff behind him nodded along. What the hell? So, they had all known the answer from the start.

Joan's nostrils flared. It was probably the desire to punch them all kicking in.

"Yes, you see," said the officer, unfazed, "the alive we took to Menogeia Detention Center yesterday. We put the dead in morgues. No one left in Ayia Napa," he said, his English reminiscent of Joan's level from middle school.

Joan forced himself to nod politely. "Menogeia Detention Center. Got it. And how do I get there?"

"You take the bus if you cannot afford taxi."

He couldn't be bothered to ask where the bus left from.

A bus passenger told him that the barracks were situated like yellow splashes in a barren landscape, which far from matched the idyll of the journey. The buildings were relatively new and surrounded by a steel fence, and in front of the buildings, there were man-sized signs with site information. "You can't miss it," the unexpectedly friendly man had said to him. It didn't make Joan feel any more comfortable with the place that the site information was written entirely in Greek, and that he had been unable to find a telephone number or any contact names on the Internet.

He directed himself with the utmost humility to the first person inside the main building, aware of how arrogant a uniform could make its wearer in these parts. Rejection wasn't an option he could afford.

"Yes, of course. We've been expecting you, Mr. Aiguader; the immigration officer from Larnaca airport was kind enough to call us and announce your imminent arrival." He stretched out his hand in a cordial fashion, leaving Joan speechless. "We're always happy when the wider world focuses on our problems. You understand, it's hard for our small country to accept so many refugees."

Joan saw the sweaty officer from the airport in a new light. *When I meet him on my return journey, I'll give him a bottle of seven-star Metaxa,* he thought before recalling his budget. He checked his extravagance with the decision that the five-star version would be sufficient.

"Last year we received four thousand five hundred and eighty-two applications for asylum," continued the prison guard. "Naturally, most of them were Syrians, and we're very behind with the processing. To be exact, we're behind with one thousand one hundred and twenty-three applications, which is almost twice as many as at the end of last year. So, we appreciate the attention. Would you like a tour?"

"Yes, please. But I'm mostly interested in meeting the survivors from yesterday. Is that possible?"

A small twitch from the man's mouth indicated that that wasn't at the top of his agenda, but he managed to soften the impression.

"Naturally. After the tour, okay?"

Hundreds of dark, scrutinizing faces watched him with a mixture of doubt and hope. What could his presence mean for each of them? Was he from an international aid organization? Was it a good or a bad sign that he was talking in English? Was it a sign of something positive that this man had suddenly appeared?

The refugees were squatting in the courtyard along the length of the steel fence and inside large, sterile rooms painted in earth tones and with steel tables and a distinct lack of seating. In the dormitories, where everything had the same earth tone, men were lying in bunk beds with their heads resting on their hands, giving him the same look as he had encountered outside: *Who are you? What do you think you're staring at? This isn't a zoo. Can you do anything? Can you help me? Are you just going to leave again? Can you please fuck off!*

"As you can see, it's important to us that the surroundings are con-temporary and well kept. The regrettable days when refugees were locked up on Block Ten in Nicosia's main prison are thankfully behind us. It was dismal and unhealthy in there, with little light and overfilled cells. You can't accuse us of that here," said the guard as he offered an unreciprocated nod to a couple of the asylum seekers.

"The few possessions these people had with them when they fled are naturally insufficient for a longer stay, so we've organized clothes col-lections and have a cleaning team who keep on top of hygiene."

I won't be writing about that exactly, thought Joan. "I'll make sure to remember that when I write my article," he said all the same. "And the people who were brought in yesterday, where are they?"

The guard nodded. "Well, we had to isolate them from the others. As you know already, of course, one of the deceased was identi-fied as a wanted terrorist, so we're not taking any chances. There could very well be more of them among the survivors, so we've begun investigations—and in some cases interrogations—so we can see if their individual stories are watertight."

"Is that something you can know?"

"We're very good at it, yes."

Joan stopped to scroll through the photo archive on his camera. "I'm interested in talking with these two women." He pointed at the photograph of the despondent women standing next to the man with the black beard. "They were very affected by the situation when they pulled the old woman onto the shore, so I got the impression that they could tell me more about the woman I wrote about in my article."

The guard's expression changed. "She was stabbed in the neck, but I guess you know that?"

"Yes. The police know nothing, so I want to try to find out who did it and why. That's why I'm here."

"You are aware that at this institution we adhere to all international standards for how immigrants are treated? Law one fifty-three from 2011 is not in conflict with the council's directives from 2008, only that the automatic procedures concerning legal assessment of extended detention of more than six months have been suspended."

Joan shook his head. It was all gibberish. Why was he talking about that now?

"Of course," he said.

The man looked relieved. "I mention it because we find ourselves in a dilemma. We don't have any desire to detain immigrants. Actually, we want to get them all off our hands as quickly as possible, but once they are registered here, we're stuck with them. And we won't just release people who we're not completely sure about into society; the world has to understand that. They could be terrorists, criminals, fundamentalists, the sort of people the rest of Europe wouldn't host. Even though our resources are limited, we try to be cautious. We've had enough accidents on this island in my time here alone."

"I understand, but women and children are generally innocent, aren't they?"

"Children, perhaps, but women?" He snorted. "They can be put under pressure. They can be manipulated. They can sometimes be more fanatical than the men, so no. They aren't just a priori innocent." He pointed toward the courtyard of another extension. "We'll go in there. The men and women are separated from each other, and I assume it's the women's block you want to visit."

It was very quiet inside. High-pitched voices mumbled while others quietly sobbed. The women stared at him with imploring eyes, one of them breastfeeding an infant—otherwise, there were no children.

"Where are the children?" asked Joan.

"There were no children apart from this baby. As far as we know, there was a five-year-old girl with one of the women, but the child probably didn't make it."

Joan looked again at the women's resigned faces. *Make it!* he thought. What a cynical way to put it. Somehow it explained the extent of this nightmare better than anything else.

"Is this all the women who were brought in yesterday?"

"No, two of them are in the rooms there for questioning at the moment." He pointed at two doors. "Always two at the same time."

Joan compared his photos with the faces staring at him. As far as he could see, none of them were a match with the two women who were deeply affected when the old woman was pulled up onto the shore.

"The women I'm looking for aren't here. Can I stick my nose in the interview rooms?"

The guard looked doubtful but nodded. "Well, a few seconds is probably okay. We aren't supposed to disturb them."

He tentatively opened the first door. A uniformed woman was sitting with her back to the door behind a desk with a pile of amateur-looking photos of men. A steaming cup was placed next to the prison guard but nothing was in front of the woman who was seated wearing a head scarf and staring at Joan. She wasn't one of the women he was looking for either.

Joan's thoughts about his immediate future became blurry and unpromising. What if the women weren't here at the camp? Where else could they be? Were those people who had disappeared from the crowd the other night now beyond reach? How would he be able to tell the story?

A minute later, his worst fears were realized. The other woman being questioned was also not a match with his photo.

"You're sure that there are no detained women from that group anywhere else than here at the Menogeia camp?" he asked, shaken, when they returned to the common room.

"Yes, quite sure. Illegal immigrants used to be detained at nine different police stations on the island, including Limassol, Aradippou, and Oroklini, but not anymore. I can guarantee you that everyone who was detained that night is here."

Joan looked at his camera display and zoomed in on the two women's faces. Then he held up the camera toward the first row of women and pointed at the faces.

The women slowly forced themselves to direct their vacant eyes at the photo. After a moment, they all shook their heads. They didn't recognize them, but a little farther down the line one woman was nodding slightly.

"Yes, those two women were sitting at the front of the boat," she said in English. Then she pointed behind her at another woman. "The woman sitting there was at the front of the boat with them with her little girl on her lap. But I don't think you'll get anything out of her. She's still devastated after losing her daughter."

The woman she was pointing at was wearing a floral dress torn at the side. Scratches forming red lines down her ribs were oozing, and dark blue blotches bore witness to the trials she had been through. She placed her hand on her collarbone and absently watched Joan as he approached her, not returning his nod or greeting.

"I'm very sorry that you don't know where your daughter is," he offered.

She didn't react; maybe she didn't understand English.

"Do you understand what I'm saying?" he asked.

Was there a little twitch of confirmation?

He held out his camera toward her. "Do you recognize these two women?"

She looked apathetically at the photo and shrugged. He repeated his question, only to be met with the same indifference. She was lost in her own dark thoughts.

Joan held the camera in the air. "Does anyone know these two women? They were on the same boat as you."

"Give me a thousand euros and I'll tell you," said the woman in the torn floral dress, without any emotion.

Joan was taken aback. A thousand euros? Was she crazy?

"I know who they are. Give me the money and I'll tell you. Why should you be the only one to earn from our misfortune?"

Suddenly her features appeared more defined. Her weak mouth had stiffened, and the furrows on her face were not only from the loss she had recently suffered but from the endless tragedies that had befallen her in her short life.

"I don't have that much money, but I'll happily give you ten euros."

"Now, just a minute, Joan Aiguader!" whispered the guard, tugging at his sleeve. "You shouldn't be bargaining with them. If you do, there'll be no end to it. The women you're looking for aren't here anyway."

Like the guard, Joan had expected his offer, regardless of how bad it was, to be met with greedy stares and begging hands, but the eyes surrounding him expressed only mockery and disapproval. It still wasn't promising, but he grabbed his wallet anyway and took out a fifty-euro note. "I won't be eating tonight, but here you go."

The woman took it without a word. "Let me see the photo again. Do you have more?"

Joan scrolled through to the first photo, where the women were clinging to each other, crying, while the man with the beard held one of their drenched coats.

"That's the pig who killed the old woman." She pointed at the man with the full beard. "And he was with those two women, no doubt about that. And you can be sure that he's already shaved his beard off, just like the man who drowned."

9

Joan

Outside the detention center, Joan tried to collect his thoughts. The bus to Larnaca wouldn't be here any time soon, so he might as well make a record on his Dictaphone of the information he had acquired.

The woman had pointed at the bearded man, and the ensuing commotion in the sterile room had spread down the rows as the atmosphere suddenly turned immensely volatile. Many of them had grabbed at Joan's arm to get a look while curses and shouts filled the room. A couple of women spat at the camera in his hand, leaving it dripping, while others commented on what the woman had just told him, and a cascade of terrible experiences and frustrations overwhelmed the previously very passive women. Had the black-bearded man been in the room, he would quite literally have been flayed alive.

Then one of the women said that the old woman, probably like most people on the boat, had traveled from the area around Sab Abar or a bit farther north. The two younger women in the photo had been with her, she said, but their dialect was different from the others', a strange mixture of rural expressions and a light foreign accent that was hard to pin down but that possibly originated from Iraq. They didn't know anything else about the two women except that they were mother and daughter.

"Not that you would have guessed," one of them had shouted, referring to the fact that the daughter seemed older than her mother.

"The raped wither away," shouted another.

Joan caught the eye of the woman who had shouted last in the throng of glaring faces, and the women began to whisper among themselves, nodding; others screamed in Arabic, almost in unison, as if they had all experienced the same atrocities.

"What happened to the old woman?" Joan asked the woman in the floral dress when the outbursts subsided.

"I'm certain she knew the man, just like she also knew the two women. The three women were servile toward him, scared even, and he ordered them about and lashed out at them if they didn't do what he said. I don't know exactly why he stabbed the old woman to death, but I noticed that she'd vanished when the dinghy started to capsize."

She turned to the other women and asked questions in Arabic, to which several of them replied angrily. Two women started to scuffle right in front of Joan, ripping each other's clothes and pressing their dirty nails into each other's faces. The skirmish immediately spread through the room, insults turning to slaps, which in turn led to punches to bodies and faces. Joan didn't understand what was happening, only that the situation had escalated out of control when the first woman fell to the floor bleeding.

The doors of the interrogation rooms suddenly swung open, and uniformed officers with determined expressions started to throw punches at those closest to them to signal to these aggressive women that the party was over and that they should get down on the floor if they didn't want to receive even worse.

"I'm afraid you'll have to go now," said the guard. "You're agitating them. I hope you got your money's worth."

He had sacrificed fifty euros, and what had he actually found out that could help him in his search? Nothing! So no, he definitely hadn't received his money's worth, but he did at least have a clear goal.

The bastard with the black beard had murdered victim 2117, and nothing would stand in the way of Joan's finding him.

Though that would be easier said than done.

Joan turned off the Dictaphone and looked at the parched landscape around the detention center. What should he do now? Neither the two women nor the murderer was behind the metal fence of the center, so where were they? The Greek part of the island was one hundred sixty kilometers long and eighty kilometers wide, and then there was the Turkish part to the north. They could have been anywhere. The Troodos Mountains had before hidden people who did not want to be found; they could even have found some way or other into the Turkish side if they had had help. Even though as an EU citizen he could obtain a visa and follow them over, what would he do there without so much as a single lead?

Joan inhaled the dry air. He was really under pressure now. He had thirteen days left, and he had already used too much of his limited budget getting to this backwater.

He turned toward the fence. What if he went back and gained entry to the men's area? Was there a chance that he might obtain more information? Would they even let him in while the interrogations were under way?

He remembered the look on his editor's face when she gave him her ultimatum, and then he made the only decision that made sense under the circumstances. From now on, he would lie shamelessly and invent a colorful and captivating story about the old woman and what had befallen her. The man who had murdered her had been identified; based on that and the terror to which he had subjected the two women, Joan could easily spin a believable yarn. The motive for murder would require a little more time to conjure up, but imagination was not exactly something he lacked.

Yes, it was actually a good idea. The world media would buy the next chapter in the story of a murderer on the loose, especially now that he could be identified on the basis of the photograph. If there was someone in the editorial office with the necessary know-how, they could easily manipulate the picture in Photoshop and anticipate the possibility that he had shaved off his beard.

With all this in mind, he would head for Nicosia and spice up his fabricated story with some folklore and tales from the civil war–like fights that sprang from Cyprus's status as an independent nation. One thing was for sure: There wouldn't be a single euro left to pay back to the paper when he returned to Barcelona. Maybe he could even find someone on the island who could produce a few fake receipts so there was a bit of cash left to afford him some time back home while he searched for a new job.

All that remained for him to do just now was to take a few more photos of the exterior of the detention center, and then he could look forward to lying down on a soft bed in a decent hotel.

He was just about to take a couple of shots of the center when he spotted a woman with a bucket in her hand walking across the court-yard behind the fence and directly toward him.

As he went to photograph her to give the coverage a little life, she froze and raised her hand in the air to stop him.

"This will have to be quick," she said when she reached the fence. It was the woman who had shouted something about how old the two missing women looked in relation to each other. "Give me a hundred euros and I'll tell you what I know, and it's more than what the others can tell you."

"But I—" was all he managed to say before she stretched her fingers through the fence.

"I know who the man is. And I know what happened, so make it quick." She wriggled her fingers toward him. "They mustn't see me here."

"Who, the guards?"

"No, not them. I'm giving half the money to one of the guards, so they're in on it. It's some of the other women I'm worried about. They'll all be out on yard exercise in a minute; if they see me with you, they'll kill me."

"Kill you?" Joan fumbled for his wallet.

"Yes, some of the women aren't like the rest of us; they've been planted by the militia and don't talk to us. They're on the run from the Syrian troops and appointed to carry out acts of terrorism around Europe in the countries where the quota scheme distributes them."

Joan shook his head in disbelief.

"I'll give you fifty now, and if you convince me, I'll give you the other fifty, okay?" Anything that could make the story more sensational was worth it.

She took the money and stuffed it under her head scarf. "I heard the old woman call the man with the beard by his name, and I'm certain that's why he did something so terrible to her. He was protecting his identity because he's a terrorist pig, just like the man who drowned. The only reason that they helped us across the sea was so they could disappear in the crowd. No other reason."

"What name?"

She stretched her fingers through the fence. "First the other fifty, hurry up." She stomped her sandal, causing dust to rise up in a cloud. "I have more to tell you."

"How do I know you're not lying?"

She looked over her shoulder. Why look so anxious if there was no danger?

When he produced the note, she placed it this time between her breasts; it must have been the one she would keep for herself.

"When our group were gathered on the beach in Syria waiting for the dinghy, the man with the beard came over and gave us orders," she said. "He called himself Abdul Azim, 'Servant of the Mighty,' but the woman in the boat called him Ghaalib, which means 'the Victor.' He went crazy when she shouted that name out at sea and stabbed an awl in her neck without hesitation. He knew exactly what he was doing and how to do it, and he seemed prepared, almost as if he would've done it no matter what. My blood froze when I saw it, but thankfully he didn't see me." She put her hand firmly over her mouth to stop an outburst of emotion.

"What do you mean, prepared?"

"The awl he suddenly had in his hand. The position he sat in next to her to make it easier to stab her in the neck. It was probably also him who punctured the boat just after that."

"What about the women who were with the woman he stabbed to death? Why didn't they intervene?"

"They were sitting with their backs to us, so they didn't witness it, but they screamed when they turned around and saw she had disappeared into the water. The youngest was about to jump in after her, but Ghaalib restrained her. When the body washed ashore, they accused him, but he hushed them up with a warning that they should be careful if they didn't want to suffer the same fate."

"How do you know that? Maybe you're just saying all this for the money. How can I trust you?"

In the blink of an eye, her expression turned from compassion to anger. "You can! Show me that photo of the man and women once more!"

Joan scrolled through the photos on the camera display. "You mean this one?"

"Look at the two women and the man! Who is standing right behind them? Me! I heard everything they said."

Joan zoomed in. Her features were somewhat unclear, but it *was* her. And suddenly this anxious, slender woman had become his witness to truth, every journalist's dream of a primary source for a true story. It was no less than fantastic.

"What's your name?"

"What do you need that for? Do you want to get me killed?" She pulled away from the fence, shaking her head.

"Where did the two women and the man go?" Joan shouted after her. "Did you see how they got away from the group and the people watching over them?"

She stopped ten meters away from him. "I don't know, but I saw a photographer wearing a blue uniform jacket and Ghaalib signaled to him. He was up with our group taking pictures of Ghaalib and the two women before heading down and photographing the body of the old woman when it washed ashore. On the surface, Ghaalib appeared agitated. He didn't say anything, but I think he was pleased that the woman washed ashore where she did at that very moment."

"I don't understand. He murdered her. Wouldn't it have been better for him if she'd never been seen again?"

"The sight of the old woman broke the two women, and that suited him well, I think."

"You mean he deliberately had photos taken of himself, the women, and the body?"

She looked over her shoulder and nodded.

"But why?" asked Joan. "He was on the run and was supposed to disappear in the crowd somewhere in Europe. Surely he wouldn't want to be identified?"

"I've been wondering if he wanted to send a signal to someone that he was alive. But I now know that you've made sure that the whole of Europe got the message. Maybe because you were there the German photographer wasn't necessary for Ghaalib."

"The German photographer. He was German?"

"Yes. He came over to us for a moment and said something to Ghaalib in German. He pointed down at you when you were walking around the dead woman, then Ghaalib nodded and handed him something. But I didn't see what it was."

She flinched when a door slammed up at the building and immediately began running. No explanation, no good-bye. She needed to make sure that she wasn't spotted.

Despite her express wishes, Joan took a photo of her anyway as she ran off with her dress flowing behind her.

The guesthouse in Nicosia was situated in the city two blocks from Ledra Street and cost forty euros a night, so he would be able to stay there for a few days without busting his budget. He already had enough facts and information to flesh out the story and enable him to send it to *Hores del dia;* however, maybe some further probing in this colorful area could gain him even more column space, possibly even enough to cover several days in a row.

All in all, he now had a very concrete lead to follow, even though it might have seemed vague. It was the shaved German-speaking photographer in the blue uniform jacket. As far as he could remember, he had also taken some photos of him.

Joan placed the camera on his lap and took a couple of pictures of his pulled-pork sandwich. Now that he had copied all his image files from the camera to his mobile and laptop, it felt safe to swipe through the image files on the camera itself. With this material, he should be able to get himself a permanent job at *Hores del dia*. Who except him had ever managed to secure that rag of a paper front-page press in the world media? It brought in a good income for the paper's greedy shareholders, so maybe he could be bold enough to demand a permanent job for continuing with his research. Montse Vigo wasn't a god, so why should he be scared of demanding something that was only reasonable?

He inadvertently laughed out loud at the thought of her annoyed expression while he swiped through the images and came to the photo he had taken of the German photographer.

Joan frowned; it wasn't very usable, to say the least. Apart from the man's hunched back in some kind of blue uniform jacket, there was nothing by which to pinpoint his identity. Not even the shaved head was visible due to the way he had positioned himself over the body to get a good shot.

Damn it, damn it, damn it!

Joan shook his head and squinted closely at the camera screen. What was it about the jacket that made people assume it was a uniform jacket? Was it the cut? The particular shade of blue? The black collar and lapels, or maybe the masculine shoulders? There were no distinctions or insignia on the arms or shoulders, but it did look like a uniform. Was it conceivable that the jacket had been stripped of rank and distinction and sold in an outlet? Was there an outlet like that here in town? He doubted it.

He opened his computer and Googled where you could buy uniforms. There were seemingly no shops in Nicosia specializing in military apparel. Maybe it had simply been purchased at a flea market; yes, it might even have been a jacket the photographer had been wearing for years and that could have been bought anywhere in the world.

Joan sighed and looked again at the photo series from Ayia Napa. Had he taken any photos when the photographer was standing up with the exhausted refugees on the beach? No, he hadn't. Why the hell hadn't he taken some?

He found the picture again of the hunched photographer. Was there nothing that could help him?

On closer inspection, the jacket resembled not a military jacket but rather a blazer of the sort that used to be used in civilian contexts. The material appeared to be woolen like the uniforms from the First World War, but it definitely wasn't that old. Besides, it wouldn't be suited to the field of modern warfare.

If he were to assume that a German would buy a German uniform in Germany, who could he ask? And how did you even say *black lapel* and *blue uniform* in German?

Schwarzer Kragen and *blaue Uniform,* according to Google Translate after a couple of attempts.

There was nothing for it but to make a start. Joan searched and quickly found a lot of debate forums on the Internet where people discussed uniforms of all sorts and shared information about where they came from. He posted his photo of the photographer in the blue jacket on a couple of forums and wrote, *"Is there anyone who can tell me where this uniform comes from?"*

And when he had finished, the night was still young.

The answer was on the screen the following morning when he opened his eyes to the burning heat and a light that threw shadows as black as coal in the small room. A pair of sleepy geckos had already capitulated and were sitting under the curtain poles waiting for the cool evening air.

        Ich weiss nicht wie alt diese Foto ist,
     aber mein Vater hat so eine gehabt. Seit zehn

Jahren ist er pensioniert von der Strassenbahn
München. Es ist ganz bestimmt dieselbe.

The woman had signed her name Gisela Warberg.

Joan jumped out of bed and translated on his computer. She didn't
know how old it was, but she recognized it as the uniform her father
had worn back when he worked for Strassenbahn München trams.

What do I do, what do I do? he thought, and Googled *Uniform Strassenbahn München.* Perhaps he had expected to spend a few hours researching, but after only a few seconds he found a uniform for sale on
eBay that looked exactly like the one the photographer had been
wearing.

"*Alte Schaffnertasche, Uniform, Abzeichen, Strassenbahn München
Trambahn Konvolut, 399,00 Euro,*" read the advert.

It was definitely the same uniform, but what the hell should he do
now? Fly back to Barcelona with his notebook full of notes and a reasonable set of assumptions that could stretch out to two or three articles? No, it wasn't enough. But how did he follow up on this lead and
finally find the man in the uniform so he could confront him about his
connection with the disappeared refugee who was supposedly a holy
warrior and was now loose God knew where in Europe?

There was a knock at the door of Joan's room.

The boy at the door looked momentarily confused when he saw Joan
standing in front of him with his body sparsely covered with a sheet,
but then passed him the envelope he had in his hand. The second Joan
took the envelope, the boy made a run for it. Joan didn't even manage
to shout anything before the boy was down the stairs in a couple of
jumps.

Perplexed, Joan sat on the bed and opened the envelope.

Inside, there was a scrap of paper folded over a photo.

Joan took it out, and with no more than a quick glance, he knew
what he was guilty of.

He swallowed a couple of times with his eyes closed before he dared
to look at the photo again. It was dreadful and left no room for doubt.

The body was on its back with a slit throat and dead, dull eyes. A couple of notes were sticking out between the woman's pale lips. Two fifty-euro notes, to be more precise.

Joan threw it on the bed and looked away while fighting back his compulsion to vomit. This woman had bet her life for a measly fifty euros and lost. If he wrote about what had led to this unfortunate woman's death, the finger would be firmly pointed at him. It was a fact that if he hadn't taken on this assignment, she would still be alive.

Joan stared into thin air. But he had.

He sat for a long time with the scrap of paper in his hand before mustering the strength to read the English text.

Joan Aiguader, we know who you are, but you have nothing to fear if you do what we tell you.

You will follow your leads and write everything to your paper. As long as we know we're one step in front of you, we'll give you instructions along the way about what to do. And as long as you don't give up, we'll let you live.

And remember to tell the world that when we strike, it will be unimaginably painful.

You'll be hearing from us.

Abdul Azim, heading north

10

Assad

Assad was shivering all over, but what was it? A dream or reality?

All too clearly, he saw his daughters standing in the doorway in their lavender dresses: Nella, six, and Ronia, five. They waved to him with fine, subtle movements while the ailing Marwa stood between them with tears in her eyes, both hands on her arched diaphragm, a third baby on the way. Her expression said farewell. It wasn't a goodbye that expressed lovers' loss at a brief parting but a sad farewell that took root in Assad with unending pain, and a moment later Saddam's security police dragged him into a black van. It was now more than six thousand days ago. Days and nights, summers and winters, full of countless moments of pain when he thought of nothing except what had befallen his family, and always without answer. And now here he was, powerless with an overwhelming shock that almost stopped his heart from beating. Sixteen terrible years with the isolation of his uncertainty were torn from his consciousness in a split second because he finally had a sign of life.

Then the image changed; Marwa was standing in front of him, just twenty-one years old and as beautiful as the blushing dawn. Samir had his arm around his elder sister's waist and was smiling proudly. "I can't imagine a better brother-in-law than you, Zaid," he said. "In my father's place, I happily put Marwa's life and destiny in your hands, knowing we will all be blessed with happiness, *alhamdulillah,* thanks be to Allah."

And she was fertile and loyal. And everything a little Iraqi refugee boy could have hoped for in life had come true. Seven years together in harmony with God and the world, and then it was all over.

Half-asleep, Assad whispered her name and immediately felt a body cling to him; in relief, he stretched his hand behind him and felt its softness and warmth, the warm breath on the back of his neck, and the rhythm of a sleeping woman breathing—a sensation that could both make his heart rush and relax him. All disruptive thoughts were dissolved by the end of years of neglected sensuousness and intimacy, making him turn around with his eyes shut and recall the scents and challenges of the female body. In this slumberous state, his hands moved slowly down her back as her breathing grew more intense. The skin on her lower back and hips was moist and hot, and with a jerk she turned a little and parted her thighs so he could notice his effect on her.

"Are you sure?" a lazy voice appeared to whisper as if from nowhere.

Assad raised his head up to hers and felt her warm mouth, lips, and tongue embrace his kisses with desire, and her hands slid down and awoke his body.

When he opened his eyes, he felt himself welling up, but he didn't know why. It was the sort of disquieting feeling that serves as a warning that it isn't a day worth waking for. Like the thought of an upcoming exam you can't pass, like you've just been diagnosed with life-threatening cancer, or like your lover has cheated on you and left you. Like life has suddenly fallen apart and left you in emotional and financial chaos. That was how he felt in one unreal moment, and then he realized that he was lying on his side staring at Rose's wall, that she was naked and pressed up against him, and that half a meter from his head lay a newspaper front page with a somewhat out-of-focus photograph of his long-lost wife.

This was reality, and it left Assad gasping for air.

The body behind him moved a little, and he felt a hand on his shoulder.

"Are you awake, Assad?" said a quiet voice.

"Rose?" He clenched his teeth and frowned. "What happened?" he asked without wanting to know the answer.

"You passed out on the bed, and then you lay here seemingly unconscious but sobbing. I tried to wake you to stop whatever nightmare you were having but had to give up in the end, so I just went to sleep next to you. Later during the night, we made love, and then you finally fell into a deep and peaceful sleep," she said, unaffected. "Nothing else. But why did you faint, Assad? Is there anything wrong?"

He sat up with a jolt, his eyes moving between her face and the newspaper clipping at the foot of the bed.

"You do know that you're exposing your brown bits right in front of my face?" She laughed.

Assad looked down at his exposed, naked genitals.

He looked at her apologetically. "I didn't know where I was. You're my best friend; if I'd known, I . . ."

She knelt in front of him, still completely naked, and put a finger against his lips.

"Shh, silly chocolate man. You're still my best friend, and a good fuck never hurt anyone. We aren't tied to anyone, are we? We're just two camels who bumped into each other when their paths crossed, so to speak." She laughed heartily, but her jovial mood didn't rub off on Assad.

"It's not true, Rose. I am tied to someone; that's what affected me so much last night and now this morning."

She covered her breasts with the duvet. "I don't understand. Who are you tied to?"

Assad picked up the clipping and examined it closely. For so many years, he had been faithful to his one true love in the hope of finding her, and now on the same night that he discovered that she was alive, he had surrendered to another woman.

Assad noticed the date at the top of the clipping. It was only a few days old, and now it was very clear to him that it *was* Marwa standing in the floodlight with her face distorted in pain. He had to force himself to look at her despair and hopelessness, the clothes hanging off her, and her face, haggard from years of hardship. But despite everything, it appeared as if she had enough energy to give some sort of comfort to the female figure standing next to her. But who was the woman beside her? An adult, that much was clear, even though her face wasn't in focus. Could it be Ronia or Nella, now taller than Marwa? he asked himself.

His tears were uncontrollable again. Assad didn't even know what his daughters looked like. And if that was one of his daughters standing there, where was the other one? Where was Nella? Where was Ronia? And who was who?

11

Carl

"Look at this, Carl," said Gordon, as white as a sheet. He pointed at a small, red swollen mark on his cheek. "I'm worried it's skin cancer because I was in the sun a lot last summer."

Carl took a closer look. It was bloody disgusting.

"If you want my opinion, you should stop touching it; I've never seen anything so gross."

Had he said it with any more emphasis, the nervous wreck would have broken like a twig. He looked horrified, and his voice was trembling.

"Stop touching it? So, it *is* cancer?"

"Well, I'm no doctor, but I can tell you that if you keep scratching it, it'll explode with pus, and you aren't doing that in here. It's a real bitch of a pimple, Gordon."

Strange how a face could express relief at the thought of something so disgusting.

"Was there anything else? I'm actually rather busy," said Carl, and he wasn't lying: His nicotine gum needed chewing, his feet needed a good rest on the table, and he needed to close his eyes for a suitable length of time before the news flashed on the flat-screen.

Gordon hesitated for a moment before composing himself to speak. "Well, it's just that the creepy guy called again! Not a day goes by without him calling to tell me what he's up to."

"Okay!" Carl sighed and reached out for the nicotine gum. "Tell me. What did the loony have to say for himself today?"

"He repeated that when he reaches his goal, he's going to decapitate his father and mother with his samurai sword. And then he's going to head for the streets and attack as many people as possible."

"A samurai sword, how interesting. Is he Japanese?"

"No, just a normal Dane, I think. I've recorded him, if you want to hear."

"Good God, no! So, you still believe that he's serious?"

"Yes, otherwise he wouldn't call every day, would he?"

Carl yawned. "You'd better contact our colleagues upstairs, Gordon. We don't need a lunatic palmed off on us down here. I don't imagine you'll want to take responsibility if you don't manage to stop him and he slays twenty people."

Gordon looked worried. He obviously didn't.

"Just a second." Carl sighed again at the sound of the telephone ringing and reluctantly reached for it. It was from the third floor.

"We have to go up to the command center right now," he said wearily. Yet another nap neglected. "Seems we have to be there when they present Bjørn's successor in five minutes. Pray to God it isn't Sigurd Harms."

It was the second time in the space of a week that Carl found himself standing in the parole hall tightly packed in with a mass of reeking colleagues whom he'd rather have seen shipped off to the other end of the earth. Had those unrivaled noses of the world engaged with inventing the myriad of scented waters and perfumes never spared a thought for what became of their well-meaning ambitions to create the perfect euphoria for the senses when their scents emanated from a body that had been bathed in sweat all day, not to mention when the seniors' Old Spice was mixed with younger colleagues' sissy scents like Hugo Klein or whatever the hell that shit was called?

Carl was almost knocked out.

The chief constable came forward. "It might seem insensitive to present Lars Bjørn's successor before his funeral; I would have waited had it not been for the volume of open cases in Department A or the fact that I've managed to persuade a very special person to take on the role. I can say with certainty that he'll carry out the job better than anyone else."

"It'll be Terje Ploug, then," Carl grunted to Gordon.

But Gordon shook his head and pointed behind him. Terje Ploug was standing there and didn't look in the least like someone who had been offered anything.

"I know that everyone here will agree with the appointment." The chief constable turned toward her office door. "You can come out now, Marcus."

A gasp of shock went through the room when Marcus Jacobsen, their former boss, stepped forward. It must have been six years since he'd retired to care for his wife, who had been ill with cancer; yet, despite the extended absence, the sight of him caused a couple of spontaneous claps, followed a few seconds later by a deafening applause, whistling, and stamping on the floor, the likes of which had never been heard in the honorable surroundings.

Marcus looked touched, but only momentarily; he put both fingers in his mouth and whistled so loudly that no one could ignore it.

"Thank you," he said when the room was quiet. "What a welcome to return to! I know that most of you here probably think I've passed my sell-by date, but for once the politicians have come to the rescue in demanding that we all have to work a little longer. So, despite my age, you're stuck with me for a while yet."

He called for quiet with a raised hand when people began to cheer again.

"I'm deeply saddened by the circumstances; Lars Bjørn was a reliable and honest policeman, and he should've had many years left ahead of him. A few hours ago, I spoke with his widow, Susanne, and I can tell you the family are having a tough time, not least because Lars's brother, Jess, chose to take his own life yesterday." He paused to let the news sink in.

"I'll be taking on the role of chief of homicide for the foreseeable future, and it's a task I take on with pride and in the old spirit of Department A. The chief constable uses the correct name for the department, of course; however, as some of you know, I can be a contrary bugger, and so with her permission, I've decided to call Department A 'Homicide' as long as I'm the one occupying the corner office. Politicians and their reforms can't dictate what we call our workplace."

Now the cheering was unstoppable. Even Carl clapped along. Things were wonderful with a little uncivilized disobedience.

Gordon was the first to react to the strange smell in the basement. As if he had just been bashed in the face, he stopped and let his nostrils vibrate. At least it smelled better than the orgy of aftershave upstairs.

"Rose?" Gordon said quietly, full of optimism. He hadn't seen her for months, even though he was the one who had taken her collapse the hardest. But hope, as they say, springs eternal, and it is often all one has.

Carl patted him on the shoulder. "It's probably just Lis who's been down here in the archive, Gordon. You shouldn't expect to see Rose at HQ again." He was just about to give him another pat when Rose stepped out from his office.

"Where the hell have you been? We've been waiting here for half an hour!"

And that from someone who had been absent for two years.

"Rose! Good to see you! Welcome back, even though it's just for a short visit," said Carl with an unusually broad smile to make sure she knew she was really missed.

Judging by her expression, Carl's welcome was nonetheless a little over-the-top. She was happier with Gordon's embrace, but then they had had their liaison together.

"We sat in here because there's more room. Come in, both of you."

Carl snorted. Two years she had been gone, and now here she was commandeering them and taking charge of his office. And what did she mean by "we"? Was she talking about Assad?

She was. They found him sitting in Carl's chair with streaks of tears on his dark face.

"Good grief, man. You look beside yourself. Is this because of Lars and Jess?"

Assad looked blankly ahead but managed to shake his head.

"Look!" Rose placed a couple of newspaper clippings on Carl's table and pointed at someone in one of them. "Assad is in total shock, Carl, and with good reason. He's spun us some yarns over the years, including that he had a wife and kids living here in Denmark. But have we ever seen them? Have we ever been told anything specific about them? Has he even spoken about them in the last few years? No, he hasn't, but today Assad decided to tell me the truth about his family. He lost touch with his wife, Marwa, and his two girls sixteen years ago, and since then he slowly came to accept that they were no longer alive. But yesterday evening something totally unexpected happened. And that brings us to why I'm pointing at the woman in this clipping."

Carl was confused and looked at Assad, who was sitting with his face turned away.

"I can see what you're thinking, Carl, and you're right," said Rose. "Yesterday, Assad saw his wife, Marwa, in this newspaper clipping."

Carl looked at the photo and read the text, which was about yet another fatal escape across the Mediterranean, this time to Cyprus.

"Are you sure, Assad?" he asked. Assad turned toward him and nodded.

Carl tried to interpret his expression. He felt he had learned to read the lines on his face over the years. When his seriousness was replaced by pain, how his smile lines became deeper immediately before liberating laughter, whether the furrows on his brow expressed thoughtfulness or anger. But the expression on Assad's face was not one he recognized. The twitching eyebrows spoke of despondency, the ripple by his mouth quivered, and his eyes were dull and lifeless. He didn't even blink.

Carl didn't know how he was supposed to react; this was no time to be diplomatic. Wasn't it the case that they had maybe never really known the man in front of them? Their hunches were one thing, but what about the future? Could they live with the truth when it was finally revealed?

He hoped so.

"Well," he said, and took a small pause. "You finally opened up, then, Assad; that must've been a relief. It'll give the rest of us something to relate to. Just a few sentences will change how we see you, and maybe we'll finally see the real you. At least, I hope so."

Assad took time to compose himself before he could answer. "Sorry, Carl. I'm really sorry. So very sorry," he said, and placed his hand on top of Carl's.

It was burning hot.

"It had to be that way, Carl. There was no other way."

"I see, and if I understand correctly, that's not the way it has to be anymore?"

"No, not anymore."

"Maybe you're ready to tell us all about it now?"

Rose lightly squeezed Assad's shoulder as he looked Carl straight in the eyes with beads of sweat on his forehead.

"My name is Zaid al-Asadi," he quietly began.

Just that was enough to unsettle Carl. Zaid? Al-Asadi?

Rose noticed his reaction.

"Assad is still Assad, Carl. Just let him speak."

Carl nodded, shook his head, then nodded again. As if he hadn't yearned for this for years. But Zaid? Is that what he was supposed to call him now?

"I assume we all agree to give Assad all the time he needs to find his Marwa?" she asked.

"Hell, of course," growled Carl. Who did she think he was? Adolf Eichmann? "Assad, it genuinely hurts me to hear about what you've been through," he said, and meant it. "It must've been really difficult for you."

Carl glanced at Gordon and Rose. Did this tough woman have tears in her eyes? And was Gordon looking at her tenderly? Even though

Rose had filled out, she was obviously still able to get Gordon's blood rushing.

Carl took a deep breath, because his next question would not be without consequence.

"Assad, I hope you understand that I have to ask you directly. Does this mean that everything that has happened in here between us was a deceit? Of course, I knew that your past is problematic due to your reluctance to talk about it, and I knew you had a lot of secrets. But your odd way of speaking, all the misunderstandings, the references to Syria. What is true and just who are you?"

Assad sat up in his chair. "I'm glad you asked me, Carl, because otherwise it would be hard to begin. But you need to know that there has been a good reason for everything. Once again, I'm sorry. You also need to know that I am your friend, just as I hope that you are mine, and that I've never said or done anything intentionally to hurt that friendship. Most of my misunderstandings with the language have been genuine; even though today I'm as Danish as the next person, I've spent most of my life in an environment where Danish wasn't spoken very often, and it's rubbed off. It's the same for a lot of bilingual people, Carl. So, you can count on more of the same, don't worry on that score. That way of speaking has become a part of me, sometimes as a role and other times totally naturally," he said, and scratched his beard. "But of course, you know what happened to the camel when it tried to learn Arabic and walked around the herd practicing all day?"

Carl looked at him, puzzled. Did he really have the energy to crack one of those now?

"The other camels thought it was weird so they began teasing it, and the Bedouin couldn't stand listening to its strange Arabic and thought it sounded awful, so it ended up as steak."

He smiled at his own parable and then turned immediately serious again.

"I agreed with Rose this morning to tell you my account to the extent I think you need to hear it. It'd be too much just now to try and include everything, but it'll all come out sooner or later."

Carl looked at Assad. It would be interesting to hear how many more camels he could weave into his account.

"And Assad will need our help to find Marwa; are you all in?" continued Rose.

Did she say *"our* help"? Was she suddenly part of the team again?

"Of course, Assad," said Gordon, and Carl tried to nod as naturally as he could.

"If we actually can help with anything," added Carl, and scrutinized the clipping. "This is abroad, and we can't carry out a police investigation just like that; you are aware of that?"

"Give it a rest, Carl," said the mother duck. "We can do whatever the hell we like as long as we don't pretend to be on official duty. Go on, Assad."

Assad nodded. "I'm sorry, you'll have to be patient because there's a lot to tell." He took a deep breath. "Perhaps I should start in 1985, ten years after we arrived in Denmark. I was an elite gymnast at the time and became friends with Samir, who was a few years younger. You know him; he's a policeman today. In 1988, I finished high school, where I'd focused on languages, and then I was called up for military service. I got on well and my superiors recommended me for officer training, but I declined and went on to be a sergeant in the military police. That's where I met Lars Bjørn, who at the time was an instructor at the military police academy in Nørresundby. He persuaded me to continue my military career and train as a language officer because I spoke Arabic, German, Russian, and English fairly fluently."

Carl tried to take it all in. It was a lot to digest. "Okay, well that maybe explains your connections in the Baltic. Is that where you were stationed after the Eastern Bloc collapsed?"

"Yes. Back then, Denmark had a policy of great-power politics, pumping billions into the Baltic states. So, in 1992, I was in Estonia and Latvia and later Lithuania. That's where I met Lars Bjørn's brother, Jess, who was an intelligence officer; I worked for him for a short period." Assad bit his cheek and sighed. "We became close pretty quickly; he was a sort of mentor and recommended that I apply to join special forces."

"Why?"

"He was special forces himself, and he obviously saw potential in me."

"And you were accepted?"

"Yes, I was one of the ones who was accepted."

Carl smiled. Of course he was. "You learn a bit of everything there, so I'm told. That explains your skill when the shit hits the fan."

Assad thought for a moment. "Do you know the special forces motto: *Plus esse, quam simultatur*?" he asked.

Rose and Carl shook their heads. But then Latin wasn't exactly the main interest of a hillbilly from Brønderslev.

"Isn't it, er . . . ?" attempted Gordon.

Assad smiled briefly. "It means 'Rather to be than to seem.' Do you get it? You learn to keep your mouth shut in all situations, but apart from that, there have been other and more pressing reasons why I haven't been open with you, Carl. I hope you understand. First and foremost, it's been to protect my family, but also myself."

"Okay, we'll try to understand, Assad, but you'll have to reveal how it got to that stage. Because if we are going to be able to help you, you need to drop the secrets completely. We've waited for—"

Carl wasn't quick enough to dodge Rose's slap to the back of his neck. "For God's sake, stop pressuring him, Carl. He's getting to it. Are you deaf?"

Carl rubbed the back of his neck. It was a good thing that harpy wasn't working for him anymore. On top of interrupting him midsentence, she had the audacity to signal Assad to continue.

"At that time, I'd completed all the qualifications needed to be commissioned as an observer and interpreter in the field; so, in 1992, I ended up in the Tuzla district of Bosnia in the middle of the civil war between Muslim and Serbian Bosnians," continued Assad. "It was the first time I was witness to how extremely abominable and atrocious humans can be."

"Yes, it was sick, what went on down there!" commented Gordon.

Assad smiled at his choice of words, and then his face froze with an expression Carl had never seen before.

"I saw far too much and learned the hard way that survival in war is totally dependent on your level of foresight. I hated it, so, when I came home, I planned to quit as an active soldier. It wasn't easy to work out what I should do instead, but then, on the back of my language qualifications and exemplary army papers, I received an offer as an instructor at the special forces barracks in Aalborg; it was the right thing for me at that point in my life." He nodded. "I was single at the time"—he smiled—"and Aalborg can be a fun place to live. But when I visited my parents and my old friend Samir Ghazi in Copenhagen on one of my weekends off, I met his elder sister, Marwa, for the first time and fell madly in love. The next seven years were the best of my life."

He let his head fall and swallowed a couple of times.

"Do you want something to drink?" offered Rose.

He shook his head. "We got married, and Marwa moved to Aalborg. Within two years, we had Nella and Ronia. I was really happy with my job as an instructor and wanted to stay in North Jutland, but on New Year's Eve at the millennium my father died suddenly, so we moved back to Copenhagen in my parents' flat so we could help my mother. Neither my mother nor Marwa was working, so I became the breadwinner for five people. I didn't want to continue in the military because there was a risk I'd be stationed abroad again. So I searched high and low for a civilian job."

"And you didn't find one?" asked Rose.

"No, what do you think? I wrote over a hundred applications, but with the surname al-Asadi I didn't get a single interview. Instead, I was offered a meeting with Jess Bjørn at Kastellet military fortress. He suggested that because I speak so many languages fluently, I should apply for a vacancy at the Danish Defense Intelligence Service under his command. Jess was a major and for a time worked for the Department of Middle East Analysis and coincidentally needed an Arabic-speaking and seasoned soldier like me. I knew it would risk being stationed in the Middle East, where Saddam Hussein was still wielding his reign of terror, but Jess assured me that if that were the case, it would be under fully controlled conditions. In other words, I wouldn't be exposed to any danger." Assad looked down. "Of course, it didn't work out that way in the end."

He looked up at Carl with a forlorn expression. "What I didn't think through was what consequences my military past could have for me if we suddenly found ourselves in a disaster-like situation, which we unfortunately did on several levels. My mother died of cancer two days before September 11, 2001, and on that day the world went crazy. And my world with it."

"Why yours? What happened?" asked Gordon.

"What happened? Task Force K-Bar, Task Group Ferret, and Operation Anaconda happened."

"You're talking about Afghanistan now, right?" asked Carl.

"Afghanistan, exactly. And it was the first time in the history of the Frogman Corps and special forces that they were sent on active war duty. From January 2002, those two corps were suddenly part of the international coalition, with me as an interpreter but also as a special forces soldier with a machine gun under my arm. And I'm telling you in confidence that it was used frequently. After a few months, I knew everything about how to kill and be killed. I saw people blown in half, found decapitated civilians and defectors, took part in suppressing the Taliban and al-Qaeda militia, and all the while without our family or friends knowing the horrors we were personally involved in."

"You could have refused," suggested Rose.

Assad shrugged. "When you've fled from the Middle East like I have, you always dream of one day seeing the region liberated from wrongdoing and evil. The Taliban and al-Qaeda stood for—and continue to stand for—the opposite. You also have to remember that I didn't know what I was getting into; none of us did. Back then, I already thought I'd seen most things—what could possibly surprise me? And despite everything else, it was a good, safe income, right?"

"How many times were you stationed in Afghanistan?" asked Carl.

"How many times?" Assad smiled wryly. "Only once, but it was for five months and in tough conditions with heavy equipment, a constant heat wave, and threats from the locals, who you never knew where you stood with. I wouldn't wish it on my worst enemy."

He paused to consider his next sentence.

"As it turned out, worse was yet to come. And that was my own fault."

12

Assad

"If the other inspectors can't do it, I'll bloody well prove where those assholes are hiding the shit myself," said Major Jess Bjørn to Assad late one night after yet another long, hot day when they had made no headway toward their goal. It was only a few weeks since Jess had been sent to Iraq as a UN weapons inspector, taking Assad with him.

Along with the rest of the international team of UN weapons inspectors, he had been deployed with one aim—to prove that the US president was right when he convinced not only himself but much of the rest of the world that Saddam Hussein had secretly hoarded weapons of mass destruction. But they had found nothing, and among Jess Bjørn's colleagues on the weapons inspection team, doubt was spreading about their mission. It was at that time that their boss, Hans Blix, expressed significant misgivings about the evidence on which the US intelligence services had based their assumptions, or rather their convictions. But Jess Bjørn didn't doubt it for a second.

"Saddam's people are simply too cunning for that old-school Swedish diplomat," he explained to Assad. "Hans Blix doesn't understand that when the Iraqis see our UN uniforms approaching, they've already hidden what we're looking for. Don't you think there's a shitload of bunkers under the desert sand where they can hide all sorts of machinery and dirty weapons?" he asked.

Assad didn't know. The Iraqis they had already met and questioned in the area seemed genuine. The nuclear plant engineers and administrators could clearly account for their stock of uranium and other radioactive elements, as well as for their intended use. The military bases they had visited did have enormous stocks of conventional weapons, remnants from the merciless war against Iran, but they had found no evidence of anything that contravened the Geneva Conventions. Despite the Americans' unwavering belief in the existence of weapons of mass destruction, there was still no certainty about where they might be. Saddam Hussein was probably reveling in the chaos, and he exacerbated the situation with frequent cryptic statements. But there were not many who were prepared to take a public stance on whether or not it was all just a cock-and-bull story, not even Major Jess Bjørn. Wasn't the attack on the World Trade Center a reality? he asked himself. And hadn't those behind the attack been from the Middle East? Didn't that prove what sort of people they were dealing with?

So why should this dirty dog Saddam Hussein be any different?

Such obdurate conclusions should've been met with normal skepticism. But if you can instill anxiety in a man, his powers of deduction and natural filters such as common sense are easily put in checkmate. This was exactly what the president of the United States and his advisers had exploited to the fullest in the period after September 11, 2001. The world was readied for a new enemy, new business opportunities, and, most important, the opportunity to cover up that the Bush administration had taken its eye off the ball and failed to realize the scope of the international and local tensions that had arisen from the situation in the Middle East. All resources had to be put into action, no matter the consequences. Bush adapted to the situation with new terms and aggressive rhetoric like *war on terror* and *axis of evil,* through which he skillfully created a popular desire for military action while also paralyzing the opposition. If, after the invasion of Afghanistan, it was possible to convince the world that the brutal despot Saddam Hussein had enabled the growth of his military strength based on weapons of mass destruction, what other option was there but to demand they be demolished?

Despite Saddam's persistent denials, he was threatened with harsh sanctions if he didn't allow weapons inspectors access to inspect military bases in Iraq, planting the seed of doubt that Iraq was harboring enormous quantities of weapons of mass destruction. For the average citizen in the West, the phrase had a magical quality and could cover almost anything: nuclear weapons, apocalyptic bombs, chemical and biological warfare. And the suspicions were based on reality, so they were told. Hadn't the loathsome dictator shown what he was capable of countless times? The chemical attack on Halabja alone, where at least three thousand civilian Kurds had been killed, was answer enough. What further evidence was needed?

And the Danish prime minister willingly went along with this rhetoric. When the American president told him that there were weapons of mass destruction in Iraq, he agreed that they had to be found and destroyed as quickly as possible, and with Denmark's assistance.

Regardless of the cost.

From the beginning, the intention was that Jess Bjørn, Assad, and the other subordinate UN employees would help with the inspections and investigation, even though it might take some time. And when Marwa's family in Fallujah caught wind of the fact that her husband would probably be stationed in Iraq for some time, they sent a message to Denmark without Assad's knowledge suggesting to Marwa that she and the girls come to Iraq to visit them in the town west of Baghdad so she could introduce them to the latest additions to the family. It was a happy reunion, not least when she told them that she and Assad were expecting child number three. She might have been only a few months pregnant, but news was news, especially when it was good.

Marwa wanted it to be a surprise that they were in Iraq, and it certainly was a surprise. She was suddenly standing with the girls outside Assad's tent. They greeted him with beaming smiles, sweat forming on their brows, anticipating his arms around them, and Marwa was excited at the thrill her husband would feel that they were together again in the country that had raised them.

But Assad was far from thrilled; Iraq was a brutal country to be in, and no one knew what the next day might bring. He urged them to say good-bye to the family and travel quickly back home. But Marwa had other ideas. If Assad was going to be in Iraq for months anyway, why couldn't they meet once in a while with the family in Fallujah? He had been stationed abroad for so much of their marriage, so why not grab such an obvious opportunity to make up for it?

Assad was like putty in Marwa's hands. She was his heart and desire and, together with the girls, the world he lived and breathed for. So, Assad gave in to her wishes, and it was to be the biggest mistake of his life.

"We agreed to see each other once a week, and that's what we did for a month. But then Jess Bjørn was arrested by Saddam's secret police."

Assad looked around at Rose, Gordon, and Carl and was about to continue with his account.

"Hang on a minute," said Carl. "Jess was arrested? He was a weapons inspector, so why didn't it end up in the press?"

Assad understood why he asked. It had been a really nasty affair.

"Jess did something stupid. He dropped his UN uniform and forced his way into places where he wasn't invited. He bribed people working there. He broke in when possible. He photographed machines and facilities in legitimate companies and then manipulated the photographs to give the impression of something suspicious."

"Did you have anything to do with it?" asked Rose.

Assad shook his head. "No, quite the opposite. I warned him time after time; in the end, he disappeared without telling me what he was up to. I knew he was in deep, and then one day he didn't come back in the evening."

"They'd arrested him?"

"Exactly, and sent him to Annex One."

"That was a terrible place, right?" said Gordon.

Assad nodded. A really terrible place. He knew that better than anyone.

Assad reported to his superiors and informed them about his fears that Jess Bjørn had been captured. He was told that there was nothing they could do in the current climate; the man had removed his UN uniform and engaged in espionage, so he was on his own. Despite the family's pleas for diplomatic intervention to persuade the Iraqis to drop the charges, there was no reaction. It was inevitable that they would have to turn their backs on him, otherwise it could jeopardize the entire UN operation in the country.

Assad knew they were right. Jess was reaping what he had sown; when it came to spying, Saddam's judges seldom showed mercy. It wasn't until the death sentence had been pronounced, only a week before it was to be carried out, that the hopelessness of the situation really hit Jess and Assad.

With visible sadness, Assad relayed how Jess's brother, Lars Bjørn, had arrived the day before the verdict.

He certainly hadn't wasted any time. Three independent Iraqi defense lawyers sporting Western dress were in turn threatened, rebuked, and finally promised the moon if they could secure his brother's release. Their reactions were identical: They looked contemptuously at Lars Bjørn and the dark sweat stains forming under his arms, informing him without hesitation that bribery of the sort that could set an advocate against Saddam's judiciary didn't exist. They couldn't risk being on the side of an idiotic Dane with a death sentence. Did he know how many people simply vanished in the anonymous graves in the desert without anyone's ever knowing what had happened to them?

After two days of threats and pleading in vain, Lars Bjørn realized that there would be no mercy. His brother would be led to the scaffold, his head covered with a black hood, and then he would be dropped a couple of meters through a trapdoor with a noose around his neck to break his cervical vertebrae. A quick and certain death.

Lars Bjørn didn't rest at all that night in his hotel room; and the following day, he summoned Assad to inform him of his plan.

"I'm sorry to get you mixed up in this, Assad, but you speak Arabic and you're a trained soldier. If anyone can rescue Jess, it's you."

Assad was worried. "What do you mean?"

"Have you been inside the prison where Jess is being kept? It's located west of Baghdad near Fallujah, your wife's hometown."

"Is it Abu Ghraib? I know only too well where it is, Lars, but what would I be doing there? It's hell on earth."

Lars Bjørn's hands were shaking as he lit his cigarette. "No, it's a concrete annex a few kilometers from there. But you're right, it's hell on earth. There are no human rights, just torture, abuse, and suffering beyond belief. Many innocent people have been executed there over the last few years, and once you find yourself in Annex One, you're doomed. So, what you would be doing there is a fair enough question. And that brings me to why I've asked you here. You're going to help me get Jess out."

Assad stared at him in disbelief as a shiver ran down his spine. Who did he take him for? Superman?

"Lars, this isn't somewhere you would voluntarily choose to visit. How would we even get in, let alone get Jess out, without them noticing? Aren't there soldiers and guards on the other side?"

"Assad, we aren't going to get him out undetected. One way or another, we're going to get them to let him out."

Assad closed his eyes and imagined a compact prison with huge concrete walls and barbed wire. What was the man thinking? Had he lost his senses?

"I can see what you're thinking, Assad, but the plan isn't impossible. We need to convince the security police that Jess is their best chance to put an immediate stop to the weapons inspection. I've already contacted the judge who sentenced him and made a deal so long as Jess is compliant."

"I don't like the sound of that, but let me guess. You're going to tell them that Jess was spying with the UN's consent, is that it?"

Bjørn nodded in acknowledgment. "Yes, and that will compromise the entire mission to such an extent that the UN will have to cease with the inspections. Jess will be the Iraqis' best weapon in that maneuver."

"I understand that you'll do anything in your power to save your brother, Lars, but it's a lie. They'll find out."

"Find out? The Iraqis couldn't give a shit whether it's true or not as long as they have a confession. They've already had a good go at him, according to the judge. But he's a tough man to break. They whipped him until he fainted, then brought him to again with cold water, only to continue whipping him repeatedly. They claim that he caved in and said whatever they wanted him to say. But now they know for certain that he actually is part of a weapons inspection team, and that will have an impact when he provides them with a statement that his superiors ordered him to spy, regardless of whether it's true or not. Iraqi intelligence is based on lies, Assad."

Assad pictured Jess. He had seen him in a vicious fight in Lithuania and knew that he could take more pain than anyone else he knew. It didn't seem right that a day of whipping would break him.

"Lars, if Jess has revealed anything about who he works for, they must have used the most brutal torture possible. If they want to put him in front of a camera, it'll be days before he's up to it." The thought of what those bastards were capable of made Assad shiver. "Maybe they'll tie him to a chair in an enclosed room and force a confession out of him on tape and then execute him straight after. What's to stop them once they have what they want?"

"If my plan works, they won't do that. And that's where you come in, Assad. You'll go in and get him."

The idea made the hair on Assad's arms stand on end. People went missing every day in Iraq's prisons. Once you were in, you needed a lot more than luck to get out again.

Lars pushed a blueprint of a building complex toward him that read: "*Baghdad Correctional Facility, Annex 1, Abu Ghurayb Prison.*"

"I don't believe that Jess is as battered as they claim or as you fear because I've managed to get permission to see him for ten minutes before the execution, and for you to come along as my translator. Officially, ten minutes is what you get to say good-bye to someone, but in reality, most people never get that chance. I'm not going simply to say good-bye; I'm going to get him out."

He pointed at a row of smaller cells at the bottom of the blueprint. "This is death row. They pull them out, torture them, and when they have what they want, they hang them or slit their throats. The undeveloped area behind the buildings is used as a mass grave. The bulldozers dig deeper and wider ditches to make room for more bodies. I know exactly what goes on in there."

Lars pointed at a large square in the top right of the drawing.

"The square in this corner is close to the passage that leads to the exit—the only one for the whole prison."

He pointed at a cross close to the exit.

"You and I will be standing here in the square. When they lead him out from the death row cell, they'll come directly over to us. The camera will be placed right here, which is where Jess will make his confession. And to document that he isn't being coerced, I'll step in front of the camera and ask him directly if he's speaking under duress, which he'll deny. That's what I've agreed to with the judge. After the confession, he'll get up and we'll escort him out to the front yard, where my driver will be waiting to take us away."

"The way you put it makes it sound very promising and optimistic. But what if something goes wrong?"

"Then you step in and make sure we get out alive. You speak the language. You'll keep your ears open so we can react before it's too late."

"I don't understand, Lars. We won't be allowed to carry weapons on us when they let us in. How will we be able to defend ourselves?"

"Assad, you're a special forces soldier. Trust your instincts. If things go wrong, you'll know how to disarm people around you and incapacitate them."

Assad wiped the sweat from his forehead and turned to Carl with a grimace. He didn't know why all this was so hard to say, only that he was close to collapsing with exhaustion.

"That's how it was back then. Lars Bjørn was totally desperate. I'm afraid I need to take a break, Carl. Is it okay if I say my prayers and rest for an hour?"

13

Alexander

They had attempted to gain access to his bedroom to see him.

He had heard whispering outside his door and had seen the door handle slowly turn downward.

But Alexander didn't give a damn because he had taken precautions. On the first day he had ensconced himself, he had considered the topic of doors. Regardless of whether they opened inward or outward, they would always create problems for someone who wanted to keep them closed, even though he had locked the door with a key that couldn't easily be pushed out.

In this case, the door to his bedroom opened out toward the corridor, and with the use of a crowbar in the casing by the lock, it would be easy enough to gain entry. Alexander knew better than anyone, however, that his father would never smash such a magnificent door on his account, not to mention that he was too cheap and pedantic and didn't think his son was worth the effort.

Alexander still clearly recalled the pride and joy his father had exuded on first presenting his new acquisition.

"Behold our new house, son: It's a genuine symbol of noble craftsmanship. Solid doors, stucco ceilings, stairs with handmade banisters. Just look! You won't find any plastic door handles, plywood tricks, or peeling walls here. No, this is the work of people who had the will and the skill to create a unique and beautiful house."

"The will and the skill" was his father's mantra. When he spoke of other people, he divided them into categories according to whether they had "the will and the skill" or not. And those who in his opinion had neither the will nor the skill were written off as inferior underlings who would never be welcome in the same country as him.

Every mealtime was accompanied by his bleak views on those who didn't pull their weight or refused to submit to his philosophy of a well-functioning country. And when Alexander finally exploded one day, shouting at his father that he should shut the hell up and help those who didn't have the will or the skill rather than constantly making out that he was better than everyone else, his father gave him the first serious slap of his life. He had been only thirteen at the time, and it was to be the first of many because tensions ran high in that house, and no one should be in any doubt that his father would have preferred any normal Danish boy as his son rather than Alexander.

And here they now lived in a house built almost a hundred years ago by people who had had both the will and the skill. And regardless of whether the door could be secured from the inside on account of its atypically opening outward, the door was also endowed with a genuine and heavy brass knob that couldn't easily be removed. This doorknob was the key to Alexander's peace in the home; in a fit of practical home improvement, his father had fitted a steel wire on the stucco in Alexander's bedroom, from which he had hung a row of halogen lamps; the wire was fitted with a tightening device, but Alexander had long since pulled it down and tied one end of the steel wire to the doorknob and looped the other end around the regulator on the cast-iron radiator at the opposite side of the room, thereby preventing anyone from opening the door enough to gain entry. It took Alexander all of ten seconds to undo the mechanism and open the door when the house was empty. So, when his parents stood whispering outside the door, he simply smiled— they weren't going to be coming in.

"I'm fine," he shouted through the door. "I just need a few more weeks and then I'll come out."

That resulted in the whispering's ceasing, but Alexander was lying, because deep down he actually wasn't fine.

In the course of the last day, he had lost his life in the game, which had set him back so much that he momentarily considered whether he should drop his ambition of reaching level 2117. He just wanted to give the anonymous woman on the wall the attention to which she and all the others who had died on the beach and in the sea were entitled. When the time came, he planned to inform his contact in the police exactly what his intentions were and then go out and chop off his parents' heads and those of anyone else he came across. Then no one would *ever* be able to forget that number and that innocent woman.

That was his idea.

Get a grip, Alexander, he admonished himself, looking at the screen. *You can do this. Get it together. Shoot and kill without mercy; you've just been too tired lately. Change the rhythm and you'll get there.*

There was noise outside the door again.

"Your friend Eddie is standing out here, Alexander," shouted his mother. "He's here to say hello."

That was a blatant lie. First, Eddie wasn't his friend, and second, he wouldn't just pop by to say hello. Maybe if he wanted to borrow something, which he never returned anyway, or possibly if he wanted a tip for some good porn sites, but not simply to say hello. Not in a million years.

"Hi, Eddie, how much have my parents paid you?" he shouted back. "I hope it's a lot. But if you're smart, you'll take the money and run, because I don't want to see you. Not even for a second. Bye, Eddie."

The poor guy tried to earn his money, shouting back that he had missed him. They had certainly coached him well in what to say.

"Just ten minutes, Alexander," he said, his voice more hoarse than usual.

Alexander reached up for his samurai sword on the wall and pulled the blade out of the sheath. It was so unbelievably sharp. If only that imbecile Eddie knew what awaited him if he somehow managed to gain entry. His head would fall heavily to the floor, and the table, chair, and rug would be splattered with every last drop of blood his heart pumped from his body.

"Just five minutes, then," the idiot tried again.

Alexander didn't answer. The best strategy for disarming someone was simply not to answer them. Being ignored drove people totally crazy, and it paralyzed them too. "Silence is the best weapon," he had heard someone say once. Relationships between people broke down due to silence; friends disappeared on account of silence. Politicians' best weapon was silence, followed closely by lying.

A few minutes went by with the pleas from both his mother and Eddie growing shorter and shorter, and then the sounds from the corridor dissipated.

Alexander placed the sword back in its sheath on the wall and returned to his game. He had a good one hundred and fifty wins to go before he reached his goal. On good days, he managed around fifteen wins, and only a couple on bad days. But if his luck returned, and if he made a concerted effort, conserved his powers, and increased his concentration, he would be able to reach his goal in a couple of weeks. It was all a question of motivation, and Alexander knew exactly how to focus on that.

He took his cell phone and found the number he had had so much success with over the last few days. He didn't manage to get ahold of his contact every time, but this time it was only a few seconds before he heard the slightly nasal voice on the other end.

"It's you again," said the policeman. "Tell me your name because I don't want to talk to you before I know what it is."

Alexander was on the verge of laughing. Was a policeman allowed to ignore someone who told him that he shortly intended to kill? What did he take him for?

"Okay. I'm just calling to let you know that I haven't made as much progress as I'd hoped. You might have to wait a little longer before I reach twenty-one seventeen because it's hard to make headway. I get killed all the time, you know, which sets me back and wastes time. And then I have to build up my points again."

"What game are you playing, and why is it so important for you to reach number twenty-one seventeen? What's the deal with that number?"

"You'll know when I reach it. And when I *do* reach it, you'll also know my name. That's a promise."

And then he hung up.

14

Carl

"Do you know more than what Assad has just told us, Rose?" asked Carl when Assad had left to say his prayers and take a rest.

"No, nothing. It's the first time I've heard most of this."

"I understand you're back here at HQ because you want us to help Assad. Does that mean you're returning to Department Q?"

"Do you think I look like someone who's up to that?"

Carl took in her appearance. The previously disciplined and athletic woman was a shadow of her former self. He was actually shocked by her shapelessness and sluggish movements. Her question was fair enough.

"You look good," said Gordon from the back. "You can manage, Rose."

Was the guy close to drooling when she smiled back at him?

"I don't mind saying we've missed you and your insight, Rose, and even your cheek to some degree," said Carl. "And the fact is that if we're going to use man-hours on Assad's case, we have to insist that you come back. The choice is yours. Are you in or out?"

A familiar but unexpected voice in the corridor interrupted them. "Is who in or out?" asked the figure when it appeared in the doorway. It was Marcus Jacobsen.

He walked over to Carl with an outstretched hand and greeted each of them with a smile that promised news.

"As you've probably figured out, I'm conducting a charm offensive in the various departments. Were they talking about you, Rose?"

She looked at him with respect but forgot to nod. She had always had some sort of soft spot for this seasoned man.

Marcus flashed her his trademark beaming smile, which had left him wrinkled. "It would be good for everyone if you feel strong enough to come back. I know you've had it tough, so it's obviously something you'll need time to think over."

He turned to Carl. "I'm starting with your department, and you might think it's because I'm going through the building floor by floor, but you'd be wrong; it's because Department Q is probably the most effective and successful investigative unit we've had at HQ, and it's my hope to not only keep you all on but to improve and modernize your working conditions. With that in mind, I've got a little present for you and Assad, Carl."

Carl could hardly believe his ears.

"You and Assad work very closely together, Carl, and as part of a pilot project intended to strengthen exactly that sort of relationship between colleagues, we're equipping a few of you with these."

He handed Carl two boxes.

Carl looked at the packaging. It was one of those super-modern watches that could do everything. How the hell had their newly appointed old chief of homicide gotten it into his head that Carl would be able to use something like this? He couldn't even figure out which remote on Mona's coffee table was for what. Was he really going to have to read a manual? He shook his head. Not likely! He would have rather read a feature on cleaning habits in Mongolia. It was a good thing he had Ludwig to teach him. This would be right up his alley.

"Um, thanks," he said. "I'm sure that Assad in particular will be really pleased with it."

"It has a GPS so you can always find each other. For example, you could find out where Assad is right now."

"Is it that accurate?"

Marcus Jacobsen looked at him, confused.

"Well, right now he's approximately eight meters from here in his so-called office on the other side of the corridor."

Jacobsen smiled. Something Lars Bjørn would never have done.

"Well, the point is that it should be seen as an appreciation of your work. And if you ever have anything on your mind, you can always come to me. Remember that."

Carl looked at the other two and counted the seconds to himself. One, two, three . . .

Only four seconds, and Gordon was first.

"I have a problem," he said. "I have this young man on the phone every two minutes threatening to kill his parents and random people on the street just as soon as he reaches a specific number in a game he's obsessed with. I think he means it, so we're discussing what we should do about it."

"Okay, good to know!"

"He calls from a cell phone using a prepaid telephone card. He probably has several."

Marcus appeared to agree with that assumption; he probably hadn't imagined anything else. "How long has this been going on?" he asked.

"Some days now."

"Have you contacted the telephone companies?"

"Yeah. But unfortunately, the guy only talks to me for short bursts. He's probably changing the prepaid cards every time, and you can bet he's turning the phone off when he's not using it."

"Well, then we can probably also guarantee that it's a shitty old phone without GPS," added Rose. "Everyone will need to be more on the ball if we're going to detect him using cell towers. And even if we're successful, it won't be within a radius of ten meters like people think. It's not like those watches you've just been given."

"Does he speak Danish?" asked Marcus, directing himself to Gordon, unaffected by Rose's obvious and envious glances at the watch boxes.

"Yes, fluently, I'd say. He sounds like a teenager or perhaps a little older."

"What are you basing that on?"

"He talks like a teenager trying to sound clever, but then he uses words that demonstrate a certain maturity. Maybe he's been well brought up."

"What do you mean?"

"Well, once, for example, he used the word *dispatch* instead of *kill* or *murder*."

"Hmm, does he speak in an affected manner?"

"A what manner?"

"Like people from Rungsted or Gammel Holte?"

"No, I wouldn't say that. But he also doesn't have the Copenhagen accent you hear young people using in Nørrebro or Rødovre, for example."

"No discernible Funen, Jutland, or Zealand accent?"

"No, I don't think you could pinpoint an accent like that."

"You're ready to record him next time, I assume?"

"Yes, of course. I'm already doing that. I've only managed to record him once, but he didn't say too much that time."

"A little can go a long way, Gordon."

Carl agreed. The police had experts in linguistics and dialects, so Marcus had a point. It was worth looking into.

"Have you contacted the police security and intelligence service?" asked the chief of homicide.

Carl took it upon himself to answer. "No, we haven't contacted PET yet. But we're considering it, of course."

"Do you know why this guy is calling Department Q in particular?"

"No, but I *have* asked him," answered Gordon.

Marcus beamed again. "This young man has no doubt read about you. Perhaps he knows how effective you are and really wants to be caught before it's too late."

Wow, bull's-eye, thought Carl. Now Gordon wouldn't give up this case for anything in the world.

The lanky beanpole was scratching his head. "So, what should I do now other than record the conversations?"

"Contact PET and ask them to listen in on the line with you."

Carl frowned. Hell no, he wasn't going to have them checking his telephone lines.

"We'll manage ourselves, Marcus," he said. "We have our ways to catch idiots like that."

Gordon was about to protest but noticed Carl's glaring eyes. Carl changed the subject. "We have another case that requires me, Rose, and Assad to give it our full attention over the next few days, possibly more."

Marcus sat down and listened while Carl and Rose took turns explaining what Assad had revealed about himself.

For a man who throughout his professional career had experienced more than his share of most things, the chief of homicide was more affected by this account than Carl had expected. No doubt about it.

"Good God!" Marcus responded before sitting in silence for a moment in an attempt to allow what he had heard to sink in. It was obviously no easy task.

"Right then," he finally said. "Of course, it explains a lot about who Assad is and why Lars Bjørn went to such lengths to create a new identity for him and secure him a job that matched his talents." He directed himself to Carl. "And he did a good job sending him down here to you, Carl. No coincidence there."

"Show Marcus the clippings, Carl. Let him see what started the whole thing," said Rose.

Carl pushed the pile of clippings over to him and pointed at the photo of the women in the first clipping. "That's Assad's wife, Marwa, and probably one of his daughters standing next to her."

Marcus took his reading glasses from his breast pocket. "The photo was taken in Cyprus a few days ago, I see."

"Yes, in Ayia Napa. That's where the refugees came ashore."

"What about the other clippings? What do they say?" He picked up a couple of them and read the headlines. "Have you read them all?" he asked.

Carl shook his head. "No, I haven't had time yet. But Rose has read them all, haven't you?" he said. "She collects that sort of thing."

Rose blushed. That was a shock! Was she really capable of being embarrassed?

She pulled out a clipping from the bottom of the pile. "This one was hanging on the wall in my bedroom; that's where Assad saw it, and it almost paralyzed him."

Did she say in her bedroom? What on earth was Assad doing in there?

"A moment later, I understood why," she continued. "Assad recognized the drowned woman. She was a sort of second mother to him."

They all looked at the headline on the clipping. VICTIM NUMBER 2117.

"What the . . . !" exclaimed Carl, and Gordon was sitting speechless next to him with his mouth wide open.

"Twenty-one seventeen!" Gordon managed to utter. "That's the exact number the boy who keeps calling me is trying to reach in his game before murdering his mother and father."

A familiar and welcome change of expression was discernible on the chief of homicide's face. It was still a mystery what it meant, but he was no doubt pondering connections, which had always been his forte. But what was he thinking just now? Presumably the same as Carl: This couldn't be a mere coincidence.

"That number has obviously made an impression on the boy. But where could he have seen it?"

"It was a front-page headline in newspapers across the world, Marcus," said Rose.

He frowned. "When did he start calling you, Gordon? Was it before or after these headlines?"

Gordon glanced at the date on the newspaper. "Definitely after. A day, more likely two."

"Could the boy have known the connection between the drowned woman and Assad and that way also indirectly with Department Q?"

"No, impossible!" said Rose. "Assad saw the photo for the first time yesterday, I'm certain. But the message about the awful things happening in the world to these refugees is really strong in the article; you'd

have to be very cynical not to be moved by it. That's why I hung it on
my wall," she added.

"Well, the boy is certainly moved in a very cynical way, if you ask
me. Even though I might want to, I don't chop my mother's head off just
because she's a nightmare and drives me nuts," grunted Carl.

The chief of homicide looked pensive. "Okay, Gordon. When the boy
calls next time, tell him you're familiar with the photo of victim twenty-
one seventeen. Tell him you understand why he's outraged and see if
you can get him to open up."

Gordon looked nervously at him. Maybe he wasn't the right one for
the job.

"And, Gordon," continued the chief of homicide, "you can go and
get Assad now, or Zaid al-Asadi, if that's the name he prefers. And I
don't think you should tell him about the boy and the number; there'll
be plenty of time for that. He has enough on his plate just now, or what
do you think, Carl?"

Carl nodded and pictured Assad the day he had started down here
in the basement over ten years ago, how he had introduced himself as
Hafez el-Assad, a Syrian refugee with green rubber gloves and a bucket
by his feet. But inside, he was really Zaid al-Asadi: a special forces soldier, language officer, Iraqi, and almost-fluent Danish speaker. The man
was one hell of a gifted actor.

They turned toward the door as Assad walked in with his disheveled curls sticking out in all directions. His eyes were tired and bloodshot when he briefly greeted Marcus Jacobsen and congratulated him
on his new job. Then he sat down and listened as Carl explained that
the chief of homicide was now informed about his situation and that
they would appreciate it if he felt up to continuing with his account.

Assad cleared his throat a couple of times and closed his eyes, but it
was only when he felt Rose's hand on his shoulder that he continued.

"Lars Bjørn and I weren't able to meet his brother in prison until there
were only two days to go before the execution. And when Lars saw him

sitting with his hands cuffed behind his back and his face almost unrecognizable, he knew that the Iraqis had extracted everything from him."

Assad opened his eyes and looked directly at Carl. "His nose was never the same again, and one of his ears was half flayed off. He had cuts and bruises all over his naked torso. His fingernails were dark blue. No wonder Lars was shocked. They weren't allowed to speak Danish with one another, so he couldn't inform Jess of his plan that way. However, he had been given more than the allotted ten minutes when suddenly the guards pulled back, which they had more than likely been instructed to do. Lars told me that Jess seemed very apathetic when he heard about the plan. Lars was convinced for a moment that Jess would rather die than betray the UN mission, but then he began to cry. He was a broken man."

"I don't get it," said Carl. "What was the problem? When he was freed, he could just tell the press that he had acted independently."

"You're not a professional soldier, Carl. He would be dishonored. Do you understand? In his world . . ."

"No, I don't understand anything."

"He knew that the Iraqis would say his retraction was a lie. That they had extracted the truth from him, and that this would remain the unquestioned record."

"But he went along with the plan, so what happened in the end?"

Assad doubled over slightly as if the memory gave him a stomach cramp. And then he continued.

15

Assad

The following day, the sun shone mercilessly and spread an unbearable heat across the country. Tarmac melted, and the locals remained indoors. It was warmer than Assad had ever experienced, and only two minutes after they left Lars Bjørn's hotel, both their shirts were drenched with sweat.

The road to the prison annex felt endless, and the armored car Lars had hired felt like an oven. Even their seasoned driver, a Lebanese mercenary Lars knew from the past, had sweat dripping from his beard as if he had drunk a glass of water and was drooling it back out again.

He parked ten meters from the concrete wall that ran around the entire complex and where a pair of unsmiling soldiers were waiting for them at the entrance gate. A quick body search conducted with bellowing commando orders set the mood, and when they escorted them in, Assad gagged.

The two guards led them through a five-meter-wide and twenty-meter-long passage flanked by both an inner and outer wall that finally led to a deserted square, which on one side bordered a conjoining row of concrete buildings.

A short distance from them, they heard an inmate briefly shout that Allah was great followed by some dull thuds, after which the silence returned.

The radiating heat caused the walls surrounding the empty square to dance. It was almost impossible to breathe.

Then they were commanded to stand quietly and wait while the two soldiers stood behind them, each with a machine gun hanging by their side. Assad noted their alert and penetrating eyes. Even though the heat made them drowsy, they wouldn't hesitate to react in the event of an unexpected situation.

Assad turned to Lars Bjørn; he wasn't looking good with his bloated face and short, shallow breathing.

It was always difficult to be confronted with anxiety that could not be tamed.

Ten minutes later, two prison guards with bare chests dragged out Lars's brother, Jess, and let him fall to his knees in front of them. He was followed by two official-looking men in black suits, without doubt members of Saddam's security police, and finally by a robed Iraqi carrying an oversized camera.

While the two prison guards left the square, the two men in black stood behind Jess, who could barely lift his head, kicking him until he finally did and looked directly at his brother. He looked so despondent and full of regret and fear that it was hard to imagine that he would be able to offer his testimony without giving away the deceit.

Then the cameraman stepped closer and gave Lars Bjørn the signal to position himself between the camera and his brother.

Assad took a few steps back, bringing him closer to the soldiers behind him. Three long steps he reckoned, without looking back.

Lars Bjørn, bathed in sweat, was standing in front of him facing the camera. He was silent, a little unsteady on his feet perhaps, but then the temperature was a challenge. In the flickering heat of the dusty square, the two men in black stood expressionless behind the kneeling Jess Bjørn. The soldiers immediately behind Assad were like robots, ready to end the whole affair at a moment's notice. Assad and Lars had not put themselves in an easy position.

Assad stood completely still and tried to ascertain from which direction any threat might come.

Come on, Lars, he thought, and wiped his forehead with the back of his hand. *Say and do the right thing.*

But from the moment the cameraman gave the signal to when Lars Bjørn opened his mouth felt like an eternity. And when it finally did happen, it sounded as if he did so under duress. His sentences were mechanical, and he struggled with the English words. What was supposed to be an unequivocal testimony to his brother's willingness to betray the UN mission became an unconvincing farce.

It was then that Jess showed them what he was made of. It was then that the despairing figure raised his head and looked directly at the camera.

"My brother is only saying what we've agreed," he said in English with a faltering voice. "You can see how affected he is by the situation. But the reality is that I acted on my own initiative. I have spied, that's true, and I haven't found anything that can justify this UN mission."

He took a deep breath. "That's the truth, and I've been sentenced to death. Not because I've broken into sensitive Iraqi sites without wearing a uniform but because during my last mission I came close to killing a guard. So I surrender myself to my fate and apologize to everyone for my intentions and actions."

He paused and spat a few bloodred drops in the sand in front of him. It was only then that Assad realized what Lars Bjørn's real plan was and why he hadn't told him about it, instead simply instructing him to follow his instincts. And now was the time to use them; he knew that the minute Jess's bloody spit disappeared in the sand.

There were only two possibilities after Jess's unexpected testimony. Either the verdict of the Iraqi court would be carried out, in which case Jess would be hanged, or the punishment would come more promptly. One thing was for certain: Action would be taken. And when the elder of the two men in black gave the soldiers behind Assad a stern look, Assad's instincts kicked in. And the very second the youngest security officer loosened his jacket and reached with his right hand for his weapon, Jess exploded with incredible force, jumping up from his kneeling position and throwing himself back against the men so they fell to the ground.

Without hesitation, Assad did the same, throwing himself backward and into the nearest soldier behind him so they ended up in the dust with Assad on top. In a split second, he thrust his elbow into the soldier's larynx, made a grab for his machine gun, pulled it to one side, and fired a single shot into the other soldier's abdomen. Meanwhile, Jess was fighting the officer who only seconds before had been ready to murder him in cold blood with a shot to the back of the neck. Now the officer was on the ground, looking confused and waving his pistol around while Jess grappled with him in a brutal headlock, twisting his arm until the neck broke.

The second security officer only managed to let out an inarticulate cry for help before Assad shot a quick salvo into his thigh and he fell over. Less expected was the attack from the cameraman, who in one movement threw the camera to one side, jumped out of the line of fire, and turned to face Assad with a knife in his hand and a crazy look in his eyes that testified to his ability to use it on live flesh.

In that moment, the bond between Assad and Jess became unbreakable, because it was Jess who, with the security officer's pistol, saved Assad with a single shot to the cameraman's neck, killing him before he even hit the ground. While that was happening, Lars Bjørn hadn't moved an inch from where he was standing to avoid getting in the way. But there was nothing wrong with his eyes. "They're coming from the other end. Watch out!" he shouted, pointing toward a couple of guards who appeared from nowhere and who were now aiming their weapons at them.

"I'll cover you," shouted Assad, wrenching the machine gun from the soldier lying on the ground holding his mutilated throat. Then he picked up the video camera and hung the strap over his shoulder.

Jess and Lars Bjørn had leapt over the wounded security officer and were now dragging him along as a shield. A few shots were fired from the farthest wall, which Assad responded to with a short salvo that brought down one of the soldiers.

Now there was also the sound of gunfire from outside.

"That's our driver!" shouted Lars. "This is you, Assad," he commanded.

From the moment they could see the entrance at the end of the buildings, Assad fired constantly, all the while wondering how many rounds were left.

A few steps ahead of him, Jess pushed the wounded Iraqi in front of himself as cover, blood still pouring from his leg.

He must be important if the soldiers aren't shooting him, thought Assad.

A salvo from above caused the sand by Assad's left foot to rise up in a cloud.

"Take cover!" he shouted to the brothers and the prisoner. He and the brothers threw themselves close to the inner wall and crawled along the edge, dragging the security officer behind them, to avoid the line of fire from above.

How many people Assad eliminated before they reached the gate and the driver, who was standing behind his armored vehicle firing off salvos from a smoking machine gun, he only found out later. But guards and soldiers fell in all directions.

They sped off at full throttle in a cloud of dust and with the repeated hollow sounds of projectiles hitting the armored tailgate.

When the prison was out of sight, they pulled the wounded security officer from the vehicle and laid him on the ground.

"Fasten this tightly around your thigh so you don't bleed to death," Assad said to him, and threw him his belt. "Remember to be thankful that we spared your life!" The feeling he had as they drove toward Albu Amer and changed vehicles should have been one of relief, but it wasn't. So many dead, so many fatherless children who would cry themselves to sleep.

That afternoon, Lars Bjørn reported the episode with regret to their closest UN observer, disappearing into thin air with Jess immediately after. They walked for a month through wild terrain toward Kurdistan, and then from Turkey to home, before they were heard from again.

Assad was supposed to leave Iraq immediately with Jess and Bjørn, but, just as they were about to leave, his younger daughter called him in tears, saying that their mother was sick and was worried about losing the baby.

Assad stopped when a telephone rang in Gordon's office.

"I bet that's the boy," said Gordon.

"Remember to record it," Carl shouted down the corridor.

Marcus Jacobsen looked at Assad. "You didn't make it out of Iraq?" he asked.

Assad looked at him with a pained expression. "No, I didn't."

"And that had consequences for you? Dire consequences?"

"Yes. Unfortunately."

"But not for the Bjørn brothers? I don't understand."

"The Iraqis never breathed a word about this to anyone because they were worried about Saddam's reaction. They put it down to a prisoner uprising and dragged a mass of random prisoners into the yard and executed them in retribution."

"I see." The chief of homicide took a deep breath. "That must've been hard to live with when you found out."

"Yes, it was. I found out later that day when they caught me. Everyone in Annex One hated me like the plague."

Carl spread out the newspaper clippings in front of him.

"You're sure? Your foster mother, Lely from Syria, is victim twenty-one seventeen?"

"Yes! But I don't understand how she ended up fleeing on the same boat as my wife and daughter."

"They fled from Syria—that much we know."

"Yes, but I thought my family was in Iraq."

"Did Lely and your wife know one another?" asked Marcus Jacobsen.

"Yes, we visited Lely in her home shortly before Ronia was born. And until the civil war broke out in Syria, we wrote to each other regularly. We sent each other photos, and she followed Marwa's pregnancies and called herself a grandmother because she didn't have children or grandchildren of her own. I don't know how she and Marwa later came in contact with each other. It would've made more sense that Lely had fled to Iraq than that the others fled the other way."

"And you're also certain that it's your wife standing there, Assad? The photos are very unclear with this grainy resolution."

"This one isn't," said Rose, pulling out a clipping with a smaller photo. "This is from a different newspaper. The matte colors and resolution give a better result."

"I haven't seen this photo," said Assad, moving closer.

"Haven't you?"

He shook his head and fell silent, almost as if he were caressing the woman's red-eyed face with his eyes.

"No, I haven't seen it before, but this *is* her," he said with quivering lips. "And the young woman next to her is one of my daughters. I'm sure of it."

Assad's hands were shaking with emotion as he gently stroked his wife's face with his fingertips.

When he removed his hand, it froze in midair. It was the man standing next to them.

"What is it, Assad?" asked Rose.

Assad was trembling. The man was so clear in this photo. Too clear. It was too terrible to grasp that he was standing there next to his loved ones.

"Allah have mercy on me," he moaned. "I'm staring at the man I fear and hate more than any other person in the world."

16

Joan

The taxi driver, who was waiting outside Munich Airport, looked briefly at the address Joan had scribbled down. In a heavy dialect, he mentioned what it would cost to drive there, but Joan didn't really catch what he said, though he assumed it would be far too expensive for his tight budget.

"Just drive," he said anyway, and pointed at the windshield toward the hectic traffic that flowed past the terminal.

He had hoped to find a photography club or association of photographers in Munich who might be able to recognize the German photographer by his uniform jacket. So he had called the national association in Dillingen and attempted to explain himself in English. He had asked if they might know where he could gain further information, but neither the English of the person who answered the telephone nor Joan's was sufficient.

Afterward, he Googled everything he could think of but had to resign himself to the fact that Germany's third-largest city didn't appear to have an institution or photo agency that could help. His final conclusion was that he should try with various newspaper offices and photographic businesses, but only after trying museums that specialized in photographic art. He would show them his photo of the bald man in the uniform.

The big question was whether or not the man even had a connection to Munich apart from the origin of the uniform. Joan hoped so, because regardless of what his investigations led to, he was forced to provide daily texts about his research to his newspaper and, what was worse, now also to this Ghaalib, who called himself Abdul Azim.

The latter scared Joan, with good reason. Hadn't Ghaalib shown exactly what he was capable of? The bastard was a merciless sadist who had murdered victim 2117 without hesitation and ordered the throat of a woman who was incarcerated in a well-guarded refugee camp to be slit. How was that even possible? Joan didn't dare think about what sort of formidable network Ghaalib had.

So it wasn't unreasonable that Joan repeatedly checked the rear window to see if they were being followed. Were there black Audis, BMWs, or Mercedes on their tail? Or what about the white Volvo that had driven out behind them from the airport? Wasn't it about time they turned off?

He had taken precautions like this ever since he left Nicosia, and he intended to continue.

The warnings from Ghaalib had been indisputable and clear. Joan was to follow his instructions to the letter if he didn't want to end up like victim 2117 or the woman whose throat had been slit. For that reason, his visit to the Menogeia refugee camp was fastidiously reported in his article featured in *Hores del dia* and accompanied with a photo of the murdered woman. He had played down his own role in her misfortune, but hopefully not more than that devil Ghaalib could accept.

A few hours later, he could see on the Internet that his article about his hunt for the murderer had become big news. As quickly as he had delivered the final draft to *Hores del dia,* they had sold the story to myriad European newspapers hungry for sensation. The photo of the murdered woman was now eye-catchingly and scarily plastered on all the newspaper sandwich boards in airport kiosks with the slit throat blurred out and the eyes covered with a gray strip.

Joan's editor was naturally ecstatic about the article, which definitely brought in a good income and positive attention. That the newspaper didn't give a damn that its foreign reporter was in the lion's den was just something he would have to live with.

Through the windshield, he glimpsed the grand buildings of the city center as they came into view from behind the Isartor gate. As the first stop in his search for the photographer's identity, he had chosen Münchner Stadtmuseum, which prided itself on its substantial photography collection. There must be someone there who could give him a tip about where to focus his search. Wasn't it reasonable to assume that a photographer with a shaved head who went about in an old blue railway uniform would generate some attention in those circles?

Joan pulled out the piece of paper that the boy had handed him in Nicosia.

"As long as we know we're one step in front of you," it read. But what if he did actually find the photographer? Would he then suddenly be too close?

"Achtundfünfzig euro," said the taxi driver, more clearly this time, when they arrived at the museum.

Joan was relieved. The driver could have demanded double that without his even knowing if he had been conned.

From the outside, Münchner Stadtmuseum resembled an old warehouse that stood out from its surroundings like a geometric game the architect must have played with himself on a bad day. But then, Joan was also from a city whose trademark was Gaudí's visions and fantasies.

One of the museum's inner courtyards was adorned with a fountain figure, which required you to squint your eyes in order to understand its beauty. From there, Joan entered the museum and continued into the main hall with the ticket counter.

Despite informing the woman at the ticket desk of his reason for being there and showing her his press card, he still had to part with the seven-euro entrance fee.

"Hmm, I don't really know who you should talk to," the woman answered. "You really ought to talk to Ulrich or Rudolf in the department upstairs, but neither of them is here today. Maybe you can ask someone on the second floor, where we have a couple of temporary photo exhibitions."

Joan looked around the hall. A few meters from the counter, there was some information on the project Migration Moves the City, which was the museum's special exhibition on the ground floor.

Joan wondered if could there be a connection between the photographer's presence in Ayia Napa and this exhibition. If that was the case, perhaps the contact between the photographer and Ghaalib wasn't intentional and their conversation was simply a coincidence.

Was this all just a wild goose chase?

Joan sighed. If he had written a made-up story from the beginning, facts would be irrelevant. But after Ghaalib's letter in Nicosia, that ship had sailed.

He found the photography exhibition on the second floor, where a group of German-speaking visitors was in the middle of a tour of the hundreds of framed portrait photos covering the white walls in several rooms created by partitions.

Joan approached the tour guide. She definitely had the look of a museum employee.

"Excuse me," he interjected in the middle of her speech, for which he received an angry stare.

"You'll have to wait until we're finished," she said harshly, and turned her back on him.

Joan looked around. There was nowhere to sit in the room, so he leaned up against an empty patch of wall by the entrance and did as he was told. *She won't get away without talking to me,* he thought, and kept an eye on her yellow skirt in the middle of the throng of followers.

He smiled amicably at the visitors, who passed him as if he were an employee, and a few of them even asked him questions, which he politely responded to by pointing over at the yellow skirt. In return, he received smiles and recognition, which made him think that there might be a job for him in the Museum of Modern Art or the Picasso Museum in Barcelona if *Hores del dia* didn't have a position for him.

The thought appealed to him.

A Middle Eastern–looking man entered the room and smiled at him. And when Joan returned the smile, the man walked over and offered his hand. Joan was momentarily baffled but then thought that the man was merely uncommonly polite and shook his hand.

When the man disengaged his hand, Joan had a folded piece of paper in his palm. Joan looked up in confusion, but by that time the man was already walking around a group of Chinese visitors gliding past the entrance like a shoal of herring, and then he was gone.

"Hello," he shouted after the man so loudly that several visitors turned to look at him in disapproval. He gestured his apologies, and, amid a commotion of protests, he pushed past the Chinese visitors and out onto the stairwell.

A few quick glances toward the permanent exhibitions and down the stairs were sufficient. The man had vanished.

Joan leapt down the broad stairs, took a few steps on the herring-bone parquet flooring on the landing below, and continued down until he reached the main hall.

"Did an Arabic-looking man just walk past here?" he asked the woman at the ticket desk.

She nodded and pointed at an exit.

What on earth? he thought when he stormed out into yet another inner courtyard, this one an enormous cobbled yard with coffee tables on one side and a stack of stone cannonballs on the other.

"Did you see an Arabic man run past here?" he shouted at a blond woman sitting on a bench, writing a text.

She shrugged. Why the hell did people today never notice anything going on around them?

"I just saw him run in the direction of the synagogue on the square," shouted a young cyclist who was swinging around the corner and into the yard. Joan ran as fast as he could to the square in front of the museum where the synagogue was situated. He spotted the man on the main road only thirty meters away as he got into a white Volvo.

It looks exactly like the Volvo that was driving behind my taxi from the airport, he noted to his horror. *They* are *following me! They know where I am and what I'm doing!* he thought as he was overcome with nausea and the square began to spin. He gasped for air and grabbed a drainpipe to stop himself from collapsing.

When he had managed to regain his composure, he finally understood the situation. He was merely a temporary and very vulnerable link in that murderer Ghaalib's sickening game.

Only then did he muster the courage to unfold the note.

> *Well played ending up in Munich, Joan Aiguader. Just be careful that you don't get too close.*

It was exactly as he feared.

The tour guide in the yellow skirt upstairs in the photo exhibition didn't appear to be in a forgiving mood when he approached her for the second time. She had now dispensed with the group and was talking instead with a young man with imploring eyes and a hefty portfolio under his arm.

"No, I don't know him," she answered dismissively when Joan showed her the photo of the photographer in the blue uniform.

Joan's shoulders sank a little.

"Isn't there someone I can consult with a decent knowledge of photographers in Munich, or possibly all of Germany?"

She shook her head and was visibly uninterested in doing a favor for someone who had brought chaos into her territory, but that was probably just her nature; she was equally unfriendly toward the man with the portfolio.

"You have to understand, *we* invite our artists; they don't invite themselves. When you manage to have a few separate exhibitions here and there, we'd be happy to take a look," she said bluntly.

And with that she turned away from him with such effect that the yellow pleats spun around her legs.

"*Scheisszicke*," whispered the man to Joan. It obviously wasn't a compliment. "I heard what you asked her about. You'd be better asking the man standing over there writing in his notebook. He's an art critic specializing in photographic art."

Joan did just that but was once again met with an arrogant look and a shrug of the shoulders. Not even so much as an "I'm sorry, I can't help."

Joan sighed. He knew this conceit all too well from his colleagues at the newspaper.

"Really, darling!" interjected the critic's athletic and somewhat younger doe-eyed partner in English. "Can't you see it's the man who was assaulted by an actor in front of Münchner Volkstheater?"

The art critic returned the dreamy stare and then glanced at the photo on Joan's outstretched mobile.

They giggled knowingly to each other.

"You're right, Harry. *Mein Gott,* it was so funny," he answered over Joan's shoulder. "Wasn't the actor the guy who was making out with an extra in the middle of the street while being photographed?" He laughed. "Wasn't it just three weeks after his wedding? Yes, yes, I remember it now. What was that actor's name again?"

His partner whispered something to him by way of an answer and then turned to Joan. "The photographer took a really good beating." He laughed. "And the actor was convicted for violent behavior and received a not-particularly-uplifting letter from his wife's lawyer. Munich really is a jolly city at times. Look in some old newspapers and magazines and you'll find the story. As far as I remember, it was just before the start of the season last year."

And then they walked on.

"Hey, the start of the season?" shouted Joan. "When is that, roughly?"

"After the summer break," shouted back the doe-eyed one.

Joan nodded to say thank you and passed the woman in the yellow skirt without even deigning to look at her.

A few quick searches on Google confirmed that the season started in September at Münchner Volkstheater, which meant the attack had probably happened a few weeks before.

He typed *tabloid* in Google Translate, which translated it to *Boulevardblatt,* which then led him to find a couple of glossy magazines that reported the attack for which an actor named Karl Herbert Hübbel had been convicted. The victim was described as a photographer, who'd received a small cash compensation for the incident, but in spite of that was also fined for harassing a public person in a public place. The fine was appealed, however, and the man was acquitted.

According to the magazines, the photographer was a forty-two-year-old man, Bernd Jacob Warberg—the same surname as the woman who had answered Joan's question about the uniform on the Internet forum. So, there was a connection; perhaps it was his sister. The guy was also known as "B.J.," after his initials, and it wouldn't be a big stretch to imagine that those initials also reflected his other nickname, "Blaue Jacke," which was his signature dress code.

Joan felt a tingle down his spine. It was definitely the man he was looking for.

It took him all of three minutes to find an address for Bernd Jacob Warberg, and the place was only ten minutes' drive away.

For the first time ever, Joan felt like one hell of a guy.

It felt amazing!

17

Assad

Assad normally looked at others with warmth and empathy, but today was anything but normal. He didn't look at anyone, but he did sense them. Standing there on the metro like sardines in a tin, they were just empty shells. People on their way home from work, their thoughts already fixed on dinner, TV series, the few intense minutes with the children, a moment alone on the toilet, and subsequent sex. They stood there, emanating meaningless routine, habitual ritual, and hierarchical lives that had to be perfect.

In contrast to them, he was standing trembling with a green cardboard folder under his arm as testimony that people only understand how to live when all their senses gravitate around survival.

Assad was experiencing inner turmoil in every possible way. He had again asked his colleagues for a break in telling them his account to give himself peace to rest and pray, but this time the truth was that he was about to explode. Inconceivable sorrow and senseless anger led him to clutch this small folder as if it were pure gold that could be taken from him at any moment.

He clenched his teeth when ten minutes later he was standing in front of the dark building, staring up toward the light coming from the windows, which like a blazing fire shone from Samir's family's apartment.

The moment Samir opened the door, Assad broke down. Not with uncontrollable crying or a powerless and weak body, but with a mixture of inarticulate groans as he was faced with a torrent of Arabic words conveying curses and hatred.

They hadn't seen each other in several years, and their last meeting had been one without reconciliation. So, Samir's initial reaction was confusion and a desire to protect his family, who like waxwork figures were sitting around the dining table staring at him.

"Go to your rooms," he shouted to the children, and gestured for his wife to follow them.

Then he turned to Assad with a menacing look and seemed more than prepared to push him backward and out onto the stairs.

"Here," said Assad, and handed him the folder.

And while Samir looked at it in puzzlement, Assad sank down and buried his face in his hands.

Every little sound Samir made as he opened the folder and took out the copy of the photo and turned it over hit Assad like a sledgehammer.

Samir gasped and with his back against the wall slid down toward the floor next to Assad, his eyes still glued to the picture from Cyprus.

"Marwa is alive, Assad," he said repeatedly when they had sat down facing each other at the dining table.

Assad gave in to the intoxicating words that had also come to him the first time he saw that photo.

As Assad had done, Samir caressed his sister's hair in the photo with his fingertips. He cried when he stroked her cheeks and eyes, expressing sorrow for the distance and all the lines life had etched on her face.

Then his expression changed and stiffened.

"It's your fault that things turned out this way, Assad. Yours alone! You don't deserve her to come home to you. Do you understand me? Maybe she won't want anything to do with you." He looked at him with hatred. It had been this way between them for many years now.

Assad pushed the evil prophecy out of his mind. "The man next to Marwa is Ghaalib," he said, pointing at the man with the beard standing next to her. "He doesn't plan for me to see her again either. They're still his hostages, and he won't give them up voluntarily, trust me."

Samir looked intently at the photograph, his eyes penetrating the dark face. He immediately understood. This man was the devil whom Samir had never met in real life but who had murdered his elder brother and crushed his family when he abducted Marwa and the girls.

Despite his overwhelming anger, he remained silent but pressed the nails on his trembling hand hard against Ghaalib's face.

Assad took a deep breath. He felt exactly the same way.

"Be careful that you don't ruin it, Samir. If you lift your hand, you'll see one of your nieces standing next to Marwa."

Assad's brother-in-law didn't seem like he had taken it in. It was almost as if the last sixteen years had to be relived in glimpses before he could believe that this grown woman was part of his family.

"Which one of the girls is it?" he asked.

Assad's voice faltered. He said he didn't know. He really didn't know.

"What about Marwa's other daughter?"

Assad didn't react to his choice of words. As things had turned out, he understood Samir, because he was right after all. They were Marwa's daughters, not his. Not the daughters of a man who had forsaken them and left them to their fate.

"You have to help me, Samir," he whispered to contain his anger. "We need to find them. Do you hear me? You have to come with me to Cyprus. We'll find them and kill Ghaalib. We'll flay him alive and throw him to the dogs. We'll rip out his eyes and—" He stopped short when he noticed Samir staring down at the table.

"You have to help me, Samir. Please?" he implored again.

Samir sat up straight. Over the abandoned dinner with dirty plates and the remains of cold vegetables and marinated fish, he regarded Assad with glazed eyes and a look of contempt and shook his head.

"Coming from you, Assad? You're the one who's looked for this monster for more than fifteen years. You've searched but never found him. You've never even come close to a lead. You haven't even known if they were dead or alive. Are you really saying that to me?" He scoffed. "You're forgetting who he is, Assad. You're blinded by anger. Do you really think he's still in Cyprus? Ghaalib? He could be anywhere. Just not in Cyprus. Are you listening to what I'm saying?"

When Assad departed the apartment, he left the folder on Samir's dining table. Not because the anger and sorrow had dissipated now that there were two of them to share it, but because he couldn't keep the photo of that devil Ghaalib so close to his body. Just the smell of the photocopy made him nauseous, and the folder had been burning his hands. Just now it was Samir's turn to suffer. Perhaps it would help him change his mind and remember his responsibilities.

When Assad offered his hand to Samir and was snubbed, he knew that as soon as the door shut behind him, Samir would fall to his knees for the second time that evening.

Assad hardly slept that night. No position allowed him to escape the unbearable feeling of being awake. No darkness could shelter him against the events of the previous day, which had been burned into his soul.

When he had been lying there twisting and turning for hours still fully dressed, and had swiped the clock radio and papers from the bedside table and kicked the duvet onto the floor, he finally went to the bathroom, looked at himself in the mirror, and threw up. His exhaustion only got the better of him ten minutes before the clock radio on the floor informed him with a robotic voice that the time was seven o'clock and that a wonderful day awaited him. Then he finally lay down to rest, curled up in a fetal position, hugging the sheet as if it were a living being.

The last thing he did before leaving home was to let out a tirade of hateful abuse at the clock radio while smashing it against the kitchen floor.

No man-made gadget was going to tell him that the day awaiting him was wonderful.

18

Ghaalib

"It was Allah's will that we found Zaid al-Asadi so quickly last time. If the idiot had fled like the cowardly Danish brothers, we would never have found him," said Ghaalib to the photographer sitting in front of him like a king in his castle of a messy Munich apartment.

But if we had never found him, then this would never have happened, he thought, stroking his scarred lower face while losing himself for a moment in the memories of all the humiliations the encounter with Zaid had cost him.

Revenge!

Ghaalib smiled to himself, because now the time for retribution was approaching. He was sure of it.

"How long is it since it happened?" asked the photographer from the sofa, pointing at Ghaalib's chin.

"How long?" Ghaalib looked at him sternly. "Hundreds of sins and millions of breaths ago. Oceans of blood have been shed in the sand since then. So, long enough."

Now the women in the next room began shouting again. Ghaalib turned toward the man standing behind him.

"Shut them up, Hamid," he said in Arabic to a heavyset man who had been following their conversation. "Kick them or punch them until they get the message, and tell them to lie on the bed and wait until I come in. Force them to take sleeping pills. We'll be leaving in ten minutes."

The photographer smiled derisively. "You're finding it hard to control your women, aren't you?"

A single look from Ghaalib wiped the smile off his face.

"You'll be relieved of their crying very soon, because we have to get going."

The photographer looked at him insistently. "First, you have to tell me about what happened back then once you found Zaid al-Asadi."

"What happened? The man became weak and wanted to take his wife and daughters home with him, that's what happened. And it helped that they lived with their family on the outskirts of Fallujah, where my family also comes from." Ghaalib shook his head. "Just a few hours after the killings in the Abu Ghraib annex, he entered the town with stains on his clothes. Maybe the idiot thought that no one would notice, but in our country even the smallest child recognizes the sight of dried blood. That sight, and the sound of high-pitched shouting from inside the house where his women were. No one could be in any doubt that something unusual had happened."

Ghaalib smiled. "No, if there was someone who couldn't control his women, it was Zaid al-Asadi. But then, he had grown up in a country where too much attention is paid to women's opinions. And that was their downfall."

The photographer leaned back in the sofa. "And the secret police came for him the same day? Is that what happened?"

A couple of hard, dull thuds were followed by muffled screams from the room behind them. When everything went quiet half a minute later, Ghaalib's helper reentered and positioned himself behind him.

Ghaalib nodded in acknowledgment and turned again to the German photographer. "Yes, that's exactly what happened. The police came the same day. The idiot thought he could manage to escape the country with his family, but his wife was ill, so they were easily able to find him there with her family. And when they dragged him to the prison yard, the bodies of the men he and the brothers had killed were laid out in a long line on the ground. In total, he and the brothers and their assistant outside the prison wall had massacred fifteen men. The bodies were not shrouded so he could clearly see what he'd done."

"Why didn't you just kill him immediately?"

Ghaalib shook his head. Did these white dogs understand nothing?

"You have to understand that Zaid al-Asadi possessed a mountain of untold knowledge that had to be extracted from him, and that was exactly the area we specialized in at the Abu Ghraib annex. The security police in my country existed back then for the sole purpose of extracting information that would satisfy Saddam. The employees in the annex had to make amends for what had happened earlier that day. Do you understand?"

"So, you tortured him?" asked the man.

"Torture, mutilation, body demolition, call it what you will. But the man was tough. That's why the whole affair isn't over yet. But now we have to get going. My friend behind me has learned that the Spaniard is in town and looking for you."

The photographer sat up with a jolt. "For me? What does he know about me?"

"How would I know? But the little Catalonian is obviously smarter than you think." Ghaalib stood up. "I'll be in touch if I need your services again."

"Hey, hang on, Ghaalib. You can't just leave. You owe me a lot of money."

Ghaalib looked surprised. "Owe? I don't follow. I've already paid you what we agreed."

"Then we didn't agree to the right amount. You paid me to travel to Cyprus but not for your stay in my flat or to keep the women locked up in my bedroom. And you haven't paid for the fact that a man is now coming to ask me questions. It all adds up, Ghaalib."

"Ghaalib doesn't pay for beds to sleep in; we've discussed that."

"And the two women? The blood on the bed? The food you ate? What about that? It all costs money, Ghaalib." He leaned toward him with glaring eyes. "You're wanted all over Europe, and only I know what you look like without a beard. Don't forget that. So, if you don't pay up, you might regret it."

Ghaalib glanced at his helper before looking back at the photographer and the pulse in his neck. "Very well, I hear you, Blaue Jacke. And what do you think I should pay for all that? A hundred euros?"

"Yes, a hundred euros, and five thousand to keep my mouth shut."

"To keep your mouth shut? Hmm, you appear to have misunderstood." He nodded briefly to the man behind him. "Don't you understand that I'm like a decoy goat tethered at the edge of the jungle to entice the tiger? And when the tiger finally comes, it unexpectedly meets its end. The tethered goat waits patiently, and you should never underestimate an animal with horns."

Ghaalib felt the handle of the knife that his assistant had placed in his hand, which he was concealing behind his back.

"But you're right. You should have something for your services and for keeping quiet. We couldn't settle for anything less, could we, Herr Warberg?"

Then he thrust the knife forward so violently that the photographer jumped backward, landing on the top of the sofa with his eyes fixed on the sharp, engraved knife blade.

They waited until the side street was empty. Despite the pain from their battered ribs, the two women followed the men without a sound, only protesting feebly when they were pushed into the Volvo.

"Drive over to the other side of the main road and park on the corner, Hamid, so we can see who comes in and out of the house," said Ghaalib.

He turned to the back seat, where the two women were lying cheek to cheek next to each other and already sound asleep.

"We ought to get going; we have a long distance to cover to reach Frankfurt," said Hamid.

Ghaalib looked at him. "I know, but the people expecting us have time."

They waited fifteen minutes without a word, while the shadows slowly crept up the facade of the yellow building and people began to return from work.

"What did happen with Zaid in the Abu Ghraib annex?" asked Hamid, breaking the silence. "Were you there when they arrived back with him?"

"Yes. I worked in the annex and had since I was twenty-one."

"Were you a prison guard?"

Ghaalib smiled. "Yes, that too. A prison guard with special authority, you could say. I made people talk. I could turn my hand to winning the confidence of the inmates or beating them until they almost burst with information."

"And Zaid?"

"Yes, Zaid was something special, not just one of the spoiled idiots who screamed and bawled when they had a noose around their neck for blaspheming against our president. Zaid had been sent by the UN, so everything we could extract from him would be like a flaming sword in the stomachs of the conceited and self-righteous infidels who mocked our leader and the entire regime by their presence."

"But he's still alive. I don't understand how. . . ."

It was true, Zaid was still alive, and Ghaalib had only himself to blame. May Allah have mercy on him.

He turned to the side window of the vehicle and made eye contact with the man who was waiting patiently on the street corner in his large winter coat and long blue scarf.

And then Ghaalib let his mind wander.

While the soldiers forced Zaid's head down toward the faces of the dead so he could look each one in the eyes, they spat on him and mocked him to make sure he understood that the revenge for every one of the murdered men would hit him tenfold.

Even though darkness was descending over the inner yard of the prison, it was clear to Ghaalib that sweat was dripping from him, but the man didn't utter a word, and he maintained his silence when the first interrogation began. Only when they attached electrodes to his nipples and turned on the current for the fifth time did he open his mouth. And despite the pain and his hopeless situation, his words were clear, spoken in an Arabic that, while understandable, had a pronunciation and intonation that wasn't a perfect Iraqi dialect. "My name is Zaid al-Asadi, and I'm a Danish citizen," he said. "I'm here voluntarily, and neither my affiliation with Denmark nor the UN delegation has anything to do with what happened here earlier today. We acted independently with the sole purpose of rescuing a prisoner. You won't get anything else out of me, just so you know. Do what you want to me; it won't change anything."

He held out for five hours before he fainted and was dragged to death row and put in solitary confinement. They had lost a prisoner under similar circumstances, but it couldn't happen this time, which was where, once again, Abdul, alias Ghaalib, came into the picture.

"You need to win his confidence, Abdul, and just now I need you to do two things," said the interrogation leader. "Tell him that your family lives in the same neighborhood as his wife and children. And you need to ensure that by tonight the mother and children are separated from their family and taken hostage. Can you do that?"

"We have a suitable place, yes. I'll tell them that they're in danger because the husband won't speak and that I want to help them."

The interrogation leader looked satisfied. "Make sure you tell Zaid al-Asadi the same thing. Early tomorrow morning, just before we drag him over to us, whisper to him that you're on his side and that you just want to help his family. That you've taken them to a safe place so they can't be used against him."

It had been child's play to carry out. The man's wife, Marwa, was ill and terrified when Abdul arrived late that night and informed her that it was unfortunately normal practice for the security police to return and hold the entire family accountable for the actions of the head of the household. So the wife packed their belongings as quickly as she could and did not say good-bye to the rest of the family in order to protect them. That way they could honestly swear that the woman and the girls had just disappeared and state in all truthfulness that they did not know where they had gone.

It was only when the woman and her girls were thrown in a mud-built shed used for slaughtering goats that she realized that they had fallen for a trap. The girls cried and screamed, but they soon stopped when their mother was beaten every time they opened their mouths.

Before sunrise the following day, Abdul stood ready outside Zaid's cell door. He had seemingly slept well, and even though his eyes betrayed his fear and his body was mutilated, his movements were calm when Abdul stepped forward to the hatch in the door and whispered his name.

"I live in Fallujah, and my family knows your wife's family," Abdul said quietly. "We are close acquaintances, and even though we're Sunnis, none of us are loyal subjects of Saddam Hussein." He looked down the corridor before pointing his index finger at him. "If you ever mention that I've said this, I'll have to kill you. It's important you remember that. I've taken your family to a safe place. Trust me, and I'll do everything in my power to get you out. I don't know how yet, but if you hold on in there, we'll think of something."

Ghaalib took a deep breath and allowed his eyes to refocus on the building where the photographer lived.

Yes, Zaid was still alive, but Ghaalib did not answer Hamid's question. Not all stories were suited for other ears.

"I assume all the arrangements have been made in Frankfurt, Hamid?" he asked instead.

"Yes, we have spread the martyrs out between five different hotels in the center. They all have different appearances like you ordered. None of the men have full beards, and none of the women are wearing veils. A couple of those we recruited at the start protested about our demands, so we've dropped them."

"Did you end with fifteen in total?"

"Twelve. There are still a few interned in Cyprus, but two of the best escaped, so they're here too."

Ghaalib took Hamid's hairy wrist in his hand and gently squeezed it. He was a good man.

A taxi turned onto the street and stopped outside the main door of Bernd Jacob Warberg's entrance.

For a minute or two, it just waited there, and then a thin man got out. Even from a distance, it was easy to spot when a man was nervous. Movements, despite being controlled, became a little staccato and aimless. A hand slipped past the pocket a couple of times before going in; the head scanned the area with a jerking motion. Even the slightest drop of sweat was wiped away.

Joan Aiguader was definitely nervous and clenched his hands several times before stepping backward onto the road to look up at the photographer's windows. What had he expected to see? A face spying on him? Curtains suddenly being drawn?

When he observed nothing, he went over to the intercom, found the name, and pressed the buzzer a couple of times.

Ghaalib had expected that he would hesitate when no one reacted, and he was impressed when Joan then pressed the buzzer for every apartment in the building.

When he finally succeeded in getting the street door open and went inside, Ghaalib knew that his message would find the right receiver.

"You can drive now, Hamid," he said with satisfaction. "And drive carefully. The last thing we want is to be stopped. We can be in Frankfurt in four hours. That's good enough."

19

Joan

A woman was waiting for Joan in the entrance with her arms crossed. Her floral dress was faded, much like herself, but her eyes were glaring and her voice sharp. Even though he didn't really understand her German, the meaning was clear. Why the hell had she been disturbed by a total stranger, and why had he rung her doorbell? Did he even have any business in this building, and which apartment was he visiting?

He shrugged and moved his index finger in a circular motion against the side of his head. "I'm sorry, wrong floor," he said without any indication that she understood as he trudged past her and up the stairs, feeling daggers on the back of his neck.

Two floors up, he finally saw a brass plate engraved with the name B. J. WARBERG, and underneath it, a sticker with the pompous name INTERNATIONAL PHOTOGRAPHIC BUREAU, MUNICH.

Joan hesitantly raised his finger to the doorbell and then noticed a small strip of light on his shoe—the door was ajar.

He put his ear to the mail slot and listened but only heard the woman downstairs finally slamming her door shut.

His instincts made him pause, and holding his breath, he leaned against the wall between the two front doors for the apartments on this landing. *Be careful, Joan,* he thought. *A door isn't simply ajar unless the person living there has popped out quickly or there's something horribly wrong on the other side.*

Joan waited. Fifteen minutes later, and with no sign of life on the stairs or behind the door, he carefully pushed it open and stepped inside.

No one had ever accused Joan Aiguader of being a tidy person, and you certainly couldn't say the man who lived in this apartment was either. Slippers were strewn all over the floor in the entrance; a worn leather briefcase hung from the door handle of a half-open door, behind which was the not-so-welcoming sight of a urine-stained toilet with the seat up. Piles of old newspapers and photographic magazines had been lazily stacked up against the walls, meaning every step had to be taken with caution to avoid their tumbling over, not to mention the rubbish bags that had been left ready to take out.

There was a cool breeze in the hallway coming from a larger room in front of him. Joan assumed that it must be the photographer's living room.

"Hello, Mr. Warberg," he said in English. "May I come in?"

He waited a moment before shutting the front door behind him and repeated his question, this time a little louder.

As there was still no answer, he pushed the door to the living room open and immediately recognized an IKEA sofa identical to the one his family had had over twenty years ago. He noted that the window that looked onto the street was wide open before walking into the room.

He was met by an insanely shocking sight; it was so overwhelming that his legs gave way and he was suddenly on the floor in a pool of half-coagulated blood that spread from the figure in the uniform jacket, over the glass table, and across the floor.

Even though the man's cheek was resting directly on the glass table-top, it was easy to see that his throat had been lethally slit from ear to ear, giving the impression of a laughing mouth. He hardly had time to process his gag reflex before he was throwing up so much that the pool of blood between his knees was as good as covered in the contents of the uninspired morning buffet he had eaten.

How do I call the police? Is that even a good idea? he wondered when he was back on his feet and had almost regained his composure. *That bitch downstairs saw me. She'll think it was me who did it,* he reasoned.

And what if the police don't believe my explanation? What if they arrest me for murder?

He imagined Montse Vigo's stern face when she had to deal with this new situation. Would the newspaper provide an interpreter or a lawyer, and who would pay his bail if it came to that?

There was nothing else for it; he would have to get out of here before it was too late.

Joan looked down at his shoes and trousers, which were so drenched in blood and sick that everything he stepped on or touched would leave a trail.

I have to change, he thought, and stepped out of his shoes and walked across the section of the carpet that didn't have blood on it. Then he carefully removed his trousers, ensuring they didn't touch him or the floor, and, holding them in front of him, walked into the entrance hallway and threw them, along with his shoes, into one of the rubbish bags.

In the bedroom, which adjoined the living room, he found a similar state of disarray. The room stank of sweat, several duvets were thrown on the floor, and the unmade double bed suggested that more than one person had slept there.

He opened a distressed wardrobe, where he found a heaped pile of clothes and shoes, and two minutes later he was wearing a stranger's things, which were all a little too small to fit him properly.

God, what do I do now? he thought just before the shrill ringtone of a cell phone made him jump.

He peered into the living room and tried to work out where the sound was coming from. He noticed a narrow sideboard with a coin dispenser that must once have belonged to the conductor uniform Bernd Jacob Warberg had always worn.

The phone was lying on top of it, and on top of that, there was a note: *"ANSWER THE PHONE."*

Joan answered with a sense of foreboding.

"Good evening, Joan Aiguader," came the expected voice from the other end. "You're probably shocked over the condition of our photographer, but that's what happens if you break an agreement with me. Remember that!"

Despite his reluctance, Joan automatically turned to look at the body and felt his stomach constrict. If only he could avoid throwing up again.

"It has to be said that you've done a good job, Joan Aiguader. You've managed to get us in the newspaper, and now the whole world knows that we're going to cause a lot of pain. And you've cleverly tracked us down." The speaker laughed unpleasantly. "Yes, it was us who answered your question online about the uniform and kept your story going, and that's the way it should continue for a few more days, but you understand that, don't you?"

Joan was unable to speak, but he did nod.

"We're heading north, Joan, and we need a few days before we give you your next tip about where we are and what we're planning. In the meantime, we'll give you some information for your article so you can keep the interest going to our mutual benefit. Now take the photographer's cell phone and put it in your pocket, and make sure it's always fully charged so we can contact you whenever we want. You'll find the charger next to his bag. And just so you don't get any ideas, we'll change the prepaid telephone card every time we call you. And get out of there now before the police arrive and make things difficult for you. I'm sure you know the German police aren't to be messed with. Keep this conversation to yourself, and write what you dare in tomorrow's paper."

Joan looked at the sick on the floor, his footprints in the dried blood, the trousers and shoes that didn't belong to him.

"Yes," he finally answered.

He exited the apartment carrying the trash bags, left the door ajar, snuck down the stairs as quietly as possible, threw the garbage in a container on one of the side streets, and sat at a café opposite the building with an Americano in his trembling hands while he waited for the police to arrive. Ten minutes had gone by since he'd called them anonymously and informed them of what he had seen. But he still didn't know what he would do when they arrived.

He looked at the photographer's phone. It was much newer than his own and also more advanced. A Samsung Galaxy S8 with a fantastic camera; the sort of phone he probably couldn't afford until it was five years old.

He unlocked the telephone and looked at the different icons before opening the photo gallery. It was empty, but what had he expected of a professional photographer? That he went around taking photos with his phone? He was on the verge of hysterical laughter at such an absurd thought. And that was exactly how he felt. . . .

Hysterical.

He began opening the other apps that he thought might contain something interesting for him to write about in his article. First, Samsung Notes, but there was nothing. Mailbox. Nothing. Secure Folder. Nothing. Facebook. Nothing. Instagram. Nothing. Nothing at all. There wasn't even a video icon.

It was only on the very last page of apps that he found something that looked promising. It was a blue icon with a camera called Finder. When he clicked on the icon, the first things he looked for were photos or videos that had been saved somewhere.

He hadn't expected to find anything, so when a single video file popped up on the screen, his eyes lit up.

He opened the file.

It was a very dimly lit recording of two men talking under their breath in a corner of the photographer's living room. The bad lighting meant he couldn't make out the faces, and as they were speaking in Arabic, he also couldn't understand what they were saying.

After half a minute, the position of the camera was changed, making it clear that the recording had been made in secret, and something that seemed like loosely woven material covered the top third of the lens. Then there was a rustling sound that presumably came from somewhere outside the camera's view, and a few seconds later, a person appeared on the right side of the picture and pulled the heavy curtain covering the window slightly to one side, allowing a faint light into the living room and to fall on the faces of the men talking. Joan didn't recognize the men, but he did recognize the jacket of the person who had pulled back the curtain. It was the photographer, ensuring the best documentation of what he was doing.

The men talking were around fifty. One had a distinctive face and equally distinctive irregular marks across his chin and neck. Maybe it was a trick of the light, but it looked like discoloration and scar tissue. The second man appeared to be subordinate to the first, judging by his demeanor, and sported a rather unusual haircut for an Arab. His body language was reminiscent of an experienced boxer with upward-jabbing arms. His flat nose completed the image.

They spoke quietly and purposefully. They ignored the photographer and were deeply engrossed in the topic they were discussing. They occasionally used gestures, which especially in the case of the second man looked exaggerated—as if punching the air to knock someone out—and then they both laughed.

When a sudden ray of light caught both the men's faces, Joan paused the video and used his own phone to take a close-up photo of the faces on the screen.

Their expressions appeared calm but cold. *One of these two will shortly slit the throat of the condemned man,* he thought with terror. That poor, poor man, standing there unsuspectingly looking out his window.

Joan started the video again and listened intently to what they were saying to each other. Maybe there would be a single word he could recognize. Lost in concentration, Joan forgot about the world around him. The words were spoken in a staccato and sometimes barking tone, a world of difference from his own soft language. And then he heard what the man with the cropped hair called the other man, because he repeated the name. All the same, he had to go back a few times to be sure. No, there was no doubt.

The name was Ghaalib.

Holding his breath, he paused the video again. Was this really the same person as the man with the full beard on the beach in Ayia Napa? Was he the puppet master who held people's lives in his hands? The one who had murdered the old woman and whose power even reached far inside a refugee camp? The man who crushed everything that stood in his path?

If it was, then this was the man Joan had to fear more than any other.

Joan looked up from the telephone when a series of blue flashes caught his eye and a patrol car almost silently pulled up in front of the building where Bernd Jacob Warberg's body was growing cold.

Joan looked down again at the frozen image of a menacing-looking murderer. This man was still on the loose.

After briefly considering his options, he made a split-second decision and forwarded the file. Then he typed a few words into Google Translate, repeated them to himself, stood up, and crossed the street in the direction of the two green-uniformed police officers who exited the patrol car and put on their hats as yet another vehicle with blue flashing lights came from behind and dropped off a couple of seasoned-looking plainclothes officers.

They nodded to their colleagues and pointed up toward the windows with a seriousness that seemed frightening. It made Joan stop and rethink, but then one of the investigators noticed his hesitation with a professional glance that told him that this man might not be completely unimportant.

Joan nodded back, walked the final steps toward them, and then slowly said in his best German:

"Ich habe diesen Mord gemeldet."

I reported this murder.

20

Carl

Assad had been unusually affected yesterday when explaining who the man standing next to his wife was.

Afterward, he had become distant and couldn't continue.

"It's too much," he had said. "Even a camel has to sink to its knees once in a while and seek rest. I don't know if I'm arriving or leaving."

"'Coming or going,'" corrected Rose.

He looked at her with heavy eyes. "It feels more final than that with all the unease going on inside my head. I need time to think, sleep, and pray. Is that okay? When we meet up tomorrow, I'll try to tell you the rest even though it'll be difficult. Can you give me some time?"

At home that night with Mona, Carl tried to retell Assad's shocking account.

"But, Carl," said Mona afterward, "if Assad had told you all this years ago, we might have been able to help him. So why didn't he?"

"Good question. But when you think about it, how could he say anything? Lars Bjørn ensured he had a new identity, and there have no doubt been lots of reasons why he kept it secret."

"You think he was worried about losing his job?"

"No, but he's definitely been worried that the truth about his identity would slip out."

"*You* would never have exposed him; he must have known that."

"I think there were times when he was just about to tell me. But he was somehow paralyzed by all the evil that was let loose in the Middle East, all the radicalization that has taken place in Europe. Shia against Sunni, civil war. He's been seeing enemies everywhere."

"It's so horrible," she said. "Can you imagine your family being kept hostage for so many years, not knowing where they are or whether they're even alive? I know I can't."

Carl held her hands. "No, it's cruel. And on top of that, he's lived with the knowledge that the man holding them captive would do anything to find him and kill him. That's why he's had to work undercover and keep moving. I understand that now. Maybe Lars Bjørn and his brother didn't even know where he was when he wasn't at HQ."

"Do you think he's taken advantage of all the opportunities available through Department Q to try to find his family?"

"Absolutely. I assume that was the reason behind Lars Bjørn giving him a job with us. But when I look back, I'm afraid he might have given up on ever being reunited with them." He shook his head. "And then this happens. Imagine what it must have felt like to be confronted with the old woman's fate in Ayia Napa. It must have been a hell of a shock."

"Do you think he'll tell you the rest now?"

"Yes. And if not, we'll just have to convince him. We've got Rose back on the team." The thought made him smile. Something good had come of Assad's misfortune.

Mona pulled her hands back and looked at him with a serious expression.

"Carl, there's something I want to ask you. Something completely different." She took a couple of deep breaths. "What do you think will happen if this trip Hardy, Morten, and Mika are planning to Switzerland doesn't work out? I mean, if Hardy's situation doesn't change. Will you move back to Allerød?"

"Move back?" He stuck out his lower lip and thought for a moment. "No, I don't think so. Why do you ask?"

"Because I . . . I love you, Carl. You've been here for me so much over the last year. Do you know how much that's meant to me?"

He examined her expression. *Does her expression match her question?* asked the investigator in him.

"Please tell me why you're asking, Mona," he said. "Are you keeping something from me?"

She lowered her head in an unusually humble manner, almost as if she was embarrassed. What was she hiding? He was becoming alarmed.

"Are you sick, Mona?" He reached for her hands.

Then she turned to face him with dimples that were so pronounced that he thought she was going to burst out in hysterical laughter.

"Sick?" She stroked his cheek. "Call it what you want. When Samantha died . . ." She composed herself momentarily. "Oh God, Carl, my daughter was so full of life, so talented, she . . . When she died, something also died in me. My soul was crushed. With my job, I should have been the first to know what sorrow can do to someone, but I spiraled downhill. I was advised by my doctor to take antidepressants, but you already know that I didn't, right?"

He nodded. He was even more worried now.

"I was in a really bad way, Carl. My soul and body were totally out of balance. I felt like I was aging at lightning speed, but then I was prescribed hormones and they actually helped a lot. But you don't take something like that without consequences. I'm afraid the doses I took were too high."

"Consequences? I don't know what you mean. Can it give you blood clots? Is that what you're worried about?"

She smiled and squeezed his hand one more time. "I'm fifty-one years old, Carl, and I'm pregnant. So you can't move back to Allerød. Will you promise me that?"

Carl leaned backward. A few years ago, he had suffered an anxiety attack that abruptly ripped him from his everyday existence and drained him of any sense of reality.

Right now, he felt like another attack might be on its way.

———————

If there were two people who didn't get much sleep that night, it was Carl and Assad. Assad was on his knees in the prayer position with his cheek on the prayer rug, sleeping like a log when Carl arrived in the basement at HQ the following morning.

"You'll wear that rug out, Assad" was the first thing Carl said when he bounded in with a cup of coffee for him.

Assad looked with confusion at the coffee cup Carl handed to him.

"Thanks," he said, and took a sip. It looked like it caused an extremely unpleasant sensation in his throat. He looked at Carl with indignation, as if his boss had finally avenged all the times when Assad had been the one brewing the coffee.

"It's just to wake you up," said Carl. "I can make more when you need it."

Assad grimaced. Apparently, there was no one on earth who was that desperate.

"It's going to be a tough day for both of us, Assad. That's why I'm here before the others."

"For both of us? What do you mean?" Assad sat on the stool in his broom cupboard of an office and rested his weary head against the wall.

"I'll just spit it out. Mona has told me that I'm going to be a father. I found out last night."

"*His eyes are as big as saucers,*" wrote Hans Christian Andersen about one of the dogs in "The Tinderbox." And that's exactly how Assad looked.

"Yes, I know, Mona is fifty-one. It's really . . . really . . ." Well, what could he say? "Unusual"? "A miracle"?

"We're both a bit in shock," he said instead. "I mean . . . we definitely want to have the baby, but given our age? Mona's grandson, Ludwig, will be fifteen years older than his uncle or aunt. That's wrong, isn't it? And can we even have a healthy, normal baby? Do we want to take the risk? And if we can, and we hope we can, we'll practically be seventy when the child goes to high school."

Carl stared straight ahead.

Mona had been eighteen when she had Mathilde, and the following year she'd had her younger daughter, Samantha. And on top of that, Samantha had also been eighteen when she had Ludwig. Strong, young, healthy mothers, so that was all right. But now Mona was fifty-one, so it was suddenly thirty-three years since Mona was first pregnant. Thirty-three years, for goodness' sake! It was a dizzying thought. And now at the age of fifty-four he was going to be a father for the first time to his own biological child.

For one scary moment, Carl pictured his parents and sister when they heard the news. That wouldn't go down quietly in Brønderslev.

Then Assad stood up like a sleepwalker, swaying for a moment, and looked at Carl as if he were ready to spout out a tirade of well-meaning advice about why it was a terrible idea to go through with it. Carl was already feeling defensive and was about to get mad when Assad slowly started crying.

"Carl," he said, taking Carl's head and squeezing it against his forehead. "Carl, it's the best thing that could happen." Then he stepped backward and stared teary-eyed at Carl with a smile dancing on his lips. "It's a sign, Carl, do you understand?"

And Carl did understand.

They didn't mention the pregnancy to Gordon or Rose, but if those two had been a little more alert, they would have noticed the energy that suddenly filled the room.

"I'll try to keep it short and not go into too much detail," said Assad. "But I don't think you'd like that anyway."

"Do whatever works for you, Assad," said Rose.

He put the newspaper article from the day before on the table and pointed at the photo. "The man next to my wife is called Abdul Azim. Maybe I said that yesterday? He's an Iraqi and comes from my wife's hometown, Fallujah. And he's the one who's ruined my life. I just hope I've also ruined his."

On death row, the stench of sweat, sick, and piss was so stifling and stinging that it turned his eyes bloodshot, and Assad was scared. Earlier that morning, they had led five men past his cell and out to the gallows in the concrete building opposite. He had heard their desperate pleas and felt the fear of death while the guards dragged them along.

When the hatch on his door was opened, he was certain that his time had come, but it was Ghaalib who appeared, for the first time. With few words, he discreetly told Assad to trust him and that his family knew his wife's family well. That he would help him; he just had to hold on for a few days.

The next time Assad saw that man was in a blood-splattered and filthy low-ceilinged interrogation room, and that was when he realized he would have to fear the worst. His training had told him that when being tortured he would be tied to a chair or hung up, but that was wrong.

A man in a traditional white dishdasha robe had entered and was standing in front of him under a flashing ceiling lamp. He smiled when he looked Assad in the eyes, and then snapped his fingers at four large men with naked, hairy torsos who had followed them in. They had thin canes in their hands and, in a manner that suggested this wasn't the first time they had done this, formed a ring around Assad.

The interrogator's first question dealt with who he was and if he was aware that his crimes would cost him his life. When he didn't reply, the interrogator snapped his fingers again.

The first blows from the four men were relatively easy to bear for Assad's well-trained torso, just so long as he tensed his muscles before he was hit. When the interrogator's questions about his rank, his mission, his origin, and what he knew about the UN observers' next move weren't answered either, the strokes grew harder and harder and moved closer to his abdomen and head with every hit.

At that point, the man who had just assured him that his family was in safety entered the room and stood by the back wall.

Without anyone else's seeing, he looked at Assad in a way that could have been understood as meaning that the caning would soon be over.

And it was. After the last minute of strokes that were so hard that Assad tried to shield himself from them, they stopped.

"You're a tough man. But we'll make you tell us everything later today," said the interrogator.

Assad pushed out his lower lip and blew warm air into his face. He tried to appear calm, but his adrenaline was pumping and his heart was beating ten to the dozen.

They wouldn't break him.

Assad sat slumped in his chair without looking at any of them. He took a rest from talking, as if to muster the energy to continue.

"They came three days in a row and beat me until my blood ran, and they threatened to drown me by holding my head underwater in a tub, but I said nothing. It was only when they attached electrodes to my nipples and turned on the current that I opened my mouth. Then I told them what my name was and that the UN mission didn't know anything about our plan. That the aim was simply to rescue a friend."

Assad described the Iraqis' rage and how the next few days' torture had been so awful that he wished he would just die.

It was at that point that the head interrogator gave up and said that the death penalty would be carried out the following morning.

Carl and Rose looked at each other and then at Gordon, who seemed like he was struggling to get enough blood rushing to his head. As long as he didn't faint.

"That evening, the bastard came to my cell again. This time he was angry with me and his story had changed. Now he said that they had taken my wife and two daughters hostage and that if I didn't confess to everything they demanded, they would also feel the edge of the knife. I was shocked, but what else could I say? Maybe I didn't believe him; I don't know."

Carl had momentarily lost his focus and hadn't noticed how Assad's account was affecting him or that his jaw muscles were twitching and his fists were clenched.

"Sorry to interrupt, Assad, but do you know the man well enough to know where he might have gone after Cyprus?"

He shook his head. "No, not at all. But somehow or other he knows that I'm somewhere in Europe. Maybe he even knows I'm in Denmark, although not exactly where. I have no doubt that he's trying to lure me into the open and will stop at nothing. And he has my family in the palm of his hand and can seriously hurt them at any moment; I have no doubts about that anymore."

He pointed at a couple of the photographs. "Look at Marwa's face. She's terrified." He gulped and tears streamed down his face. "How can I find them without them getting hurt? I have no idea. At one time, Marwa and Samir's elder brother was trying to find out where they were being held prisoner, and it ended up costing him his life. They threw him like a butchered animal with its throat slit in the dirt in front of their house. That's why Samir hates me so much." He turned to Carl. "Don't you remember how we were at each other's throats at the main train station when he asked to be transferred from HQ to Glostrup because he wanted to get away from me?"

He sat looking away from them for a moment, trying to control his breathing. "That's also why I've had sleepless nights for so many years, and why countless times I've had to say sorry to my father-in-law on Skype. And now the old man is dead," he said with his voice trembling. "It's a wonder that Samir hasn't long since revealed where I am. He's afraid it won't help his sister or nieces, and he's probably right."

Assad buried his face in his hands. It was all too obvious how he was feeling.

"Courage, Assad. This is difficult, very difficult, but we're here for you." Carl turned to the other two. "Isn't that right?"

Gordon and Rose nodded.

"So, now we'll do things systematically. I know time is not on our side, but look here, Assad." He pulled all the newspaper articles in front of him. "The articles are written for a daily in Barcelona, *Hores del dia,* and all by the same man, Joan Aiguader."

"Yes, and I've found out that the news editor is a woman called Montse Vigo," added Rose. "I have the telephone number here."

"Good. Now we find all the articles Joan Aiguader has written over the last few days, and when we know a bit more, we'll call the editor and ask her, like the police investigators we are, how her foreign correspondent can know so much about a fugitive refugee."

21

Joan

"**Good morning, Joan Aiguader.** My name is Herbert Weber," said a corpulent man wearing a turtleneck sweater. "I'm the coordinator for the region's anti-terror unit. I apologize that we had to detain you here last night, but naturally we had to run a thorough check of your story and background. I hope your stay hasn't been too uncomfortable."

Joan shrugged. A night in a German jail wasn't the worst research to which a journalist could be subjected.

"I assume you're aware that you're playing with fire?"

Joan nodded.

"Yes, of course you are. I can see from your articles that you've entered into a sort of, shall we say, agreement with this Ghaalib, also known as Abdul Azim, and that in that short time he's already guilty of, or has been an accomplice in, no less than three murders."

Joan sat up straight and looked over the intelligence officer's shoulder. If this was a place where his employees worked, it was in desperate need of an interior designer. No decoration on the empty walls, useless and cold lighting, green-painted floors. So, where were they? Not an office, that much was certain, and it worried him. Did they maybe suspect that he had murdered Bernd Jacob Warberg? Was he going to be subjected to questioning or maybe something even worse?

"They weren't acts I could have known about beforehand," he said with an imploring look. "I've told you that several times already."

"No, of course not. But, all the same, you've been alarmingly close to the events on all three occasions. I completely understand that as a journalist you have to chase stories and sometimes get too close, but if you're considering writing about your stay here at the station and your questioning yesterday and today, I would seriously advise you against it. We're of the opinion that it would make this Ghaalib man nervous and go into hiding, and we obviously don't want that. Have you seen what's on the wall behind you?"

Joan made a half turn in his chair and looked up at a list of city names written directly on the white wall with a thick marker pen; it made for very somber and frightening reading for someone who followed world history.

It read:

Munich, Grafing, 10th May 2016 (*)
Bayern Bundesbahn, 18th July 2016
Munich, Moosach, 22nd July 2016 (*)
Ansbach, 24th July 2016
Berlin, 19th December 2016
Hamburg, 28th July 2017
Münster, 7th April 2018
(*) Terror relation not indisputably established

And underneath:

Paris, Lyon, Nizza, Toulouse/Montauban, Saint-Étienne-du-Rouvray, Brussels, Liège, Burgas, Madrid, London, Stockholm, Copenhagen, Manchester, Turku, Istanbul, Strasbourg, Oslo (**)
(**) Right-wing extremist terrorism

"It isn't a coincidence that this is the first thing you see when you enter the room. You'll understand that with an awareness of the terror attacks in these cities over the last few years, we have to apply the strictest precautions when something like what happened yesterday takes place in our city and our country. As recently as the eighth of April this year, we averted some atrocious knife attacks during the Berlin half marathon, and if it wasn't for people like us and our colleagues, a lot more cities and dates would unfortunately have ended up on that wall. And that is exactly why we need to find out what this Ghaalib is up to. Are you with me?"

"You must know something. Haven't you translated the conversation on the photographer's video?"

"Naturally. And you'll have to forgive us, but we'll be keeping the photographer's phone and the information we obtained from it for ourselves. With all due respect, you might be tempted to quote from the translation."

Joan shook his head. Did he think he was stupid enough to admit that?

"You'd very possibly be signing your own death warrant if Ghaalib suspected you might write about that information. So let's say we're protecting you. Agreed?"

A few hours later, Joan was standing on the street with a GPS sewn into the lining of his windbreaker so the German intelligence service always knew where he was. A team of serious men in black suits had sat in a row in front of him and inculcated a list of guidelines if he wanted to avoid arrest, and then they had given him clear instructions about what he could write in his articles for *Hores del dia* in the future. Last but not least, they had checked and edited his phone and added the numbers he could call if he needed them. In other words, there was a professional intelligence service backing him up with their knowledge and resources if in return he kept them informed about everything. It also meant that no articles would be sent to *Hores del dia* before they were okayed by the German intelligence service.

Joan scanned the street and tried to take it all in. Here he was in Munich after a night in custody with one of the world's most effective intelligence agencies. He still had some money left, and he had experienced more in a few days than in his life so far. Suddenly, he was important. People were relying on him. They wanted articles at the newspaper, and people all over the world read what he had written because he had become a key link in the hunt for a very dangerous man. Victim 2117's murderer! It was hard to believe that only a few days ago, he could have been brought down by one wrong word, and that his self-esteem had been so low that suicide seemed almost unavoidable. And now here he was, one hell of a guy, and currently the most interesting agent in the German intelligence service.

Agent! Joan smiled at the thought. If only his ex-girlfriend knew the heights to which her measly sixteen hundred euros had brought him.

And as he followed the throng of people down toward the train station as the city awoke to a new day, he repeated what the intelligence agent had said.

"Inform your paper that you've traced the photographer to Munich but that he's no longer alive. State that the culprit is still on the loose, and that it's presumably the man called Abdul Azim, alias Ghaalib, and that he's heading north. According to your information, he has now shaved off the long beard that had covered his heavily scarred jaw. Don't mention that you were in possession of this video, which Ghaalib presumably isn't aware of, and also don't mention that you've been in contact with us. In the meantime, we'll inform the public of what we know about the man. It isn't too much at the moment, but that'll change when we receive more information from our colleagues in security agencies across Europe and in the Middle East. So, before you know it, we'll issue a missing person's report in the press with all the data we have on this man. We might also include a photo of him if any of our international colleagues can supply us with one; if they can't, we'll manipulate the photo from the video in such a way that he won't be able to work out where it came from. I imagine it will take twenty-four hours and then you'll see the results. We have the police on alert all the way from Munich to Frankfurt, so we have forces ready to apprehend him."

"Did they say anything about the route on the video?" Joan had asked.

There was no answer, so they must have done.

"Can't I write about what the police investigation has revealed about the murder?"

Herbert Weber spread out his large arms. "Yes, all right. Why not? People were already able to read about it in *Süddeutsche Zeitung* this morning."

Damn it. How was he supposed to explain to Montse Vigo that another newspaper had stolen his story and that he was subject to crippling restrictions? It was so irritating!

On the other hand, he could congratulate himself that he had forwarded the photographer's video file to his Hotmail account before he handed himself in and that he had deleted the sent e-mail.

So now it was just a question of how he would manage to secure a translation of the audio without the translator's suspecting what it was all about.

22

Carl

If someone had to guess Rose's name, all they would have to do is look at her cheeks and neck. In that moment, her entire being was flushed with righteous indignation, and had she been a boxer, it would have been advantageous to bet on her. Of course, Carl was familiar with her explosive temperament from the old days, but contrary to expectation, absence hadn't mellowed her.

"Bloody hell, that chief editor at *Hores del dia* is one unsympathetic bitch. And I assume I'm allowed to call the woman a bitch given that I'm a woman myself."

"What did she say?" asked Carl.

"That she was honored that her newspaper could get the ball rolling, but she would always protect her sources and employees, and an inferior police force in an inferior country like Denmark couldn't change her position on that one bit."

"Inferior," is that what the woman said? As if she could talk. It wasn't as if she was the editor in chief of The Washington Post.

"Did you explain to her why it's so important for us to get ahold of the journalist?"

"I didn't go into detail about Assad's situation and the women. But she had the cheek to say that she was proud that their story was inspiring new leads, but apart from that, the story would have to run its course. It's how they make their living, after all."

"Really? How unethical," said Gordon.

Unethical! That was exactly what it was.

"So, we still have no contact details for the man! Doesn't the newspaper have a website where you can find him?"

"Joan Aiguader is a freelancer, so no. I've checked him on different search engines, of course, but I don't think that'll get us anywhere. As far as I can tell, he hasn't recently had his own address in Barcelona."

"Hmm! The man's latest article ends in Munich with the description of a murder. So, the next step has to be to direct our inquiries to the police down there. Surely they must know something about his whereabouts and movements."

Rose looked at him with an air of slight indignation. "I've already done that, and they refused point-blank. Apparently, they know nothing about where Joan Aiguader is staying."

Carl frowned. "That's hard to believe, don't you think?"

"Yes, and I told them as much."

There was a noise in the corridor. Assad must have been back.

"Did you manage to talk to Samir again?" asked Carl.

Assad nodded.

"What did he say? Has he calmed down?"

The answer was written all over his face. "Well, he's obviously still very worried. He asked again and again about his nieces and couldn't understand why only one of them is in the photograph. But then neither can I."

"But what do we actually know about that, Assad? These photos are snapshots. Perhaps she stepped into the frame the second after the photographer pressed the button."

Assad looked despondent. "That's true, but Samir and I scrutinized the photos we have, and you can sort of see the whole group in a couple of them. My other daughter just isn't there, Carl. Like me, Samir hasn't seen his sister or nieces in sixteen years, so we don't even recognize this woman in the picture. The girls looked very similar back then, but Samir thinks it's the youngest, Ronia, who is missing. Nella was a little darker than Ronia when they were children, and the woman with Marwa is very dark." He looked at them with a forlorn expression. "It's so unbearable that I don't even know what my own children look like. And now they're adults, Carl. The bottom line is that I know nothing."

"You're worried about whether she's still alive, aren't you, Assad?"

"Of course. I'm so afraid that she's been murdered just like my foster mother."

"Assad, you mustn't think like that," said Rose. "There will always be hope."

Carl looked at Assad. "Samir hopefully understands that he needs to keep this quiet?" he asked. "We can't have him starting his own investigation, and we certainly can't have him revealing anything in relation to you."

Assad sighed. "The first thing we can't control, but going over to see him today for the second time mended our relationship a bit, I think. He's very grateful to know that his sister is alive and that I will do anything to—"

"Listen, Assad," interrupted Carl. "He needs to understand that under no circumstances can he mention this to the family, okay?"

Assad sighed. "There's no one to tell, Carl. Samir told me that my mother-in-law died a few months ago, so there's no one left except me and Marwa and . . . and my daughter."

"We're really sorry to hear that, Assad." Rose took his wrist in her hand and gave it a squeeze. "We're here for you, and we won't stop until there's a happy ending to all this. So even though we're at a bit of a dead end just now, things will change, all right?"

He looked away and nodded.

"Isn't it about time that you told us the rest, Assad? Maybe it can help us get closer to Ghaalib and understand the way he thinks. Are you ready?" she asked.

Assad sat up. "Yes, but you need to understand that it'll just be the main points. The details are . . ." He folded his hands and put them in front of his mouth as if to keep the words from coming out.

"Well, let's just say I'll keep them to myself," he said.

———————

Around five in the morning, when Assad was due to be executed, there was a rattling noise outside his cell door, so Assad readied himself for the last few minutes of his life. He knew that the distance to the building where the hangings took place was just a few meters, so he threw himself on his knees and prayed a final short prayer.

Assad had not slept that night. From the neighboring cells on death row he had heard quiet voices at first, but they quickly turned into shouts and curses aimed directly at him. There was no doubt that they held him responsible for twenty people being hanged to cover up Jess's escape as a prisoner uprising. He shouted back that he was deeply sorry, but that they should curse the people who had carried out the atrocities instead. That just incensed them more.

Assad covered his ears. Mankind's greatest sin had always been unjust actions, and he wasn't going to let that fact, or his awareness of what awaited him, steal his final hours and memories of past happiness. Shortly, he would no longer be part of this world, and what would become of Marwa and the girls? What was this hell he had brought on them?

Assad was still on his knees in the praying position when a cold light from the corridor spread across the cell floor around him.

Ghaalib walked in, his skin sallow and his breath stinking of garlic, and without warning he kicked him in the ribs with his boots.

"Get up, you dog!" he shouted while an older prisoner was pushed into the cell by a soldier holding a gun to the back of his neck. When he saw Assad writhing on the floor, there was panic in his eyes.

Are they planning to kill this poor sod while I watch? Assad wondered. *Are they trying to break me with another man's death?*

Then Ghaalib kicked him again. "You should know that I intend to force everything out of you before the noose is around your neck. I tried to make things easier for you, but now it's too late."

He signaled to the soldier, who with one hard blow to the prisoner's back slammed him against the cell wall.

"You can come in now," shouted Ghaalib, and a man dressed in civilian clothing and holding a camera stepped into the cell.

"Wait outside and shut the door," he said to the soldier, who immediately followed the order. It was only now that Assad realized how high up Ghaalib was in the prison hierarchy.

"We no longer have our photographer from last time, but then you know that. He was a good man. But now you can say hello to this photographer instead. He's come a long way to be here with the sole purpose of meeting the man who killed his brother."

Assad let his gaze move up to meet a pair of eyes that emanated such hatred that it was almost blinding. What good would it do to tell him that it wasn't him who brought an end to his brother's life? None whatsoever.

Then the man lifted the camera and began filming.

"Are you ready to make a full confession, Zaid al-Asadi? Were you part of a UN mission?"

Assad cradled his ribs and stood up slowly with his eyes fixed on the camera lens.

"No, I wasn't. And I hope you and all the other bastards in this forsaken country burn in hell," he said, spitting out every word.

Ghaalib turned to the photographer. "You can delete that," he said calmly, and pulled out his gun from the holster. "Come over here," he said to the older prisoner in the corner. Then he turned to face Assad. "Last night, we heard Mohammad here shouting that he wanted to poke your eyes out, and that he would make you choke on your own tongue. And Mohammad has every possible reason to do that because two of his family members swung from the gallows because of you and your attack." He turned again to the prisoner. "Now I'm giving you the chance to make good on your oaths and curses, Mohammad."

Assad looked at the prisoner's lifeless eyes. He almost looked like a zombie, devoid of willpower and resistance.

"Do what you have to do," whispered Assad. "But you need to know that he will also be your executioner. Forgive me for the pain I have inadvertently caused."

Ghaalib smiled. "Mohammad and I have a deal. He helps me with you, and then I help him. Right, Mohammad?"

The man gave a slight nod. A dark blue bruise stretching from his throat and down his chest, visible from his open shirt, attested to the fact that this was not a deal he had made voluntarily.

"We will inflict immense pain on you if you don't talk, Zaid. And when you're no longer here to defend them, we'll also inflict that pain on your family. So start cooperating. It's the only thing that can save them now." He put his hand under his robe and produced a small brown bottle.

"Concentrated phosphoric acid, Zaid. One of the most painful things your skin can be subjected to. It will make you beg for mercy and plead to be taken to the gallows as quickly as possible. And it will disfigure the faces of your wife and daughters forever if you don't talk. So, may we have your confession now?"

Assad shook his head. "Whether I produce the lie or you manufacture it is all one and the same. I can't say anything other than that I deserve my fate and that my family has done nothing wrong. So I beg you in the name of Allah to spare them. Shoot me now and let's get this over with."

Ghaalib looked at him expressionlessly and passed the bottle to the prisoner, who with drooping shoulders and fear in his eyes stepped forward and took it.

Ghaalib lowered the gun and pointed directly at Assad's stomach. "You're going to feel unimaginable pain if I shoot. Talk, or we begin."

Assad clenched his teeth. *That bastard won't break me. I won't let my family or the rest of the world see me begging,* he resolved. When the time was right, he would show them all what he was made of.

Ghaalib shrugged. "Start with the back, Mohammad. We'll make this frog croak."

Assad clenched his fists when the prisoner grabbed his collar and tore at the material. Some drops hit the open wounds on his skin from the whipping, and while he writhed from the blinding pain, he heard his skin sizzling.

"Mohammad, my friend, don't do this," he moaned. Then more drops.

Assad tilted his head back and began hyperventilating, while the smell of the bubbling flesh caused the man behind him to splutter.

In a second, he would attack Ghaalib and spare himself from any more pain.

"Don't stand there fiddling with it," commanded the bastard in front of him. "Pour it! Let's see how he copes. Remember what we agreed, Mohammad, otherwise . . ."

But when Ghaalib pointed his gun toward Mohammad to stress that he expected to be obeyed, the situation exploded.

"*Maleun yakun Saddam wakul kalaabuhu!*" shouted the prisoner behind him: *Cursed be Saddam and all his dogs.* And before Assad could attack their tormentor, the prisoner threw acid on the hand with which Ghaalib was holding the gun.

The searing pain caused Ghaalib to involuntarily pull the trigger, and the prisoner behind Assad stopped and fell to the floor.

Ghaalib's eyes were wild as he took the gun in his other hand and tried for all he was worth to wipe off the acid on his robe.

The prisoner behind him pressed one hand against his stomach while he pushed the other hand with the bottle under Assad's arm.

The photographer's warning came too late, and before Ghaalib knew what was happening, Assad had grabbed the bottle and thrown the contents in his face.

He didn't scream this time. It was as if his body short-circuited and every part of him was paralyzed. In that moment, as the shadow of death left Assad, he grabbed Ghaalib's gun, pried it out of his hand, and pointed it directly at the photographer, who had raised the camera above his head ready to use as a weapon.

Assad shot him before he could react, and he fell to the floor like a rag in a pool of his own blood. The shot awoke Ghaalib's defenses, and he was suddenly alert with a curved, engraved knife in his hand and shouting for the guard outside.

Assad aimed the gun at him, but the injured Mohammad pushed him aside and threw himself at their tormentor.

"What's going on?" shouted the guard when he stepped into the room, but he didn't get any farther before he looked down in disbelief at the lethal wound in his chest from Assad's shot and then collapsed.

Assad stepped over him, closed the cell door, and turned toward the men on the floor just in time to see the prisoner lifting a knife to Ghaalib and plunging it in his abdomen, pulling it down into the groin as they fell.

Mohammad and Ghaalib lay still and entangled for a moment before the prisoner looked up at Assad with a mixture of sorrow and clarity in his eyes. "Now you and I are both dead," he said. "More soldiers will be here shortly, and the will of Allah will be done."

"Are you badly wounded?" asked Assad as he put his ear to the cell door. As far as he could tell, the only noise was coming from the neighboring cells. They obviously feared that they had listened to Assad and Mohammad being executed, and in a way they had.

He looked at his fellow prisoner, who stood up with difficulty as the bloodstain on his robe steadily spread.

His hands were shaking. "If I'm lucky, I'll bleed to death before they arrive," he whispered.

Assad pointed at the two bodies lying on the floor. "We'll change into their clothes. You take the photographer's and his camera. Hurry, we don't have long."

Assad looked around at the others, who had been listening in total silence. "And that's how we got out. As a safety precaution, I hid Ghaalib's gun under the black robe so we could attempt to shoot our way out, but the robe and the camera Mohammad was carrying on his shoulder proved sufficient. We shouted hello to the soldiers at the wall and the one standing by the entrance gate, and they shouted hello back. The darkness proved to be our best friend. We found the car keys to a Škoda in the cameraman's robes, and there was only one of them parked outside the walls. It was slow, but thankfully it took so long before anyone reacted that we were long gone."

Assad paused and looked at Gordon. He had been silent throughout Assad's account and had turned increasingly pale.

"Are you okay, Gordon?" he asked.

He nodded but was evidently troubled. "I don't understand how . . . that you did . . ."

"What happened to the other prisoner, Assad?" asked Carl.

Assad looked away. "A few kilometers from the prison, he asked me to stop. He couldn't go on, he said, and when I looked over, I saw that everything around him was soaked in blood: the passenger seat, his trousers and shoes, the floor."

"He died?" asked Carl.

"Yes. He opened the car door and just let himself fall out. By the time I got to the other side of the car, he was dead."

"But what about Ghaalib?" Rose looked down at the clippings in front of her. "He looks very much alive and well in these photographs."

Assad shook his head. "Biggest mistake of my life. We left him for dead, but we didn't finish him off."

"And your wife and children?"

"I did everything I could to find them, but Fallujah is a big city, and it was as if they'd just vanished. I used all my money on bribes trying to get information, but it didn't help. Then the UN delegation got involved. Word had gotten back to them about what had happened, so they sent me home. They said my presence in the country could quickly become explosive."

"But did you already know that Ghaalib was still alive before you realized that he was the one in these photographs?" asked Rose.

"Yes. Not long after I returned to Denmark, my father-in-law contacted me on Skype and told me what was going on. Abdul Azim, as he was called back then, had survived and taken Marwa and the girls as hostages. My father-in-law wanted me to come back and turn myself in so they'd free them. I obviously considered it, but then they killed Marwa's elder brother, which both crushed my father-in-law and sowed a hatred in him that made him change his mind."

"He advised you not to go back?" she asked.

"He said that my life's mission would be to find Ghaalib and kill him. It was the only solution he thought would work if we were to have any chance of getting the girls back."

"That was sixteen years ago, Assad. Why did it take so long?"

"When they captured Saddam Hussein in 2003, everything in Iraq went haywire. Many Sunnis went into hiding, and Fallujah was bombed. Since then, the only thing I've heard from there is that Ghaalib had been recruited by the Sunni militia, been promoted to an even higher rank, and was now located in Syria. That's when I gave up any hope of ever seeing my family again."

"Who told you that?"

"He told me himself. He sent a statement to my father-in-law for him to read to me."

"What did it say?"

A sort of vacuum filled the room, which Carl knew all too well from the times when he had driven to the relatives of road traffic victims. From the moment he saw the front door open until the moment when the realization of the absolute catastrophe was mirrored in the relative's face, the world stood still. Assad's expression was just like that, and the pause he was hiding behind was just as heartbreaking. How long had it been since he had formed the words of that message? What price had Assad paid to avoid thinking about it every second of every day? The answer was clear from the expression on his face.

He had never told anyone else about Ghaalib's message.

He cleared his throat a couple of times, but his voice was faltering. "What did it say?"

He hesitated again. He stared up at the ceiling with glazed eyes and sighed. Then he leaned forward, took a deep breath, and placed his hands on his knees as if his entire body was charged with adrenaline.

"It said that he made sure Marwa lost our third child, and that he raped Marwa and my daughters every day, and that every time they gave birth, he immediately killed the child. That he was waiting for me and that he would make sure things ended badly for me."

All three of them sat just staring at Assad, unable to utter a word.

"And that's what I think he's trying to accomplish now," he said quietly a minute later. "And I didn't even think they were still alive."

Carl was shaken. Was this the Assad he had joked around with so often before? The man he had laughed with and who had helped him recharge his batteries? This tormented man whose past was so crushing that Carl didn't know how he could even function normally?

Carl pictured Mona with a newborn baby in her arms. His first child. That frail life that knew nothing of the horrors of the world and whom he would shelter with all his might from reality. But the world was a horrible place and this account was truly—

Carl stopped his thoughts from racing and looked directly at Assad. He had no idea how Assad could keep himself together with the shadow of this terrible knowledge hanging over him. But maybe he hadn't kept it together. Perhaps the whole thing was an act just in order to survive.

Carl opened a drawer and fumbled for the cigarettes that he knew were in there. Despite his colleagues and Mona's aversion, smoking was the only thing just now that could rescue him from this paralyzing atmosphere.

"Save yourself the trouble, Carl," said Rose. "If it's cigarettes you're looking for, you'll have to check the incinerator. I'm afraid they've already gone up in smoke, so to speak."

She smiled, and Carl made a mental note of what she had done.

Then he turned to Assad. "Listen," he said. "I'm going to go up to Marcus now and explain why we need to immediately use the paid time off we've accumulated over the years and that we'll need a travel allowance and money for expenses. Shall we say two weeks to start with?"

23

Joan

Joan saw his reflection clearly when he leaned forward toward the window and the white ICE train carriages on the opposite track at Munich Central Station.

"You're looking good, Joan," he whispered to himself. Hadn't the events of the last few days made his features more defined, his eyebrows darker, and given his expression more depth? Yes, they really had. He was going to have some fun when he got home. He would sit at the waterfront restaurant Xup, Xup in the Barceloneta district with a wineglass nonchalantly resting in his hand while eyeing up the women who walked past. If he sat there long enough, he would pick someone up; he could sense it in his groin. Joan felt reborn.

He looked down the first-class carriage and smiled, opened his laptop on the table, and observed the busy but silent businesspeople who were all sitting with their heads buried in their laptops and paperwork. For a paltry four euros extra for a first-class seat on the early-afternoon train, he had finally climbed the social ladder, and he had no intention of coming back down. Here he was, the man with the hottest journalism of the day in his head, and soon people would remember Joan Aiguader as the man who had risked his own life in averting catastrophe.

Risked his own life; that was what he wanted the world to believe. The knight in shining armor, the cavalier who arrived in the nick of time, the Dutch boy with his finger in the dike, that's who he was.

Without Joan Aiguader people would die. Without him, who knew where the lightning would strike in all its horror, spreading chaos across Europe. He could just imagine it. If Ghaalib's plans were put into effect, people would flee from open city spaces, men and women would retract into their shells, and children wouldn't be allowed to go to school.

Yes, that's exactly how he imagined it. Naturally, it was only right that the German intelligence service would take their share of the glory, but who had given them the information on which they acted?

Again, it was Joan Aiguader. And like so often over the last few days when his thoughts went in this direction, he sent a grateful thank-you to victim 2117.

He leaned forward toward his laptop and was thinking for a moment about the article for the next day when a man with a blue scarf and thick winter coat sat down on the seat next to him on the opposite side of the aisle.

Joan nodded politely to him and received an unusually pleasant smile in return, not exactly something he was used to, but he just put it down to this being the way things were in first class. People in here understood and respected one another for who they were and what they could do. So he smiled back.

He was a rather dark, rugged, and handsome man. *Probably Italian,* Joan thought while admiring the man's shoes. When he was sitting at Xup, Xup, he would be sure to remember to flaunt a pair of shoes like those. They were presumably expensive, but if *Hores del dia* wouldn't give him a decent and well-remunerated offer, others would. He was certain of it; after all, there were more than enough newspapers in Catalonia. But what if he received an offer from a Madrid-based newspaper? Should he accept? Joan was on the verge of laughing out loud. Of course he should; there was no need to be a fanatical Catalonian.

The translator he had hired in the city center to translate the video file from Bernd Jacob Warberg's cell phone had initially shaken his head and complained about having to work before ten in the morning on the tight deadline he had been given. But Joan had pressured him,

after which the man had quoted two hundred euros more than the going rate, which Joan told him he couldn't stretch to. He explained that
there wasn't enough money available because the text was just for a
read-through for a couple of actors in a TV production, and that the
reason he needed it was because they had forgotten to give him the
English text. They agreed on an extra hundred euros, but he was given
no assurances for accuracy due to the poor sound quality of the video.

Despite whatever inaccuracies there might be in the translation, it
left no doubt that Ghaalib was a terrorist and that he had spent years
fighting for the militia in Iraq and Syria, rising to a very-high-ranking
position in the organization. But now that the war had turned, he had
been given other objectives that could still lead to chaos and misfortune
wherever he was sent. Even though it didn't reveal exactly what the
plan was, it appeared from the conversation that everything had been
planned down to the smallest detail. People were waiting for his orders,
and it was clear that Frankfurt and Berlin had terrible events in store.

Joan placed the map of Frankfurt from the train station kiosk on the
table. Ghaalib and his assistant Hamid had mentioned a violent attack
in a square in Frankfurt, but whether it was Römerberg, Rathenauplatz,
Goetheplatz, or somewhere else altogether, they hadn't mentioned. Only
that the square was large, open, and full of people. But which square
was the right one? There were so many to choose from.

Joan looked up and caught the eye of the man on the other side of
the aisle. The man had apparently been eagerly following what he was
doing.

"Are you a tourist?" he asked Joan in English with a strong accent.

"Yes, in a way," he answered, and looked down again.

As far as Joan understood from the translated text, Ghaalib wouldn't
personally take part in the operations, but Hamid might. He certainly
had a very detailed knowledge of everything.

"Excuse me, but am I right in thinking that you are perhaps planning what to see in the city?" continued the man, pointing at the translation and the map. "May I suggest that you go to Römerberg first? It is
without doubt the city's coziest and best-preserved square."

He couldn't put his finger on it, but the man suddenly didn't seem quite so Italian anymore, so he thanked him for the information and packed away the map and translation.

When the train was approaching Nuremberg, where he was supposed to transfer, he had been typing aimlessly for almost an hour without managing to find any spark of inspiration.

"Damn it," he whispered to himself. How could he write eloquently and freely when he had so many people keeping an eye on what he wrote? If he followed the various directives, what choice did he have but to simply repeat what he had already written: that he was on the trail, had witnessed terrible things, but didn't know what he was on the trail of, or who they were trying to catch, or even anything about what might happen or where. If he revealed even the slightest knowledge of the conversation between Ghaalib and Hamid, he would have the German intelligence service and Ghaalib after him. Herbert Weber would probably come with a fabricated murder charge, and Ghaalib with a sharp knife to slit his throat. On the other hand, if he didn't circumvent these restrictions, he would lose his momentum and the backing of his editor. He had actually thought it would be possible to navigate these obstacles, but now it seemed hopeless.

Joan looked despondently out the window. If he was going to hold on to the belief that he would one day be a famous and celebrated reporter sitting at Xup, Xup and eyeing up the ladies, there was no other option. He would have to write whatever the hell he wanted, regardless of the risks. To his surprise, he realized that he had the courage to do just that. Yet another thing for which he could thank victim 2117.

Joan turned his attention back to the screen and started the job of amending his article; this time he would call a spade a spade. First the headline. Then the main text. Names were given; he described the murder of the photographer in Munich in detail, as well as the blood he fell in, the town he was headed for, and the man he was trying to stop before he committed an act of terrorism.

When the train slowed down and finally came to a halt, he had reached the point in his article where he had to decide if he should mention his meeting with the intelligence service and not least his discovery of the video file on the photographer's phone.

That decision will have to wait until after I've changed trains, he thought, and was just about to put his laptop in his bag when the man who had been sitting across the aisle from him leaned over and with a smile whispered in his ear that he was grateful for all the useful information he had obtained.

It only took a millisecond before Joan's defenses kicked in, and he turned to see the man in the large winter coat leaping down the aisle in a couple of steps before disappearing down the platform.

Over the course of the twenty-seven minutes before the next train for Frankfurt left from Nuremberg station, Joan's mind was filled with urgent questions. Exactly what useful information had the man thanked him for? From the distance at which he had been sitting, it would have been impossible for him to read what Joan had been writing, so he couldn't have deduced why Joan was on that train or what his business was in Frankfurt. He hadn't asked him about his profession or where he came from, so wasn't it likely that the only reason he knew Joan was traveling to Frankfurt am Main was because of the map?

But Joan couldn't get things to add up in his mind. Who the hell was that man? Was he friend or foe? A journalist who wanted to steal his story or one of Ghaalib's men? Joan was sweating profusely as he used his waiting time to push his way to every corner and searched the main hall and platforms in the station in an effort to get some answers. Where had the man disappeared to, and why had he been in such a hurry to get away? Could this possibly be a clear hint that the security agents were not letting him out of their sight and that it wasn't just the GPS in his jacket lining that told them where he was? He sincerely hoped so.

The first-class carriage on the ICE 26 to Frankfurt resembled the previous one. Splendid working conditions, serious men in suits, and the sort of silence that facilitated the peace of mind needed to plan and think ahead. He would stay somewhere central in Frankfurt so that the distance to the various squares he had in mind was as short as possible. He would work systematically and acquaint himself with all the locations, and not least their potential as terrorist targets. If he used his imagination and observed the movements and density of people in each of the squares, he might be able to see into the future. The question was when this future would be. In theory, the catastrophe could already have happened before he arrived in the city. Ghaalib and Hamid had a head start after all.

He took out his laptop and skimmed through his article.

They certainly won't be happy at the LfV if I include too many facts and start making predictions, thought Joan. But wasn't it every journalist's duty to speak up and warn the public when in possession of information on forthcoming catastrophes, regardless of what the intelligence service thought about it?

It was clear that the man with the scarred face wanted to create fear with the articles sent to the newspaper, but how would he react if Joan put obstacles in his way with his article in the next day's newspaper? Would he adjust his plans? Would he take advantage of the opportunity to create a false sense of security and move his terror attacks to a different place altogether where it was least expected?

Joan tried to envision the entire picture. Hopefully, Ghaalib didn't know where he was at the moment. If he was careful, what could possibly happen if he sent a factual article to *Hores del dia*? Hopefully nothing. But his present problem was that there was a whole series of essential facts about which he knew nothing. Where was Ghaalib, and what were he and his team up to? All he knew was that this most dangerous of men was probably already staying in one of Germany's most industrious and populous cities, and that he wouldn't hesitate in eliminating any obstacle that stood in his path. So, what the hell was he supposed to write?

He had been weighing the pros and cons for some time when a man stepped into the carriage and stopped in front of his table.

"Joan Aiguader?" he asked politely.

Joan frowned and looked up at a small, thickset man who, given the time of year, was conspicuously tanned.

"Yes, who's asking?" he replied.

"I'm here to deliver this," said the man, and handed him an envelope. Then he cocked his hat, apologized to those sitting nearby for the interruption, and left.

The envelope was white and neutral, but the contents were not.

It read:

> *How did you know to go to Frankfurt? And what were you doing with the police last night? Didn't I give you direct orders to keep away from them? We know everything you do, Joan Aiguader, so be careful. One wrong move and it will be game over, and you'll be history. You'll know how in Frankfurt.*

Joan held his breath. "*One wrong move and it will be game over.*" In this case, the word *over* meant something absolute and definitive, no doubt about it. *Over* as in a slit throat. *Over* as in apprehension and torture. *Over* as in the end of something that had already gone too far. And then he would be history.

What should I do? he wondered in desperation. Would he be able to jump from the train when they were nearing the station?

He clenched his mobile. If he called Herbert Weber at the intelligence service, they would think he was of no use to them anymore. They would charge him and take him into custody until the case was under control and any dreams of greatness or picking up women on the beach in Barcelona were gone. He would immediately be back at square one and the futile existence that he had been close to ending forever only a few days ago.

He read the note one more time. Could *over* mean anything other than death?

Joan's head was spinning. Should he jump from the train while it was moving? No! Maybe jump when they were approaching the station, but when exactly? Wasn't the main station in Frankfurt one of the world's busiest? If he jumped, he might be smashed against the tracks or run over by another train. He couldn't just hang out of an open door when they were approaching the station and wait for the right moment because Ghaalib had people watching him and they would grab him; he realized that now. And he couldn't call the German intelligence service if he wanted to continue with his coverage; he had just been over that. But maybe he could pull the emergency brake and try to jump off before he was apprehended.

Joan looked around. It wouldn't take more than five seconds for these strong and resourceful men to grab him, so it was hopeless. But what if he allowed himself to be accosted by the people here in the carriage? Wouldn't the local police be waiting for him on the platform? Yes, they definitely would, because pulling the emergency brake without good reason was an offense; everyone knew that.

But what if Ghaalib had more men on the train than the one who'd delivered the note, and what if they suspected something was awry? Maybe they were in the next carriage keeping a close eye on developments. If so, weren't they capable of killing him silently and discreetly with a lethal injection and then disappearing?

Don't let your imagination run wild, Joan told himself while clenching his fists and trying to think straight. If he looked at it rationally, why would Ghaalib's men have given him the note if they were intent on killing him? It didn't make sense, but he didn't intend to wait around for the answer. Death, torture, apprehension—he had to escape from here no matter what it took.

He looked at the map in front of him and searched for a way out. Between Nuremberg and Frankfurt am Main there were lots of small towns but only one where he imagined the train could stop in an emergency, and that was Würzburg.

I've heard of that one, he thought, and Googled it. It had 130,000 inhabitants and several hospitals and clinics; it sounded perfect.

Joan sighed with relief and calmly stood up, put on his jacket and placed his phone in the inside pocket, closed his laptop, and put it in his bag along with his papers before putting it over his shoulder.

"Arghhh," he suddenly moaned, and grabbed his chest. He repeated the moaning sound and let his head fall backward so only the whites of his eyes were visible and began to grapple for something to grab on to to support himself.

As expected, everyone in the carriage stopped what they were doing and a couple of passengers ran over and propped him up.

"Is there a doctor here?" one of them shouted without anyone's reacting.

"Is it your heart? Do you have medication? Where is it?" asked another, but Joan didn't respond.

In a few seconds they'll contact the train staff. It's all going according to plan, he thought. Then they would stop the train in Würzburg and move him to an ambulance. And when he reached the hospital, he would vanish before they knew what had happened.

Joan sank to the floor, ending on his back with his eyes closed, which caused a lot of commotion around him. Someone rushed out to the next carriage while another fumbled in Joan's pockets and bag, looking for the nonexistent medication.

It was actually a very peaceful experience to witness all this care and attention, so Joan passively went along with it and made sure to only breathe superficially and imperceptibly. What he hadn't thought through was that if a person displays symptoms of a heart attack, no one, especially in this circle, and regardless of their skills, would hesitate in taking drastic action, and suddenly there was a gigantic man kneeling beside him.

Joan was terrified when he felt the first press and the crushing weight on his ribs followed by the man's warm mouth on his.

"Ahhh," he complained, at the feeling of his ribs being crushed. In a second, he would no longer be able to keep up the charade.

"I've got it," shouted a voice. Through his half-closed eyes, Joan caught a glimpse of the outline of a man in a conductor's uniform leaning over him with a determined look in his eyes while someone else rolled his shirt up to his shoulders.

"Have you done this before?" someone asked.

And when Joan heard the conductor say yes and that he had taken a course, and finally realized what he intended to do, it was too late to protest. The shock from the defibrillator caused his entire body to jerk and all his nerve endings to explode as the pressure from his heart moved up toward his throat like an undigested lump.

For a few seconds, the countershock caused his upper body to tighten, and when it stopped, his body jerked and the back of his head slammed against the floor.

He heard them shout, *"Mein Gott,"* before everything went black.

24

Alexander

It had been an absolutely dreadful night. Alexander had struggled for hours with the game in vain. For every step forward, he was kicked two steps back.

Alexander banged his hand against the keyboard, but that didn't have any positive effect; he let his fingers rip on the keyboard, but to no avail. He reluctantly made the radical decision to click away from the game and opened the settings function to analyze the status of the computer. As he had feared, it didn't bode well, and even though he had only been playing for a few hours, the machine was overheating and was now in the red danger zone. Maybe he had been too tough on his hardware and now the motherboard was worn out somehow or another, even though that sounded crazy. He had only had the machine for twelve months and the guarantee was for three years, but if he handed it in for repair, how long would it take to get it back?

Calm down, it's just something that happens every now and then, he thought, trying to comfort himself, while the machine cooled down. Hopefully, that would work and put him back on track, because if waiting and allowing the computer to cool down didn't help, he had absolutely no idea what else to try. The thought alone drove him to biting the skin around his nails until he bled, while his legs were tapping like drumsticks on the floor.

The seconds felt like an eternity.

After twenty minutes, the computer had cooled down enough for him to restart it, and he looked nervously at the screen.

Come on, come on, he thought as the perspiration began to build in his armpits. Nothing was happening. A white square appeared in the middle of the screen, but that was all. The system appeared to be totally dead.

He fumbled with the cables, rebooted it, thought until his head hurt, sobbed in frustration, and then rebooted it again. And still nothing.

Alexander could have thrown himself out the window.

He woke up with a start and the uneasy feeling that his world had collapsed. With trembling fingers, the first thing he did was to press the ON button and concluded that nothing had changed with the shitty machine. His precious gaming PC was finished.

Luckily the game is saved on the external hard disk, he reassured himself as he looked up at the image on the wall of the old woman who had drowned.

"Sorry, I burned out the machine," he said to the photo. "But don't worry, I'll manage. My father has a laptop I helped him buy. It isn't as fast as my Shark Gaming, but the FPS is still high enough." He smiled. "Yes, you're right, I fooled the idiot. He didn't know what to buy or why it should cost double what he'd expected."

Alexander laughed momentarily and shook his head. "Yes, sorry for my endless yapping. You probably don't know what FPS is, but it stands for 'frames per second,' and if it's over sixty it's good enough for this game." He smiled to himself. The graphics card in his father's Lenovo was fairly good, and the FPS was seventy, so it should be all right. When his parents left for work shortly, he would leave his room and grab it. He knew the code because he had set it up himself. He smiled. There was no doubting that his father would be furious, but what could he do about it? Scratch the varnish on the door a bit more?

From behind the gray blinds, Alexander could glimpse the dawning of a new day, and on the other side of the door his parents were already busily going through the motions of their usual morning ritual while dragging their feet in their slippers, shouting at each other, and making a general racket. In ten minutes, when they had left, it would be quiet and he would go and fetch the laptop from his father's office; connect it to his external hard disk, mouse, and gaming monitor; and start again. As soon as the system was back up and running, he would reach his planned victories for the day.

"Alexander," shouted his mother from the hallway. "I'm off now. I'm going to the conference in Lugano, remember. I've left the usual ready meals in the freezer for you and your dad. And, Alexander! Surprise me for once and come out while I'm gone, won't you? It would make me happy."

Lugano! Alexander snorted. Yet another reason he hated these sick hypocrites. She had been pulling this number with the conference for years, and while she was gone his father would rarely be home. Why couldn't they just admit they were fucking other people? He hated them.

Alexander put his ear to the door and couldn't hear a sound. His father must have left already, but, just to be sure, he would wait ten minutes before removing the steel wire that was wound around the radiator regulator. That way he wouldn't be caught unaware if they had forgotten something and came back to find him strutting around.

Out in the corridor, it stank more than usual of heavy perfume and deceit. It was sickening. He couldn't wait to put an end to it all; all that remained was to complete his mission and reach the victory number 2117.

Then they would get what was coming to them.

Normally, he would have eaten breakfast, emptied the pot, and done all the usual things, but the thought that something might go wrong with the transfer led him to walk straight past the kitchen and into the office.

He stood for a moment in front of his father's desk and thought about what he would do if things didn't go according to plan. About a year ago, one of his gaming buddies from Boston had experienced the same thing with a game he had been playing for years, and when the computer burned out, the dumb fucker went haywire, threatening in frustration to commit suicide.

Alexander shook his head. How stupid and futile. Suicide? No danger. When the time came, better to take a whole load of others with you to hell.

He had just taken the cables out of the hardware to disassemble it when a shadow crept over the desk and an iron grasp fixed on his shoulder.

"Got you!" said the well-known voice in a harsh tone.

He had hardly turned around when his father began shaking him like he was a child.

"What are you doing?" he shouted. "Did you really think you could get away with stealing from me on top of all the other stunts you've pulled, Alexander? Really?"

Alexander didn't answer. He just allowed himself to be shaken and pushed. What else could he do just now? Promise repentance and say it was all just a game? Hell no.

"I'm not letting you go before we've sorted out this disgusting mess you're living in," threatened his father.

It had been weeks since Alexander was so close to his old man's pallid skin, sickly breath, and body odor. How he had managed to live an entire life under the same roof as this laughable man was a mystery. But now it was time for that to end.

"Look around you, for Christ's sake," hissed his father when he pushed him into the bedroom. "Is this the thanks we get for all we've done for you, for giving you this room? It's a pigsty. Do you think this is what we've taught you? Well, do you?" he shouted, and kicked a couple of empty Coke bottles strewn on the floor. "It smells like a sewer in here. Everything reeks. Take a look, Alexander. Look at all the rubbish. What does that say about you? That you're okay upstairs? No, not really, does it? Then maybe you'll understand why we're embarrassed of you. What the hell should we do with a son like you?"

"Don't worry yourself about that," said Alexander as he pushed his father away from him. "You'll be rid of me before you fucking know it."

Whether it was due to the swearing or his lack of respect, his father took a step back and looked at him as if he had been punched in the face.

"Rid of you? You know what, I think I'll take you up on that," he said coldly after composing himself for a moment. Then he pulled a money clip full of notes from his pocket. "Here, take this. Now get lost! We don't want to wait around until it suits Your Highness. You'll find a youth hostel; you certainly aren't staying here anymore."

He turned toward the door and caught sight of the limp steel wire hanging from the door handle. "So that's how you did it!" he said, gauging the distance to the radiator. Then he unhooked the wire from the handle and wound it around his wrist. "There we go! That'll put a stop to you holing yourself up in here, got it? You'd better start packing your shit. If you forget anything, I'm sure your mom will bring it over when she gets back from her trip."

"Surely you mean when she's finished fucking the guy that she likes more than you. Isn't that what you meant?"

It wasn't the first time Alexander had seen his father turn white with anger. It conveniently happened just before he gave him a good beating and it usually scared him, but this time he didn't give a shit. The punch came quickly, but it didn't feel hard even though it was, and nor did the second or third punch. What he really felt was the satisfaction of the expression in his father's eyes growing more and more desperate because he could no longer scare his son. The blows simply confirmed that the power relation between them had finally turned.

"You're crazy," gasped his father as he pulled back. "Crazy!"

Alexander nodded. *Maybe he's right, who can say?* he thought as his father continued his tirade and he set about collecting clothes from the floor and slowly moved toward the samurai sword on the wall.

When Alexander unhooked it from the wall, his father began to laugh.

"Are you really thinking about taking the sword to the hostel,

Alexander? You think they'll let you in with that? Are you really that stupid? You're in a worse state than I thought."

His face distorted into a mocking laugh that continued until the moment Alexander drew the sword from its sheath.

The grin on his father's face stuck eternally when his head was cut clean off and landed softly on Alexander's bed.

He looked up at the clipping on the wall and smiled. "It's begun," he whispered.

That's the first one, he thought with satisfaction when his father's heavy head was placed in the chest freezer and the body dragged out to the utility room with a plastic bag over the neck so the blood didn't get everywhere.

"You'll be comfortable here, old man," he said as he wrapped the headless body in cut-open trash bags. A little gaffer tape here and there and the body could stay here forever without the stench spreading to the rest of the house.

Alexander nodded contentedly and pushed the bundle a little closer to the washing machine so there would also be room for his mother on the utility room floor when she deigned to come home.

His entire body was shaking with joy as he carried his father's IT equipment into his room. He had done exactly as planned, and it had gone like clockwork. He could easily do it again. And again. And again.

He connected everything and turned it on. Funnily enough, he was no longer worried that it wouldn't work. Of course it would.

From now on, everything would work out for him.

And when he had made sure that the Lenovo was purring like a cat and the game was running smoothly, he raced through the entire next round without the slightest hitch.

Time for an update, he thought as he leaned over for his phone and called his contact number.

The policeman who went by the name of Gordon sounded irritated and tired, but that soon changed.

"Well!" teased Alexander. "I haven't reached the victory number twenty-one seventeen, but I think you should know that I've already begun."

He could clearly sense the question mark forming in the man's head. He found it dead funny.

"Already begun what?" came the anticipated question. "Shooting your way toward twenty-one seventeen, is that it? Is it difficult?"

Alexander laughed out loud.

"Difficult? LOL. You haven't got a clue about what is and isn't hard, have you, you stupid police retard?" He counted the seconds until the man on the other end digested the insult. It took a little longer than he had anticipated this time.

"Well, I guess it's possible that I haven't got a clue," he answered. "However, I can tell you that we know what the number twenty-one seventeen refers to. It refers to the unfortunate victim who was washed up on the shore in Cyprus a few days ago, doesn't it? But tell me, why does that old woman mean so much to you?"

Alexander froze. How could he know that? He looked around. Had he missed something? Could they have traced his calls? Hadn't he been cautious enough when changing prepaid telephone cards? Had they managed to trace his IP address or something else he didn't know about? But how? It was impossible.

"Come again?" he said, but even he was aware that his voice had lost its bravado.

"Stop the games now," said the voice. "Or we'll come and stop you, understood?"

There was a momentary pause. Were they tracing him at this very moment?

"Bummer. You're already too late," answered Alexander, ready to hang up.

"Too late? It can never be too late," said the policeman.

"Can't it? Try saying that to my dad's head that's laughing in the chest freezer as we speak. This is no game," he answered, and hung up.

25

Gordon

Death is the ultimate *completion of life, much like capers are to Wiener schnitzel,* Gordon's father had always joked until the sad day when he was admitted to a hospice, stiff, ashen, and with plastic tubes sticking out from almost every available orifice.

That sort of made the comparison fall flat.

Gordon, on the other hand, saw death as anything but the completion of life. For him, awareness of death had become the eternal nightmare of life and a source of grief. He had spent days trying to understand why Lars Bjørn, who had meant so much to him, had died so shockingly suddenly. And while his question remained unanswered, he had checked his pulse at least twenty times every hour out of fear of the day when his heart would stop and everything else along with it. Slowly but surely, the fear of his final heartbeat began to consume him. Not only did it haunt his thoughts both day and night, but he now began to experience physical pain in his chest.

Am I breathing properly at night? was one of the many questions he asked himself. *If my resting heart rate is always eighty, will I wear my heart out?* was another.

And the thoughts of this inescapable fate, which could hit him at any time, terrified him.

It didn't make it any easier that he had now seen death etched in Assad's eyes. Wasn't he the man who, until the Bjørn brothers' demise and the new worry for the safety of his family, had always had a smile on his lips or an ironic distance from the vicissitudes of life? The man who always greeted each new day with optimism? Gordon felt all too clearly how Assad, behind his otherwise very stoic appearance, was considering the outcome of the next few days. No one who had heard his account could be in any doubt that Assad was preparing to kill Ghaalib to avenge his family or that he was aware that the same fate might await him.

And now Gordon was sitting in the safety of his office chair with these depressing thoughts about life and death at the back of his mind, constantly checking his pulse to make sure it was still okay. It was so pathetic and embarrassing.

Gordon stood up and walked around the table a couple of times. The incident room was where Department Q kept all its open cases lined up on bulletin boards with notes, prints from journals, and photos. A gruesome place in the basement that could rid anyone of their personal considerations for their own well-being. Yet his mind was preoccupied with the idea that if he just jumped on the spot or did fifty push-ups, everything would be better and death kept at bay.

He had managed ten push-ups and was bathed in sweat when the telephone rang.

"Hello," said the voice at the other end.

It only took one word for Gordon to know it was the boy intent on killing.

"Yes, it's me again, copper," said the boy.

Like a dangling puppet, the lanky body drew itself up toward the telephone and pressed the RECORD button.

The boy sounded uncomfortably smug and euphoric in contrast to how uncomfortable he otherwise was with living in harmony with the rest of the world.

Now I'll ask him his name and what this game is he's playing, thought Gordon. The plan was to come across as friendly, polite, and understanding, but he didn't get far before the boy's tone grew more intense and arrogant. And when he then also began laughing at Gordon and mocking him, Gordon couldn't stop himself from taking a tougher approach.

The boy was clearly unsettled when Gordon said he knew what the number 2117 referred to in the real world, but that was nothing compared to Gordon's shock when the boy retorted that he had decapitated his father and thrown the head in the freezer and then hung up on him.

Gordon began to shake. For the first time in his no-longer-quite-so-young life, he had spoken with a murderer. A maniac who boldly declared that he would murder again. It was really unsettling to think about because the responsibility would rest on his shoulders alone when Carl, Rose, and Assad left to look for Assad's family. It made him a sort of lord over life and death, but what if he couldn't cope with the situation?

His pulse began racing uncontrollably again. Gordon collapsed into the office chair with his head between his knees and prayed that the telephone would never ever ring again. Of course, he could pull the phone out from the socket, but then there would be no doubt where to pin the blame if reports came flying in one day about a young man who had gone crazy in public.

Oh God! What should he do?

All four of them were sitting in silence in Carl's office, listening to the recording of the conversation. Even Carl looked serious.

"What do you think?" asked Carl afterward. "Has he done it? Has he decapitated his father?"

Rose looked at Gordon and nodded. "He's called you before, but the difference now is that he's displaying severe emotional instability. I mean, one moment he's laughing at you and the next he has a very aggressive tone just before hanging up. The conspicuous change in his voice when you shouted that you knew what the number stands for. Don't you think he's telling you the truth, Gordon?"

Gordon had to say yes.

"Then we agree that he isn't acting on impulse or fantasy; it would appear that everything he says refers to something real and calculated. What do the rest of you think?"

Both Carl and Assad nodded.

"But have I done something wrong?" Gordon asked tentatively.

Carl patted him on the back. "It's only now that we know what we're up against. Up until a moment ago, you couldn't have done anything differently, Gordon. Don't beat yourself up. And well done for sticking with it despite my skepticism."

Gordon let out a sigh of relief. "I'm just worried that I can't cope with this," he said. "I don't want to be responsible for more people dying."

"Let's remain calm and analyze what we've just heard," said Carl, leaning back in his office chair. "Does the guy live in an apartment or a house? What do you think?"

"He lives in a house," answered Assad with certainty.

"Yes," added Rose. "He didn't say 'freezer' but 'chest freezer.' Who on earth has room for one of those monstrosities in a flat?"

"Exactly." Carl smiled, but Gordon didn't follow. How did it make the case easier that he didn't live in a flat when the alternative was that they would have to check thousands of houses?

"This reminds me of those young Japanese people who sort of imprison themselves. You remember what it's called, don't you, Rose?"

"Yes, they call it *hikikomori*."

"That's it. You haven't heard of it, Gordon?"

He shook his head. Or maybe he had and couldn't remember it.

"Anyway, they believe there might be as many as one million young people in Japan living in isolation like that. They live with their parents, but they don't communicate with them. They just sit in their rooms lost in their own small worlds. It's a huge problem in Japan today."

"A million?" Gordon felt dizzy. That was the equivalent of saying there were as many as fifty thousand people like that in Denmark.

"It's very embarrassing for a Japanese family with all their concepts of honor, so they normally hide it from everyone."

Rose gave him the thumbs-up. "And it would definitely be the same here."

"Do they ever come out of their rooms again?" asked Gordon.

"As far as I know, it's not uncommon," answered Carl. "But it can take years. However, I've never heard of anyone threatening to kill people when they do. But that happens too, I guess."

"They're psychologically ill, right?" Gordon nodded in answer to his own question.

Carl shrugged. "Some more than others. This guy certainly isn't all there."

Gordon couldn't have agreed more. Thankfully, this boy wasn't the average citizen.

"Can we agree that he's quite young and presumably lives in the Copenhagen area?" he asked.

"Yes. He said *LOL,* 'laughing out loud,' so he must be very young," said Assad.

Carl scratched his neck. "Exactly. But doesn't *LOL* mean 'lots of laughs'? At least that's what I thought it meant."

"And he doesn't have any real dialect. My guess is he lives in the Copenhagen area."

Carl and Assad nodded again.

"But he also doesn't sound working-class, so he probably isn't from a working-class area," said Rose, feigning a working-class accent.

Carl shrugged. He didn't have the best ear for sociolects. But then, he was from Vendsyssel.

"So, where do you think he might be from originally?" he asked.

"Denmark," said Rose and Assad almost in unison.

"Again, I'd tend to agree." Then Carl turned to Gordon. "So you're looking for a young Danish man, presumably around twenty years old, whose father probably isn't turning up for work anymore, lives in a house with a chest freezer, and, in my opinion, comes from a nice middle-class home. Next time you talk to him, change your strategy and taunt him. Call him Kurt-Brian or some other stupid name. If you keep at it, I'd be surprised if it didn't frustrate him. And if you can get him just a little riled, you might be able to provoke him into arguing with you. It's easy to get people to screw up once they're angry.

Afterward, our linguist can have a listen. A language expert will definitely be able to deduce a lot about the boy from that sort of conversation."

Now Gordon began to feel queasy. He had had lots of assignments of all different sorts, but this one was . . .

"And find out who sells prepaid telephone cards in the Copenhagen area. When you know, call everyone and ask if they remember a young Danish man who recently bought a lot of them. Can you manage that?"

Gordon looked wide-eyed. He would have to run to the toilet in a minute. "But, Carl, he could've bought them from different places and far from the place where he lives," he said, but Carl ignored him.

26

Carl

Carl had never seen so many medals, distinctions, and pompous finery. Row after row of at least a hundred black uniforms, officials with hats and dark jackets, colleagues in full dress uniform with newly cut hair and stern faces, and women with modest skirts, some even with veils.

Hypocrites, he thought. While, professionally, Lars Bjørn deserved the honors, when it came to it, he was also a detestable, unfaithful bastard who was to blame for Assad's awful misfortunes. So, when everyone else removed their hats in respect for the deceased, Carl kept his on. *That would have annoyed Lars Bjørn,* he thought momentarily until he noticed the chief of homicide staring at him.

This is one hell of a state funeral, he thought, and removed his hat.

In front of the coffin stood Lars Bjørn's widow with the children, trying to hold back her tears in front of the solemn representatives with starched creases. Behind them stood Gordon, red-eyed and with lines down his face, and at the back of the assembled group stood a small, dark man with tousled curly hair and such an expression of grief etched on his face that Carl had to look away.

In a few days, it would be Jess Bjørn's turn to be buried, doubtlessly with significantly fewer mourners. Perhaps it upset Assad that it would also be without him.

He turned to look up at Gruntvig's Church, which, with an orgy of organ pipes in yellowish brick, stood majestically in the background.

During the service, the aisle had been covered with wreaths and bouquets, and the male police choir had made the Danish flag flutter and the interior of the church echo. The priest had balanced on the edge of exaltation as he fired off one honor of the deceased after the other until Carl was about to throw up. Over the years, he had lost many good colleagues in the service to either illness or accident and seen them to the grave in more humble fashion, so what the hell made Lars Bjørn such a superstar?

And then it hit him: He was standing in front of a church, and a year from now, he might be doing the same but with a small child in Mona's arms wearing the family-heirloom christening gown that his mother had proudly mended in preparation.

Then the gang in front of him could kiss his humble behind.

"You almost look good in full dress," Rose said tartly at the wake. She had been this way since Carl had made it clear she would not be accompanying him and Assad to Germany.

"Yes, you have to make an extra effort for such an unbelievably popular corpse," answered Carl, opening his arms to indicate the eagerly talking dignitaries, the national police commissioner, the minister of justice, the chief constable, and the whole pack right down to the lower ranks such as an inferior detective inspector like himself.

"*Popular* isn't a word you can say about certain other people," she said even more tartly and directed at him.

Carl walked over to the large group of tedious funeral guests who were salivating in front of a table with red wine and tapas. He tried politely to reach the booze, but nobody reacted or acknowledged him.

In the end, he straightened up to his impressive North Jutland stature and pushed his elbow forward like a spear. "Sorry," he said as people were forced to the side while cursing at him.

Then he grabbed a whole bottle of wine from under the nose of an apprehensive waiter and left. He deserved something for his efforts.

The editor at *Hores del dia,* Montse Vigo, was a bit of a tough cookie. Vague, dismissive, and not exactly on a charm offensive.

"Like I told one of your colleagues, we don't give out contact details for our staff. You could be anyone, and Joan Aiguader is involved in what might be regarded as a very sensitive job. He's actually been injured, and you shouldn't go snooping into that either."

"Fine, let's say that. But it'll come back to bite you in your presumably fat ass."

"I beg your pardon!"

Carl considered the way he had chosen to express himself in English and shrugged. At least he had her attention now.

"You won't give me the information, but the whole world has read Joan Aiguader's articles and knows that he's on his way to Germany and has probably already been there for several days," he said. "The Copenhagen police are investigating a very serious terrorism case in which knowledge about this Ghaalib and his movements is of vital importance, so if you don't put me in touch with Joan Aiguader immediately, you risk being guilty of the death of many innocent people."

She laughed dryly. "And that from a man who comes from the country whose Mohammad cartoons have set the world ablaze. How many innocent people have perished on account of that?"

"Listen here, you! Let me tell you something, and I advise you to pay attention. If you think that it's acceptable to put the interpretation of the unlimited freedom of speech of a few crazy people on the shoulders of an entire nation, then you're just plain stupid. However, as I don't actually think you are, but simply got caught up in the heat of the conversation, I'll ask you again. I have a colleague who I care about very much, and his family is being threatened by this Ghaalib that Joan Aiguader is writing about. If I promise that you'll be the first one to get the story afterward and that I won't take advantage of Joan Aiguader or his work, can I please have his number?"

―――――――――

Carl was satisfied with himself, but no one answered the number Montse Vigo had given him.

Hmm, I'll have to try again, he thought while eyeing the red wine tempting him on the table.

"Cheers, Lars Bjørn," he'd just managed to say when the chief of homicide appeared in the doorway as he still had the glass to his lips. Bloody bad timing.

"Quite," was Marcus Jacobsen's only comment, and it was more than enough. "Carl, I spoke with Gordon and Assad after the funeral," he said.

Carl put the glass to one side.

"In contrast to you, but like many of the rest of us, they were deeply affected by Bjørn's death, so next time you might want to show a little more respect." He tipped his imaginary hat, but Carl had already gotten the message. "I understand that you're thinking of conducting police business in Germany during your time off. Is that correct?"

Carl glanced at the glass of red wine. A small sip would be good just now. "Police work? Nooo," he said. "We just want to follow some leads, but no different from how a civilian would do it. Relax, there won't be any arrests."

"Hopefully, all three of you are aware that police business must be carried out by the national police of the country you're in."

"Of course."

"But you're going there on police business?"

"Well, it's more personal than that."

"Carl, I know you, so listen. If you're there on police business, you have to inform the local police. Understood? And if for some reason an arrest is necessary, remember that there has to be a local police representative present during questioning."

"Yes, but—"

"And remember in particular that under no circumstances can you carry weapons in a foreign country! Leave your gun in the firearms storage, got it?"

"Marcus, we know all this like the back of our hand. You don't have to worry that we'll compromise the Danish police."

"Good. But if you do, don't count on any support from here."

"Of course not, Marcus."

"Another thing. As I said, I spoke with Gordon today. When were you thinking of informing me about the developments?"

"I thought he'd done that."

The chief of homicide didn't look impressed. "You think a violent murder has been committed, if I understand correctly. And the indication seems to be that this will be followed up by a wave of violence and very likely more murders. So, let me ask you, do you think this is a minor case, or is it possibly one PET should be informed about?"

"Isn't that your decision? Anyway, I doubt PET will be able to make a difference in this case."

"Go on."

"We're dealing with a deranged boy, and even though his actions can be interpreted as terrorism, I don't think PET will have anything on him. He's a lone wolf, Marcus, but his motivation doesn't seem to be fundamentalism, more of a misguided political message. We're not sure what exactly, but we're getting there."

"And you think an office assistant down here is capable of getting to the bottom of it?"

"Rose is staying here with Gordon."

That softened his face a little. "But Rose is also an office assistant, Carl."

Carl tilted his head. "Really, Marcus?"

"Yes, yes, okay, we're all aware of Miss Knudsen's talents. But make sure you keep track of the case no matter where you are. Understood?"

Carl emptied his glass in one gulp when the dust had settled from the chief of homicide's visit. Then he called the number again that was supposed to belong to Joan Aiguader. It rang a couple of times, and then a male voice finally answered in German.

Carl was confused. "Er, I am trying to get hold of Joan Aiguader. Is he there?" he asked in English.

"Who am I talking to?"

Is he going to steal all my lines? thought Carl. "I am Detective Inspector Carl Mørck from the Copenhagen police," he said gravely. "I have some questions in connection with an investigation."

"*Jawohl,* and you are talking with Herbert Weber from LfV."

LfV? It sounded like a spare wheel warehouse for four-wheel drives. Had that bitch really had the audacity to give him the wrong number?

"*Jawohl,*" repeated Carl. "What does LfV stand for?"

"Landesbehörden für Verfassungsschutz, *natürlich.*"

He would give him *natürlich!*

"Which is?"

"That is what we call the intelligence services in the German states. We cooperate with BfV, who operate all over Germany. And in what capacity exactly are you contacting Joan Aiguader?"

"I would rather tell him that directly."

"Joan Aiguader has suffered a serious head lesion and a minor hemorrhage to the hindbrain. He is currently lying unconscious here at the clinic, so that isn't a possibility. Good-bye."

"Hey, hold on a minute. Where is Joan Aiguader just now?"

"At the university hospital in Frankfurt, but you can't speak with him unless you come here personally, and, even then, only once we have given you clearance."

Come here personally. That was something he could bloody well count on.

He had only just put the receiver down and cursed out loud when the phone rang again.

"Well, had a change of heart, have we?" he almost shouted down the receiver in English.

"Carl?"

Not many voices were so recognizable that a single word could give the person away; however, this voice pronouncing his name like it was a mediocre gluten-free foreign dish could only belong to his ex-wife, Vigga.

"Er, yeah!" he answered.

"What are you playing at frightening me like that, shouting down the phone in English? I'm actually in a right state here. My mother is dying."

Carl's head sank to his chest, but it wasn't due to shock or grief. His almost ninety-year-old ex-mother-in-law, Karla Alsing, drove people crazy, and roughly every two months, the retirement home announced that they were reconsidering her situation. No one was safe from her whims. Arson, sexual advances on anyone regardless of gender or age, and premeditated theft of any sort of fur, even if it was still attached to the pets of visiting relatives. Despite advanced osteoporosis and weighing in at only forty kilos, she stole furniture from her defenseless neighbors with dementia, redecorating her own flat with the loot quicker than the staff could react. Karla had given new meaning to the diagnoses Alzheimer's and dementia, and no one knew what direction her mental state would take from one second to the next. So, if she really was dying, there would definitely be some people who would envisage a more manageable future, Carl included. The fact was that an old financial agreement between Carl and Vigga meant that he was responsible for everything to do with his mother-in-law that Vigga didn't want to deal with, of which there was more than enough.

"Dying, you say? Goodness, Vigga, how sad. But she's only eighty-nine, so no need to panic."

"Carl!" she shouted. "Get down there right this minute! You haven't visited for three weeks, so you already owe me three thousand kroner. And I promise you, if you don't get a move on, I'll cancel our agreement, got it? How much is half your house worth now? One and a half million kroner?"

Carl gasped, put the cork back in the bottle of red wine, and popped it in a plastic bag. He would need that by the time he got home.

Karla's prognosis was delivered just as tersely as a weather report on a gray day in February. If it weren't for the care assistant's ruddy cheeks, he would have assumed she was a robot whose batteries were running low.

"But then again, she is very . . . well, old," said the woman after pausing to choose her words.

He tentatively opened the door to Karla's room, expecting to see a pale dying body in a nightgown lying on the bed, but nothing could have been more inaccurate. Karla was lying on the bed right enough, but with her head buried under the pillow and wearing her legendary kimono, which she had won fifty years earlier in a bet on which of the women in the bar where she worked could snog the most men over fifty within twenty minutes. According to legend, there wasn't a middle-aged man in that bar or within twenty meters up and down the street outside who got away.

"Yes," said the care assistant, looking at the kimono. "You'll have to excuse it being a bit open, but you know the lady."

A bit open, yes. But he didn't have any desire to be this familiar. If it were any more open than it already was, it could almost be mistaken for a blanket on an unmade bed.

She covered Mrs. Alsing a little, at which the dying woman began moaning from under the pillow.

"She's actually very weak, so we had to confiscate her cognac. She resisted, of course, but we couldn't risk the death certificate stating that she drank herself to death."

Then she lifted the pillow and the dying woman's heavy eyelids opened to reveal a pair of blurry eyes looking at Carl as if he were the archangel Gabriel himself come to collect her.

A few times she seemed like she was about to say something, so Carl listened with great concentration. If he missed her final words, Vigga would never forgive him.

"Hello, Karla, it's Carl. Are you tired?" He knew it was a stupid question, but then deathbed conversations hadn't exactly been part of the curriculum at the police academy.

She made a couple of wheezing noises again as if she was about to draw her final breath.

He put his ear right next to her dry lips.

"I'm listening. What did you say?"

"Are you my friend, little policeman?" Her voice sounded like she had almost given up.

He took her hand and squeezed it. "You know I am, Karla. Your friend forever." His voice was as smooth as chocolate, just like in an old film.

"Then get that fucking bitch out of here!" she said with a weak but crystal-clear voice.

"What's she saying?" asked the care assistant at the end of the bed.

"She wants to say a final prayer with me in private."

"She said all that?"

"Yes, we spoke Esperanto."

The care assistant looked very impressed.

Just as she shut the door behind her, a withered hand reached out from under the duvet and grabbed Carl's wrist.

"She's trying to kill me. Did you know that?" she whispered. "You might as well arrest her straightaway."

Carl looked at her with compassion. "I can't do that before she's done it, Karla."

"Then I'll call you and let you know when she's done it."

"Okay, Karla, that sounds like a good plan."

"Have you brought me presents?" She reached out greedily for the plastic bag.

Carl pulled the bag toward him and heard a sloshing sound.

"It's bleeding," she said with surprising clarity.

Carl leapt over to the sink, pulled the bottle out, and threw the plastic bag in the sink. The cork was still in the neck, but it was loose.

"Ooohh, red wine!" his mother-in-law said as she sat half-upright in bed and reached out for it.

What the hell, thought Carl, and gave it to her.

If Assad had been present, he would have had a suitable camel joke, because she drank it as if she had been wandering in the desert for weeks, and her metamorphosis was instantaneous, so her confession could wait. It would also have been never-ending given the life she had lived.

All the way down to the care home's offices, he could still hear her resonating soprano voice attempting something reminiscent of opera.

"What's going on?" asked a nursing assistant when Carl passed her on his way to the exit.

"Er, it's coming from Karla Alsing," he said. "And you can prepare yourselves for a protracted show. That swan isn't singing its last song yet."

"Assad is picking me up before dawn, Mona," he said when he was finally lying in bed.

"Will you be home before the amniocentesis?" she asked tentatively.

He pulled up her blouse and stroked her stomach. "We agreed. Of course I will be."

"I'm scared, Carl." He caressed her cheek and gently pressed his face against her protruding stomach and could feel that she was shaking.

"Don't worry, Mona. I'm sure everything is just fine. Just look after yourself. Promise?"

She looked away and nodded very slowly.

"Who will look after me and the little one if something happens to you?"

Carl frowned. "I'm just going to Frankfurt for a few days, Mona. What could happen?"

She shrugged. "Anything. People drive like lunatics on German highways."

He smiled. "Assad isn't driving, so don't worry."

She took a deep breath. "And then there's the situation with Assad, the dead woman, and his family."

Carl pulled his head up from her stomach and looked her straight in the eyes. "What do you know about that?"

"I spoke with Gordon. He called just before you got home."

That idiot. He had no right to tell her anything.

"I can see what you're thinking, but it isn't his fault, Carl. I dragged it out of him. He wanted my help so he could get through a case that's bothering him."

"About the killer boy?"

"Yes. And then he told me about the number and the woman who was murdered. Actually, he told me everything when I asked. About Assad's past, his family, and how they've been kidnapped. And that it's the reason you're going to Germany." She reached out for his hand. "Find them, but come home alive, darling. Promise me."

"Of course I will."

"Say it like you mean it. *Do you promise?*"

"Yes, Mona. I do. If we find them, we'll leave all the hard work to the German police."

She leaned back against the headboard. "Do you know that Morten has arrived back from Switzerland with Hardy?"

"Heck no. When did that happen?"

Why on earth had they not called him to tell him how it had gone?

"Yesterday. Hardy is in treatment. But they say they don't know if it will help him. They didn't sound very optimistic, if you ask me."

27

Assad

Assad had only managed a couple of hours of sleep when he awoke freezing cold, as if his circulation had stopped. He rubbed his arms and legs in vain and wondered if there might be some internal reason for feeling so cold.

The answer hit him immediately.

Today was the day the hunt began. The thought made him nauseous; the likely outcome was that some people would have to die. And with Lars Bjørn gone, there was no one at HQ who had any idea about what he and Carl were getting involved in or what they were up against. Not even Carl. They would have to make on-the-spot decisions about life and death, and no matter what, the outcome would be merciless.

Assad rolled out his prayer mat and knelt down. "Almighty Allah, help me to act justly, and give me the strength to recognize and accept my fate," he prayed quietly.

On the floor beside him, there were newspapers with Joan Aiguader's photos and everything else he needed to pack and take with him. It was so painful and incomprehensible to see his loved ones pictured there. Lely Kababi, his guardian angel. Marwa, whom he had left alone with the girls and the little one in her womb. His beloved wife, whom Ghaalib had abused until she miscarried their third child and then continued to rape again and again. That devil incarnate, Ghaalib, who ruined everyone's lives, committed terrible abuses against his daughters, and murdered their newborn children.

Over the last few days, those images had burned themselves so deeply in his soul that he could no longer remember how life had once been. Maybe that was why he awoke like one of the living dead.

Then he got up, took a thin album made from camel skin from the bookshelf, and opened it for the first time in many, many years. It was the lost reality of this album he had to travel to avenge.

Remember them as they once were, Assad. Let all the good memories guide you and you will find them, he thought as he flicked through the album.

There were photos from his wedding to Marwa, the children as infants, the times at Kastellet military fortress, and the flat in Copenhagen. Happy days and smiling faces full of hope and life.

In the last photo of Nella and Ronia, they were respectively six and five, just before he joined the weapons inspection team in Iraq. Nella, with a red ribbon in her dark hair with a sheen of henna, and Ronia, wearing a cardboard hat she had made at kindergarten. They were smiling and touching each other's noses. It was so wonderful and innocent.

"Sorry," he whispered. "Sorry, sorry, sorry." With the enormous feeling of having let them down, he simply couldn't think of another word.

"Dearest Marwa," he said, stroking her face on the photo with his fingers, the grief of what he had lost hardening him to what lay ahead.

He took a deep breath and was about to put the album down when his eyes caught sight of something he had long since repressed. He saw that what he had thought was a shadow from Ronia's cardboard hat couldn't be that, because she was standing close to the window and the shadows were on the other side of her face. No, this dark mark was no shadow; it was Ronia's birthmark, which stretched from her jaw and up toward her left ear. Now he recalled it only too well. She had been upset about the birthmark when she was young, but a boy in kindergarten had said that it looked like a very, very dangerous knife and that it was cool. He had said he wished he had a beauty spot like that.

"Beauty spot," that was how he described it, and Ronia never spoke about it again.

How could I have forgotten, my sweet Ronia? he thought, but knew all too well why and when repressed thoughts could be a person's only defense against madness.

He turned his attention to the clippings on the floor, pushed the prayer rug to one side, and leaned in closely. He squinted his eyes and stared from different angles at the daughter who stood next to Marwa in the clippings.

"Oh God," he exclaimed as the tears rolled down his face. Instead of a feeling of liberation or relief, his body trembled with despair and pain.

Based on the photos from the beach in Cyprus, he hadn't been able to know which of his daughters was alive up until now, and that had subconsciously consoled him. When he didn't know, it could be both of them. But now that he knew the truth, he was sure who his tears were for. They were for his younger daughter, Ronia, the one with the birthmark, because the young woman standing next to Marwa didn't have one.

He jumped up, pumped with anger and thoughts of revenge, but who could he take it out on? In pent-up frustration, he smashed his glass table, tore books from the bookshelf, threw all the furniture around, and only stopped when half the flat had been ravaged and the neighbors began banging on the walls and from the floor above.

He collapsed to his knees sobbing, flattened out his prayer rug between the shards of glass and puddles of mint tea, lay down on it, and prayed to his god for Marwa and Nella—and Ronia.

The way Carl was standing waiting in the parking lot, he didn't look like a travel companion you would want to sit with in an enclosed space for many hours, but what could be expected? He was pale from lack of sleep, taciturn, and definitely not in a good mood, which Assad's experience told him was a sign to keep a safe distance.

"You've got a lot of stuff with you," commented Carl dryly, observing the pile of plastic bags on the back seat.

"Yeah, it's just some provisions. We can't hope for food expenses, can we?" he said as Carl walked around the car and opened the trunk so he could put his suitcase in.

"What the hell, it's packed back here as well. What is all this, Assad?"

"Just different things we might need," he answered.

"This sports bag takes up nearly the whole space." Carl moved it a bit to make room for his suitcase. "It weighs a ton. What've you got in here, Assad? One of your camels?"

"Don't touch that, Carl," he said, and put his hand on the trunk.

Carl looked at him gravely. He had seen through him already. "Open it, Assad."

Assad shook his head. "You need to understand that if we don't have these things with us, we'll have nothing to defend ourselves with. If you're not on board with that, Carl, you'll have to let me go alone."

"Are there weapons in it, Assad? Because if there are, you risk losing your job."

"Yes, I know. That's just something I'll have to live with."

Carl took a step back. "Open it then, Assad."

He hesitated, so Carl did it himself.

For a long time, he stood there silently in the morning fog assessing the contents of the bag. Then he turned to Assad.

"I assume we agree that I've never seen what's in this bag, right?"

28

Joan

It's so white here, thought Joan with his eyes half-shut. In the background, he could hear voices speaking in a foreign language, and the smell was indefinably sour. The voices drew closer; they seemed warmer but also more distinct. Had he been sleeping?

He kicked out slightly with one leg and felt resistance, almost as if he had something over him. Then he opened his eyes fully.

"Hello, Joan Aiguader," a man said in English. "So, you're finally awake."

Joan glanced down at the outline of his body under the sheet, confused. Why was he lying in a bed with white linen and a white headboard, surrounded by white walls and white light? What was he doing here?

"Thankfully, it went quicker than we dared hope," said a squat man who took a step closer.

"What went quicker?" He was confused. Hadn't he just been on the train?

"You have been through what we can only describe as an extremely unusual situation, and we apologize profusely."

Joan felt his right wrist with his left hand. Had they stuck a syringe in the back of his hand? It felt uncomfortable.

"Am I in the hospital?" he asked.

"Yes. You've been admitted to Universitätsklinikum in Frankfurt. You've been here since the day before yesterday."

"Who are you?"

"Me? I represent Deutsche Bahn. Naturally, we'll pay for all your costs in connection with your hospitalization and your treatment. I'm here to keep you company and discuss the compensation to which you are naturally entitled. Just whenever you're ready to talk about it."

Now doctors and nurses were arriving. They had beaming smiles. What were they up to?

"Your surgery exceeded our expectations, Herr Aiguader," said the man in the white coat standing closest. "We have to thank Deutsche Bahn for transporting you here as quickly as possible so that the damage to the back of your head wasn't permanent."

"The man said that I've been lying here since the day before yesterday."

"Correct. We've kept you in a light artificial coma since your surgery two days ago."

"Two days!" Joan didn't understand. "But I can't be here! I have to get up. I have to send the article I was writing." He attempted to thrust a leg over the edge of the bed. It didn't go well.

"I'm sorry, but that will have to wait, Herr Aiguader. We have informed your employer that the hospital will be keeping you in for a few days yet."

"But why am I here? What happened?" he asked.

It was the squat man who spoke again. "The day before yesterday, you experienced a painful indisposition on the train, which your fellow passengers mistakenly took for a heart attack. The doctors don't know the cause of your seizure, but we're very clear about what happened afterward, and we're terribly sorry about the actions that were taken. We've already fired the individual who used the defibrillator on you."

"I don't understand."

He smiled. "It is difficult to understand. The person in question, a certain Dirk Neuhausen, trained as a medic, and it was your misfortune that he was the conductor on the train to Frankfurt that day."

Joan tried to remember. It was true that he had simulated a heart attack and there had been a good reason for it. Now he also remembered why.

Joan clenched his fists and looked around the room. There was a dark-skinned nurse behind the others, but she was the only one who stood out.

"Dirk Neuhausen was well aware that defibrillators haven't been allowed on Deutsche Bahn trains since 2016 because all forms of alternating-current magnetic fields can interfere with the electronic circuits in the advanced systems used on modern trains. But Dirk Neuhausen had apparently always had a dream of saving lives, and then he found himself almost doing the opposite. When the ban was implemented, the idiot stole an old professional defibrillator from the local hospital, which he took with him in his bag on all his shifts. You were the first one he had the opportunity to use the machine on. Unfortunately, Herr Neuhausen's defibrillator was an older version, so it was unable to register that there was nothing wrong with your heart."

"Yes, Herr Aiguader," added the doctor. "You have a totally healthy heart and no other problems as far as we can see. But the shock your body received from Neuhausen's use of the defibrillator caused you to experience cramps, tighten up, and subsequently bang your neck on the floor and, unfortunately, directly down on the buckle from your shoulder bag, which pierced a hole in your head. You fainted and lost a lot of blood."

The Deutsche Bahn representative placed a hand on Joan's. "Very unfortunate, yes. As I said, we assume you'll want to discuss compensation with us just as soon as you've taken legal advice. Until then, on behalf of Deutsche Bahn, I can only tell you how much we regret the whole episode." He pointed at the bedside table, where there was a lavish collection of bouquets. "In the meantime, we hope you enjoy a little splash of color from nature. The roses are from Deutsche Bahn."

There was a noise from the door to the corridor, and a man walked in whom he recognized but certainly hadn't reckoned with seeing again. The man whose body filled the best part of the doorway was Herbert Weber, his contact with the German intelligence service.

Weber smiled authoritatively to those standing in the room, which evidently meant that he wanted them to leave.

"You recognize me, I see," he said when they were alone. "So, I guess you're in a better state than we might have feared."

What was Herbert Weber doing here? Didn't they have enough to do looking for Ghaalib?

"Naturally, we wondered why the phone's GPS position stopped moving. Actually, we were convinced you had been killed and dumped in some remote place. Thank God the reality wasn't quite so gruesome." He tried to smile but wasn't very good at it. "When we traced you to the ward here, we took the liberty of going through your things and found this."

He unfolded the paper and read aloud:

> *How did you know to go to Frankfurt? And what were you doing with the police last night? Didn't I give you direct orders to keep away from them? We know everything you do, Joan Aiguader, so be careful. One wrong move and it will be game over, and you'll be history. You'll know how in Frankfurt.*

Herbert Weber looked sternly at him. "Why didn't you inform us that you'd received this note? If you had, we would've immediately had our people shadow you, which would probably have led us to Ghaalib."

"I was going to," he lied. "Everything just happened so fast. I was sure that Ghaalib had people waiting for me at the station in Frankfurt, so I faked a heart attack to avoid them. I thought they'd stop the train in Würzburg and take me quickly to a hospital."

"But then there was an idiot with a defibrillator instead." Now Weber was smiling quite naturally, almost with schadenfreude. Could it be at the thought of how much it had hurt?

He walked around the bed. "Do you know anyone here in Frankfurt?"

Joan shook his head.

Weber pointed at some white lilies that contrasted with the red roses.

"These flowers were delivered anonymously yesterday. We think they're a signal from Ghaalib to let you know that he knows where you're staying."

Joan looked at the gangly stems.

Of course they knew where he was just now. They had undoubtedly been waiting for him on the platform in Frankfurt, and his departure by ambulance couldn't have gone unnoticed.

Joan held his breath because now it really hit him.

They knew where he was.

"We've positioned an officer outside the door to keep an eye on you, which means you can forget any ideas about leaving before we give you the go-ahead, okay?"

He started breathing again. Thank God for that. Of course he was on board with that.

Then he turned his head to the bouquets. "Who sent the tulips, then? Do we know?"

Herbert Weber nodded. "We informed your employer as soon as we knew where you were, so the flowers are from *Hores del dia*. I have one last question before I leave you alone to rest."

"Okay."

"The Menogeia camp?"

Joan frowned. Why was he asking him about that?

"A woman died there. You wrote that she had her throat slit."

"Er, yes." He tried to keep a clear head, but he was feeling nauseous. That chapter in particular was something he didn't want Weber to ask too many questions about.

"The people who murdered the woman were never found. If you have any idea about the motive, you need to tell me."

"I don't really. But there was a lot of hostility in there. You could clearly feel it."

"In what way?"

"Several of their group had just drowned, and they blamed each other for being accomplices. They didn't name names, but still . . ."

"If you have a theory, out with it. We also have our own theory."

"There were militia sympathizers among them. I've written about that, haven't I?"

"And the woman who was murdered, what had she done to harm them?"

"She had spoken to me, and that was enough. I was looking for the two women who had been standing on the beach next to Ghaalib because I thought they could lead me to him and the story behind everything."

"So, we can assume that the person or persons who killed the woman in the camp were in one way or other sympathizers of Ghaalib and his plans, or at least not opposed to them. Could they be the ones who escaped from there? I'm asking because we believe that the escapees have already been smuggled into Europe and probably without good intentions."

"I can't know that, can I? I didn't even know that some of them had escaped. Are we talking about women or men?" The questions were beginning to worry Joan. Did the man think that he might be involved in all this?

"The camp administration has sent us pictures of the two women who escaped and disappeared." He put them in front of him. "Look! Do you recognize them?"

Joan wasn't good with faces, but he recognized them immediately. It was the two women who had begun fighting when the atmosphere in the room at the camp went crazy. So, the fight had been a sham.

"Yes, I recognize them. They fought at the camp."

Weber tilted his head. "As if they were enemies?"

"Well, that's what I thought, but maybe they weren't after all."

Weber pursed his lips. He appeared to be satisfied, so, thankfully, it ended there.

Then Weber handed him a cell phone.

"We'll hold on to your phone, so you can have this one instead. We've programmed in all the important numbers, for example the latest number Ghaalib used, the local numbers for the German intelligence from Munich all the way up to Berlin, and, of course, the number for your editor at *Hores del dia*. She asked me to say she'd be grateful if you'd give her a call just as soon as you regained consciousness."

Joan took the phone. It was the same make and model as his own.

"This time we've chosen not to sew a GPS into your clothes but had a GPS built into the phone, which works whether it's turned on or not. So now we'll know where you are once you're finally discharged from here. In the meantime, get well soon."

And then he left.

Joan leaned forward in bed and felt the smoothly shaved back of his head and the dressing that went from ear to ear. It must have looked terrible from behind.

He looked around. An empty bed next to his told him that the room was intended for yet another patient. At the end of the bed, there were a table and two chairs, presumably meant for potential visitors, and then there were the bedside tables, each with its own little shelf. To his great relief, he saw that his laptop was on the shelf of the table with all the flowers.

Joan reached out for it and turned it on; fortunately, the battery still had some power. Then he opened the document he had been working on in the train carriage and read it with satisfaction. Even though he was behind, there was still enough substance to give *Hores del dia* what they had paid him for. He thought for a moment and then took his mobile and rang Montse Vigo. He would show her that it would take more than a hemorrhage to stop her star reporter. "Thanks for the tulips" was the first thing he said.

"Ahh, Joan Aiguader, splendid." Did she sound surprised or irritated at the interruption? It was she who had asked him to call. "I just heard from the hospital that you were awake," she continued. "Are you okay?"

He smiled. Finally, his well-being meant something to her.

"I'm okay, thanks," he answered. "I'm quite dizzy, but that's all. The hospital and intensive care unit have taken good care of me. And ill weeds grow apace, as they say." He laughed.

"That's good. Have you read the card that came with the flowers?"

He looked over at the tulips. Was that white dash between a couple of green leaves a card?

"No, not yet."

"Well, never mind. I've got you now, so I can say it myself."

"Okay, but let me tell you first that obviously I'm sorry I had to miss a day, but I'm already back on track. I won't be able to write everything I want over the next few days because there's a strong suspicion that a terrorist act will be carried out shortly, so the German intelligence service have to okay all the pieces I write. But I have an article I wrote on the train, and—"

"We know, Joan. We've already gone public with it. We had the Germans forward it to us after they had censored it a little. So, thank you."

Joan frowned. "You've printed it?"

"Yes, isn't that what we've paid you for?"

He wasn't quite sure if he should be happy or something else.

"But it isn't the Germans who decide what we print in *Hores del dia,* so from now on we won't accept more censorship," said Montse Vigo.

"But that's the agreement I have with the intelligence service. I won't get near Ghaalib if I don't follow their rules. They'll just arrest me."

"That's why we've taken you off the story, Joan Aiguader. We've assigned two of our permanent reporters to follow up on it. Our print run is growing, and royalties from newspapers all over the world are flying in. Should we just stop in the middle of it all? But don't worry, Joan, you can keep the rest of the money you received as compensation for pain and suffering."

"Can you just run that by me one more time? Who is going to be writing? I'm the only one who can write this story: I have the sources, I'm the one close to Ghaalib, I'm the one speaking with the intelligence service. I'm the one who knows the backstory."

"Yes, but we're tackling the story from a different angle, Joan. It's going to be more general and therefore more theoretical than practical; more analysis than coverage, you might say. We need to have column space filled every day, and you're too unstable for us. It's simple arithmetic, Joan. Better to have daily sales to other papers than a lot of sales once in a while. Continuity, Joan, that's what we stand for at *Hores del dia*."

Joan swallowed hard. There went his permanent position, the flirting with women at Xup, Xup, his dream of a secure life as a celebrated journalist.

"Maybe you can earn a bit with someone else. There are some stupid Danish policemen who are very keen on talking to you, at any rate. That's what I wanted to tell you."

Then she hung up, leaving Joan sitting there speechless. Now someone else was going to walk in his footsteps, but what sense would it make if they couldn't also walk in Ghaalib's? And what sense would it make when they had never seen victim 2117? None whatsoever.

Could it be that Herbert Weber's people had struck a deal with the newspaper? Had they really sunk so low? Either way, he would be sure to turn that evil hag Montse Vigo's hair gray even if it ended with his working for a newspaper in Madrid.

He tried to sit up properly and slide his legs over the edge of the bed, but it didn't work out for him this time either. His legs were too heavy, his body too weak, and the back of his head in too much pain.

Joan fell backward onto the pillows and breathed heavily while looking up at the ceiling. That was why they had taken him off the job. They didn't have time to wait for him to recover, so he had simply been sidelined. He could have cried.

But what did the Danish police want with him? Denmark? He didn't know any Danes; in fact, he didn't know anything at all about the country except that some people asserted that Danes were the happiest people in the world.

Joan was almost laughing to himself at the thought when the

dark-skinned nurse from earlier came in with an equally dark-skinned doctor in a white coat and with a serious expression on his face.

What now? Bad news? He felt the back of his head. What could it be?

"We have a visit from a doctor sent by Deutsche Bahn's insurance company, Herr Aiguader. He would like to ask you some questions. Is that okay?"

Joan sighed with relief and shrugged. He would damn well make sure they understood that any compensation less than a six-figure sum in euros would not satisfy him.

The doctor introduced himself as Dr. Orhan Hosseini, after which he produced a stethoscope and helped Joan sit up on the edge of the bed so his gown could be lifted up in order to allow the doctor to listen to his heart and lungs.

"Well, well," he said every time he moved the stethoscope. "Your heart and lungs appear to be fine," he said with a certainty and authority that made a couple of the zeros in Joan's imaginary compensation fade away. "Sit still for a moment," he said, and fumbled with something in his pocket. Then he heard a bump, and Joan turned his head just in time to see the nurse fall to the floor and her body jerk a couple of times. Then he felt a violent shock himself.

What happened immediately after was hard for Joan to register, but someone came in and released the brakes on his bed and pushed him quickly out into the corridor. The officer who was supposed to be keeping an eye on him was still there but was slumped in the chair with his eyes closed.

My God, there's no one here to stop them, he thought, and tried in vain to scream as the porter behind him shouted to make room. Then he felt something being attached to the IV on the back of his hand, followed by a warm, slightly burning sensation that shot through his arm.

And then he was out.

29

Carl

Carl checked their schedule. After taking the Rødby–Puttgarden ferry, it would take them approximately seven hours, including refueling, and bathroom and snack stops, to drive down through Germany to the hospital in Frankfurt.

Seven hours in this vehicle with Assad, sweet Jesus! The prospect felt like an eternity to Carl because since their departure from Copenhagen, Assad had tearfully whispered his younger daughter's name at least a thousand times. "Ronia, Ronia, Ronia," over and over again, and Carl had had to restrain himself from shouting at Assad to stop.

And then Assad suddenly did stop, sat upright in his seat, turned to look out over the landscape of the Fehmarn Belt, and started banging his fists against the passenger door. Carl threw him a worried glance because he had never witnessed such uncontrollable anger in Assad. The blows were actually shaking the body of the car, the veins in his neck looked like they were ready to burst, his complexion grew darker and darker, and the usually calm man was sweating so profusely that it was dripping from his armpits and forehead.

Let the boy get it out of his system, Vigga had often said when Carl's stepson, Jesper, had been in the habit of throwing tantrums and banging his head against the wall as a teenager. Right now, Vigga's advice seemed appropriate, but even though they were driving a BMW, there had to be a limit to the durability of the door upholstery. Despite Assad's stature, he had always been as strong as an ox.

Poor car, thought Carl. Thankfully, the situation only lasted for three or four minutes and then it was over. Assad turned to Carl and asked with total composure if he would be able to kill someone without hesitation if the necessity arose.

Without hesitation. What was "without hesitation"? During wartime? When you or your loved ones were threatened?

"It depends on the circumstances, Assad."

"I said, 'if the necessity arose.'"

"Then yes, I assume so."

"Could you do it with any kind of weapon? With your hands, an ax, a piece of wire, a knife?"

Carl frowned. It was a very uncomfortable question.

"I thought as much, Carl. You couldn't. But you need to understand one thing: The man we're going after can, and therefore so can I. And when it happens, because I think it will come to that, you shouldn't stop me. Do you understand?"

Carl didn't answer, and Assad didn't ask any more questions about it. It was very quiet as they both sat with their own thoughts while the car cruised southward on the network of highways.

Maybe a bar of chocolate will cheer him up, thought Carl a few kilometers later when a sign with the image of a knife and fork announced that a *Raststätte* was coming up.

"What are we doing here?" asked Assad when Carl turned off the highway and parked in front of the services. "Do you have a stomach-ache or something?"

Carl shook his head. So what if he did need the toilet after several hundred kilometers? Would that be so strange? Just because Assad had a strong bladder, it didn't mean there weren't others who enjoyed using a restroom more often.

Carl found a couple of bars of chocolate and paid for them. At least it was something he would eat himself if Assad didn't want any. He showed the chocolate to Assad, who was staring at the selection of newspapers and magazines.

"I just thought we needed a little pick-me-up."

Assad looked at him in surprise. "Pick-me-up?" he said. "Isn't that a private matter?"

A private matter? Carl wasn't sure he wanted to ask for more information about that association.

"Then call it a treat, if that sounds better."

Carl turned around and noted that Assad hadn't heard his reply because he was over by the newspaper stand with a paper in his hands, in a world of his own. Carl looked over his shoulder. OPFER 2117 was written in large letters across the front page. He was clinging to the newspaper as if it would fly away from him.

"Come on, Assad, let's go," he said, but Assad remained where he was. He was, unfortunately, better at German than Carl.

"Hey," shouted the shop assistant. "You can't just stand there reading the paper; you have to pay for it."

Assad turned around and looked at the man as if he were about to ram the newspaper in question down his throat. Carl knew the signals. When Assad once in a while gave in to his anger and exploded, it could turn into a long and costly affair.

"I'm coming to pay. Thank you!" Carl shouted back. "Don't worry."

Assad placed the newspaper on his lap when they were back in the car. He rocked back and forth, held his stomach, and then bent forward and cried without either sound or tears.

After a few minutes in this state, he turned to face Carl. "You keep me grounded in reality, Carl. Thank you."

He said nothing else before turning his gaze to the windshield and watching the world go by with his jaw grinding and his feet tapping the floor with a machine-gun rhythm.

It was only now that it sank in for Carl that Assad was standing on the verge between human and killing machine.

They had reached the area around Kassel when the Bluetooth in the car reacted to Carl's phone. It was Gordon.

"Can you talk, Carl?" he asked. It was a relief amid the otherwise all-consuming silence.

"I'm on the hands-free, so talk away."

"Rose and I have been ringing around all day. We started with the kiosks in Brøndby and then Hvidovre, Rødovre, and Valby. Then we directed our attention a bit farther north and we might have found something. A kiosk owner in Brønshøj says that a little over a month ago, a young man bought all the prepaid telephone cards he had in stock. He couldn't remember how many exactly, but he thinks it was between fifteen and twenty."

Carl and Assad looked at each other.

"That's a hell of a lot, but it could have been for a group or a club," suggested Carl.

"He can't remember precisely what he talked about with the customer, but the guy didn't seem like he was buying them for someone else. He didn't seem like a sociable type who is instantly likable, he said. More of a wary, nerdy sort."

"What did he look like?"

"A very regular Danish boy with reddish, spotty skin and ash-blond hair."

Assad nodded to Carl; they were thinking the same thing.

"Then he paid by card, I hope."

They heard some grunting noises. Was he laughing?

"What's so funny, Gordon?" he asked.

"Carl! We've called around fifty kiosks or maybe double that, I've lost count, and we have a list as long as my arm of kiosks who have had weirdos buying four or five prepaid telephone cards at a time, and now we've found this one. Sounds easy, right? But do you think it's going to just be smooth sailing from here on out? *Of course* he didn't pay by card or we'd already be going through the kiosk's accounts, wouldn't we?"

Was Gordon being sarcastic? That was something new!

Carl shook his head. "What goes on in the heads of our politicians? They need to hurry up and make it illegal to sell those shitty prepaid telephone cards without registering the buyers. If they can register those sort of purchases in Norway and Germany and a whole load of banana republics, why can't we do it here? It's elementary, Watson! Criminals and terrorists and this idiot calling Gordon use them. The minister of justice needs to wake up and smell the coffee."

Assad pointed ahead at a road sign and then at the speedometer. Bizarrely, there was suddenly a speed limit of a hundred kilometers, and he was driving one hundred and fifty.

Despite the reprimand, Carl nodded contentedly. Assad was slowly returning to reality.

"Rose is on her way to the kiosk with a police sketch artist," continued Gordon. "She thinks the kiosk owner will be able to give him a detailed description."

"How can you know that? But good, worth a try."

"And what should we do with the sketch when we have it?"

"You'll need to ask the chief of homicide," said Carl. "Marcus is unlikely to agree to you going public with it. These sketches have a habit of being a bit too general, and what would be the point? We don't even know if he's the right person, or if the boy is just full of shit. Maybe he just has a lively imagination. And what would we say, and who would we say it to? You'll be inundated with calls if the media gets hold of it."

"Rose is on FaceTime, and she wants to call you in half an hour. Will you be able to pull into a rest stop?"

"Tell her that Assad and I are in the middle of an important conversation, so she'll have to wait until later. It'll also give you time to think everything through."

"Are we having an important conversation, Carl?" asked Assad when Carl hung up.

Carl shook his head.

And then the silence continued.

The sight that greeted them in front of the Universitätsklinikum in Frankfurt was seven or eight police cars with blue flashing lights blocking the entrance and a lot of hectic activity in front of the door to the hospital.

Carl parked askew on the pavement. Marcus would have to pay the fine.

"What's going on?" Carl asked the nearest officer.

Maybe he didn't understand English, but some sort of disturbed primal instinct was awoken in him when he saw Assad behind Carl.

"*Hier!*" shouted the idiot to the other officers, and then he went directly for Assad. It could have gone terribly wrong given how Assad was feeling, but thank God he didn't go crazy and beat them up; quite the opposite, he simply let them cuff him.

"Take it easy, Carl," he said when they ordered him to stand with his legs spread and began frisking him. "See it as an exercise in keeping calm when things seem out of hand."

"Idiots!" shouted Carl, and pulled out his ID. "We're police officers from Denmark," he said in English. "*Wir sind Polizisten aus Dänemark. Lass ihn los!*"

Maybe it wasn't such a good idea to call them idiots. They certainly only looked at his ID with reluctance and suspicion, and it really wasn't very impressive, to be fair. It was at times like this that he missed his old badge. There was some commotion behind the frontline officers, where stony-faced men in suits were having a discussion. Carl noticed that two of them were heading toward them, but he didn't notice how heavily armed they were before they were up close.

"What's going on here?" one of them asked in English while holding on tightly to the machine gun hanging by his side.

"I am Detective Inspector Carl Mørck. We've driven here from Denmark to meet with a certain Joan Aiguader, who has apparently been admitted here." It was hard to know if it was Carl's comment that caused all hell to break loose, but in the next second they were both in cuffs and roughly led through the main entrance and into a room where they had established a sort of interim command center. There was a tense atmosphere inside, where ten to twelve police personnel and just as many men dressed in dark clothes were busying themselves. Not exactly a place they had planned to be, and definitely not in handcuffs.

They were pushed down into a couple of plastic chairs and asked to remain calm for their own good. They sat with their backs to the wall for at least half an hour without anyone's paying the slightest attention to their protests.

"What do you think this means, Assad?" asked Carl.

"The same as you. Joan Aiguader is probably not doing too well just now!"

"Do you think he's been killed?"

"Maybe, how can we know that? We need to get out of here, Carl." He turned his head away. Why was he shaking? Was he crying because their lead was getting cold?

"Assad, hang in there. There will always be new leads to follow."

He didn't react. His body just rocked slowly from side to side.

Carl left him in peace and looked around. A few hours ago, this room that now resembled a digital wonder of an incident room had presumably been a totally normal meeting room for the doctors. Of course, Carl knew that the Germans were world-famous for their methods and effectiveness; all the same, this was something else. If his colleagues at HQ saw it, they would shrink away in shame.

One team had hung up a map of the Frankfurt area with information about the control posts the police had established on the approach roads, and at least twenty-five locations were marked with pen, including Ludwig-Landmann-Strasse, Lorscher Strasse/Nordwestkreuz, Am Römerhof/Westkreuz, Mainzer Landstrasse, and so on, all over town.

A second group was sitting with a row of monitors linked up to the video surveillance in town and the cameras in the helicopters that were circling the suburbs. The pictures in the room were constantly changing while men and women tried to keep apace with them. Several people were sitting with telephones and giving updates, while others were discussing the problems that required clarification. Carl was familiar with the scenario from back home, just not to this extent. Then his eyes caught a table only four meters away from where they were sitting. It was obviously where the preliminary interrogations were taking place. A pair of grave-looking officers were questioning the person who had been summoned, while a third was taking notes. Next to them sat a fourth person, a heavyset man in plain clothes who was listening intently.

Carl turned his ear slightly and tried to understand, but due to all the German classes he had slept through at Skolegade Skole in Brønderslev, it was difficult.

"There we go," said Assad quietly next to him. He looked at Carl and seemed calm and relaxed. The contrast to the intense silence on the drive here was striking.

Assad shook his head as if he could read his thoughts and signed to Carl to look down. His handcuffs were lying on the floor between the chairs.

"Good God, how did you do that?" whispered Carl, staring at Assad's hands, which were resting on his lap.

He smiled briefly. "I could ask you where you're hiding your key to the handcuffs."

"Er, just now in the drawer at home. It's with the handcuffs, of course."

Assad shrugged. "A camel always has its water in its hump, and I have my homemade master key stuck right under my massive new watch. That's where we differ."

Now the old Assad was back.

"Take my key and we'll get out of here," said Assad. "This isn't going to lead anywhere, and my instincts tell me we haven't got time to waste."

"Hey, Assad, come on. This is police work; they're our friends. Sit for a moment and look around. Don't you think this massive effort will be able to help us? What do we actually know at the moment? Nothing!

Only that something serious has happened. Can *you* understand what they're saying? I can't." He nodded toward the interrogation table.

"They're asking people if they've seen anything, but you probably worked that out."

"And have they?"

"Just before they mentioned a white Volvo, which is probably the one on the screen over there."

Carl stretched. They had presumably zoomed in on it a bit too much because it was very out of focus.

"They're trying to follow it from camera to camera across the city. It would seem that it isn't quite as simple as they had thought. The person they're interrogating now works in the hospital laundry or depot, I didn't quite catch it. They want to know if the lab coats come from there."

"What lab coats?" asked Carl.

"What's going on here?" It was the man who had apprehended them. He pointed at Assad's hands.

Assad raised his arms in the air. "I'm very sorry, but they were too tight," he said, and bent down to pick up the handcuffs. "Here you go, you don't want to lose them."

The policeman inspected the handcuffs in disbelief. Then he walked over to the table and whispered something to the heavyset man, who nodded a couple of times while watching them.

"I'm informed that you've identified yourselves as policemen from Denmark," he said a few seconds later in front of them. He adjusted his turtleneck and pulled up his trousers. It didn't add to his authority. "I'm told there was some concern about the validity of your ID card. In the meantime, we've done some background checks and have verified that you are who you say you are. Colleague to colleague, I apologize for the hardhanded way you were welcomed, but you don't actually have any business here, so you have to take the good with the bad."

Despite that, he offered them his hand. "As you'll have noticed, we have enough to see to at the moment, so please don't get in the way. When we've settled some more pressing matters, I'll get back to you."

"Thanks. But we don't understand what's happened. What's going on with Joan Aiguader?" asked Carl. "Why aren't we allowed to talk with him?"

"You can if you can tell me where he is. We were able to follow him to within a few blocks from here and then his GPS signal disappeared, and now we're high and dry." He unlocked Carl's handcuffs and pointed at Assad. "And now tell me how you managed to free yourself, Houdini."

Assad showed him the key. "It wasn't an exact match, but with a bit of fiddling in the right places, it works, you know." Then his expression changed. "Is Joan Aiguader dead?"

"Well, that's exactly what we aren't sure about. He was abducted from his hospital room a couple of hours ago. Presumably in the white Volvo station wagon that we're currently trying to locate."

30

Carl

"It's late, Rose, why haven't you two gone home?"

Carl might well have been from Vendsyssel and he certainly wasn't getting any younger, but talking with this sourpuss on FaceTime and staring at a screen that was smaller than a five-euro note would have been a challenge for anyone, he imagined. Apart from that, the activity in the German incident room had grown increasingly hectic over the last hour, so it was difficult to concentrate.

"This is what our guy looks like if the kiosk owner remembers correctly," she said.

Carl squinted and looked at the sketch she held up to her mobile. He was a very youthful-looking man with fine features and actually rather handsome. Slightly unruly blond hair and a very small bun on top like a samurai. Carl had seen it before; it was obviously the replacement for the ridiculous tiny ponytail that had been so popular among men about twenty years ago. *Every decade has its own misconceptions,* he thought. But perhaps due to his expression, it wasn't altogether unflattering on this young man. Despite his immaturity and slender physique, his face didn't look weak in the least, but rather somehow powerful and determined. Maybe it was because of his cheekbones? Maybe it was the lips? But the more Carl studied the face, the more he was convinced that a kiosk owner from Brønshøj would be able to remember a face like that.

"It's a strong face, Rose. Do you think it's a good likeness?"

She turned the phone back to herself and nodded. Why did she look so annoyed?

"Have you discussed it with Marcus?"

"Yes, he also thinks the facial composite shows something distinctive, which in the best-case scenario should be recognizable, but he also said that we can't go public with it. It's so irritating."

"So, what's your plan?"

"I complained to him, and he came back with the consolation prize of offering me a permanent job at the same wage level as a clerk with ten years' service."

Carl smiled. It would be a real benefit for Department Q to have her back on the team.

"He had the cheek to suggest right to my face that I move to the second floor and replace Mrs. Sørensen."

Carl leaned back in his seat. What the hell did she say? Marcus had no right to do this to him.

"What did you say?" he asked, and held his breath.

"I said no thank you. I don't want to be a clerk with ten years' service."

"You said no!"

"You bet I did—not that I agree with betting." She tried to smile. That was something at least. "I know you love me, Carl. It's written all over your face."

Was it?

"So now I've been given a permanent position with immediate effect in Department Q. And Assad and I are both being given ID cards and the new title of assistant inspector. Of course, the wage is less than Mrs. Sørensen's, but I'll deal with that later."

She didn't sound particularly pleased, but Carl was.

"You asked what our plan was now. Well, since we're not allowed to go public with the sketch, Gordon and I will have to trudge around all the shops in the vicinity of the kiosk to find out if that's where the boy shops on a daily basis. If that doesn't pay off, he probably doesn't live in that neighborhood."

"Probably not, no. He might have gone far from home to make sure he wasn't recognized."

"That's also our theory, but we still need to check. After that, we're thinking of making inquiries at all the high schools within a ten-kilometer radius of the kiosk."

"Hmm!"

"What?" She sounded irritated.

"This isn't an American film where you can just waltz into a high school and ask the secretary outside the headmaster's office if she recognizes a former student, which she always does—in films, at least. Rose, hundreds of students go to high school, and he might actually be twenty-three, which means it's been a long time since he graduated. He could have been enrolled in a community college or have specialized in a technical course, and he might not even have gone to high school, for that matter."

"Thanks for nothing! That's just the encouragement we need. Don't you think we know that it's a shot in the dark? Right now, Gordon is sending the sketch as an attachment to a list of educational institutions and requesting their respective offices to pin it up on a central notice board and in staff rooms. The text reads, '*Do you recognize this face? If so, contact . . . ,*' and then our number. But my instinct is that this boy has a high school education, just FYI."

"Well then, happy hunting," he said, expecting that she would say the same back. She obviously forgot.

"These chairs aren't exactly comfortable," he said afterward to Assad. He nodded. One of his feet was stamping on the linoleum as if he were keeping beat on the bass drum to a heavy metal number.

"I'm going crazy, Carl. Nothing is happening, and we're losing time." He spread his arms and looked at the room, and Carl could only agree. Everyone here was close to exhaustion. It had grown dark outside, and no one had spoken to them in a long time. He understood Assad; their mood was hitting rock bottom, and it didn't help that since this morning they had consumed no more than five hundred calories.

"*Ich hab'es!*" someone shouted at the back of the room, and everyone ran over to him, followed by Assad and Carl.

It was a very clear security camera image of a white Volvo station wagon in a parking lot. People were pointing between the monitors so they could compare it with the screen image of the car taken by a security camera close to the hospital exit.

"That *is* the car," said the man closest to the monitor. "Look at the scratches on the hood."

Carl agreed. They had found it, and it was still in Frankfurt, thank God.

He glanced at Assad. Their wait had paid off.

"When is the recording from?" asked a uniformed investigator.

"Two hours ago," answered the monitor operator.

"Is it parked in one of the immigrant neighborhoods?" someone asked.

"No, it's in a residential area with a mixture of rental apartments and family houses."

The investigator turned to the people in the room and started delegating. "You, Pueffel, get surveillance on that Volvo immediately. Meanwhile, Wolfgang, you analyze the tenant composition in the area. You, Peter, check if there are immigrants with a Muslim background and a criminal record at addresses in the area. And you, Ernst, go through the registries so we know where the car originates from and who owns it. Is it stolen? Is it a rental? Was it purchased recently? Where from? That's enough to be getting on with."

He clapped his hands. "Everyone else, into the adjacent room with me."

And then Assad and Carl were alone in the room with Herbert Weber.

The canteen wasn't the most well stocked, but everything went down without issue. If Assad's food had been served on paper plates, he would have eaten them too. And while they ate, Herbert Weber filled them in.

"The young nurse was rendered unconscious with a stun gun, and we're certain that something similar happened to Joan Aiguader. The guard stationed outside the door, however, was rendered unconscious with a single blow to the back of the head. They had placed him in the chair as if he had just closed his eyes and was momentarily dozing. That's why it took some time before the abduction was noticed. We can see from the video surveillance that they transported the unconscious Joan Aiguader down the corridor in a wheelchair after abandoning the hospital bed, and we can also see that the two people who carried out the abduction had dark skin, but that's all. They were good at keeping their heads down when they walked past a camera."

"What about the wheelchair?" asked Carl.

"We found it pushed to one side out by the entrance, and on the video surveillance we can see when and in what he was driven away. The license plate was covered in dirt, of course, and impossible to read, or we would've had a much better lead to work with."

"Why was he abducted?"

"Presumably because they found out that he contacted the police in Munich a few days ago."

"I don't understand," said Assad with his mouth full of everything the menu could offer.

"Joan Aiguader received his instructions directly from Ghaalib. It's a form of misalliance we normally strongly disapprove of, but in this case, Aiguader became an important source for us, and he still was until Ghaalib put a stop to it today. I think that he was using Aiguader's access to the media to create panic and scare people shitless, but we don't know why exactly. It certainly isn't the normal procedure before an act of terrorism."

"But do we actually know if it's his intention to commit an act of terrorism?" asked Carl.

Weber nodded.

"Why do you think that?" asked Assad.

"Aiguader provided us with a video clip that more than hints at that. As I'm sure you know from Aiguader's articles, Ghaalib has killed several times. The man is seriously determined and dangerous."

Carl looked at Assad. His eyes had never looked so gloomy.

"I know him," said Assad, putting down his knife and fork. "His name is actually Abdul Azim, and he's a monster. He's taken my wife and daughters hostage and tormented them in captivity for sixteen years, so Carl Mørck and I need to know everything you know, because otherwise he'll kill them."

He placed the newspaper clipping in front of Herbert Weber and pointed at Marwa and Nella. "Do you know this photo? That's my wife and my eldest daughter, Nella, and that's Ghaalib right next to them. From the first moment I met him, he's been the incarnation of evil on earth, and his affiliation with terrorism cells in Iraq and Syria won't have mellowed him."

"So, you're telling me that he's got total power over these two women?"

Two vertical lines joined between Assad's eyebrows as he tried to hold both his anger and tears in check. It was no easy task.

"What's his motive?" asked Weber.

"Revenge for something that happened between us many years ago."

"I see. I'm terribly sorry to hear that. What did you say your name was?" asked Weber.

"I call myself Hafez el-Assad, but my real name is Zaid al-Asadi. I'm Danish, but I was born in Iraq. I was incarcerated in the prison where Ghaalib was employed, and I'm the reason his lower face is disfigured. It's one of the reasons why he hates me more than anything else in the world. And listen to what I'm telling you! Everything he's doing is to lure me out into the open. That's also why he put Joan Aiguader up to writing his articles. Ghaalib wanted me to find out that my loved ones are still his hostages."

Herbert Weber put his hand up to his turtleneck again and began rubbing it; it was obviously something he did to help him concentrate.

"But you said all this occurred many years ago. So why is this all happening now?"

"The fight for the caliphate is suffering right now from one defeat after another in both Iraq and Syria, so it's become a very dangerous place to be for people like Ghaalib. Maybe he's lost too many fights in his life, and this one he wants to fight to the end and win."

Weber looked as if he was suddenly onto something. "Zaid al-Asadi, is that what you said?" He pulled his oversized leather portfolio onto the table and produced a plastic folder. "Here's the transcript of the sound file from the German photographer." He flicked a few pages ahead and then pointed at a name highlighted with a blue marker pen.

"Zaid al-Asadi" was written there.

"What we're going to do now is put these two cases together. Are you in?" Weber looked out over the group to gauge their reaction.

"You've heard Zaid al-Asadi's account. And I'm certain Ghaalib's weak point is that he's partly driven by his personal desire for revenge. But we mustn't be in any doubt that what he has started could also result in an act of terrorism if we don't stop it in time. The conversation on the video, which I've had translated for our Danish colleagues, is about an act of violence that will cost the lives of many, many people. We don't know when or even how, so that's what we're working hard to establish."

He turned around to face Assad. "Zaid here is our sitting duck. I've informed the Danish police that Detective Inspector Carl Mørck and Hafez el-Assad, as Zaid calls himself officially, are now part of the investigation team."

Carl nodded to his new colleagues. In front of him, Assad was sitting silently. Carl worried what the words *sitting duck* might involve, but that was what Assad had decided. He would step out of the shadows and confront Ghaalib directly. "Anything to save my wife, Marwa, and my daughter Nella," he had said in front of the whole group.

"We have to assume that there will be an act of terrorism very soon,"

Weber continued. "So it's of the utmost importance that we quickly find the people who kidnapped Joan Aiguader, and preferably before we make it public that Zaid al-Asadi has received Ghaalib's message."

Carl stretched out his hand and placed it on Assad's shoulder, and Assad turned and nodded.

His eyes were expressionless.

31

Ghaalib

There in the middle of the living room sat the pathetic being with a laughable dressing on the back of his head, begging for his life.

Ghaalib hated that sort of weakness. Couldn't people understand that their lives here on earth were temporary and that it wasn't his job to convince them otherwise? Cowards had stood in front of him and begged in vain for mercy hundreds of times, and just as many times as they had begged, he had made short work of their suffering.

It wouldn't be like that this time because Joan Aiguader was an important link as a mouthpiece in his game. He was the one who had ensured the world's attention and who had paved the way for Zaid to be shaken to his core. And he was the one who, like a professional witness at a state-sanctioned execution, would finally describe their ultimate attack in all its violence and terror.

"Give Joan another dose," he said to the Swiss woman. "We don't want the neighbors wondering what's going on in here. But give him a bit less than you give the women."

"No, no!" shouted Joan in the background to no avail.

Now they could have a rest from him for a while.

Ghaalib turned toward the group that was sitting tightly packed on the sofa and on the floor. The group was smaller than he had originally calculated because three of them were still interned in Cyprus, but he would make do with twelve. Ghaalib smiled. Twelve was a special number for the Christian dogs. How ironic.

"*Alhamdulillah,* thanks be to Allah that you have all come; feel at ease, we are safe here."

He produced a box. "This is a lead-lined box and inside it we have Joan Aiguader's phone. Some wise guys have tampered with it so that it still sends out a GPS position even when it's turned off. We found out when we scanned his clothes for chips."

He smiled.

"But even though our hideout is safe, we've decided to change our plans. Allah has willed it to be so."

A slight feeling of disquiet spread through the room, but they were good people. They knew that martyrdom did not have a specific deadline but one must simply embrace it, and so there was no one who wavered.

"We got Joan Aiguader out of the hospital, but it was a setback that he was there in the first place. We don't know what went wrong, but we know that the police and intelligence service are now fully prepared; their inability to keep a better eye on him in the first place is to our advantage."

He looked at the group. What only a short time ago had been a group of thoroughbred holy warriors—men with full beards and veiled women—had changed in appearance to resemble the essence of Western decadence. As they looked now, no one would suspect them of having hidden agendas in their tightly fitting clothes, suggestive makeup, and trousers with immaculate creases down the center. Any trace of their Muslim background was no longer visible.

"You'll enter paradise dressed like dogs. But Allah is great, and you'll be cleansed and brought to glory like the holy warriors you are."

A couple of them bowed their heads and stretched out their hands in gratitude.

"You've all checked out of your hotel rooms, which is good. We'll stay in the house now for a day or two until the main roads are secure, and then we'll implement our plan B."

The holy warriors looked at one another, smiled and laughed. Ghaalib knew that this was what many of them wanted, even though Frankfurt would have been a good place to start. Afterward, they could travel back to Frankfurt, and to Bonn, Brussels, Strasbourg, Antwerp, and the five other cities where preparations were already well under way. That the order had changed slightly was down to fate. *Alhamdulillah*— thanks be to Allah.

"It's approximately five hundred and fifty kilometers to Berlin from here, so we should estimate seven to eight hours' travel time because we'll all go together in a bus instead of using cars."

He turned toward his trusted right-hand man.

"Hamid here will brief you when the time comes. Until then, follow the prayer times and get some food and rest. You have to remain indoors, but that won't be any problem. This is a very well equipped villa that Hamid has rented for us, and besides, it's very cold outside. We don't want any more of you coming down with a cold."

Ghaalib turned to Joan, who was strapped to a wheelchair with his head hanging. However, there was nothing wrong with his eyes. Despite his slender frame and hopeless situation, he dared to emanate hatred. Peculiar how extreme situations could be the making of someone.

"What a perfect audience. Could we wish for anyone better, Joan? You hear me loud and clear but you can't speak or move, which is good for us."

He parried Joan's lightning gaze with an overbearing smile.

"Yes, it's hard for you, but as consolation you don't need to write anything at the moment. We'll take over that duty, and we have a couple of good people for the job. So don't worry yourself about the stream of news you've obligated yourself to; we'll provide *Hores del dia* with more than enough so that I can lure Zaid al-Asadi into the open."

He looked over to the door where one of the group was entering the room, pushing a wheelchair.

"Well done, Fadi. Now all the resources are ready. Has everything arrived safely?"

He nodded and sniffled. So, he had also fallen victim to the cold north European weather.

"And the two women? Are they calm?"

He nodded again.

Ghaalib was extremely satisfied. The last phase had required extra transport, and while expensive, it had been worth every penny. Then he turned to the map of Berlin hanging on the wall. A series of white pins marked the route and a red one the final destination.

At some point in between, Zaid would meet his maker and his god.

32

Assad

The bag was on a chair next to Assad's bed, and inside there was an assortment of equipment from his many deployments abroad. Over the years, the bag had grown heavier and its contents significantly more effective, but Assad had left the heaviest weapons in Denmark. If Carl had had the slightest suspicion of how many people's lives had ended with only this selection of weapons, he would never have looked inside the bag when he saw it in the trunk of the car.

Assad took out his best knife. He had acquired it in Estonia, and if he honed it right, it could split a hair but also cut through neck guards and bulletproof vests. When he was at his saddest, he would take it out and sharpen it on the whetstone until he fell into a trance. Just now, this distraction from reality was his best defense, because otherwise, his mental state could have been compared with the poisonous cocktail of desperation and apathy that makes people in trenches walk into a bombed-out landscape and meet the enemies' bullets with open arms. If he didn't look after himself now, only the fall from his bedroom window on the top floor of B&B Hotel Frankfurt City-Ost and down onto Hanauer Landstrasse could take the pain away.

But Assad had never actually seen suicide as an appropriate way out from the pain he had lived with for sixteen years. As long as there was the slightest hope of seeing his loved ones again, he kept his chin up and his head level. Now he knew that his beloved Marwa and his elder daughter, Nella, were still alive, but if everything ended in tragedy and it all went wrong, he wouldn't hesitate. Then he would go to his bag, find a suitable weapon, and put an end to it all.

Even though it wasn't necessary, he plugged in his new GPS watch to charge. Since he had received it, he had gotten on top of a lot of things: number of steps per day, stress level, pulse. All with a very depressing result recently, but it had other functions too. If he had a call, it vibrated, and if someone sent him a text, he could read the first few lines of the message on the face.

Then there was a knock at the door.

"Hey, open up, Assad!" It was Carl. "They've found the house where Ghaalib was staying," he said when he entered the room. He glanced at the whetstone and knife on the bed, and then he took Assad, who was putting his GPS watch back on, by the arm.

"They're driving there now, and we're going with them."

On a gray weekday like today, there wasn't much activity in this neighborhood where the houses were tightly packed.

Assad looked at his watch. It was still morning, and by taking a good look around, it was possible to gather a rather telling impression of the residents of the area.

There was only light from a few windows, so most people were presumably at work. The only visible activity was a solitary cyclist and a pair of young immigrant girls who were going around sweeping in a couple of cafés that weren't yet open. There were very few cars in the driveways and, as far as it was possible to ascertain, even fewer that had been built on German assembly lines. In other words, the area was extremely average and dead.

"A good example of a sleepy town," said Assad.

"Yes, out here both the husband and wife work," said Herbert Weber. "They've tried to make the area attractive with cafés, wide driveways up to the houses, and evergreen bushes in front of the apartment complexes. There are childcare services nearby, and it's also relatively close to public transport. When you take all these benefits into account, the houses and apartments are actually reasonably priced, but not exclusive enough to attract people who work in the city. We thought that Ghaalib and his people had gone into hiding in one of the more modest immigrant neighborhoods, but they had more room to maneuver out here, which they obviously needed. But they aren't here anymore."

He gave his team some guidelines for cooperating with the police and forensic technicians inside the house.

"Where did you find the Volvo?" asked Carl.

"Just four or five streets from the house, but it was far enough to make tracking them down difficult. We found the house after door-to-door inquiries all day yesterday. And it didn't make it any easier that people here come home late from work."

Assad looked up at the house, which looked very insignificant and anonymous. Nothing stood out from the uninspiring overall impression, except from what in the end had given away that there had been a lot more activity in this house than in the other bourgeois bastions.

"After the bins were emptied, it was only three days before they were so full again that the lids wouldn't close properly. It was partly the enormous amounts of trash and partly the fact that normal garbage was thrown in the recycling bin that caught the attention of the neighbors," said Weber.

Too late, thought Assad. Why couldn't it have been sooner? It was all too heartbreaking. Someone in this house would have been able to tell them where Marwa and Nella were. Maybe they had even been here, but where were they now? Where were they?

"Are you joining us?" asked Weber.

Rhetorical question, thought Assad as he nodded. Did he think they had driven almost a thousand kilometers for a short sightseeing trip in this godforsaken, tedious neighborhood?

They rounded the property to a lawn, which apparently no one had tended for quite some time. The angular modernist house was of the cookie-cutter variety without decoration, and the land completely square and surrounded by a man-height wicker fence, which was presumably intended to allow the residents to move freely outside without being disturbed. A perfect place to go into hiding and wait for safer times ahead.

It was immediately apparent that there had been both men and women inside, and also that there had been many of them; this was evidenced by the contents of the bins, which the forensic technicians had spread out over the terrace in front of the living room. There was packaging from disposable razors, sanitary pads, dozens of ready meals, paper plates, disposable cutlery, empty bottles of mineral water, and used tissues and paper towels. Everything told a story.

"At a quick guess, how many are we talking about?" one of Weber's men asked a forensic technician who was kneeling in the pile of trash in his white overalls.

"Well, if we assume that they've been here for some days, which is confirmed by both Airbnb and the neighbor, and that they each ate three meals a day, of which at least one was a ready meal, then we're talking about at least ten people," calculated the forensic technician. "We've counted the used sanitary pads, and if only one woman was on her period, we believe that woman was here for three or four days, which also ties in with the number of ready meals and people. We know that at least one of the residents has had a severe cold, judging by the snot on at least two packets of tissues, and that the infection was about to stop, given that the snot in the tissues from the top layer of rubbish was no longer green."

Assad inspected the microwave meal packaging.

"Well, we also know that for sure, then," he said.

Carl tried to follow his line of thought. "What do we know, Assad?" he asked.

"That the whole group were Muslim. There's only packaging here with chicken and lamb. Do you see one with pork?"

"Hmm, well spotted, Assad," said Carl.

Weber turned to the forensic technician. "Yes, every little detail counts, but you know that better than anyone. Can you give us a picture of the ratio between men and women, their ages and appearance? That would be essential information for us, just like your good observation that one of them has a cold. Any facts like this that can help us to define the makeup of the group are important, especially for those in charge of security at the place we'll hopefully discover the group intends to strike."

"I can see at least one thing that will help us identify this group," said Assad. He picked up the plastic packaging with GILLETTE written on it and showed it to them.

"What fundamentalist Muslim men do you think use disposable razors and walk around clean-shaven?" he continued. "Those who want to look cool, or those who definitely don't want to stand out from the crowd in Germany?"

Carl nodded. "Then we can assume that both the women and the men are dressed in a Western style. So, no veils, no black burkas, no full beards, no leather slippers. A mixed group of at least ten people who could be anyone. No small task, if you ask me. It's actually pretty frightening."

The man next to Weber sighed. "Yes, and then there's unfortunately also the question of whether they intend to stay as a group or split up."

"I think that in terms of the ratio of men and women, my colleagues inside the house might be able to help you more," said the forensic technician from down among the garbage. His rubber gloves were almost worn through from his energetic efforts. The hope of uncovering an essential hint that could tell them about the residents' plans going forward—perhaps a record, a word on a piece of paper, receipts, maybe even a map of something—was what kept them all going.

They stepped into a large, nondescript living room without frills. Vacuumed and clean. Sofa cushions at an angle, an armchair nicely arranged beside a pair of teak tables, wineglasses on shelves in glass cabinets, an older TV. Everything was completely neutral.

"They made sure to clean up after themselves," said a forensic technician who was wiggling out of his white suit. "But there are fingerprints everywhere, so they obviously didn't want to hide them, just like they haven't made any effort to remove traces of DNA. There are dirty tea towels and towels in the laundry basket. The beds have been made, but the sheets haven't been changed. It makes you wonder why it wasn't a priority for them."

"Yes, but who is unfazed by leaving their trace behind?" asked Assad with a bad gut feeling. "Those who are going to die anyway."

The forensic technicians in the room turned to him; it was evident that they were reacting with significant unease, some even with fear.

Herbert Weber took Assad by the arm and pulled him in close. "Most people here are affiliated with the police in Frankfurt, and only a few of them need to know at this point just how dangerous these people are," he whispered. "Can we agree that there's no need to create unnecessary panic?"

Assad nodded; he was right, of course.

"Does anything stand out in here?" Weber asked the closest forensic technician.

"Yes, something does." He pointed at some almost undetectable parallel marks on the floor.

"Marks from a wheelchair," said Carl.

The forensic technician nodded. "There are actually two of them. There's a similar mark here, but the tire pattern is different."

"Could the marks be old?" asked Weber. "From a previous tenant or perhaps the owner?"

"We're investigating, naturally, but my personal opinion is that they're relatively new. They tried to remove them by cleaning the floor, but because the floor was wet, they didn't notice that they left traces." He bent down and rubbed hard with his thumb on the mark. "See? It's very easy to remove it." He showed them that his thumb was black, so the mark couldn't have been too old.

"Given that they otherwise didn't clean up their tracks, doesn't it stand out that they cleaned the floors? We're obviously not supposed to know that they had wheelchairs in here," said Carl.

"What I said was that they are relatively new. The floors could have been washed by the owners or the previous tenants."

"Have we asked the owners?" Weber asked the man next to him.

"No. We've tried to contact them, but they're in Gabon at the moment, deep in the jungle. They're insect researchers, entomologists, as far as I understand, and they aren't due back in Libreville for another two or three weeks."

Herbert Weber sighed audibly.

"But not to worry, we'll follow the lead no matter what," he continued. "We've photographed the marks and are trying to trace the makes and origins."

Weber shook his head. "It would be weird if there were disabled people among the group. I don't get it."

Assad was staring blankly ahead. An unusually horrible image was beginning to form in his mind.

"Who says they're disabled?" he asked quietly. "A wheelchair can carry healthy people, and they can be used to carry explosives regardless of how innocent they might appear." He took a couple of abrupt breaths before coming out with his conclusion. "They could be ten times as destructive as an explosive vest."

Assad looked despondently at Carl, who didn't really look well either. Just now he looked like he would rather have been anywhere other than here.

Assad wiped the sweat from his brow. "Tell me what you're thinking, Carl."

"Nothing, Assad."

It obviously wasn't true, but Assad knew why he avoided answering the question.

"No, come on. Out with it, Herr Mørck," probed Weber. "Everyone here is free to say what's on their mind."

Carl looked at Assad with sorrow in his eyes. It was terrible.

"I'm really sorry to have to say it, but the wheelchairs could be intended for people who aren't voluntarily part of this; isn't that what you're thinking, Assad?"

He nodded. It was his worst nightmare.

Carl turned to the forensic technician. "Do you have any idea how many women were in the house?" he asked.

The forensic technician shook his head. "We have a room in here where everything points to at least three women having slept. There were long dark hairs on the pillows, and the beds are made very neatly with aligned duvets." He pointed at a door at the other end of the room. "There were also women sleeping in there, but it's a bit different. Just like in the other room, there are long hairs from women, but the beds haven't been made. On the contrary, the sheets are crumpled and pulled away from the mattress in one corner as if they had been kicking."

Assad took a deep breath. "May I go in there?" he asked.

"Yes, we're finished in there, so be my guest."

Assad put his hands in front of his mouth when he walked into the room. The sight of the disheveled sheets alone could have made him cry. Was this where Marwa and Nella were held prisoner? Was the sheet kicked to the side because they had tried to escape? With his heart racing, he looked at the bedposts. Was there damage from something being tied to them? Not as far as he could tell, and the forensic technician would have told them if there was.

He leaned over the pillows on the bed, but there didn't appear to be anything there. They must have removed all the hair as technical evidence.

Assad sat heavily on the edge of the bed and caressed the sheet with his hand. Then he raised one of the duvets up to his face and inhaled deeply. "Oh, Marwa and Nella," he whispered when he sensed a weak but lingering scent. He didn't recognize it, but why should he? Yet it affected him deeply, because if those two had been in this bed, then this fading remnant of a scent was the closest he had been to them in sixteen years.

"Hey," someone shouted. "We've got something."

But Assad didn't want to get up. As long as that scent was there, he could rest in the hope that his loved ones were still alive.

He clenched his fists and imagined the wheelchairs and what Carl had said.

If the wheelchairs were intended for Marwa and Nella, it must have been Ghaalib's plan that they should be sacrificed as part of the attack;

he was sure of it, not least because it would be the worst thing he could do to Assad.

He pressed his fists into his stomach. *Sacrificed as part of the attack,* he thought. He could not allow that to happen.

Then he stood up, sniffed the duvet one last time, and went in the direction of the commotion.

They were all standing in the utility room in front of a sideboard where a small pile of clean clothes had been spread out.

"If we assume that the intention was for the group to take their personal belongings with them, I think that one or several of them wanted to have clean towels with them, and we're probably talking about women," said a plainclothes policeman Assad hadn't seen before. He was probably the crime scene supervisor.

"Do you think they forgot that the laundry was still in the tumble dryer?" asked one of Weber's colleagues.

"Yes. Who doesn't forget clothes in the tumble dryer?" he answered. "And we found this towel among the others."

He folded it out and turned it over. "The logo isn't very big, but it tells us a lot."

They moved closer. It was a towel with a hotel logo.

"Where was this person staying before they came here? Shall we say that the person concerned stayed at this hotel, which is only three or four kilometers from here?"

"Hang on," blurted out one of the plainclothes investigators. "It will take forever to find out who stole it. Was it a woman or a man? What false name did they use? Was the thief there three days ago? Or four days? These are parameters that can result in all sorts of answers. Just imagine how many guests the hotel has had over a two-day period. The hotel isn't the biggest in Frankfurt, but still."

"That's right," said the crime scene supervisor. "We won't get far with that. But nevertheless, we need to do something because I don't think we have much time."

"Don't waste your time on that; just forget it," came a voice from behind.

They all turned toward Weber's assistant, who was standing in the doorway. "I'd like to ask our Danish colleagues, Herr Herbert Weber, and the crime scene supervisor to come in here; there's something you need to hear."

He sat on the edge of the bed and lifted his iPad toward them. "*Frankfurter Allgemeine Zeitung* has received a sort of press announcement supposedly written by Joan Aiguader, but I very much doubt that to be the case," he said. "It's in English and was uploaded half an hour ago. *Frankfurter Allgemeine Zeitung* has decided not to make it public but contact us directly instead. I assume that not all the media outlets it's been sent to will afford us the same courtesy." He looked directly at Assad with an expression that made him feel uneasy.

"I'm sorry, but you're named several times. You'll have to brace yourself for some of the information in the text that might shock you."

Assad reached out for Carl's arm.

"Let's sit down, Assad," said Carl, pointing at the sofa.

Weber's assistant continued. "The fact that it's been sent directly to a German newspaper rather than coming from *Hores del dia,* who Joan Aiguader otherwise has written for, and always in Spanish, tells me that this text has a totally different goal than previous ones, and that it isn't written by Joan Aiguader."

"Have you got our team tracing the IP address?" asked Weber.

"Yes, naturally. That's the first thing I did. But I'd be surprised if that leads us anywhere."

"Are you sure you want to hear this, Assad?" asked Carl.

He nodded and realized his entire body was shaking. How would it help Marwa and Nella if he lost courage now? He *had* to hear this.

"The heading is neutral," he said. "'*Islamic group escapes,*' it reads. It's dated yesterday at twenty-three forty-five, and the byline reads, '*Joan Aiguader.*'"

He read. "'According to the Iraqi man Ghaalib, who is wanted for questioning by the German police, the planned action in Frankfurt has been postponed indefinitely. The group, consisting of seven holy warriors, has come to Germany to protest against the disgrace that people from Arabic countries and their peers in North Africa and Asia are increasingly subjected to in the European media. They demand that the world's media desist from this besmirchment immediately starting tomorrow morning and show respect for their faith and culture. If this demand is not complied with, they will come down hard on random places. The holy warriors are heavily armed, and according to the group's spokesman, Ghaalib, the first hit will be carried out by their brave sisters Marwa and Nella al-Asadi, who are thankful for the opportunity to honor Allah with their lives.'"

He put down the iPad. "I assume we all agree that this form of manipulation in connection with terrorism is something totally new. I'm convinced that this has nothing to do with any existing terror organization."

"Shall we talk about what we don't think is true in this?" said the crime scene supervisor. "He mentions that there are seven of them, but what motive can he have to publicize that? They could be fewer or more. I don't think we can trust that number."

"You've seen the photo of the two women who escaped the internment camp in Cyprus," said Weber. "I'm certain that those two are part of the group, so we've sent their descriptions to absolutely everyone. Naturally, I've also assumed that they fled from Cyprus, and why shouldn't that have been possible? Ghaalib managed. Apart from him, there is his helper, Hamid, which brings us to four. Then, unfortunately, we have Assad's family, which is two more. That's a total of six. We can't dismiss seven as a number, naturally, but I think you're right; we know nothing about how many there are, so it's probably higher," said Weber.

Assad didn't comment; he felt dead inside. All he could picture was Ghaalib's loathsome smile, but what could they do? Regardless of the means, they had to trace the evil group, and he didn't care how. He had hoped that the bastard would have exposed himself just a little, but there was nothing to go on except that Ghaalib was intent on killing Marwa and Nella.

"I can't remember any instance when suicide bombers have revealed their names *before* they've committed an act of terror," continued Weber.

Assad nodded. "But have you understood the message? All that non-sense about taking revenge on the European media is secondary; he's coming after me personally, and he can bring it on. This is a game of cat and mouse. But I'll make sure that the tables are turned. Even if it costs me my life."

33

Alexander

He hated that sound, and he had always hated it. When his father's phone rang, he and his mother made themselves scarce.

"Haven't I told you two to keep your damn mouths shut when I'm on the phone!" his father would shout afterward if they had disturbed him. And then he would shake Alexander, as if yet another physical assault would enable his brain to remember or understand things better. Even his mother was subjected to an earful if a kitchen appliance was running in the background or if the radio wasn't immediately turned down. It was *his* phone and *his* conversation, and nothing could compare with its importance.

Alexander was a teenager before he discovered that most of the conversations were insignificant and that his father was a self-important nobody who demanded to be taken seriously on every occasion. And now the phone was lying there again on the hallway dresser chiming with its ridiculous sound of the church bells from Westminster Abbey. Even now, he flinched by reflex, and that despite the fact that the head that used to have the phone next to its ear now lay with crystallized eyes in the chest freezer at minus twenty. It had been four days since his father had been to work, and there was no doubt that such an absence would have been noted. So, if Alexander wasn't careful, he risked one of his father's colleagues' suddenly standing outside the door asking for an explanation. As tempting as it might have been to throw up on the corporate drone's polished shoes and fling the truth in his face, he couldn't let that happen under any circumstances, so he got up. He had just finalized his strategy for win number 2067 and could hardly wait to try it out, but reason prevailed.

"I'd like to speak with William," said the voice when he answered the call.

"Unfortunately, you can't. He's moved."

It went silent at the other end, and Alexander smiled. If only he knew.

"I see. I'm sorry, but it's strange that he hasn't mentioned anything at work about this. When did it happen?"

"Four or five days ago."

"Do you know if he has a new telephone number?"

"No. He just up and left. He has a lover somewhere, but I don't know more than that. Hasn't he been to work at all?"

"No, that's just it. Is this Alexander I'm talking to?"

"Yeah."

"I didn't recognize your voice, Alexander. Sorry about that. So, you have no idea where he is?"

"No, he just left. He's totally crazy about his new bit on the side; my mother thinks that they've run off to France, where she apparently has a place somewhere or other."

"And your mother? Is it possible to talk with her?"

Alexander thought for a moment. Did the man really want to talk with her after he had just told him that her husband without so much as a good-bye had run off with someone else? What an ass.

"My mother doesn't want to talk about it. Anyway, she's away on a business trip. I'm at home alone, but I'm used to it."

That pause again. The man was simply dumbfounded.

"Well then, thank you, Alexander. I'm sorry to hear that. Please give your mother my regards and tell her I'm sorry for both of them and that when she knows more about your father's whereabouts, we'd very much like to know."

He promised, of course.

He looked at the clock; it was nine twenty. He reckoned that in two hours he would only have fifty wins left to reach his goal.

In thirty hours, his mother would let herself in the door, and the first thing she would see was her husband's cell charging next to where she always put her gloves. She would be confused and call out for him. "Honey!" she would shout a few times, as usual, before giving way to an irritated outburst.

"Back to normal," she would say. But that's where she would be wrong.

Alexander leaned back and stared at the screen. It had been an insane game. It had taken him three hours to reach his latest victory, and now the statistics were there in yellow, green, red, and blue numbers. Beautiful digits, impressive digits. No one could do what he had done; he was sure of it. Let his classmates brag about tales of Machu Picchu and condors in flight at sunset. He couldn't have cared less about Machu Picchu, Ayers Rock, the pyramids, or the girls they had fucked in Paris, Amsterdam, and Bangkok. None of them could better what he had just achieved in the game, and none of them would ever experience the same satisfaction in anything they did.

He glanced at his phone. Fifty wins to go! Wasn't that a victory worth celebrating? Should he be the only one who knew what was soon to happen?

Alexander laughed. Time was passing, and it was sure to be worrying his policeman. He was probably rocking on his office chair, unsure about what to do. But Alexander would comfort him by saying that there was nothing he could do about it. What had to be would be.

And he would tease him and confuse him. Try to get the better of him by offering explanations he hadn't seen coming, send him on wild goose chases that were both plausible yet far out. The idiot wouldn't know what to think. Such unimaginable power! It was enough to give him goose bumps.

Alexander found his number and was pleased when the man answered.

"Department Q, Gordon Taylor. Is that you again, Kurt-Brian?" Alexander was confused. Kurt-Brian? What did he mean?

"We can't be bothered with any more calls from you, Kurt-Brian. We don't believe a word you say. You're just wasting our time."

Wasting their time? Had the man gone crazy?

"Okay. Call me whatever you want; I don't give a toss, because I haven't got a loser name like you. Gordon Taylor! Where are you even from? Are you a little immigrant boy who was adopted by a couple of idiots who couldn't give you a proper name?"

"Perhaps, Kurt-Brian. Tell me, have you decapitated anyone else recently?"

There was a voice in the background. Was there someone whispering to him? A woman's voice? The guy certainly sounded different than usual.

"Do you have a prompter, Gordon Taylor-Boy?"

"Prompter?" Then there was a very telling pause. "Of course I don't have a prompter, Kurt-Brian," he said coldly. "If you don't answer my question, I'm hanging up."

"Put the bitch on or it will be me hanging up."

Another pause.

"I'm hanging up!" he warned, and then he could hear fumbling from the other end.

"Hi, Kurt-Brian. You're speaking with Rose. And you can do your worst with my name; I'm above that pubescent bullying. Answer the question. Have you decapitated anyone lately, or are you just sitting there beating one out while you think about all the girls that you'll never get your hands on, you smarmy little git?"

Alexander was relishing the moment, because now he knew for certain that they were taking him seriously, and the thought made his skin tingle. No one could hurt him with words. His father had attempted to bully and tyrannize him with words since he was a boy, and he had experienced the same from his friends all through school.

Words were just hot air.

"You're shooting with blanks, cock-tease," he said. "Listen to what I'm saying or put Gordon back on."

"I'm listening but make it snappy. We're busy here with cases that are more important than yours."

We'll see about that, he thought.

"Let me give you a tip, tulip. Shall we say my name's Logan—then we all have English names—and that I intend to outlive myself by exactly one year? Now everything makes sense, right?"

"Okay, your name's Logan! Were your parents obsessed with Johnny Logan from the Eurovision Song Contest?"

What the hell was she talking about?

"Okay, I can hear you don't know Johnny Logan. That tells me that Logan isn't your real name. Am I right?"

Alexander tilted his head back and began to laugh. And as the question was repeated a couple of times, his whole body began to shake from laughter. In fact, this feeling of well-being matched, in a way, the feeling he had just experienced winning for the two thousand sixty-seventh time.

"Today, I only have fifty wins left to go, and I thought we should celebrate that together. I'm having a cola in honor of the occasion, but you two are welcome to drink champagne or whatever the hell you like."

"Kurt-Brian Logan, you're laughable," said the woman. "We don't celebrate with crazy people."

"If you say so. And congratulations for working out that Logan is a surname. Well done, Rose Red. And as for your question, which you're so horny for me to answer: no. The next decapitation won't be until tomorrow around eight. Good-bye, Mommy!"

34

Rose

"**Did he mean to** give us a hint, Rose?" asked Gordon after they had listened to the recording for a second time.

"I think so. It was certainly very strange that he said he planned to outlive himself by exactly one year. Very strange."

"He gave me the creeps. Do you really think that he'll make good on his threat to decapitate someone else tomorrow?"

"Yes, his mother apparently. Then he'll have eliminated his parents so they can't stop him from turning on the rest of the world with his dangerous, sick ideas."

"Do you think that he'll carry out his threats to kill random people when he's reached twenty-one seventeen victories in his game?"

"Yes, that's what I'm afraid of. That crazy imbecile."

"Shouldn't we finally get someone on the case now, Rose? I don't like the idea of us sitting alone with this responsibility. What if he really does carry out his threats? Marcus did say that maybe we ought to contact PET."

She looked at him for a long time. If Gordon broke down in the middle of the investigation, it would definitely be too big a task for her. But who could help them? Homicide was up to its neck in it. Too many shootings and too many murders took their toll on their resources. And what did she and Gordon actually have besides their suspicions? The boy obviously wasn't right in the head. But couldn't his biggest crime just be that he had an overactive imagination? That his warped brain was just enjoying the excitement of a crude telephone prank that they should probably just shrug off?

"Okay," she said to appease him. "I'll inform PET, even though Carl thinks they should keep their noses out of Department Q's business."

"And if they do get involved?"

"What of it? We'll keep working on it like we always do, right?"

He nodded.

Now she would have to remember to call PET at some point or other, but it certainly wouldn't be right now.

"The guy hasn't mentioned other family members; do you think that means he's an only child?" asked Gordon.

"Definitely, yes! A dysfunctional boy who's had a really shitty childhood, if you ask me."

"But not because they didn't have money?"

"Hell no. Quite the opposite. He's the stereotype of someone who has compensated for a lack of love and affection by wasting his life in front of his computer. And who has that luxury? Only someone who doesn't have to work hard for their keep."

"Are you sure? He could be someone on benefits who just sits around doing nothing."

"No, I don't think so. His vocabulary and language hint at someone who comes from a home that tries to keep up the pretense of some sort of standard."

"What the hell do you think he meant by outliving himself by one year? Does it have anything to do with the number twenty-one seventeen?"

"I don't know. Maybe we've been barking up the wrong tree in seeing a connection with the victim from Cyprus. It *could* just be a year, right?

"Do you think there was any discernible reaction when you mentioned the drowned woman?" she then asked.

Gordon shrugged. "Hard to say. He did pause when I mentioned it."

"Hmm! But if we're wrong and it is a year, what should we make of it?" she asked.

"That it's a long way in the future."

"Google the number, Gordon."

"How?"

"Just type the number, for God's sake."

"Numbers or letters?"

She pointed to the numbers on the right-hand side of the keyboard, and then he typed.

"Apart from being the media name for the woman from Cyprus, 2117 is also a Swedish clothing brand," he said after a few seconds. "And an asteroid. There are loads of hits for that number."

"Okay, it's a wild goose chase. Write 'year 2117' instead."

It took him two seconds.

"There's an article in the *B.T.* newspaper: '600,000 people to move to Mars in 2217,' it says. But that's a hundred years out."

Rose put her face in her hands. Move to Mars? How long would people be subjected to this sort of nonsense? Colonizing space would never, ever, ever happen. A total waste of faith, hope, and a lot of money.

She thought for a moment while Gordon scrolled through one doomsday prophecy after another for the next century.

"Is there anything that makes sense?" she asked.

"There are a lot of doomsday prophecies. Maybe there's some sort of symbolism in it. Maybe he wants us to think that his world will also cease to exist."

"Yeah, but he could have referred to so many different years. Try typing 'Logan 2117.'"

Gordon typed in the new search.

Rose had her face right next to the screen when his hands stopped midair.

"Bingo," he said. "There's a Hollywood film with Hugh Jackman from 2017 called *Logan.*"

"Damn strange coincidence; but now it's a hundred years too early because you typed it in wrong, Gordon. Try again, and type it right this time. 'Twenty-one seventeen' and then 'Logan.'"

He typed.

"Okay." He laughed. "Now we have a load of hits for 'Logan Avenue 2117' in the USA. Does that make any more sense?"

Rose sighed. "How many are there?"

He scanned the list. "I'd say it's in the hundreds!"

"Forget it."

"My feet hurt," complained Gordon.

Rose looked down at her Skechers sneakers and thanked the lord for their existence. Her feet were feeling much better now than when she had just been sitting in her flat, and she felt she could still tramp around the area for hours, but it was beginning to look like it might all be in vain.

There were hairdressers who thought they recognized the young man from the sketch, but they had never cut his hair. Could he be a model with Copenhagen Models? one of them had asked.

A busy menswear shop owner complained that you could only see the guy's head, while a random couple in the shop thought they had seen him on the TV in a Swedish film set on an island in the skerries.

"Yes, that's my son," said a wrinkled woman on the street, and then burst out laughing. The smell of alcohol was potent.

After three hours, Gordon and Rose had to admit that they had made no progress. This neighborhood, where the guy had bought his prepaid telephone cards, was definitely not a place he frequented.

"Do we need to continue?" asked Gordon.

Rose looked out at the multitude of signs and glowing shop windows on Frederikssundsvej.

"If we do, it would take an entire army to check them all. Frederikssundsvej alone is endless. And that's not including all the side streets. How could we ever manage it even over a couple of days?"

"So why don't we send e-mails out to all of the education institutions within a one-mile radius instead, just like Carl suggested? Do you think that's what we should do?"

"Well, it was actually me who suggested that. The problem with the sketch is that if Marcus Jacobsen won't give us permission to go public with the guy's face, there's no other obvious way to do it than e-mail it to specific target groups." She shrugged and reached for her mobile, which was buzzing in her pocket.

"Hello, Rose Knudsen speaking, assistant investigator on a low pay scale," she said with a wry smile that quickly dissipated.

"Oh no, Assad," she said several times. "In Frankfurt too?" She kept nodding and shaking her head.

Gordon took her by the arm and pointed at the speakerphone icon on her mobile.

She pressed it. "Gordon is listening in now, Assad. What are you going to do now?"

It was easy to hear how distressed he was; his voice was shaking, and his words weren't as considered as usual.

"We wait. What else can we do?" he said, exhausted. "All I can think about is where Marwa and Nella are right now and what Ghaalib intends to do with them. Another little piece of me dies every time I think about it, Rose."

"You have no idea where they might be?"

"We've got nothing. The intelligence service has placed a GPS in the journalist's phone that runs on the mobile battery whether it's turned on or not, but the signal disappeared just a few streets from the hospital."

"And the other emergency services?"

"They've all been briefed. There are hundreds out looking for them. There isn't a town left in Germany that isn't in a state of emergency."

"I don't understand, Assad. Ghaalib should be easy to spot with that face he's got."

"I know you're trying to keep me optimistic, Rose. Thank you. But just before we came over to the hotel here, one of the forensic technicians found a tissue with makeup on it. They laughed about it and assumed that one of the women had taken the leap to wearing makeup to try and appear harmless, but Carl and I didn't buy it."

"Ghaalib is hiding his scars, isn't he?"

"Of course he is."

Rose looked imploringly at Gordon. Now it was his turn to think of something.

"Er, Assad, Gordon here," he said. "We've got a problem with the sketch; no one recognizes the guy."

Rose looked at him despairingly. That was the last thing he needed. She grabbed the telephone from him.

"Sorry, Assad. You've got bigger problems to worry about. I'm sure you and Carl will find something that can put you on the right track. Let me know if there's anything we can help with."

"There is."

"Anything, Assad. Out with it!"

"I want you to send out a press release to all the big European newspapers. I want it to read that Zaid al-Asadi has received Ghaalib's message and is waiting for him in Frankfurt at Hotel Maingau on Schifferstrasse."

"Is that a good idea, Assad?" said Rose. "Won't it put Marwa and Nella in serious danger if he knows where you are? I'm sorry to be blunt, but why should he keep them alive?"

His reply was very subdued. "Ghaalib has had no idea where I've been for the last sixteen years. So he knows full well that I'd never tell him something like that without having an ulterior motive. He'll know I'm on his trail but also that I have a plan. He'll check the hotel and, of course, won't find me there; he knows that. I'll have checked into the hotel, that's easy for them to find out, but I won't be there until a few days later. He'll think I'm waiting somewhere nearby so that I can follow his men back to where he is. And that's exactly what he wants because he can control that, or so he thinks. It's the only way the cat's game with the mouse works in his world. And he'll enjoy the wait and suspense in the meantime because he knows for sure now how much I'm suffering. So, rest assured that he'll keep Marwa and Nella alive as long as possible. The only thing I'm worried about is whether I can get to them before he puts his terrorist plot into action. But that's the Germans' plan. There's a lot to arrange before then."

"Are you finished, Gordon?"

Rose pointed at his printout on the table.

"Yes, Assad's press release has been sent to just around a hundred different European news media. So, surely some of them will publish it."

She looked at the text and nodded.

"The headline will make sure of that. Good work, Gordon." She gave him a pat on the shoulder. "In the meantime, I've been thinking about this Logan character, and I think I'm on to something."

"Okay. What is it?"

"He said he's going to outlive himself by a year, but what did he actually mean by that, Gordon? Could the very precise year in which he's outlived himself possibly be the year two thousand one hundred and seventeen? What do you think? Do you follow?"

He shrugged. He didn't know where she was going with this.

"Listen. If he has outlived himself by a year in 2117, it brings us back to 2116, which is a fictional present, right? So, search for that instead."

"Isn't that stretching it a bit . . . ?"

"Just do it, Gordon, for goodness' sakes. Write 'Logan 2116'!"

He did.

"I'm getting almost the same hits as before, Rose."

"Yes and no. Look a bit farther down. It says 'Logan's Run' on Wikipedia."

"Okay, yes, it does." He opened the page and nodded, impressed.

Rose read the text aloud. "'Logan's Run. A novel by William F. Nolan and George Clayton Johnson from 1967. It describes a dystopian future in 2116 where the population increase is kept under control by killing all young people when they reach twenty-one.' The novel was made into a movie in 1976, and in the film, it's not until they reach thirty, but I think the guy is referring to the book. Do you see?"

"Yes. Good find, Rose. But what do you think he's trying to tell us?"

"His age, Gordon. He's given us a crystal-clear hint about how old he is. If he has outlived himself by a year in 2117 in Logan's world, he's twenty-one plus a year, right? Yeah, I know it seems a bit far-fetched, but isn't that the way his mind works?"

"So, twenty-two years old?"

"You're bloody quick on the uptake today, Gordon. Yes, exactly! He's twenty-two years old. A bit older than we thought. Now we're getting somewhere, Gordon. We're getting somewhere."

35

Joan

They look good, thought Joan.

Beautiful golden skin, red lips, curvaceous and mature forms accentuated by fashionable clothes. They could pass for anyone with these looks. Upper-class ladies, well-educated academics, or artists at a certain level. But looks can be deceptive—none of the others in this large house had behaved anywhere near as vulgarly or sadistically toward him as these two women.

When they had all assembled in the house in Frankfurt, it took less than an hour before Ghaalib's two female accomplices came over to him and spat in his face for nearly exposing them in the Menogeia camp. As far as he could tell, one of these two furies spoke German without an accent while the other spoke French in a dialect, but otherwise totally fluently, as if she came from Switzerland or perhaps Luxembourg. Joan understood the French-speaking woman best; it was often that way for Catalonians. However, she was also the worse of the two—of them all, in fact. The first time she paralyzed his face with Botox injections, she jabbed the needle in so deeply and randomly that he would have screamed had he been able. He couldn't because the cursed drip that was still stuck in the back of his hand, and that was slowly becoming infected, contained a liquid that paralyzed his speech and most of his motor functions. He could still control his eyes and turn his head slightly, but that was all. So, when they hit him on occasion, there was nothing he could do to defend himself.

In a strange way, Ghaalib was the one who treated him best, and Joan didn't understand why. Wasn't his work for Ghaalib over with? Why not rid himself of the problem and just kill him? Joan was scared, of course, but when he was paralyzed, it affected everything inside him and he became defeatist, indifferent, and passive.

The men didn't talk to him at all. Some of them spoke only Arabic, and did so passionately. Only a couple of people in the group seemed apathetic, but the others acted as if they were already in paradise. He would have given his right arm to be able to understand them.

The bus pulled up in front of the house in Frankfurt very early in the morning. It was a white, well-equipped tourist bus with air-conditioning, a minibar, and all sorts of other benefits, though from the outside it looked like an outsized minibus in which the only luxuries were a tiny toilet and some curtains that could be drawn back and forth in a myriad of combinations.

When they lifted him into the aisle, he was facing backward. And only those two damned women who tormented him were sitting farther back in the bus than him. The objective was obviously that the furies should keep an eye on him throughout the trip to make sure his condition didn't change.

He avoided their gazes. He tried to sit still, and if he felt a small sensation in his legs or parts of his torso, he made sure he didn't react even though he sometimes felt jolts of pain. He just sat completely still and looked down at the very back of the bus, where the rear window and the last two rows of seats were hidden behind a dark, densely woven curtain.

When they had driven for a couple of hours, it began to get light. The traffic grew more and more intense. A normal day for normal Germans had begun, and Joan envied them more than ever. It would have been less painful if he had ended his life in Barceloneta's waves a week ago.

When a car overtook them, he could just make out the people sitting inside. *Look at me,* he thought. *Can't you see that something is wrong? Call the police and tell them there's a suspicious-looking bus. Can't you see that these are people with evil intentions? Can't you see that the man in the wheelchair is at their mercy?*

It was only when it was fully light that he noticed the mirror positioned above the rear exit. And in the curved surface of the mirror, he saw himself and understood. Who hadn't seen buses for the disabled like this one, and who hadn't avoided making eye contact with people who were unable to signal or move? Hadn't everyone done that? And now he was suddenly one of these poor people: so pale that it seemed as if the summer sun in Barcelona had never arrived, so motionless it almost seemed like he was unconscious or sleeping, so hopelessly anonymous and helpless in the blue institutional clothes they had dressed him in.

They see right past me in this condition. They'd rather look at the two beautiful women sitting farther back in the bus. No, he couldn't count on help from other drivers, so the outcome of the trip was already decided. He wouldn't be able to make contact with the real world; he was destined to be directed with the rest of the group toward the fate that Ghaalib had mapped out for them all.

Joan looked up at the driver through the mirror at the back of the bus. He was just a little spot, and yet that little spot was the only one who could put an end to all this. He could jump out at a service station and call the authorities. He would be able to stop it. But the spot just sat there like a fly on the mirror even when the others went to the toilet.

What was it with this driver? Couldn't he sense that something was horribly wrong? Couldn't he get it into his thick skull that the two poor paralyzed women sitting in the other two wheelchairs nearer the front of the bus didn't belong to the rest of the group? Couldn't he see the panic in their eyes or that every fiber of their being was screaming for help?

Maybe he didn't care.

Joan felt sorry for the women, just like the times when they had wailed and cried for mercy when Ghaalib's two abominable furies came into their room and did things to them. He couldn't know exactly what they did to their fellow sisters but assumed it couldn't be much different than what he was subjected to. Maybe their bodies had been pumped full of sedatives, because he hadn't heard a peep from them when the bus arrived or when everyone took their seats.

No, the bus driver, that little spot in the mirror, wouldn't be coming to their rescue. He was in on it.

In the middle of the second day in the house in Frankfurt, the furies had pulled the two poor women out of the room in which they had been locked and into the bathroom, where they washed and dressed them. Like everyone else, they were dressed in Western clothes to ensure they didn't stand out. But new clothes or not, Joan noticed an irrational yet strong bond between them when he finally saw them. It took some time before he figured out why, because recognition is sometimes a slow process.

When Joan finally understood that these two poor women were identical to the ones that he had photographed together with Ghaalib on the beach in Ayia Napa, he realized that things were even worse than he had thought.

There were questions looming again for which he wasn't sure he wanted the answer. How had the women from the beach ended up here against their will, and why were they medicated? Why had Ghaalib taken him on the bus? Why was he even alive?

Very slowly, the story of these refugees began to take shape into a plausible explanation of their despair. Just like other refugees, they had risked their lives at sea to escape from the most tormented and feared region in the world at the moment: Syria. In that war-torn and chaotic country, they had witnessed things that people were not meant to live with or understand. They had been close to death in the Mediterranean Sea, and in the most brutal way had lost someone dear to them: victim number 2117. They had witnessed how she had disappeared in the watery depths and now they had ended up here in Frankfurt. Joan now knew that when he had seen the women standing, drenched and ex-hausted, on the beach next to Ghaalib, they hadn't been there volun-tarily, and they hadn't come to Frankfurt by choice either. So now these sedated women had become his only allies on this bus. They were doomed just like him.

Seat by seat, he used the mirror to count the necks of the people on the bus and tried to recognize them from the house in Frankfurt. Apart from Fadi, who was recognizable from his sneezing, it was no easy task, because the bus was shaky and the mirror distorted everything and made it small. He could just make out Ghaalib in the front seat next to the driver.

Joan had no idea where they were, but the signs on the other side of the road that disappeared quickly behind them as they drove past gave him constant hints about which town they had just passed. Unfortunately, he didn't know the area they were driving through, so what good did it do him?

KIRCHHEIM 5 was the first sign he noticed when it began to get light. Then there was BAD HERSFELD 5. And after he woke up from dozing for a while, the sign read, EISENACH. If only he recognized the names. They were like points of reference in a make-believe land where the fairy tale slowly turned into a nightmare. Was this how the Jews had felt on their way to the concentration camps as they pressed their faces against the cracks in the cattle cars to read the names of the train stations they had just passed? Or had they sat the whole way in the dark, mesmerized by the rhythmic beating of the railroad ties as they journeyed toward the unknown from which there was no escape? Joan opened his eyes wide and tried to remember a little. He had heard of Weimar; wasn't it a re-public of some sort? But where were the other places located that disap-peared from view as they drove past: Jena, Eisenberg, Stössen? It was only when he spotted LEIPZIG 10 that a map began to take shape for him. Were they more than halfway now? Did he have any chance of surviv-ing this nightmare of a journey? He didn't think so.

The bus stopped in a forested area at yet another modest and un-manned rest stop. When those who needed to pee were back on the bus, a figure stood up from one of the front seats and turned toward them. It was Hamid, as far as Joan could tell in the mirror; he reached out his hands to the other passengers in greeting and seemed to recite a short prayer, after which the words continued to flow from him. Joan didn't understand what he was saying, but the group was totally silent and listening intently. The two furies at the back of the bus were wide-eyed. Small muscles under their eyes tightened as if they had to make a con-certed effort in order to understand. But the message was evidently clear enough, because suddenly everyone was clapping simultaneously and cheering as if something wondrous had been proclaimed.

The she-devils in front of him looked at each other and nodded, and to his surprise they clutched one another's hands, and he was suddenly aware of their strong bond.

Intoxicated by the words they had heard, the two women started to quietly cry. Something in them had been released, and with a greater sense of ease than before, they began to talk to each other freely.

Joan closed his eyes and tried to follow what they were saying.

Their mutual language was a mixture of German and French with some Arabic words thrown in, so while Joan wasn't able to pick up everything, he understood the gist, and that was more than enough.

When they first mentioned how unconditionally they were looking forward to following their friends toward the seven heavens, where a single day was like a thousand days on earth, where there was no sor-row, fear, or shame, where nothing rotted and where no one experi-enced hunger, Joan opened his eyes and felt himself breaking out in a cold sweat. They called it paradise and Jannah, and their eyes emanated a feeling of true and pure happiness, which Joan secretly envied with all his heart. But it also made him terribly uneasy.

They referred to themselves as "holy warriors" and almost couldn't wait to be given the cue to carry out the deed they so longed to com-plete. They clasped each other's hands again as if they were sisters who had been separated but were now reunited.

"Our mission in life is complete," they said, confirming Joan's worst fears. With every sign they passed, they were all approaching their death.

Joan tried to avoid the women's gazes when, as simultaneously as Siamese twins, their euphoria disappeared and they remembered their task.

"What did he hear?" whispered one of them to the other.

Joan had heard everything and tried to concentrate on controlling just some of his muscles. The people on the bus were so sure of their drugs that they hadn't even taken the trouble to tie him down. So, if he could just stretch his left arm a little so that the cannula in the back of his hand or the tube in the cannula slipped out, the paralysis might wear off just enough to enable him to shout for help when the bus stopped.

Joan closed his eyes and tried to concentrate on regaining the feeling in his arm. And when he still couldn't feel anything, he turned his concentration in vain to his hand and fingers. Everything was like dead flesh.

He had been sitting like this for a while, seemingly far away, when the two furies began whispering to each other again, one of them with the strangest smile he had ever seen.

They laughed quietly as they recapped what would soon happen. As far as Joan could understand, they would all pretend to be tourists and send hundreds of people to hell. And then they discussed Ghaalib, their spiritual leader, with a warmth and affection that made it sound like they were his lovers. The thought that this person would be with them in their final hour and behold their pure and justified sacrifice whipped them up into an excited frenzy.

And Joan screamed inside with the full essence of his being for help and mercy.

A few minutes later, everyone in the front seats got up in unison as if by command and assumed the prayer position in the aisle. Even the women behind him seemed to disappear into themselves. Joan opened his eyes wide and turned his head very slowly toward the window and the road outside.

Cars were speeding past like migratory birds, stubbornly and quickly heading toward the day's duties. Every now and then, there were a couple of children in a back seat, presumably traveling with their parents on the way to school or wherever they were going. A couple of times, he managed to catch the eye of a curious kid with their nose pressed against the window, but the gaze quickly disappeared in the other direction.

Then he made himself cross-eyed, rolled his eyes back, and blinked furiously, but he was met with only smiles and laughing faces.

Why should they react to that?

Look at me, he said to himself over and over, and they did see him but just not properly: not like a man who would shortly take people with him to their deaths.

"Ladies and gentlemen," announced the driver. "We have reached Berlin." Several people clapped as the bus drove into an anonymous residential area that in no way resembled a capital or world city.

In this jumble of blocks, they left the bus parked across several parking spaces in front of a playground.

For a moment, he looked at his fellow passengers as if they were aliens. Their movements were considered and their eyes were glazed like those of zombies. Everything was like an assembly line: mechanical and rehearsed.

When most of them had been taken away in private cars, a second disability bus arrived for him and the other two in wheelchairs. Hamid oversaw the procedure, so it was obviously important that this part of the transportation went without a hitch.

Just like last time, they positioned him in the aisle, but this time facing the two paralyzed women in wheelchairs, which afforded him the chance to see their faces and the terror in their eyes.

Despite the paralysis, the elder of the two tried to turn her head to the younger presumably to create a bond of shared experience and feeling, but she didn't manage. The younger woman, on the other hand, could turn her head a little more, and she stared longingly at the elder woman's cheek. They looked so alike. Were they mother and daughter? Why were they here?

It was only now, while sitting in the aisle, that he realized the full extent of the tragedy to which he inadvertently had become a part. These two women were sacrificial lambs for the holy act—and so was he.

There was a clattering sound from the white bus next to them, where a couple of the men were struggling with something at the back of the bus. He saw a hatch being opened and a large transport box removed and emptied. Then the plastic-wrapped contents were arduously carried to the back of the new disability bus. A light shake to the bus told him that the goods were now in place, while Hamid's shouting and screaming made him too nervous to think about what the contents of the box might be.

They drove purposefully for ten minutes through the streets of Berlin, and when they stopped at a set of traffic lights in front of an immigrant kiosk with Arabic signs written on the shop window, he caught sight of a newspaper board on the pavement.

Joan didn't manage to read the headline, but the photo underneath said it all, because it was a picture of him, lightly smiling as if he had been instructed by a photographer from *Hores del dia*.

Joan took a deep breath. They were looking for him. Did that mean there was hope?

At that moment they pulled a hood over his head.

36

Carl

Carl looked at Assad with concern. His face was ashen, and there wasn't the slightest hint of a smile. Like a soldier with post-traumatic stress disorder, he flinched at the slightest sound. It was clear that the waiting was driving him crazy.

"I feel like I'm waiting for my family to be dragged up the steps to the scaffold." His lips quivered. "And the frightening thing is that this is reality, Carl. It's happening right now, and what can I do to stop it? We're powerless."

Carl looked over at Herbert Weber's cigarettes. Right now, the urge to start smoking again was stronger than ever before. His hands were wavering between them and Assad's arm, which was resting heavily on the table. He took Assad's arm.

"Listen, Assad, you're already doing something. You've done exactly what Ghaalib wants you to, which is a move in the right direction. You're out in the open and have made yourself known. Now he knows you're watching what he's doing, and he knows you're in Frankfurt. You're moving in on each other; there's nothing else you can do just now."

"I'll kill him when I get the chance, Carl," he said in a thick voice. "I have so much to avenge."

"You have to be careful, Assad. Keep a cool head, or he'll be the one plunging the knife."

Assad turned to look at the film screen that the police had obtained at the request of the intelligence service. It seemed like they had again waited far too long for something to happen, so Carl knew how Assad felt. It was enough to drive anyone crazy.

After another fifteen minutes, Herbert Weber returned with a group of men dressed in black, who, apart from Herbert's weight, looked exactly like him.

"Gentlemen," he said when everyone was seated. "The situation is this: We are now optimistic that we are a bit closer to pinpointing where the group is. A couple of alert policemen stood guard last night at the house where we know the group stayed, and while there they came in contact with Florian Hoffmann, who is a seventeen-year-old paperboy. He was able to tell us that while he was cycling around the area three nights ago, a bus was backing up toward the house. He was delivering the morning paper to the people across the street, and in the one and a half years he's been doing that round, he has never seen anyone driving around the area—and especially in such a large vehicle— so early in the morning."

Carl observed the people in the room sighing with relief. Finally, there was something concrete to go on. He should call and let Marcus Jacobsen know.

"It was still dark, so Florian didn't notice anything distinguishing about the bus, but he did observe that it was very white. And when it drove past him, he noticed that it had a sort of lift used on disability buses. My colleagues have shown him many different photos of disabled lifts on bus tailgates, and he's very sure that it was this type of lift."

He clicked to the next picture on the screen. It was a very ordinary lift of the sort seen everywhere but with a very visible sign stuck to it that read, U-LIFT.

"The boy thought it was funny. He's a dedicated skier and goes skiing with his family every winter, and he thought that if it was a ski lift it wouldn't get you anywhere. That's what made it stick in his mind."

There were obviously more than a few people in the room who didn't get it.

"Yes, a U-lift," said Weber, smiling. "Like a lift where you get on and end up back in the same place. That wouldn't get anyone very far."

A couple of the slowest on the uptake had an aha moment.

"Smart boy. He also noticed that the bus didn't have any other distinguishing characteristics. In other words, it was totally bare, as he put it. No advertisements or anything that could lead us to the owner, which is actually not very normal. So, we can now assume that the bus the police have just located is identical to the one we've been searching high and low for."

He clicked to the next picture on the screen. "A couple of hours ago, we managed to obtain a security camera image from the highway."

The photo wasn't very clear but the bus was white without any other features and had a U-lift on the back.

"Yes, I know what you're thinking. But we're now fairly certain that this is the same bus and that the group left Frankfurt at around four thirty in the morning based on the distance and a rough average speed to the location of this video camera. We're currently going through all our vehicle registers to see if we can find the owner. As you can see, the bus isn't very big. It's presumably intended for twenty passengers at most."

"Can we see anyone in the video if we zoom in?" someone asked.

"We're working on the video, but it's unlikely."

Weber clicked again, and a street map of Frankfurt and the area to the north appeared. He pointed directly at the screen.

"The rest stop where the image is from is up here."

Those assembled reacted again. They could have been heading anywhere, but Berlin was close and a good guess.

"Potsdam is also nearby, as are other important cities," he continued. "So we've had to intensify our efforts in those areas. We have to assume that the bus will be hidden somewhere before they reach their final destination, but just now, the task is to find it."

Weber paused and turned toward Assad.

"Our Danish friend here is very involved with several of the people we assume to be on the bus. As you know by now, he shares a very bleak past with the leader, Ghaalib, and they've been enemies for years. Our hypothesis is that Ghaalib has chosen this moment to kill two birds with one stone: a well-planned act of terrorism and a confrontation with his enemy sitting here, Zaid al-Asadi. He's given clear indications of this by killing someone very close to Zaid and ensuring that a photo of this woman has been printed in the world press. And to underpin his terrible intentions, he's holding Zaid al-Asadi's wife and daughter hostage."

He pointed at Assad, who then stood up.

"I'd prefer it if you'd call me Assad." He attempted a smile. "Tomorrow I'll check into Hotel Maingau here in Frankfurt under my birth name, Zaid al-Asadi, where we expect that Ghaalib will provoke a confrontation with me and possibly try to kill me, although the latter is very unlikely. In the best-case scenario, the confrontation will be with Ghaalib himself, or at least with his people, who will then hopefully lead us to Ghaalib. That's why we're still here in Frankfurt. Herbert Weber and the local police have naturally made sure that I'll be afforded every protection. I also know that a couple of you sitting here will be there, so thank you for that. I hear that the place has been under surveillance since yesterday, but nothing will happen before I get there."

He looked up at the photos that had been taken of the hotel and the park in front of it. The plan was that he would go early in the morning and stroll from the south into the park across from the hotel, walk slowly through it, and wait momentarily at the playground. He would wait there for a confrontation, but if nothing happened, he would enter the hotel and sit in the restaurant and, after a light meal lasting half an hour, go back the same way through the park. If someone still didn't try to attack him, he would go back again and check in at the hotel.

Herbert Weber thanked him and continued along the same lines. "We have a common task to ensure that no pedestrians are injured during this operation. If any children from the nearby buildings come to play in the playground, we have to get them away from there. The police have positioned a couple of plainclothes female officers in the side streets who can easily step in and pretend to be either mothers or friends of the parents."

"What about the hotel?"

Weber stepped to the side so that he was standing shoulder to shoulder with Assad. "There won't be any episodes there. Naturally, we'll make sure that the guests at the hotel are identified and cleared. Just so that no one is in any doubt, the operation will be exclusively executed outside."

"Yes. Of course I hope that you'll stop him in his tracks, but also that you'll bring the person or persons who Ghaalib sends to confront me alive," said Assad. "I don't think Ghaalib will be nearby. He's too much of a coward for that."

"Will you be armed?" someone asked.

Assad nodded.

There was a good deal of murmuring in the room. The situation was irregular, and Carl was aware of it.

"I assume that Assad doesn't have authorization to shoot first?" one of them said.

Weber confirmed.

Assad continued. "It's been decided that if nothing happens during my two trips through the park, I'll go back and stay in my hotel room until three. At that time, I'll take the elevator down and go back to the park for a third time. My guess is that that's when they'll strike. I'll be wearing a bulletproof vest, but they'll probably aim for the head. I certainly would."

It was unpleasant to hear, but Carl nodded. After the meeting, they would carefully go through the details and the area one more time to ensure that they took all eventualities into account. They had to make sure nothing happened to Assad.

Weber thanked him and stressed that if Ghaalib took up the gauntlet, they would have to be prepared for the worst. Even if they were only able to apprehend one person with a connection to Ghaalib and the operation, they would be a good step closer.

"Our colleagues in Cyprus have sent us some important and very useful information," he added. "Firmer measures are being taken with the refugees who were washed ashore on the beach ten days ago. Some people might protest about their methods, but in a situation like this we've decided to turn a deaf ear."

Carl frowned. Was he talking about torture?

"I'm not talking about torture," he said, as if he'd read Carl's mind, "but rather a form of pressure that's hard to resist. Physical pressure has been used, yes, but what really brought results was promising asylum to these refugees if they spoke candidly. They were subsequently promised a transfer out of Menogeia under a false name. The authorities quickly found out that their silence was due to fear."

"Couldn't there be opportunists among them who've given false information?" asked Carl.

"Yes, of course. There were several examples of just that, but they were reported by another passenger from the boat. She's now been placed in safety at another location but has provided us with essential information about the women who escaped from the camp."

He clicked forward to a couple of new photos on the screen.

"These are the camp photos from when they registered the refugees who were washed ashore, and here we have the two women who escaped. By correlating the information from the informant about their accents and their difficulties with Arabic with the information we have from the Syrian intelligence service and a few European countries, we are now able to positively identify them."

He pointed at one of the women. She looked to be in her forties, with thick black hair, beautifully shaped lips, and slightly dark skin.

"She looks like the actress Rachel Ticotin." He clicked to produce a photo next to the suspect. The similarity was incredible.

"I'm sure this beautiful American actress will forgive us the comparison. The woman we're looking for is now in familiar surroundings on her home turf and wearing normal Western clothes, so the actress's photo gives us a very accurate guideline for her. The woman's name is Beate Lothar but she is known as Beena. She's German, forty-eight years old, and comes from Lünen in the Ruhr district. We think she was radicalized three years ago after her conversion to Islam and countless trips to the Middle East over the last decade. You've all been sent a copy of her photo, as have our colleagues in Potsdam and Berlin. We have a strong suspicion that she'll be taking part in the operation and that she's one of the bus passengers."

"Do we know exactly when she made contact with this Ghaalib?" one of them asked.

"Afraid not. But as far as we can tell, she was in Syria until fairly recently. She has assumedly been recruited specifically for this operation."

"And the other one?"

"A bit more difficult because this woman has gone under several names. Born in 1973 as Catherine Lauzier, she's also gone by the names Justine Perrain, Claudia Perrain, Giselle van den Broek, Henrietta Colbert, and so on. We know that she's Swiss and that she was something of a tough nut under the pseudonym Jasmin Curtis in the women's prison in Danbury, Connecticut, where she was doing time for assault, from March 2003 until October 2004. There wasn't much she didn't do in there: threats of violence against fellow inmates, hunger strikes, bribery, and a whole lot more besides. Strangely, she was released early on probation and vanished. We believe that she's been linked the whole time with a terror cell, but nothing is proven. When she turned up in Menogeia"— he clicked to the next photo—"she looked like this. Let's compare it with the one from the file we received from Danbury yesterday."

Carl was speechless. Even though there was no immediately striking similarity between the two photos, it was the same woman. The eyes gave her away, just like they always did.

"Yes, it would seem that she's had all the hair colors under the sun, so ignore that. But note her smile. Could we call it crooked? No. Broad? No. She has the sort of smile that can make a beautiful woman ugly. Her eyes are somehow mean-looking. Her lips almost curl."

Then he clicked to a new picture. "Here we have a photo of the actress Ellen Barkin, who is a very attractive woman. But in seconds you can see her transformation. like here in the film *Sea of Love,* where she plays a cunning murderer, unless I'm mistaken."

He clicked again and the screen was filled with smaller photos of the same actress. "Here we have Ellen Barkin in many different roles, from pure glamour to something much graver. As you know, sometimes makeup and hair color change a face a lot. And when it comes to our woman, Catherine Lauzier, alias Jasmin, be prepared for a lot of creativity. We don't have any up-to-date photos of her, but she's unlikely to have any signs of aging over and above what you might expect from time spent in war-torn Syria. So, focus on the smile and the eyes."

"When was she radicalized?" one of the group asked.

"We don't know too much. Of course, she's been questioned repeatedly in connection to other cases, but her ability to make up stories has blurred the real picture of who she is and why she's ended up where she is today. But there's one thing in particular we need to pay attention to. During her physical examination in Danbury, there were various signs that she had attempted suicide. Deep scars on her wrists, inner thighs, and even her neck and throat. It's a wonder that she hasn't died at some point."

"A wonder? You mean a misfortune," interrupted Assad.

Weber smiled wryly. "Well, it is what it is. We have a good grasp on her now, but I know where you're coming from." He turned to face the group. "Someone with suicidal tendencies is a threat to all of us."

He turned his attention to Carl.

"Carl Mørck here is another of our Danish friends who has joined us. He's the head of Department Q in Copenhagen, which has an exceptional success rate, and he has yet more information that can help us in our understanding of this mission and the people involved."

Carl stood up. "Yes, that's right." He looked around and nodded to the people present. If it weren't for Assad, he wouldn't have given a damn about these Goody Two-shoes. Over the past few days, Carl had realized that apart from the guys back at the house in Allerød, Assad was actually the only man in the world he would be proud to call his friend. He would do anything for him—even being polite and well behaved in the present company.

He smiled at Assad and continued. He, hopefully, felt the same way.

"In cooperation with the Police Intelligence Service in Denmark, I've focused on the first body that was washed ashore on Cyprus the day Joan Aiguader arrived in Ayia Napa," he said. "It's been of particular interest to us because the man in question was deported from Denmark. A stateless and criminal Palestinian, Yasser Shehade had exceptional leave to remain but was subsequently arrested in 2007 for a series of crimes in Denmark. To pick at random, we're talking assault, extensive dealing in hash and hard drugs, break-ins, threats. After serving five years, he was deported for a period of six years. He was escorted to the airport in Copenhagen, from where he escaped. An embarrassing incident, but he hadn't totally gone off the radar because he was observed in Zürich boarding a plane to Islamabad."

Carl looked around. The message had already sunk in.

"Yes, we're certain that when he was in Pakistan, he made contact with ethnic Pashtuns at a Koran school. We have a good picture from the Americans of how he acted in Syria. When we went through their material yesterday, we found this photo."

He nodded to Weber, who clicked again.

"And here, gentlemen, we see Ghaalib and Yasser Shehade in the same photo taken in Pakistan."

There was a buzz in the room. The two men were eating by a primitive fire on a cliff, fully armed with Kalashnikovs and ammunition belts across their chests. Yasser Shehade had a full beard that reached his chest, while Ghaalib's stubble was only days old. They were laughing with their mouths full of meat and seemed very intimate.

Carl noticed how affected Assad looked. When Carl had shown it to him the previous night, he'd cried so hard that the veins on the sides of his head had been close to bursting. Carl had never seen him like that before and had never seen a hate as intense as Assad's. "Yes, it's something of a surprise, but a lot points to Yasser having been in the field for the Syrian militia for a long time at this point, while Ghaalib, or

Abdul Azim, to give him his real name, has just arrived. Now we can clearly see how he looked at the time and probably also looks now. The scars on the bottom of his face are down to Assad here."

Now everyone was seeing Assad while he stared at the floor. He couldn't cope with looking at that photo again.

"The Americans found the photograph on a fallen holy warrior, and based on the time when the warrior was shot and from other records, we know that the photo was taken in 2014. Here we can see that the transformation from the Abdul Azim who spread fear in Saddam's jails to the high-ranking holy warrior Ghaalib happened very quickly. Ghaalib's cruelty and mercilessness led to him being promoted faster than normal, and the Americans have him high on their most wanted list. So they're now in a state of full alert and are ready to share any information that might help us find the man."

"What else do we know about him apart from the information we already have?" one of them asked.

Carl nodded. "We know his movements very precisely. How he moved southwest from northeastern Syria. And we know that he always had a harem of women in his personal entourage who no other warriors were allowed to come near."

Assad stood up and stormed out of the room. Maybe it was for the best.

37

Alexander

He was standing in the kitchen when the taxi stopped in front of the driveway, and just like the other times when his mother had been away, it took a few minutes before she got out. He could picture the scene. She had fumbled in her handbag for cash or a credit card, and when she finally found what she was looking for, after having spread the contents of her handbag all over the back seat, she had flirted a little with the driver, given him too big a tip, and showered him with compliments, which she was sure made her seem attractive. Fawning disingenuousness for which Alexander hated her all the more.

When the driver placed her suitcase on the pavement, her laughter could be heard from all the way inside the house. So, he was probably more handsome than average. To put it another way, his mother lived for sexual tension. It had been this way ever since traveling to conferences in southern European cities had become part of her life. Even Alexander had to admit that it became her, with rosy cheeks and blood-red lips whose latent desire superseded the boring life and absence of passion between her and her husband.

Welcome back, bitch, he thought, and closed the fridge.

"I'm baaaack," shouted his mother with false excitement in her voice when she came through the front door.

Alexander pictured her. The way she always hung her jacket on the hook, put her suitcase in the entrance, and tidied herself up a bit in the mirror. Then she would take a couple of steps into the hallway and prance into the living room as if everything were normal.

But this time it wasn't, and he could hear that she had stopped abruptly in the hallway.

Alexander smiled to himself in the kitchen.

"Alex?" she asked tentatively. She had reached the open door to his bedroom.

Another step. A quick glance into his room confused her, he imagined. Why was the door open, and why wasn't he inside?

"Alex?" she said again, this time a little louder.

He left the kitchen and walked out into the corridor. It was amazing to see her cower when he very quietly answered, "Yes." If he had shouted, he would have given her a heart attack. But he didn't want it to be that easy.

She turned hesitantly toward him. Her otherwise ruddy cheeks had already turned pale. Even though she tried to look pleasantly surprised, she couldn't manage to do anything other than gawp.

"You did ask me to come out," he said, walking toward her. "And here I am. Did you have a good time?"

She answered yes with a slight stutter.

"You're back a day later than I thought," he said, and noticed that she took a step back for every step he took toward her. Had she already noticed the bloodstain on the carpet?

"Er, yes. It's because we had an extra course included this year," she lied. A discipline she had otherwise mastered over the years but that failed her now. Her smile was a little too wide, her nod too eager. It gave her away.

"An extra course! Wow, that's great. But that means it's left to me to tell you that Dad's gone. He couldn't look you in the eyes anymore after all your whoring around."

The effect was immediate. Surprise mixed with badly concealed disappointment that she hadn't been the one to leave first was written all over her face.

"Okay." She took a long pause and bit her upper lip. "Do you know where he's gone?"

Alexander shook his head. "But at least it meant I could leave my room now that the bastard isn't here anymore to order me about."

She tilted her head. It might have been a long time since his parents had regarded each other with respect, but she didn't want her son talking like that about his father; that much was clear.

As if the loathsome hypocrite thought any differently about him.

"I'll call him," she said like the woman of action she so wanted to be.

"Of course," said Alexander, and he watched as her polished finger found his father's number on her telephone and pressed it. Her plucked eyebrows shot up noticeably when she heard the ringtone coming from Alexander's bedroom behind her.

"Oh dear, I guess he didn't take it with him." Alexander looked surprised, which also confused her.

"Why on earth is your dad's cell phone in your room?" she asked, and followed the sound. So, she hadn't seen the bloodstain the first time.

But she did now.

Like someone standing on stilts on the ice, one of her high heels slipped out to one side, and the movement tore her skirt from the slit up. In a fateful moment of clarity, she stared at the dark stain as she fell flat.

It was a mystery how a woman with a business degree who lived in a world of her own could deduce what the thick matter on the floor was, but she seemed in no doubt.

She placed the palm of her hand on the floor and pushed herself up with such agility that Alexander was momentarily impressed.

"What happened?" she moaned while pointing at the stain.

"Oh, that?" he said. "Maybe I got it wrong. Maybe Dad didn't leave after all. Maybe I cut his head off instead, but you definitely shouldn't count on him coming back."

She lowered her head. Whether she believed him or not wasn't what mattered most; right now, all she was thinking about was how to take down the crazy person standing in front of her—son or not, it didn't matter.

"Don't touch me!" she shouted as she walked backward toward his computer. "If you lay a finger on me, I'll smash this damn machine on the floor, got it?"

Alexander shrugged and walked backward out of the room. "Come out, Mom. It was just a prank. I took a couple of bottles of red wine when he left and had too much to drink. I'll pay for the bloody carpet."

Then he walked to the kitchen and put the kettle on.

He counted her tentative steps down the corridor. Then she stopped before continuing again after a few seconds.

He turned toward her, and in the moment where she raised the stool from the corridor above her head, ready to strike, he managed to swing the kettle into her face with such force that she fell to the floor.

"Wake up, Mom!" He gently tapped her forehead where the kettle had hit her.

She blinked a little and struggled to focus. She looked down at herself and tried to understand what had happened and why she was strapped tightly to her husband's office chair with gaffer tape. Her bloodred lips didn't help her very much now.

"What have you done, Alex? Why?"

He squatted in front of her. What a rare opportunity to look her straight in the eyes and tell her exactly why.

"Because you're shameless, Mom. You and all the other pigs on this street and in this neighborhood and in this ridiculous town and in this ridiculous country are despicable hypocrites. And your reign of crime ends here. That's why!"

"I don't understand what you're talking about, Alex. You're over-reacting. What's all this about?" She tugged at the tape to try to free herself. "Let me go!"

Alexander pointed instead at the clipping of the drowned woman.

"That's why, Mom! You and your sort think of nothing but your-selves. And that's the reason she's lying there in the sand. Can you see her?"

She looked puzzled. "Yes, and it's macabre. How can you stand look-ing at it? Is it because she looks like your grandmother that you've hung it up? Do you miss her that much?"

Alexander felt his face trembling. "That's typical of you. You can't even show empathy for a fellow human being. But the reason she's hanging on my wall is because she doesn't deserve to be forgotten. She tried to live her life in a terrible place, and when she couldn't do it any-more, she ended up dying at sea. And people like you couldn't give a toss, which is why you're here. And you can't get away."

Then he turned the office chair a hundred and eighty degrees so that she could see his screen.

"Look how far I've come, Mom. Two thousand one hundred victo-ries. And when I reach two thousand one hundred and seventeen, the same thing will happen to you that happened to this guy."

He pushed the PC screen to the side.

The scream when she saw her husband's frozen face lying on the table was so shrill that the empty glasses on his bedside table clinked.

He put a stop to her screaming with gaffer tape. Twice over her mouth and around her head. There would be no more screaming from her.

Alexander smiled, pushed her chair into the corner, and reposi-tioned his screen. His father's head could stay there for a while longer before he put it back in the freezer.

He sat down and entered the game, preparing for the next round, then opened his drawer and took out his old Nokia. He removed the old SIM card and threw it in the trash with the others.

When he had inserted the new SIM card, he opened his contacts and pressed on one he had saved as "Dumb dick."

38

Rose

It was Rose who answered the phone, because the caller was unknown and it had been a few days since the delusional boy had been in touch. Rose listened to her almost never-failing female intuition and snapped her fingers at Gordon, who immediately called the head of homicide. Now she just had to keep the conversation going for a few minutes to allow Marcus time to get down there and listen in.

"Well, well, well, if it isn't my old friend again," she said, and pressed the RECORD button.

The reaction was immediate. "I'm not your friend, and I don't want to talk to you. Put me on with the dumb dick!"

Rose looked apologetically at Gordon.

"He's listening. You're on speakerphone."

"Okay." He sounded like he was laughing. Was he feeling important now?

"Say hello, then, to Kurt-Brian Logan, twenty-two years old, dumb dick," she invited Gordon.

"My name isn't Kurt-Brian Logan!" The boy sounded offended.

"If you say so. But we do know that you're twenty-two or you would have complained about that as well."

"Is there anyone else except the idiot listening in?"

"Not yet, but the chief of homicide is on his way for a visit. Like us, he finds you really interesting."

"The head of homicide! Then you know how important this case is," he said. "That's satisfying to know."

Satisfying! Rose took a deep breath. Why on earth did it feel so vulgar talking with this crazy jerk of a murderer?

"You haven't done it, have you, Kurt-Brian Logan? You haven't killed your mother?" Rose held her breath.

He laughed again. "No, funnily enough, she's kept her head for now. She can hear what you're saying, but you can't hear her."

Actually, she could. The terrifying muffled sounds of screaming for help were almost inaudible, but they were there.

Rose began to sweat. This life was now her responsibility.

She noticed Gordon's expression. He had obviously heard the sounds too.

"If you call me Kurt-Brian one more time, I'll chop her head off, so I'd advise you against it."

"Okay, so what should I call you?"

His silence betrayed that he hadn't thought that through.

Rose said nothing. Marcus Jacobsen was on his way down, so she let the boy think.

"You can call me Toshiro," he said finally.

Then Gordon came closer. "Hi, Toshiro," he said.

"Is that you, dumb dick?"

Gordon nodded and answered yes. "I knew you were a samurai," he continued.

The boy laughed. "Why? Because of the type of sword I use? You're very quick."

"Maybe, yes. But probably more because you call yourself Toshiro. Isn't that Japanese? Don't samurais come from Japan? And didn't they use samurai swords? Yes, they did, hence the name."

He nodded to Marcus as he entered the room and sat down.

"And I think you're referring to the actor Toshiro Mifune, the greatest samurai ever to appear on the screen. Isn't that right, Toshiro?"

He was chuckling in the background. It was awful to hear that laughter simultaneously with his mother's muffled cries for help.

Gordon looked at Rose, and she nodded in agreement. He should keep going in the same vein.

"We know that you're a samurai, Toshiro. It's obvious from your blond man bun, isn't it?"

Now the only sound on the other end was from the mother. The chuckling had completely stopped.

"Hello, Toshiro," interjected the chief of homicide. "My name is Marcus Jacobsen; I'm the chief of homicide. We deal with the very worst criminals in Denmark, and my specialty is finding people like you, putting you all in jail, and throwing away the key. You're twenty-two just now, but when the justice system is finished with you, you'll be a very old man, Toshiro. Unless, of course, you slowly and calmly put a stop to what you're doing and tell me where we can find you."

"Put dumb dick on again," he said curtly. "And shut the hell up, you piece of shit! I hate people like you. One more word out of you, and it'll be the last you hear from me."

Marcus Jacobsen shrugged and gestured to Gordon to continue.

"How do you know that I have blond hair and a man bun?" continued the guy.

"I know because we have a really good facial composite of you, Toshiro. It was sketched at the kiosk on Frederikssundsvej where you bought your prepaid telephone cards. We're getting those cards registered, and then we're coming to get you."

Rose was taken aback. Was this pale lad she could seduce with one grab at his trousers now growing a spine out of nowhere?

"Prepaid telephone cards aren't registered in Denmark," he replied. "I happen to know that for a fact. Do you think I'm stupid?"

"No, not at all, Toshiro. But right now, we're finding out how clever you actually are and where you went to school. Just for your information, we've sent the sketch to every education institution in the country."

Surprisingly, he began to laugh again.

"That's a lot," he said. "But listen. I'll hold back for a while with killing my mother because I can hear it amuses you that she's still alive. Now you can practice some of that police psychology."

Did he say "amuses you"? thought Rose. The boy was completely insane.

"Great," said Gordon. "We'll play along."

"What more do you know about me?"

Gordon looked questioningly at the chief of homicide, who was sitting with pursed lips. It was clear that he also thought that they were dealing with a crazy person and that this could easily develop into a case that would backfire on the department if things got out of hand.

Then he nodded.

"Okay, Toshiro. Apart from your age and appearance, and where you bought the prepaid telephone cards, we know that you live in the Copenhagen area and probably in a nice large house. We'll find you, Toshiro, but do yourself a favor and listen to what the chief of homicide said and you'll receive a hospital order and significantly better conditions."

Rose interrupted. "And you'll be spared having your brains fucked out, pretty boy," she said harshly.

Now the guy's voice sounded piercing. "What makes you so sure I'd want to miss out on that?"

"Toshiro," said Gordon smoothly. "I promise you'll get a fair trial if you tell me who you are. Otherwise, it'll be the hard way. We're working around the clock on this. We're tireless, just so you know."

"Good! All that leaves for me to say is *perseverando,* and good-bye." Then there was a click and he was gone.

Marcus Jacobsen looked over his half-rim glasses and seemed unhappy, to say the least.

"His condition is worse than I thought," he said. "Send me the recording. I'm going to send it over to PET anyway. We need to work at full force or we'll have a mass murderer on our hands in a few days."

Rose raised her hand. "Let me hear his last sentence one more time, Gordon."

He placed the cursor on the audio track bar and pulled it back twenty seconds.

Rose kept her hand in the air until the word came.

"Did he say *preseverando*?" she asked. "Play it again."

All three of them listened intently.

"No, *perseverando*," said Marcus. "Do you know what it means? Because I don't."

Rose Googled it.

"It means 'perseverance,' it says here." She shot to her feet.

"I think the boy has given himself away." She nodded to herself with a wry smile. "Because do you know what *perseverando* also is? It's the motto for the boarding school out by Bagsværd Lake. Look."

The other two directed their attention to the screen.

39

Ghaalib

When Ghaalib joined Danish-Palestinian Yasser Shehade's group of holy warriors, it was to escape Syria alive. For years, he had been on the top of the USA's most wanted list, and not without good reason; he was proud that his ruthlessness and mercilessness toward people who got in his way was known throughout the areas of Syria where the war had raged.

Ghaalib had met Shehade for the first time several years before in a dusty training camp a few hundred kilometers from Pakistan's capital, Islamabad. Among the hundreds of holy warriors of all nationalities with whom Ghaalib came in contact, Shehade was the one in whom Ghaalib saw the most potential. Not only was he intelligent, he was infused with a brutality behind his doll-like face, with its large eyes that inspired confidence and a smile that under more civilized skies could have led to a film career and countless victories over the ladies. In other words, Shehade was a sublime killing machine who with simple facial expressions could camouflage his intentions and violent attacks. He had also lived in Denmark, which was interesting, but that recalled experiences that Ghaalib didn't want to work through just now.

In the relationship between these two men, Ghaalib was the strategist. Years of fighting against the regime in Iraq in the aftermath of Saddam's death had toughened him up and refined his methods. He lived as a nomad, never sleeping in the same place for more than a couple of nights, covering his tracks no matter the cost that inevitably followed. Ghaalib was the ideal mastermind in any guerrilla war, and that was also how he wished to be known. One moment a short-haired and clean-shaven man with makeup covering his scarred lower face and smartly dressed in Western clothes like an average businessman who could navigate effortlessly between the coalition forces, and the next in the field like a barbarian with bloodstained clothes and a deranged look in his eyes.

In these roles, he never took unnecessary chances; however, Ghaalib had one weakness that controlled him more than anything else, and that was his never-ceasing thirst for revenge. Ever since Zaid al-Asadi had disfigured his face with phosphoric acid, which had given Mohammad the opportunity to mutilate him over fifteen years ago, his mission in life had been to create balance in the equation where he had once lost. He took out his revenge on Zaid al-Asadi every day by terrorizing the three women whom this man loved most in life. The dilemma, however, was that for the revenge to have an impact on his enemy, it had to be visible, and dragging these three hostages through a war zone brought constant risk that he could well do without.

When he met Shehade in the summer of 2018 for the second time, he made an agreement with him that if he took the women with him to Syria, he could do with them as he saw fit, with the one condition that he keep them alive so Ghaalib could collect them later. Shehade agreed, and for his troubles was also given command of a group of fighters who would operate in an area of Syria where the risk of being killed was minimal and where he would therefore be able to achieve glory.

Ghaalib had regular contact with Shehade so he could confirm with his own eyes that the women were still alive, but he otherwise devoted all his energies to finding al-Asadi. Several attempts to get Sunnis in Denmark to track down Zaid al-Asadi had come to nothing, and Ghaalib came to realize that perhaps the man wasn't living in Denmark. So he went further back in time and after a few months discovered an elderly couple in Fallujah who, with a gun to their heads, were able to tell him about the family's flight from Saddam's regime. It was the last thing they ever said.

The day Ghaalib approached the bomb-damaged white house in southwestern Syria where Zaid al-Asadi's family had purportedly lived before they came to Denmark, he fell to his knees and thanked the good fortune that had led him there.

There was sporadic greenery in the garden and a solitary goat tethered and munching by a ditch, but apart from the goat, it was hard to see how they managed to get by in this house, which once, in more peaceful times, had stood like a gem in the landscape.

Inside the house, things looked different. The house had clearly been vandalized, but with the remains of the contents, the owner had restored a semblance of its former glory and elegance in sheer defiance.

In the middle of the living room on the first floor, he found Lely Kababi sitting on a threadbare sofa with a frail grip on a cigarette that had long since gone out.

Ghaalib asked politely about the al-Asadi family, but Lely Kababi denied any knowledge of these Iraqis who had supposedly lived with her. It was a lie, of course—Ghaalib was an expert in interrogations and could spot a lie straightaway—but he left her in peace. Lely had unknowingly sown the seed for an idea that would bring his plan to fruition.

Three days later, Yasser Shehade arrived in Sab Abar in Syria with a band of warriors and Zaid's three women, as he had been instructed. From the moment they arrived, Yasser and his entourage seemed warweary and exhausted, and their scars and open wounds bore witness to the sacrifices they had made in fighting their way past the massive forces of Bashar Hafez al-Assad's regime and coalition.

Ghaalib had set up camp in a disused tannery opposite Lely Kababi's ruin of a house, and it was here he met Yasser Shehade and his entourage. Ghaalib noted Yasser's unusual lack of fighting spirit once he had lodged his men and settled next to him outside the wreck of a tannery.

"We took more lives than they did, but I lost a couple of men on the way; it was hell getting to this region. Too close to Damascus, too close to everything. Ghaalib, trust me, if we stay here for more than a few days, we're through. Do you understand?"

Ghaalib nodded. He understood. The government troops' suppression of militant groups over the last few weeks had colored the land red with blood, not least here.

"Yes, we need to get away, I know. And I have an escape route. We need to head northwest and over toward the sea, and you'll all need to be totally clean-shaven as if you're escorting an important prisoner, who'll be me. Do you all have your papers in order?"

Yasser Shehade nodded.

"In a few days when we've made it across the sea, I'll introduce you to Hamid, who I've appointed to head the operations in Europe that will shock the world. But first, you and I are going to visit an old lady in the house over there." He pointed to the white house. "And we'll take the women with us. Are they compliant?"

Shehade nodded and went into the building to fetch the three women.

Ghaalib smiled when the women were pushed out. Ronia, the youngest, was a sorry sight—dirty, hunched, and with matted hair—while the mother and elder sister looked much better in spite of the fear in their eyes and the way they flinched at the slightest sound.

"What's happened to the youngest one? Haven't you been looking after her?" he asked.

Shehade shrugged. "What can I say? The men had a preference for her."

When they stepped into the living room of the white house, the old woman was waiting in her chair with a rifle on her lap and following their every move like a snake watching a rat.

Ghaalib stepped toward her with his hands behind his neck. "Lely, stay calm, I'm here on peaceful business," he said. "I have some people I want you to meet."

He signaled behind him without taking his eyes off her. He wanted to see her reaction at the moment the three women were pushed into the room, but she didn't even flinch.

Apart from the sound of his own breathing, he didn't hear a sound. It was as if time stood still, as if his hunch had led him down the wrong path.

"Push them right in so she can get a good look at them," he said to Shehade's men, all the time with his eyes on Lely's face. "You can see that you need to put the rifle down, can't you, Lely?" he attempted. "Otherwise it won't fare well for our companions here. Can't you see who they are?"

It was only then that he noticed she was squinting and trying to focus. Reluctantly, she had to acknowledge the situation.

She stood up slowly, fully aware that it could mean the end of her life but also that the reward was worth it.

She cried as she approached the women and stretched out her arms in an embrace, but the women turned their heads away.

Were they ashamed of their situation, or did they think they could protect the old woman from something unavoidable?

"I see you recognize them now, which tells me you also know Zaid," he said, and pulled the women apart.

The old woman looked at him for a long time in silence while the younger daughter fell to her knees and the others gave in to their tears.

"Yes, you heard what I said. I said Zaid. Zaid al-Asadi, Marwa's coward of a husband who abandoned her alone with her two daughters to a fate worse than death. Zaid, Zaid, Zaid."

Each time he mentioned the name, it was like a spear piercing them. But where he thought that it would break their resistance, it seemed instead, in spite of their enormous hardship and pitiful fate, to momentarily change their demeanor. The name *Zaid* alone seemed to give them strength. The distance in their eyes changed to an expression of alertness. The younger daughter pushed herself up from the floor with her frail arms. And they all looked at him as if his next sentence would bring an end to their years of uncertainty.

"Kill the bastard, Lely. Kill Ghaalib!" shouted Marwa, and pointed at him. "Let us put an end to it all."

She didn't get any farther before Shehade struck her down and she lay bleeding and defenseless on the floor.

Ghaalib pulled out his gun and pointed it at the prostrate woman's head.

"Good. Now I know that you two know each other, Lely. Tell me why or I will kill Marwa. First her, then her daughters, and finally you."

Lely stood with her finger on the trigger, but Ghaalib knew instinctively that she didn't have the strength to pull it and take control of the three women's lives, so he effortlessly wrested the rifle from her with a single grab, like plucking feathers from a bird.

"So, Zaid is still alive?" said the old woman with a strange calm.

"I have no reason to believe otherwise. That's what we're going to find out together. Answer me. How do you know each other?"

The answer came easily to her. "Zaid and Marwa visited me several times just after they were married. I'd never seen the girls."

Ghaalib nodded.

"What are you planning to do to us?" she asked.

"Some of you will be traveling across the sea, and that's all you need to know."

It didn't seem to rattle the old woman. "Then let me help the girls first. You can see how they look; they won't survive such a journey. I can tend to their wounds; I can give them food. Just a day or two."

"There's no time."

"No time? Tell me, what is your issue with Zaid, Ghaalib?"

He nodded to Shehade's men that they could take the women with them now. Then he turned toward Lely. "Ghaalib has no issue with Zaid, but I do as Abdul Azim. And if you ever call me Ghaalib again, I'll kill you."

40

Ghaalib

Over the last few days, Ghaalib had been very active on the Internet and concluded with satisfaction that Zaid al-Asadi had taken the bait from their press release.

Zaid's answer in the Frankfurt newspaper was furnished with a photo of himself and a detailed account of the day, time, and place where they would confront each other. There was no doubt about the authenticity because in spite of a face ravaged by time and sorrow, he looked the same.

Ghaalib's pulse was racing. It really was the same Zaid al-Asadi who had thrown acid in his face and ruined his life. Finally, there was a sign. Finally, he could have his revenge.

He laughed when he read that of all the places in the world, Zaid al-Asadi was now in Frankfurt am Main. So, he had been following their tracks through the press releases.

The showdown was arranged to take place at his hotel; it couldn't have been better. Of course, Ghaalib knew that Zaid had allied himself with all manner of law enforcers. What else should he expect? But Hamid had made sure that they would get what was coming to them.

Their sitting duck was an archetypal Arab. A devout young man with noticeable beard growth, dressed in a white windbreaker, loose-fitting brown trousers, and a white kufi on his head, so there could be no doubting his convictions. Hamid had instructed him via e-mail about where and when he could find this infidel so he could get close enough to execute him. Afterward, his family would never want for anything. And the man accepted the task with great humbleness and delight that he could serve this honorable cause.

The true objective was that the showdown should end with the death of this devout young man, and when he was lying on the ground in a pool of his own blood, someone would make sure they searched him thoroughly. And in the poor man's pocket, they would find hints that would inevitably drive Zaid and Ghaalib closer to each other.

That was the way it had to be.

It would make Zaid lose control.

Ghaalib's choice of base in Berlin had prompted massive protests from Hamid.

"I could find hundreds of better places. So why this flat in Lichtenberg? It isn't a good place to hide. The area is a hotbed for right-wing extremists. How many times have I said it? Have you seen a single person with Arabic roots in this area except us?"

Hamid peeped through the curtains at the street below for the tenth time, and Ghaalib knew what he saw. He had been fascinated with this part of the former East Berlin for years, and for a very particular reason.

"We would blend in with the crowd more in Wedding, Kreuzberg, or Neukölln," continued Hamid. "Those areas of town are a third immigrants, and a lot of them have Middle Eastern backgrounds. And because a lot of them are unemployed, the streets are always teeming with life. Tourists don't go there very often, at least not to Neukölln, where the Lebanese Mafia holds sway. I think it's a mistake that you've chosen this place."

"Yes, and we've discussed it, Hamid. But right now, the police and intelligence service are searching for us like crazy. And when they find the bus in Tempelhof, the search will be intensified in Kreuzberg and Neukölln, where the immigrants live, not here. We just need to keep a low profile and stay indoors until we strike, and nothing will happen."

Hamid grunted; even in this context, he knew his place.

"Did you get hold of the hats?"

He nodded. "Yes, and with accessories too. They're very authentic."

"And the beards?"

"Yes, and they were very expensive." He sniffled a little. Was he coming down with this devilish cold now? "But they look like the real deal," he continued. "I got them in different lengths."

Ghaalib smiled. The trip to Berlin had been uncomplicated, and the apartment here in the former East Berlin was ideal and situated only a few hundred meters from the Stasi prison, Hohenschönhausen. Of all the prisons in the world, it was the one whose cunning methods Ghaalib identified with most and from which he took his inspiration. His mentors in Abu Ghraib had given him detailed information about how things worked there and how carefully planned everything was. The prison was hermetically sealed to the outside world and didn't show up on any maps. Taking long detours, prisoners were brought here in sealed vans so they didn't know where they were being taken, which is how the secret police initiated its ultimate terror and control in the prison, much like Ghaalib had learned in Iraq. The prisoners were allowed to sleep only on their backs with their hands on top of the sheet, the windows were opaque, and during the day, they were only allowed to walk or stand in their cells while they awaited questioning. Most cunning of all was the guards' ability to confuse the prisoners with Christmas decorations at odd times of the year and interrogations that could last five minutes or five hours; they just never knew. And finally, to complement this image of hell on earth, they allowed many of these political prisoners to be bought by West Berlin, but only after a dental check where a heavy X-ray machine behind the headrest damaged the brains of the soon-to-be-released prisoner. When Ghaalib looked out the kitchen window, the view was toward the prison. He could stand there for hours while they waited for the right time to strike. Until the day when Berlin and Germany would feel the spirit of their ancestors' sins until it hurt.

What wonderful irony.

That morning was the first time Ghaalib had seen the Catalonian TV report on the Internet about the drowned Yasser Shehade on the beach in Cyprus. Ghaalib had scoffed when he saw his former ally's body sloshing in the wash. But how could he have known that the otherwise tough man would be beset with panic the very moment he landed in the water or that the idiot would beg for help and cling to him like a helpless baby? If Ghaalib hadn't pushed him under the water, they would both have drowned.

Ghaalib shook his head. It was a good thing he had Hamid, who had already demonstrated that he could complete the task alone. He looked at the man who had executed the complicated preliminary work so exemplarily and thoroughly. This strong, loyal man with cropped hair had been the right choice.

Agitated shouts coming from the living room puzzled Ghaalib, and the commotion appeared to be growing when he entered the room. In front of him stood one of Hamid's best men with a furious expression on his face and surrounded by a group who were presumably on his side.

"We refuse to meet our maker in the clothes he's given us," he said, pointing at Hamid.

"What are you implying, Ali?" Ghaalib asked calmly. "Or what?"

"Or we'll abandon the mission."

"Abandon? But we are holy warriors, Ali. Holy warriors don't abandon a mission."

"What you're proposing is profane. We all agree. It's haram."

Ghaalib turned his head slowly and looked at the others. "Do you agree with Ali? Will you abandon the mission?"

A couple of them were about to nod but didn't; Ghaalib could clearly tell that they were hedging their bets.

"I'll ask again! Who here is with Ali on this?"

No reaction whatsoever, even though Ghaalib knew what they were thinking.

"What do you think, Hamid?"

"You know what I think. Our plan rests on this, so Ali will just have to deal with it."

"Well, I won't." He nodded resolutely at the others to try to win their backing. It was definitely not a development that served their mission.

"This pains me, Ali," said Ghaalib, and pulled out his gun from his kaftan and pointed it at Ali's head. "You're on your own on this, so we can't use you. I'm sorry."

The two female converts who were standing behind him moved to the side while shouting at him to stop.

Then Ghaalib shot, and Ali fell to the floor like a sack in free fall while people jumped to avoid the blood that was already sailing over the floor. Only Joan Aiguader in his wheelchair was unable to move, and when the blood flowed under one of the wheels, he turned as pale as a corpse.

From the bedroom next door where Ghaalib's hostages were tied to the bed, there was the sound of crying. Only Hamid remained standing where he was, unperturbed and firm.

"The road to paradise has been paved for Ali. He faltered, and yet still I showed him mercy. Today, the doors of Jannah have been opened for him, a true son of the faith," said Ghaalib.

"He was one of your best men, Ghaalib!" screamed Jasmin, one of the two converts.

She would be the one ordered to remove the blood and clean up after this mess.

Ghaalib put the gun back in his inside pocket and turned his back on them.

Now there were only ten of them left in the group including himself. Still enough to do untold damage.

41

Assad

Assad was tormented by doubt.

Was he doing the right thing? He hadn't been able to think about anything else over the last few hours.

"Should I go through with this, Carl?" he had asked.

"Do you have any choice?" Carl had answered.

"Choice? We're here, and Ghaalib is in Berlin."

"We don't know that for sure, Assad."

"I have contacts in the city. I could go there and set them to work."

"Are you talking about people in the underworld?" Carl shook his head.

"I'm talking about people I've met here and there over the years, yes."

"Do you think Ghaalib would expose himself so much that it would be of any help?"

"I don't know."

"Then I think you should go through with it. If he wants to have his revenge, he'll turn up sooner or later where you are. We simply need something to go on, Assad. Maybe it's a bad bet, but do you want to take the chance and leave it?"

"Can you hear me, Assad?"

Assad nodded and gave the thumbs-up to Herbert Weber's man who was standing at the other end of the room. The earpiece was so small that it was a wonder it didn't get lost inside his ear; it was amazing what these intelligence people could come up with.

"Don't take any chances. Got it?"

Herbert Weber was standing in front of him pointing his finger like an old schoolteacher, but apart from his own pathetic life, Assad knew what was at stake, so he nodded.

"If you're killed, Ghaalib won't postpone the terrorism he has planned any longer. You know that, right?"

Assad nodded again. That was probably his best life insurance, unless Ghaalib turned up in person.

"Look carefully at these photos we took yesterday. If Ghaalib has decided that you should be killed, which you doubt, you can see here that there are lots of windows surrounding the park from which a sniper could easily hit you, so we're taking all that into account."

Assad scanned the facades of the houses that surrounded the little park. Curtains everywhere. Curtains, reflections, plant pots. More apartment buildings to the east, all five or six stories high with balconies and low brick parapets on top. Who in their right mind could claim that they could take all that into account in this enormous shooting gallery? There could already be a couple of Ghaalib's fanatic followers up there with rifles. Maybe there were already some lifeless bodies up in the flats—people who had trusted the person who rang their bell.

Taking all that into account, as Weber had put it. He was obviously aspiring to win a prize for the most understated comment of the year.

"I can see that you're skeptical, Assad, and I appreciate that. But we've been to all the flats, so relax; they're all being watched. We've placed five snipers in various flats, and I strongly doubt you'd be able to spot them even if you tried."

"Are we planning to bring any potential assassin in alive?" asked Carl.

Weber pointed at Assad. "That all depends on this man. We have to assume that an assassin is on a suicide mission. If things come to a head, it will be difficult, especially if the attacks come from all sides at once."

"I know the expression in a man's eyes right before he blows himself up," said Assad. "I'll bring him down before he gets to that point."

But Assad was lying. He knew nothing, because no two people who were prepared to meet their death reacted the same. He had seen people do it, but only from a distance. Always from a distance, and it was terrifying, senseless, and evil.

"What about the square, the parked cars, and the trees?" asked Carl.

Assad smiled at him. They were redundant concerns but touching all the same.

The time was precisely ten minutes to eight when Assad crossed Bruchstrasse and walked across Gutzkowstrasse toward the path that cut through the former graveyard that was now a park.

As Weber had predicted, there was nothing to indicate that there were five competent men behind windows keeping an eye on proceedings through a sight.

There was sluggish morning traffic all around. People obviously weren't in a hurry even though the working spirit in this mercantile city normally required an almost warlike bustle twenty-four/seven.

"It's just us cruising around, so stay calm," explained the voice in his earpiece.

Assad was calm. With so many of Weber's men in play just now, Assad almost felt sorry for the man or men whom Ghaalib had sent on the mission. But only almost.

"Slow it down a bit, Assad," continued the voice. "There's a man coming from behind. In a moment he'll have cleared Bruchstrasse. We're keeping a close eye on him."

Assad held his watch up in front of his eyes as if he wanted to check the time. Sure enough, in the reflection of the clock face, he saw the outline of a person behind him walking at a quick pace.

In twenty-five meters, I'll be within shooting range, he thought, and stopped. The gun in his jacket pocket could be drawn in seconds; he had practiced all last night. A quick turn and he would have to aim and shoot at the man's shoulder. First the right and then the left.

Now the figure had reached the corner of Gutzkowstrasse. He stood still for a moment.

"Is he reaching for something?" he asked the man in his earpiece.

"I can't tell." He shouted out in the room and was back a second later. "My colleagues say he's looking around. Now he's heading right. He seemed to just be unsure what way to go. We've got him covered."

"Even though there isn't a single leaf left on the trees, I can't get an overview of the whole park from where I'm standing."

"No, but we see you. Don't look up, but there's a drone above you."

"Get rid of it. If there's anything that sets alarm bells ringing, it's those bloody things."

"It's three hundred meters up, so don't worry! In a moment, a cyclist will cycle through the park from the direction of Schifferstrasse. He's one of ours, so just let him pass. He's monitoring all movements in the park."

"Are you allowed to cycle here?"

"No idea, but I think so. Who cares? Make out like you're going to go to the toilet, Assad. You can see it, right? Just to your left."

"Yeah. And I can see the playground behind it. I can hear a child playing, but I can't see anyone. Have you made sure there's no one there?"

There was a rustling sound in the background. They had, but obviously not thoroughly enough.

"Get that kid out of here before I come out from the toilet, all right?"

"Hey, something's happening, stay outside. Can you see the car approaching from the west via Gutzkowstrasse? It's moving pretty fast. A bit too fast, in my opinion."

Assad turned when he heard the car brakes screeching. A man jumped out, stood completely still, and looked over at the park. Apart from the windbreaker, he was dressed exactly like a Middle Eastern peasant. Wide, baggy trousers that stopped just above his ankles, so they were halal and in accordance with the regulations. The kufi on his head was white, and his shoes were pointy with a slightly upturned end.

Assad kept a firm grip on his gun.

"He's coming now——" the voice in his earpiece managed to say before a shot made Assad flinch and all the birds in the trees took to the sky. He didn't see where the shot had come from, but he did see a shower of glass fall from a window in the closest of the large white houses to his right.

"Damn it," said the voice in his earpiece. "We have a man down." There was a noise of intense commotion in the background. And when he heard the sound of another shot and yet another shower of glass, he instinctively spun around just in time to see his attacker only ten meters from him with his gun in the air and his kufi falling to the ground.

The guy pressed the trigger on his gun a couple of times, but both times it just clicked. Then he threw it on the ground, and when there were only a few meters between them, he pulled out a knife that was so long it was hard to understand how he could have concealed it.

Assad's shot hit him in the neck, but it didn't bring the man down. However, the shot that came from above and hit him straight in the head did.

"Are there any more like him on the way?" he shouted, but there was no reaction from his earpiece.

Assad stood still. A child was screaming in the playground, and it wasn't of the attention-seeking sort.

"Hello, what's going on?" he shouted as he flipped the body onto its back with his foot. He wasn't very old, and his eyes were still open.

There was a clattering sound in his earpiece. The voice was different, and it sounded like it was in shock.

"Get out of there, Assad. It isn't safe."

"But the child. What's going on?"

"There isn't a child over there. It's just some kids playing in Danneckerstrasse—a side street just across from the park. One of them fell and took a tumble on the concrete, that's all."

That's all! It had been enough to cause him to momentarily lose his concentration. They should have secured that street much better.

Assad slipped behind a tree. "Who shot? Where did it come from exactly?"

"We don't know. That's why we want to get you out of there."

"Why am I not talking to the same guy as before?"

"Because he's dead, Assad. Both him and his partner were hit. I'm in the room looking at them. They're dead."

Assad was in shock. The man he had just been communicating with had been killed. *Don't worry,* he had said only moments before. Why hadn't he said *Better safe than sorry* and acted accordingly?

Then there was a sound of a third shot, and this time the projectile hit Assad's shadow on the gravel. Right in the region of his heart.

There couldn't be a clearer signal of what sort of opponent they were dealing with.

Assad scanned the buildings to the west of the park.

"Are you going to do anything about the shooter?" he asked the new man in his earpiece.

"There are people on their way."

He stood there undeterred. All around him, the sound of police sirens and commotion. Weber's men and the local police, all in bulletproof vests, were already storming the building from which the shot had presumably been fired.

After more than two hours, the emergency was called off.

Herbert Weber looked almost as shocked as Carl when they left their positions at the hotel. Carl had a water bottle ready, and Weber's expression was one of both apology and suffering.

"We didn't get him, Assad. We found a couple of things on the floor: his cartridge cases and an aluminum blister pack like the ones tablets come in. That's it. We don't know how he managed to avoid our team, but the theory is that he's been there for days and that he actually greeted those in the team who went around checking the area."

"The owners of the flat have been away for at least ten days according to the neighbors, and they hadn't heard a sound from inside before the shots," added Carl. He passed Assad the water bottle and placed his hand on his shoulder.

"I'm glad you're unscathed, Assad. But, as you know, two of Weber's men were unfortunately killed, and the regrettable news won't go unnoticed. We think the killings today were intentional, with the aim of shaking security and safety all over Germany." He pointed up to the hotel. "As you can see, Schifferstrasse has been totally cordoned off, otherwise we'd have a horde of journalists on top of us."

Assad looked at the body. The blood around it had already turned dark.

"I'm so terribly sorry for your men and their families," Assad said to Weber. "But we should have anticipated something like this happening to give the young man lying here cover to carry out his mission."

Weber nodded. "I didn't tell you how many cartridges we found in the flat where the shooter was positioned."

"There were presumably three," guessed Assad. "The two that killed your men and the one that hit my shadow."

Surprisingly, Weber shook his head.

It was Carl who spoke. "They found four cartridges. It was the same shooter who shot the assassin in the head."

Assad fixed his gaze on the man lying next to him. He felt like he couldn't breathe.

"Yes, we think the shooter doubted whether your shot to the assassin's throat would stop him. The rest of us weren't in any doubt, just so you know," said Weber.

"It's unforgivable! They killed their own man!" said Carl.

Assad looked at the body. The shot to his temple was on the left side, so it had come from the same direction as the shots that were fired at the white buildings on the other side of the park, and which had killed Weber's men.

Carl's gaze lingered on the body. "He isn't very old," he said.

"No. I don't think he can be even twenty," said Assad.

What a waste of life.

Carl looked concerned. "If he'd been wearing an explosive vest, you wouldn't have lived to tell the tale. It obviously wasn't what Ghaalib wanted. And he definitely didn't want the sniper to finish you off because he had more than enough opportunity when you entered the park."

Assad shook off the thought. "May I?" he asked.

Weber nodded and handed him a pair of rubber gloves.

"I assume you're thinking the same as me that it couldn't have been a coincidence that his gun misfired both times?" he asked, and squatted down by the body.

"Hey, what's the story down there?" shouted Weber to the men who were already inspecting the weapon.

"The firing pin has been filed," one of them shouted back.

"You see, Assad? Ghaalib didn't want him to kill you."

Assad understood all too well. He carefully unzipped the dead man's windbreaker and saw a shirt that looked so brand-new and creaseless that it made him think it was straight out of the package. He had really prepared himself for paradise, and now there was one more mother who would be left crying.

"He has a wallet in his inside pocket," said Assad, and handed it to Weber, who took it with slightly trembling hands. In a short while, when he had to give an explanation for the course of events, he would be lambasted as the man who would have to take responsibility for the death of two of his own men.

"His driving license has him down as being nineteen years old and two days; it was his birthday the day before yesterday," said Weber. "It's sad to think that he didn't get much use out of his driving license; he had actually only had it for four months. Here's his card for the library a couple of streets from here. His name is Mustafa." He handed the wallet to a forensic technician. "We'll do everything we can to find out how such a young man got himself involved in something so desperate."

Another couple of forensic technicians arrived, and the deceased's pockets were painstakingly emptied and their contents placed on a plastic cover on the ground. A white pocket handkerchief, a letter from the municipality, twenty-five euros in notes and coins, keys that he would never need again. And then there was a note.

> *Congratulations on keeping your life.*
>
> *Next stop is Berlin. Keep an eye on all the green and open squares, especially where the pigeon flies low. And be aware, Zaid, that you haven't got much time. I'll be seeing you.*

"The pigeon?" Weber shook his head. "Is that a symbolic reference to the young man?"

"What do you mean?" asked one of his team.

"Wasn't the poor boy just a carrier pigeon sent to deliver a message, and with his life as the postage? How cynical is this Ghaalib bastard?"

Assad took a deep breath. Maybe now they understood what they were up against. Pure evil, nothing less.

He stared at the note for a long time.

"Haven't got much time"!

And Berlin was so immensely big.

42

Rose

While Rose and Marcus Jacobsen dug deeper into the story behind the Latin motto *Perseverando* on the Internet, Gordon was busy on his computer.

"I've sent the sketch of the boy to the boarding school in Bagsværd," he said. "Let's hope it pays off."

Rose was certain. "My intuition tells me we've got the right place. Isn't the expression 'Through Persistence,' *Perseverando,* what the boy bases his entire existence on? His persistence alone in reaching the twenty-one hundred and seventeen victories in his game tells us that. And the boy clearly knows the meaning of the word, so he has some form of upbringing. The boarding school in Bagsværd has the Latin word as its motto; there has to be a connection."

"Can't we find out what game he's playing and from there deduce where he bought it?" asked Marcus Jacobsen.

Gordon sighed. "When it comes to getting hold of software today, the most normal thing is to download the game from one platform or another. I think it'd be hopeless trying to find him that way, not least because we don't have much time. When you think about what sort of a person he is, it's unlikely that the game is a typical multiplayer game like Counter-Strike or other games like that. And also, he could've acquired the game a long time ago. I've asked some gaming experts and PC nerds, but unfortunately, they didn't have any ideas about how we could find out where he got it from."

"It's a shooting game, right? But could there be melee weapons in the game, like a samurai sword?" continued Marcus.

"Doubtful. Knives, perhaps, but not samurai swords or we're looking at a totally different kind of game. Onimusha, which was a PS2 game, for example."

"'PS'?" said Marcus blankly.

Gordon smiled. The generation gap was shining through. "PS! It stands for PlayStation, Marcus!"

"Okay." He shrugged. "You can tell I'm out of my comfort zone here. But I do know that we should ask the people in charge of the cell towers to help us. I know that it probably won't get us anywhere, if only due to the prepaid cards and the short time he's on the line, but I'll ask our colleagues in PET to see what they can do."

"Yes, maybe we could find a location within a few hundred meters. At least then we'd know what residential area he's calling from," said Gordon.

But Rose knew it was wishful thinking.

An hour after the chief of homicide had left them, they received a call from a member of the administrative team at the boarding school in Bagsværd. She was friendly and competent, had done everything she should to the letter, but the answer was disappointing.

"Just to be sure, you say he's twenty-two years old?"

"Yes," answered Rose.

"Right, because it's obviously important for us to know if it's likely that the current teaching staff at the school might have had him in their classes."

"Well, that is his age."

"Then I'm afraid that my answer will disappoint you, because none of the teachers recognized the boy in your e-mail. It perplexes us, of course, that he would use our motto in that way, but it has to be a no. The boy didn't attend this school."

After she hung up, Rose went through the list of swear words that best described her current frustration. It was a very long list.

"I've checked, and there aren't any other education institutions that use the word *perseverando* in any significant context," said Gordon.

"Significant context"! What a stupid thing to say. She would give him bloody significant contexts.

"We'll just have to wait for him to call again and ask him where he got the expression from," he continued with some misgiving. Weren't people's lives still at risk?

Waiting and waiting, thought Rose. *Is that ever a suitable tactic when the hourglass is running out?*

"Just a second, Gordon; I've got an idea," said Rose. "You've spoken about the case with Mona, so I'm going to give her a call. If anyone can help us develop this boy's profile, it's her."

She dialed the internal number for Psychology at HQ, but apparently there was no one in the office.

"Doesn't she have office hours now, Gordon?"

He looked in his notebook and nodded. "Try her at home; maybe she left early today," he suggested.

Rose called Mona's home number, but it wasn't Mona who answered. The voice was too harsh, and Rose didn't recognize it.

"Mathilde speaking," someone answered amid a cacophony of shouting in the background. "Shut up for a minute, Ludwig and Hector," she shouted to no avail.

"You're speaking with Rose Knudsen from police headquarters. Can I speak with Mona?"

"No, she was admitted to Rigshospitalet this morning."

Rose was taken aback; it was a dry delivery for such a serious message.

"Admitted? I'm sorry to hear that. May I ask who you are?"

"Typical that my mom hasn't told anyone that she has a daughter called Mathilde. A bit unfortunate for me, isn't it?"

"I'm sorry. I'm not very close with your mother. We have more of a professional relationship. I hope it isn't anything serious."

"It's serious enough when a fifty-one-year-old gets herself pregnant and can hardly hold on to the kid."

Rose pictured Carl. This was going to be difficult for him.

"She hasn't lost the baby, has she?"

"If only. I'm not ready to have a half sister or half brother at thirty-three. What do you think? Do you know where I'm coming from?"

I'm saying nothing, you little cow, thought Rose. "What ward has she been admitted to?" she asked.

"Not the fertility ward, that's for sure." She laughed hoarsely. "And shut up, Ludwig and Hector, or go outside."

Rose found Mona pale and with transparent skin in the room farthest down the corridor in the gynecological ward of the hospital.

"Rose, is that you? That's so sweet of you," she said.

Rose watched as her eyes looked her up and down, but Rose didn't care. It was a good two years since they had seen each other, more than enough time to have piled on an extra twenty kilos. Who wouldn't notice that?

"Are you okay?" asked Rose.

"You're asking if I'm going to lose the baby?"

Rose nodded.

"The next few days will tell. How did you know I was here? Mathilde didn't call you, did she?"

"Oh, you mean that loving and caring daughter who's putting her gentle touch to good use looking after Ludwig and his friends?"

Mona chuckled. So, she wasn't completely dispirited.

"No, I called you at home to establish a psychological profile, but I won't bother you with that just now, although it is a bit pressing."

"A bit?"

"Well, actually, it's very pressing."

"The boy who's been calling you. Is it him?"

Rose nodded.

After half an hour, the staff thought their patient needed to rest.

"Just another five minutes and we'll be done," said Mona to the nursing assistant, and Rose noticed that Mona was indeed in need of rest.

"You've explained what might be considered facts," said Mona. "And I can see the boy quite clearly." She tapped the sketch lying on her duvet. "And you have to ask yourself what sort of dysfunction this family has been living and breathing given that the boy killed his father in this ghastly way and is now threatening to do the same to his mother."

"Do you think he's a psychopath or just generally mentally ill?"

"Hmm, not a psychopath in the traditional sense, even though his total lack of empathy could hint at that. His intention alone to hurt other people that he doesn't even know points in that direction. But a guy like him who lives in his own little world can be suffering from a myriad of psychological conditions. He's obviously very disturbed, but in many ways seems too much in control for me to call him mentally ill according to the traditional way of giving a diagnosis. He doesn't appear to be schizophrenic, but a form of paranoia and insensitivity are often seen together and can lead to unpredictable behavior. Society produces a lot of people like that these days. Egocentrism and indifference are the curses of our time."

"Hmm, I think I can sense that you already have a theory, Mona. Out with it before they tell me to leave."

She adjusted her body with some discomfort, as if lying down was giving her pain in her lower back.

"Listen! I can also come back tomorrow if that's better, Mona. Just let me know."

"No, no, I'm fine." She reached for the water glass and moistened her lips a little. Then she smiled and placed her hand on her stomach.

"I think it will be all right. It *has* to be!"

"Shall I say anything to Carl?"

"Not now. But if this drags out, I'd like him to come home."

"Okay."

"But to get back to my theory: You're right, I do actually have a feeling about this. Have you thought about when a normal twenty-two-year-old man uses an expression like *Perseverando* or *Perseverance*?"

"He never does."

"Exactly. Unless he uses it when he's being playful. Out of mischief. And he would only do that if he felt free and on top of things. Do you follow?"

"I'm not sure. Do you mean that it might not be his own expression?"

"It *is* his own expression, but it isn't a boarding school that has pushed it on him. It's his parents. I would guess that he's an only child and that his mother, or more likely his father, has had high expectations for him during his childhood, which has made him feel trapped and caused him to hate the world around him."

Rose was following now, and with good reason. "Of course, it's the father who has beaten it into him. 'Stick to it, boy, keep going, never give up,' and all that shit. I know exactly what you're talking about."

Mona looked at her for a long time without saying anything because she knew what Rose was thinking. Rose hadn't fared well living in her father's shadow either, and it had had fatal consequences.

Mona took a deep breath. "Exactly. That's my theory. It's the boy's father who grew up with that virtuous word, and later in life he expected the same from his son as had been expected of him. And the boy disappointed him because he couldn't live up to the expression *Perseverando,* which in turn developed into disrespect and disfunction between them. That's my guess."

"So, the father could be the one who went to the boarding school in Bagsværd?"

"Yes, I think so."

"Well, that doesn't make our search any easier, Mona. I mean, who is the father? It could be any man from around forty-two upward who has gone to the school. We're talking about two hundred people or more. I haven't checked how many pupils they have in each year group."

"I know, so you can't take that route because there simply isn't enough time. But you can confront the guy with the profile I've given you."

"How?"

"Tell him that you know his father went to Bagsværd and that you're closing in on his identity. And that you understand how hard his upbringing must have been with a father like him. That it must have been really sad and lonely because he had no siblings who could act as buffers, and that you know his mother never stood up for him when his father came with his constant demands."

She considered her reasoning before continuing.

"Remember to tell him that there will be extenuating circumstances if he turns himself in, and especially if he's had such a harsh background with psychological terror, and that he should release his mother immediately to show his willingness to find a peaceful resolution. Don't let him be in any doubt that you don't have the least sympathy for his father and that he's the bad guy in every scenario. Maybe it'll be enough to save his mother and anyone else he might take his anger out on."

"What about the victim on his wall? What do you think triggered that?"

"I think it's indignation toward indifference. All the indifference and animosity he has experienced and exhibits himself to other individuals, he uses as a sort of weapon when he chooses to punish a boundless and great indifference: the one humanity itself is guilty of."

"Wow," said Rose.

"Yes, but on the other hand, it could also be that victim twenty-one seventeen reminds him of someone or other he used to like. But I think you've got enough to loosen him up. And if it works, I know that you and the team are the best people to make something of it."

"We'll do our best. Thanks, Mona. Can I do anything for you?"

She nodded. "You can look after Ludwig. Will you do that for me? Mathilde has the same way of taking care of Ludwig as a sand tiger shark that not only eats its young but actually hunts and eats its own siblings while it's still in the womb. Mathilde has no motherly instincts. So, what do you say?"

Rose gulped. This was something of a shock, and one she had to find a solution to on the spot because Ludwig was a real terror who could destroy her apartment in a matter of seconds.

"And you can stay at my place, Rose."

Rose gulped again. This was more than she was comfortable with.

"You know what, Mona," she said. "I have a better idea. I'll get Gordon to pick him up from school and he can stay with him."

This would end up costing her a fuck or two.

43

Joan

Even though it was conducted without words, it was the morning prayer that woke him. Always at the same time, always controlled. Perhaps that was what scared him most about his captors. The total discipline concerning their faith. It controlled their lives and thoughts in a way he couldn't understand. Sometimes he actually envied them. In Barcelona, the priest in charge of his religious formation hadn't instilled in him the collective foundation that a true Catholic should have.

The sounds emanating from the living room next to his room expressed the opposite. A common spirit that embraced them all as equals, which gave them hope of a paradise in the next life and made life on this pitiful earth bearable.

He turned his face to the man who had been charged with changing his nappy and tried to express a little gratitude even though the humiliation of it all made it difficult.

"You will be coming in to join us in a moment," said the guy, who also gave him his usual injection. He stood for a moment squinting his eyes and waiting for the sneeze he knew was coming, before it suddenly exploded. Then he took a tissue from his pocket, blew his nose, and left.

Joan struggled with the gaffer tape, as he had done countless times over the last few days in the precious minutes before his body was again paralyzed. And he regretted it every time. Not only were his wrists red and raw, but now the sores were beginning to get infected.

After half a minute, the injection kicked in, and Joan's head fell to one side. He could feel the pull of his neck muscles, but he had no control over them.

The prayer rugs were rolled up and stored along the skirting as Joan was rolled in. Everyone was ready and expectant when Ghaalib walked into the spacious living room of the Berlin apartment accompanied by Hamid.

"Today, we will have our first dress rehearsal. We don't know yet when the show will play out, but the more we practice, the better the final result. And we want a well-executed group effort, don't we?"

Everyone nodded. The bloodstain on the rug in front of them left them in no doubt that working with this group wasn't without its dangers.

The doors to the dining room were opened and two more wheelchairs were pushed into the middle of the room.

The two women from the beach in Ayia Napa had visibly aged since they had stood screaming as the body of victim 2117 was dragged ashore.

The older was now so pacified that her mouth gaped open all the time, with a couple of worn-down old teeth sticking out. *I could end up looking like that if they use me long enough,* he thought, but inside he was shaking his head. It was stupid to think he would live long enough for that to happen. Wasn't this charade the overture to his demise? He was sure of it.

He tried with all his might to smile at the younger one, but he couldn't. She looked so dejected in her thin dress with fear in her eyes.

What have you seen, girl? he thought as he heard a sound coming from one of the doors that led into the room.

It sounded like wheels that needed to be oiled. Everyone turned to the side door as it was opened. It was the Swiss woman, and a sigh of surprise, perhaps even relief, spread through the group.

Two of the men even clapped when an emaciated young woman with an elongated birthmark on her cheek was pushed in by a young man whom Joan had never seen before. He looked to Joan like a young boy, not even eighteen. He smiled gently as he entered, and he appeared a little distant. Perhaps the poor boy didn't know what he was walking into.

"Now our wheelchair parade is complete. And let me present Afif; he's a good boy, although a little slow." Ghaalib smiled tenderly. What was going on? It was very surprising. The way they looked at each other seemed so loving, so intimate and strangely divorced from everything else that was going on. Joan couldn't quite put his finger on it. But it was something important.

"Afif won't be taking part in our preparations, but he's a good person to have with us in the end. Gentle in looks and nature. Who could suspect a group of plotting something with a boy like him with them?"

Then there was a sound of whimpering that silenced everyone. It was the moment the three women saw one another. Even though the latest arrival was also paralyzed, all the injections in the world couldn't control the agitation that brought forth a flood of tears. Even the two other women in wheelchairs looked like this was the answer to their prayers. As if their bodies could now surrender themselves to death, and the gaze between them had been the lifeline each of them had been missing. The lifeline they were resigned to having severed at the same time.

The whimpering did not subside, but Ghaalib ignored it.

"As you can see, we have reunited the Zaid al-Asadi family, so we now have four powerless people in wheelchairs, each with their own mission. The younger daughter, Ronia al-Asadi, who is among us for the first time, has been with Afif for a couple of months now. And the wheelchair, designed for the purpose, was in the box at the back of our bus from Frankfurt."

A couple of them moved closer, and one of them squatted and caressed the brown box under the seat.

"Our clever friend here with a slight cold, Osman, has quite rightly noticed that this is no ordinary electric wheelchair battery. As you have no doubt already surmised, Ronia will be totally unable to maneuver it herself, so Afif will be pushing her from behind, because the wheelchair actually has *no* battery whatsoever." He laughed momentarily.

"Afif, you can go to your room now," he said, still with a certain warmth in his voice.

The young man mechanically patted Ronia on the cheek a couple of times. He didn't seem right in the head. Then he trudged away.

"Hamid will be able to detonate the contents of the box via remote control, so there's nothing new there," continued Ghaalib. "What is new is that the explosion is two-part. Firstly, the back of the chair will explode, followed shortly after by the box under the seat."

Joan looked with terror at the two other women in wheelchairs. A mother and two daughters who hadn't seen one another for a long time. But had their initial whimpering been relief that the younger one was still alive? Or were the weak sounds they were emitting more an expression of indescribable horror?

Joan looked again at the younger one. Her agitated heart was pumping so fast that even from a distance of several meters, he could see the pulse in her neck beating like a piston in an engine.

Then Hamid stepped forward and positioned himself in front of Ronia's wheelchair.

"You need to look at it like this: This is no ordinary suicide mission, which you might otherwise have thought. You won't be kitted out with explosive vests, and you won't be blowing yourselves up with hand grenades. We'll show the world how a real holy warrior takes their destiny in their own hands and demonstrates courage and determination."

Arabic phrases resounded in the room, and many of the people present bowed to Hamid. Proud faces turned to one another, and a couple of them looked up to the ceiling with their index finger raised.

Hamid turned to the woman and pulled up her dress; underneath she was so emaciated that her body almost disappeared into the seat.

Then Hamid's figure blocked Joan's view, but he clearly heard the metallic rustling.

"Here," said Hamid, and turned around. "Here is one of the weapons concealed by Ronia's dress."

He held up a small hand weapon.

"I can see you smiling. You're right, it's ironic that we've chosen one of the Jews' most evil and effective weapons, but the Micro Uzi nine-millimeter class three is a masterpiece perfectly suited for our purpose. Weighing in at only one and a half kilos and sixty centimeters in length, it's capable of discharging hundreds of shots per minute with a good level of accuracy within a one-hundred-meter distance. This is the weapon with which each of you will shortly familiarize yourselves. A couple of you have used it before, so you can bring the others up to speed."

Joan looked down. In his head, he had registered his hands shaking uncontrollably, but when he looked at them, they were completely still.

Hamid blew his nose. "You all know what you're wearing, so we don't need to go over that. But we need to hand out these."

He fetched a canvas sack, which had been leaning against the wall, and opened it.

"These bulletproof vests are of the finest quality, and when you notice how thin they are and how easily they can be hidden under your clothes, you can't help but respect EnGarde Body Armor for the Executive model. It's actually so well designed that you'd think it was a waistcoat from a regular black suit."

The group clapped again.

"There's even one for you, Joan Aiguader." He threw it in front of Joan's wheelchair.

"I can see your confusion, but the time has come for us to tell you your role. It isn't our intention for you to die in this operation. We'll place you at a distance from the bombing, and you'll be the first journalist in the history of the world who not only is a witness to the preparations of a terrorist act but has a front-row seat so you can describe how it was carried out. This time the world won't just see pictures of blood and body parts spread across the rubble in the hours following; no, the world will see everything through you, and you will be interviewed about it, and you'll write about it again and again."

With this harsh and cynical information, Joan's mind was filled with thoughts he couldn't process. It was so terrifying and yet a relief at the same time. He would live, and his heart pumped an extra beat, but the price was that he would have to live the rest of his life with the most horrendous images etched into his mind. Joan knew straightaway that when it happened, he would never be the same again. How could he carry on living when he knew not only that people would imminently die but that he would have to watch, hear the screams, see flesh torn apart, and be totally helpless to do anything about it?

Then Hamid produced a GoPro head-strap camera, of the sort used by the best-paid journalists at *Hores del dia* when they were reporting, and placed it on Joan's head.

"Neat, isn't it?" he said to the smiling faces around him. "Joan's innocent face and apparent disability and a sweet little camera on his head is almost touching. Just imagine how the people pushing the four wheelchairs will be met with respect and sympathy."

Hamid laughed and turned to Ghaalib.

"And then there are the last two vests. Will you fill us in on those, Ghaalib?"

He smiled again in a context where no smile should ever be seen. Joan was so enraged, his empathy for humanity so incensed, that he wished he could put his fingers in his ears and escape from this horrifying tableau.

"Thank you, Hamid," said Ghaalib. "The last two vests are for Marwa al-Asadi and her daughter Nella. Traditional explosive vests that can be detonated with a remote control, but very cleverly using the same remote as the one for Ronia's explosive charge. First, the explosive device in the back of Ronia's chair will be detonated, followed forty seconds later by Nella's, and then twenty seconds later by Marwa's."

Joan was about to be sick. Despite their paralysis, the expression in the three women's eyes was so terror stricken that Joan feared one of them would have a heart attack. Tears were streaming down their faces, and their eyes were blinking rapidly. They were no longer whimpering; they had no energy left even for that. It was so abominable and heartless that they were forced to listen to all this evil. Their anxiety must have been eating them alive.

"I can see that you all understand why we're doing it this way. You'll all have time to shoot and seek cover away from the wheelchair in question, and if things go as planned, many of you will come out of this alive, maybe even all of you. The road to paradise will be longer, but if you live to take part in our next mission, the glory and honor will be so much the greater. Inshallah."

Several people clapped again, but the Swiss woman stepped forward. She looked questioningly at Ghaalib.

"Who will be covering us when the bombs are detonated if we're all going in different directions? Shouldn't we plan a formation or all take cover in one place?"

He nodded in recognition. "Good idea, but no. We've taken every possibility into account, and the risk for each of you is less if you spread out. We have a fantastic sniper with us who will cover you. We actually used him in Frankfurt, and he more than proved his skill. You don't know him and you won't meet him, but he's already taken up his position at the appointed place today, so he's ready. And if you have any concerns about him being discovered before we arrive, let me assure you that he's the whitest convert you can imagine. The Captain, as he's known, was trained in Pakistan and has been in the field for the last three years."

Now everyone applauded like crazy while Joan's heart pounded blood to his dead limbs so hard that it hurt and caused his cheeks to burn. It was all so terrible, so unbelievably evil, that he hoped they would accidentally give him an overdose the next time they injected him. He simply didn't know if he could carry on living with all this.

Fate would have been so much more merciful if he hadn't discovered the TV crew down on the beach in Barcelona.

44

Carl

A group of forensic technicians were preoccupied with the bus parked across several parking spaces in the lot opposite the playground on Baerwaldstrasse in Berlin. They were turning the bus inside out and throwing the contents on the road: seats, luggage racks, the chemical toilet, a large box found by the rear window, apple cores, napkins, absolutely everything that wasn't nailed down or that they could dismantle.

"We'll find something that can give us a lead," the police inspector had said, but four hours later the optimism was waning.

When Herbert Weber had been awoken in his hotel in Frankfurt around four in the morning and informed that a bus had been identified north of the old Tempelhof airfield, and that it definitely was the one with the U-lift, it had only taken an hour before Weber's colleagues were driving toward Berlin with all their equipment, including Assad's bag.

Twenty minutes later, Carl, Assad, Weber, and his closest assistants were going through security at Frankfurt Airport.

Now, several hours later, the team was all assembled and eyeing the various parts of the bus that were strewn like wreckage from a plane crash along most of the right-hand lane of Baerwaldstrasse from the playground and down toward Urbanstrasse.

"We have to assume that they dropped the passengers off somewhere and then the driver drove the bus here and parked it," said Weber.

Carl nodded. "I agree. If they hadn't wanted us to find it, they definitely wouldn't have parked it so conspicuously and badly. It's been parked here so that we would find it and to make us think the group is somewhere in the vicinity. Are there many immigrants in this area?"

A man decorated with distinguished chevrons introduced himself as the police inspector, as if rank or honor meant anything to Carl as long as the man answered.

"There are a significant number of immigrants, yes."

"Then I think this is the last area we should be looking for them. Think about where they were staying in Frankfurt. That wasn't exactly the most obvious place to look either."

Assad had his doubts. "But, Carl, you never know with these people. Maybe they're staying near the vehicle again because that's actually what they did in Frankfurt. Like you said, it just wasn't in the most obvious sort of residential area."

Carl looked around. It was a boring but very pleasant and peaceful neighborhood, fairly open and without too many high-rise apartment blocks.

"I don't really know the city," he said, which was something of an understatement. Berlin for him was just an impressive collection of historic monuments and phenomena like the Brandenburg Gate and Checkpoint Charlie, not forgetting massive Wiener schnitzels and barrels of beer.

"Where exactly are we?" he asked the police inspector.

He pointed around. "We're standing in Kreuzberg, an area with a lot of immigrants; farther up toward the northwest, we have Berlin Mitte; to our east Alt-Treptow; farther up, we have Pankow and Lichtenberg; and to our south, we have Neukölln, another area with a lot of immigrants. You need to understand that Berlin is a jungle where prey and predator move freely among each other in all parts of the city. It goes without saying that we'll do everything we can to find these people, but, to put it bluntly, we're not only up against the clock, we also have to contend with the jumble of ideas, ideologies, and people of all different persuasions that you'd expect to find in a city this size. It's not so much a case of finding a needle in a haystack but more like finding a grain of sand in a desert where both scorpions and snakes are waiting to strike. Getting to grips with a situation like this takes time, which is exactly what I'm led to believe we don't have."

Smart guy. "What about video surveillance?" asked Carl.

He nodded. "Look around you and notice the streets. There are far too many alleys, too few cameras, and even less time. We might catch a glimpse of them from an illegally installed camera in one of the shops, but even that will take time."

Carl sighed. "And I don't suppose it'd help to go door-to-door and see if anyone can give us a heads-up about which direction the bus came from?"

"Hopeless," said Weber, putting a damper on the idea.

"Has anyone tried to solve the riddle of the square and the low-flying pigeon?" asked Assad.

"Yes, we've got ten men working on it," said the police inspector. "All squares with a lot of pigeons are being identified. But in contrast to other large cities, Berlin doesn't actually have many pigeons."

Carl was confused. "What do you mean?"

"Yes, it surprised me too. We have a couple of amateur ornithologists on our team, and they've informed me that the pigeon population in Berlin has fallen to less than a third of what it was only twenty years ago."

"So how many are there now?" asked Carl.

"About ten thousand. Their biggest threat comes from all the building renovations. Then there's the nets, wires, and spikes on the buildings that deprive them of nesting areas."

"Have you got something against pigeons in Berlin? Too much pigeon shit?"

"Er, are you asking me personally?" asked the police inspector.

"Yes." Wasn't he looking directly at him?

"I haven't got anything against pigeons. They're only responsible for a fraction of the excrement in comparison with dogs. Twenty thousand tons of dog shit a year in a city like Berlin is far worse, in my opinion."

Carl couldn't have agreed more. In the few years when he was a community police officer, he had annoyed his colleagues with the unmistakable stench that on an almost daily basis emanated from the soles of his shoes when he was writing up his reports at the station.

"And we have a lot of goshawks in Berlin," continued the police inspector. "They also keep the pigeon population in check."

"Goshawks?" said Assad.

"Yes, we have over a hundred pairs in Berlin. It's actually very unique."

"And the hawks nest in trees, right?" Assad asked rhetorically. "Then we should ask the team to map the areas in the city with the most goshawks."

"Why?"

"If I was a pigeon and there was a hawk in the sky, I'd fly low."

An interesting but hardly useful hypothesis, thought Carl, looking at Assad with a tentative smile. He was in desperate need of encouragement just now as he sat there on a crate frantically studying a map of the city. He looked at his watch every five minutes, as if willing time to stop.

"Are you getting anywhere?" shouted the inspector to the forensic technicians.

They shook their heads.

One of the technicians approached them. "The box that was hidden behind the curtains at the back of the bus was lined with a polythene dust sheet. We found a small piece on a splinter, but the rest had been removed. We can't know exactly what was in the box, but our puffer machine has detected explosives."

If Weber was surprised, he didn't let on.

"That's obviously worrying," he said. "What about the toilet?"

"Nothing other than the usual chemicals. They presumably used the toilets at the places where they stopped."

Weber nodded to his man. "And that hasn't given any positive re-sults either, I suppose? Video surveillance? Credit card payments?"

The police inspector shook his head. "Not yet, anyway. But we've found long hairs on a couple of the seat backs. Should we send them for DNA sampling so we can compare them with the ones my colleagues found in Frankfurt?"

The police inspector looked at Weber, who was shaking his head.

"It *is* their bus, so we can guarantee that they're a match. But to be perfectly honest, what good will it do us in this situation? Oh, just go ahead and do it anyway, but we won't wait for it."

"Have you checked the area around the bus?" asked Carl. "Maybe they accidentally dropped something or threw something away that they shouldn't have."

"The only thing we've found is used tissues. I think there was also one under one of the seats. I'll just double-check with one of the others."

"Okay," said Weber. He looked at the two Danes and his assistant with an expression that tried to convey a hope that in reality was dwindling.

Then his cell phone rang.

He stood for some time leaning slightly backward with his phone to his ear and staring expressionlessly at the sky. Then he squinted and pointed upward. Carl couldn't see anything.

"Look," he said, and pointed up again when he was finished with his conversation. "There's a hawk hovering on the air current." He was smiling but then remembered what he had just heard. "Our people in Frankfurt have a picture of him."

"Of who?"

"The sniper who killed our men."

"Bloody hell, then we stand a chance of stopping him," burst out Carl.

Weber shook his head slightly. "One of the residents in the apart-ment building took it from his balcony a few days before the shooting. You can see the man's face fairly clearly as he's heading toward the hallway entrance door with a small suitcase in his hand. His face is something of a shock. It could make things complicated."

"Why?" asked Carl.

"Why? Firstly, it isn't just any man, and secondly, the photographer sold the photo to one of our commercial TV stations. So the killer's identity will shortly be all over the media and known throughout the entire country."

"Okay! Does it get any better?"

"That's a matter of opinion. The man is actually someone everyone already knows in Germany. He's a German, Dieter Baumann, and a former captain in the German army. He was stationed in Afghanistan in 2007 but was kidnapped after only nine weeks and nothing was heard from him for a long time. Not until the Afghans demanded a ten-million-euro ransom for him."

"Let me guess," said Assad. "You didn't pay."

Weber nodded. "I think they wanted to even though it would've been possible to find an amicable and cheaper solution, but when they arrived, Baumann had disappeared into thin air. It was believed that he'd been executed like so many others."

"So, in the Germans' eyes, he was a hero?" asked Carl.

"A memorial service was held for a fallen soldier unlike anything you've ever seen. And now, eleven years later, he's back."

Assad folded away the city map. "He was radicalized; it's happened before," he said. "A hero who turned out to be the opposite. It makes for good TV for the terrorists. I can see the problem."

"Apart from the fact that I'm going to be torn to shreds again in multiple interviews that I have no desire to take part in, what problem do *you* foresee?" asked Weber.

"It will create chaos and take attention away from Ghaalib," answered Assad. "If this story develops, and that depends a lot on what messages Ghaalib sends next time, everyone in Germany will be thinking about nothing except where their antihero is now. Everyone will be looking for him. You said yourself that it would complicate things, and not only are you right, but this is exactly what Ghaalib wants. The police, people on the street, everyone will be dreaming about being the one who catches the traitor. But trust me, he'll also deliver his message before they catch him."

"There's one more thing," said Weber. "We've managed to get hold of the people who rented their flat to Dieter Baumann on Airbnb. And they insist that the aluminum blister pack for tablets hasn't got anything to do with them. So it must be something Baumann threw away."

"That was a little careless of him, if you ask me. Don't you think?" asked Carl.

Weber shook his head. "I don't think so. They were very special tablets."

Assad and Carl didn't follow.

"The type of thing someone takes when they're very, very ill. Actually, normally when you haven't got much time left, I'm told."

"Are you saying he's dying?" asked Assad.

"Yes, that appears to be what he's telling us." They looked at each other for a long time.

Now there was a very dangerous man who didn't have a life here on earth worth fighting for.

Another one.

"What are you doing, Assad?"

The bench he was sitting on was freezing; Carl felt it straightaway when he sat down next to him. There was a small notebook in Assad's hands, and two of the pages were already filled with notes. The tip of Assad's pen was resting on the paper as if he was waiting to jot down the missing clues.

"Can I see? Maybe I can add some insight."

He let the notebook fall into Carl's lap, keeping his eyes fixed on the trees in front of him.

Carl read, and as he had expected, it was a summary of the factors that could identify the terrorist group before they acted.

He had written:

1. Abdul Azim/Ghaalib is the ringleader.
2. The two known women are Jasmin Curtis, Swiss, 45, and Beena Lothar, German, 48.
3. There are possibly two wheelchairs loaded with bombs.
4. Marwa al-Asadi and Nella al-Asadi are in the wheelchairs?
5. Hamid? Is he the one who hired the German photographer, Bernd Jacob Warberg, in Munich? Is he Ghaalib's right-hand man?
6. One of them has a cold and has possibly given it to several others?
7. The group are probably not dressed like fundamentalists. Are they shaved and wearing Western clothes?
8. We need to identify a square where the pigeon flies low.
9. Find a square where the pigeons somehow or other play a direct or indirect role?
10. Who recruited the killer from the park in Frankfurt? Was it Hamid?
11. Who rented the bus? Was it Hamid?
12. Who rented the house in Frankfurt? Was it Hamid?
13. Why did Dieter Baumann allow himself to be photographed?
14. Are we looking for a place where Baumann can shoot from above, just like in Frankfurt?
15. Joan Aiguader, where is he?
16. Joan Aiguader's own mobile with GPS? Where is it and why can't we pick up a signal?
17. Where in the city are there the most goshawks? Is it relevant?

They were both staring at the list and thinking the same thing: How on earth could they find a point eighteen to make all the other points superfluous? It was no easy task.

"What do you think, Assad?"

"I think all these points are important. If we can find the location where they plan to strike, we already have a lot to go on to help us identify them when they turn up to execute their plan. The more I think about it, the more certain I am that one or two of these points are more important than the others. What do you think?"

"You mean eight and nine?"

"Yes, of course. Ghaalib has given us directions himself. 'Where the pigeon flies low' is where something is going to happen. He's pushed us in that direction, and whether it turns out to be a false lead or not, one thing is for sure, it isn't without significance."

"Just a second," said Carl, and took out his phone.

"Hey, Rose," he said in as relaxed a manner as he could under the circumstances. "So, have you caught the samurai?"

Her voice was not receptive to his tone. "I'm calling about something else. And don't even dare to tell me off because I simply won't put up with it, got it?"

What in the world was going on now? Had she smashed his TV screen? Put diesel instead of regular in a work vehicle? Beaten up Gordon?

"Perhaps I should say congratulations," she continued, "but it wouldn't be appropriate. Anyway, I know, Carl. I've spoken with Mathilde."

"What do you know? Mathilde who?"

"Mona's daughter, you idiot. When I tried to call Mona, Mathilde told me that Mona is having some problems. She started bleeding yesterday on her way to work at HQ."

Carl stared at the ground as he clutched his mobile. He was shaken. All it took was a single second for darkness to descend.

"Carl, are you there?"

"Yes, yes. Where is she now? Has she lost the baby?"

"No, but she isn't doing too well. She was admitted to Rigshospitalet yesterday, and she's still there. I think you should come home now, Carl."

When she had hung up, he stood for a moment and tried to collect his thoughts.

The last few days had worn him down despite the slow pace at which things had been moving. Carl wasn't optimistic, and especially not for Assad. He had pictured everything over and over in his mind. How

Assad's self-control was at risk of slipping away and his killer instincts were activated. How everything could go wrong. And he feared the moment when the bombs might go off and he risked seeing people killed. Even though he had experienced almost everything a Danish policeman could be subjected to, he didn't know if he was ready for what might happen. Where would Assad be in two days? Three days? Four days?

Would he even be here?

Now Carl felt a weight on his chest that he had been spared for a long time. A pain he recognized straightaway. He knew why it had returned, because the worst thing at the moment wasn't that Mona was in a bad way or that they might lose their child, even though that was a devastating thought; no, the worst thing was that he momentarily felt a deep sense of relief in finding a valid reason to leave Berlin, to get away from Assad, the pressure, and all the terrible things that might happen. It was unbecoming of him to think this way, and he felt ashamed. Not a feeling in which he normally wallowed.

Without registering what he was doing, Carl lost his grip on his mobile and it fell to the ground. The pain in his chest was unbearable, and he was feeling so faint that if he wasn't careful, he would collapse.

Summoning all his energy, he raised his head and looked at Assad, who was looking at him with an expression so full of insight and understanding that it escalated his panic attack and Carl fell to his knees.

Assad was right next to him before he fell to the side.

"I think I know what's happened. Does that mean you need to go home?" he asked with a warmth in his voice that Carl didn't deserve.

Carl nodded. It was all he could manage.

45

Ghaalib

"**Our travel guide is** named Linda Schwarz, and she'll join us at this metro station."

Ghaalib pointed at the station on the map.

"We have a photo of her, and as you can see, she's almost the epitome of an Aryan. A confident, quick-witted woman with full-bodied blond hair who'll appear completely inconspicuous in this city. She works for Charlottenburg Tours, wears a smart uniform with an embroidered logo, and, of course, carries one of the obligatory black umbrellas that we're supposed to stick close to."

He passed the photo around, and everyone commented.

She was definitely a good choice.

"Yes, she'll be a perfect shield against curious looks, and she says she's looking forward to meeting the group."

There was scattered laughter.

"It isn't the first time she's been a guide for a Jewish group, but we can make sure it'll be her last."

More laughter.

He unfolded a city map on their dining table.

"Can you start filming now, Hamid? And you, Beena, push Joan over to the table so he's in the video. It'll make it easier for him to follow the events on the actual day."

"When's it going to be, Ghaalib?" one of them asked.

"You're asking something I have no control over. But I can tell you that everything is almost in place. The Captain is in town, like I said, and he's ready. He isn't very well, but he's taking his medication and feels determined. So you can rest assured that he'll see this through. We've also arranged your transport out of the city. The plan is that those of you who make it out alive will regroup later and then Hamid will drive you on to our next goal."

"So, what does the timing depend on?"

"That Zaid al-Asadi is in the right place at the right time."

"Does he know what the right place is?" asked someone else.

"If not, we'll just have to give him a helping hand. And that will be in two days at the latest. That's a promise. Shall we begin?" He glanced at the group and pointed at four of them.

"Jasmin and you three men will make up the group who meet the guide at the metro, and you have plenty of time. Pretend you've just flown in from Tel Aviv, and ask as many questions as you can think of about the places you see. Act as relaxed and happy as possible. She'll guide you through the city to the park and farther on until you arrive at the target area."

Then he turned to Fadi. "In the meantime, you'll arrive with the disability bus, and you'll have Beena with you to do the talking. Afterward, you, Beena, Osman, and Afif will each push a wheelchair into the square, and when you reach the entrance to the monument, you'll split into three groups. The first group, which is Beena and Nella, will go up the ramp and inside, and the second group, consisting of Fadi and Marwa, will follow after you, while Osman and Ronia will stop on the middle of the ramp at the base of the tower. Meanwhile, Afif will push Joan over to this corner so that they're both safe."

"What about the guide?"

"She'll introduce herself to those with the women's wheelchairs and go inside with the first group. And all you have to remember is to keep an eye on your disguises so they don't fall off. The men need to make sure their beards are secure and that the curls from your hats are sitting right. They definitely shouldn't be hanging in front of your eyes."

He noted with satisfaction that they were laughing. They understood the operation and supported it. They were more than ready to go into battle.

He turned to Jasmin and Beena. "On the way to the destination, both of you should keep in the background of your respective groups, but step forward when something practical needs to be communicated or sorted out."

He expected moderate protests from the men, but they didn't materialize. When it came to language skills, they didn't meet the standards required and they knew it.

"Then you wait for the signal, and it'll be Hamid who starts the operation. At that point, two of you, arriving via the park, will be standing in front of the monument, and two of you will be at the far end of it. When you've taken your weapons from Ronia's wheelchair, make sure you always keep a distance from those who are with the wheelchairs so you don't seem like you're together." He pointed at the map. "And once again, make sure the three women's wheelchairs are positioned here, here, and here. Nella in the tower, Marwa outside, and Ronia just here. Afif, who will be standing with Joan over in the corner, will make sure Joan's camera is on the whole time."

Hamid took the floor. "When Marwa and Nella are inside the tower, Beena and Fadi will run out. Fadi will jump from the ramp and down into the square and will be the first one to open fire, and then Beena and Osman will back him up," he said. "You all know your positions and in what direction to shoot. During the shooting, keep moving backward to your respective positions. In other words, when the bombs go off, you'll already be making your way out of there. Of course, you'll have to expect heavy shooting from guards and the police, but the Captain will make sure our losses are kept to a minimum."

Ghaalib nodded. "Yes, we know that the police and intelligence service are on our trail. They've found the bus just as we intended, so they should know a little about what lies in store, but our job is to ensure that they arrive at the chosen site as late as possible so that they'll be unprepared for the fact that we've already struck. That's one of the things we'll use Zaid al-Asadi for. If police units or a security patrol turns up while we're there, they'll be in for a nasty surprise. The more of them we take down, the more the media will go crazy."

46

Assad

When Carl left in the taxi, Assad knew that he was now ready for anything. If he had to lose his life to save his family, then that was the way it had to be. All the pain and misfortune his actions had caused had a consequence, and Assad wasn't afraid of death. He just didn't want to die alone; Ghaalib would have to follow him.

Now he was sitting in his premium room on the fourth floor of the Meliá hotel, staring out the panoramic window at Berlin's sea of flickering lights. Somewhere out there among the mass of houses and apartment complexes, Marwa and Nella were feeling alone and scared.

Did they know that he was alive and looking for them? He hoped they did. Maybe it would give them a little hope.

All the parts of his weapons were spread out, waiting to be reassembled. His summary of the situation was also lying on top of the duvet. He had gone over the list at least ten times, and now it was beginning to worry him. If he didn't come up with an answer to points eight and nine and the area in the city where pigeons had some sort of significance, there wasn't much hope.

Assad was desperate. Where was the end, and where should he begin?

His attention was still drawn to the empty space where number eighteen would be, and he imagined that it was a common denominator for several of the other points. If he could use this point to pursue a definite link backward based on the facts he had listed, it would be like finding the end in a pile of tangled wires and slowly unraveling the knot.

Assad looked at his watch. It was after midnight, and he hadn't felt so alone in a long time. Carl was in Copenhagen, and Herbert Weber was staying in a room a couple of floors above him and was probably still indignant over the hardhanded treatment he had received from the media when they discovered the story about the convert Dieter Baumann and the murder of Weber's two men in Frankfurt.

Assad rubbed his face and tried to wake up a little. Why the hell did Carl have to let him down like this? He understood why he was worried, of course, but couldn't he have waited until he knew how bad the situation actually was? Who was he supposed to discuss things with now?

He began reassembling a couple of his best weapons while staring out over the Spree River, the lifeblood of Berlin, which quietly flowed past the hotel through Germany's most important city. Had they simply become a flock of bleating sheep dancing to Ghaalib's tune since they arrived here? That bastard!

Assad lay on his back on his prayer rug and stared up at the ceiling. The standstill of the last few days had drained him. If things continued in this vein, the catastrophe would happen without their being able to do anything. He had to make sure something changed. But how could he find the loose end in this jumble of wires?

He closed his eyes and let a sea of questions wash over him. An obvious loose end that stuck out was why Ghaalib had chosen Berlin as his target. Was it merely because it was the country's largest and most important city? The capital that had suffered so much? The world-famous city that would have the eyes of the world media on it if it was once again hit by an act of terrorism? Or did Ghaalib have a special connection to the city?

He shook his head. That wasn't the most obvious answer.

After yet another thirty minutes of futile analysis and consideration of his list, he finally made the decision to fill in point eighteen with the words: *"Hamid probably recruited Mustafa in Frankfurt. But how? Find out."*

Then his watch vibrated to let him know his smartphone was ringing.

"Are you awake?" asked Carl in his typical way. What sort of question was that to ask when someone had actually answered the phone?

"No, I was sleeping like Cinderella, Carl, what did you expect?"

"You mean Sleeping Beauty, Assad. Cinderella doesn't make any sense. How are you? Have you cracked anything?"

"I feel sick, and maybe I am. How's Mona?"

"I didn't manage to make it to the hospital before she'd gone to sleep, but she isn't doing well. She might lose the baby, but they're doing everything they can to stabilize her condition. It's too early to predict the outcome." He didn't say anything for a long time, and it was the sort of pause that didn't invite interruptions. "I'm really sorry, Assad," he eventually continued. "If there's good news about Mona tomorrow or the day after, I'll be straight back down there. I promise."

Assad didn't comment. The day after tomorrow was so far in the future that it might not even exist.

"I think Hamid is the key," said Assad to change the subject.

"Hamid? Talk me through it."

"There seem to be so many points on the list that link back to him. Like you noticed on the video from Munich, he looks very different from your typical Arab with his cropped hair and Western clothes. I actually think he lives in Germany, unlike Ghaalib. Someone must've made sure that everything went smoothly for them: renting the bus and the flat in Frankfurt, getting the group together, and finding a safe place to stay in Berlin. I'm also thinking that he must've recruited the photographer in Munich, the assassin Mustafa in Frankfurt, and the German-captain convert who killed Mustafa."

"Okay—" said Carl, and then stopped abruptly as if he had been about to say something else.

"What are you thinking?" asked Assad after half a minute's silence.

"You think Hamid could have recruited Mustafa even though he lived in Frankfurt?" Carl sounded skeptical. "Is there anything about this in the intelligence service report? It's been a day since the guy was killed, so it's probable that Weber's team have scratched the surface enough for there to be something worth reading in the report."

"I read it this afternoon but it left me none the wiser. They've questioned Mustafa's family, but they predictably didn't know anything about how he was radicalized or recruited. They said he was a totally normal boy who was led down this path out of nowhere."

"I see. Sound familiar? A totally normal boy and a couple of uncomprehending parents in shock? I think you should wake Weber and get your hands on the latest report."

"Yes, but if there's anything at all in it that would give us a definite lead, Weber's people would be following it up already."

"Of course, Assad. But Weber's team aren't you, are they?"

Another irritating pause. How was he supposed to react to them? Didn't Carl know that flattery was the food of fools?

"Regardless of what you do, look after yourself. I'll call again tomorrow. Sleep well!"

Then he hung up.

"No, I haven't gone to bed yet. Meet me on the ground floor; I'm sitting in the bar. Who can sleep after the last few days?"

Herbert Weber had sounded relatively normal on the telephone, but he reeked of alcohol and his eyes were half-closed and unable to focus when Assad found him sitting in a chair facing the street. Here was a man who had probably never experienced losing people on his watch.

"I'd like to read the report on Mustafa's parents' questioning again," said Assad.

Weber shook his head. "I don't have documents like that on me." He laughed at a pitch that wouldn't normally be ascribed to such a large man, and everyone in the bar glanced at him.

"Then who does have it?"

Weber raised a finger in the air. "One moment," he said, and fumbled clumsily in his pockets.

"Here," he said, drawling, and handed his mobile to Assad. "The code is four-three-two-one. The file is attached in Gmail under the name *qmustafa.*"

Gmail and the world's most used code! And this was the man from intelligence who was leading the investigation?

"It isn't the report, Assad. It's better. It's a video recording of the questioning. Just forward it to your e-mail address and then get me a cognac. Get one for yourself; you probably need it."

"I don't drink, Herbert, but thanks."

He transferred the file and found a secluded spot on a sofa in a corner next to the front desk.

After ten minutes, it was painful to watch the questioning, because Mustafa's parents were inconsolable. They tugged at their clothes and implored their prophet for succor in Arabic. Less than twenty minutes ago, there had been a knock at their door and then they had been informed about their beloved son's actions and death. It had been the worst moment in their lives.

Assad really wanted to fast-forward but had a feeling that the interpreter wasn't catching everything, so he listened intently instead to the parents' own words. Most of the time, the translation was a clear rendition of what the parents had said, but sometimes he spoke over their next sentence. It was clear that the interpreter was used to this sort of work because there was no visible reaction to the parents' emotional state. When the parents stuttered their love and sorrow, he left it out and only repeated what hadn't been said previously. So it wasn't hard to understand why Weber's men also weren't particularly affected.

When they came to the question of whom Mustafa socialized with and where he could have been radicalized, the mother shook her head so much that her head scarf slipped down onto her shoulders.

"Mustafa wasn't radicalized by anyone," she sniffled. "He was a pious boy who wouldn't hurt anyone, and he never went anywhere without his father. He studied hard and said his prayers; he never even went to the mosque without his father."

"We don't know what's happened," cried his father. "Mustafa was a healthy boy who played sports, just like me. He was very, very strong and boxed at an elite level. He hoped to turn pro. We were so proud of—"

Then he stopped. It was too difficult to talk about.

He stood up so suddenly that he nearly toppled the teacups on the table and returned twenty seconds later clutching a silver trophy the size of a decanter.

"Look! First place in light middleweight. He won all of his fights on technical knockouts."

He dried his eyes and turned the trophy to the camera. It was hard to watch this grown man try to defend his son with quivering lips. Assad really wished he had never been in that park. Maybe then the boy would still be alive.

"Mustafa always knew exactly how to train and what to eat. He was such a good and intelligent boy. Argh, what have we done?"

Then his arms dropped slightly and it was possible to see the engraving on the trophy. Assad paused the video and went back a few seconds.

JUNIOR COMPETITION 2016, LIGHT MIDDLEWEIGHT, WIESBADEN-BERLIN, it read.

Assad thought this might be important.

"It was the first time Mustafa won a competition, and last year he won another competition in Berlin, only this time as a middleweight. We had such a good day, just him and me," cried the father as his wife leaned into him and held him tightly.

Assad thought for a moment about what he had just seen before he got up. He waved to Weber, who was now leaning up against the window. They would probably send him up to his room shortly.

Assad tried to remember.

It had been a few days since he had seen Warberg's video from Munich, but when he closed his eyes, he could remember flashes of it that both worried him and gave him hope. He recalled the scene: In the dimly lit room in the German photographer's apartment, Ghaalib and Hamid were having a confidential conversation. It was the first time Hamid had featured in the case, and he appeared to be a resolute man for whom Ghaalib had a lot of respect. At one point, they had actually laughed together in spite of the seriousness of their conversation. He remembered it clearly, and now he also remembered why. It was because Hamid, in order to illustrate something in the conversation Assad couldn't hear, had jumped up and demonstrated a series of boxing punches, light-footed like a professional boxer. A strong reaction in the middle of a calm conversation, thought Assad. Was Hamid a former boxer? Was that how he had met Mustafa?

Assad pursed his lips and breathed out, because all his instincts told him that this had to be investigated immediately.

It only took a few search words on Google to find the boxing club that had hosted the competitions in which Mustafa had participated. He visited the website, which had presumably originally been intended as a place to list statistics, photos, and miscellaneous information. However, instead of facts and photos, all it contained was the club's address and a special offer if applying for membership before December 31, 2015, which was almost three years ago now. If Mustafa's parents hadn't mentioned a competition only a year ago, the state of the website would have led him to conclude that the club had closed.

Finally, at the bottom of the page, it listed a number to call in order to get in touch with a trainer.

Assad looked at his watch for the umpteenth time that night. It was past one A.M. and hardly the time when a trainer would be waiting for new members. Regardless, he dialed the number and waited patiently until the answering machine message kicked in and informed him that the club was open every day between eleven and nine.

Then he took his most reliable gun and stuck it in the waistband at the back of his trousers.

It didn't take long to find a taxi on Friedrichstrasse, but when the driver heard the destination, he looked alarmed.

"That's a very bad area," he said, putting the car into gear. "Very bad at this time of night," he repeated, and then drove in silence until they reached the destination.

He was right. The area actually reminded Assad of some of the worst areas he had visited in Lithuania. The building itself was situated right next to the railway and had presumably been a grand railway building before the war, with a high-pitched roof and timber framing. Today, however, it was surrounded by all kinds of rubbish and rusty steel fences that had long since collapsed.

"Are you sure this is the right address?" asked the driver.

Assad looked up at a sign with a pair of oversized boxing gloves hanging above the entrance door that read, BERLIN BOXING ACADEMY.

"Yes, this is it. I'll give you fifty euros if you'll wait for me for fifteen minutes."

"No can do," he said, and took the fare. And then Assad was standing alone in the dark.

The door resembled the entrance to a bygone public institution. The brass door handle was missing, which presumably meant it had ended up at a flea market, but the door itself was made of solid oak.

He knocked a couple of times, and when no one answered, as expected, he walked around to the back, where the remains of a narrow platform ran along the side of the building. He banged on a window and shouted to check if anyone was inside, but there was still no response.

He pressed his nose against the dirty window and peered into the large dark interior, which had probably once been the waiting room but which now had been fitted out with training equipment, a boxing ring, and seats for at least fifty people.

If it hadn't been for Herbert Weber's intoxicated condition, Assad would have called him to ask if he could find out the extent to which the club was already known to the authorities. He shook his head; a call like that would never lead to anything constructive at this time of night.

But what could he do? Clubs like this had proven before to be covers for subversive activities and attracted young men from those sections of society who had the most to fight for. Poor African Americans in the USA, poor Latinos in South America, and poor immigrants in Europe. No wonder that the boxing rings around the world were mostly filled by people of color. When he looked up at the tattered fight posters taped to the back wall, he saw that this place was no exception.

Assad nodded to himself. What was he risking if he broke in? Would an alarm go off? Would the police arrive, arrest him, and finally charge him? Would it be a charge that Weber could easily have dropped?

He found a back door that was less grand, with flaking paintwork and plywood boards that had shrunk so much that they were cracking. With a short run-up, he kicked the lowest panel so hard that the windows vibrated. He waited a moment, looked around, and then kicked again, causing the plywood to splinter and the door insulation to fall down.

After a few more kicks, the hole was big enough to allow him to crawl through.

He found a light switch on a pillar in the middle of the hall and turned on what ended up being a series of strip lights, which after flashing for a few seconds lit up the room with such a cold, white light that it resembled a place where confessions were forced out of people.

His goal now was to find something that could document that Hamid had frequented this place.

After a tough and sweaty fight, it would have been easy enough for Hamid to pat the winners on the back and tempt them with a reward. Hadn't young men across the world been recruited countless times with the right words and a cup of steaming-hot tea and cakes? And given Mustafa's sad demise, it was easy to imagine that he might have been subjected to something similar. Yes, if Mustafa's social circle really was as limited as his parents claimed, it wouldn't surprise him if Mustafa had met someone here after his last fight who convinced him of the decadence of the West and instilled in him a sense of duty as a true believer to defend his faith.

And the more Assad thought about it, the more convinced he became that this person was Hamid.

Several rooms adjoined the large hall. A couple of moldy-smelling changing rooms, one of them with a well-worn massage table; a small kitchen-dining area with coffee machines, kettles, plates, and several shelves laden with many different types of tea and spices in glass jars.

There must be an office somewhere. Maybe upstairs, he thought, and targeted a flimsy spiral staircase that went to the second floor.

He was only halfway up the stairs when a light was turned on somewhere above him, illuminating the steps at the top of the stairs.

Assad automatically placed his hand over his gun as he took the final steps. For a moment, he thought that he had activated a sensor, but a figure on the landing proved him wrong. Without warning, the figure kicked Assad in the face, causing him to tumble backward down the stairs and land at the bottom with such force that he was winded.

"Who are you?" shouted the man, standing over him.

He was large and sweaty. Maybe Assad had awoken him from a peaceful sleep. The fact he was wearing nothing but underwear certainly hinted in that direction.

"You shouldn't count on any help from that," he said, pointing at Assad's gun, which was lying on the floor four to five meters away.

Assad massaged the back of his head and half stood up.

"You asked me who I am. Well, I'm the last man in this city who needs to be delayed," he said. "I'm very sorry that I had to break in, and I'll pay for the door. Didn't you hear me banging and shouting?"

"Why are you here? There's nothing for you to steal here," he said, and grabbed Assad's collar so roughly that it made him gag.

Assad grabbed the man's wrist to loosen his grip.

"Where does Hamid live?" Assad struggled to ask.

The giant's face contorted. "We have a lot of Hamids here."

"This one doesn't come here to train. He's around fifty and has graying cropped hair."

The giant tightened his grip on Assad's collar. "Do you mean this guy?"

He nodded over to the wall, where there was a poster hanging of two boxers staring each other down. LIGHT HEAVYWEIGHT CHAMPIONSHIP 1993, HAMID ALWAN VERSUS OMAR JADID, it read underneath, along with the date of the fight.

Assad was unsure. The Munich video hadn't been clear enough to enable him to recognize with any degree of certainty what the man had looked like twenty-five years ago.

"Yes, I think so," he said anyway, and then the giant's first hit landed, throwing Assad backward toward the judges' table.

Assad assessed his six-foot-seven opponent and rubbed his chin. The punch had been precise and painful; he was probably a former class boxer. Good reach, relatively muscular upper arms and thighs, but clearly marked by age and the rough-and-tumble of the sport, with a broken nose, heavy eyelids, and fists hanging low in front of his torso.

Assad stood up. "That's the first and last time you'll do that," he said, wiping the blood from his top lip. "That guy, Hamid Alwan, on the poster over there. Is Alwan his real surname?"

The heavyweight prepared his next punch. Lack of respect was obviously punished immediately in these circles.

"Stop," said Assad with his hand in front of him for defense. "I don't want to hurt you, just answer my question. Is Alwan his real surname?"

"Did you say hurt *me*?" The giant looked as though he couldn't believe his own ears. "I'll kill you, you little shit. You can't just come here asking—"

Assad's karate chop against his neck caused the giant to keel to the side, which gave Assad enough time to land him two quick kicks to his groin and then end the triple attack with a final blow to the neck. It took no more than two seconds before the man collapsed on the floor with a thud.

Assad picked up his gun and stuffed it back in his trousers. His mountain of an opponent was lying on the floor, clutching his neck and struggling for air. The sight of this man, weighing in at 275 pounds, wearing only his white underwear and writhing on the floor with panic and anxiety in his eyes, wasn't exactly what Assad had come here for.

"Is Alwan his real surname?" he asked again. The man tried to answer but couldn't.

"Is this your place? Do you have a flat upstairs?" he asked, but still received no answers.

Assad went into the kitchen to fetch some water. Even if he had to oil his tongue, he would get him to talk.

The man drank tentatively while keeping his eyes fixed on Assad's eyes. It was clear that he was still in shock. Assad almost felt sorry for him.

"Is Alwan his real surname?" he asked for the fourth time.

The giant closed his eyes. "He'll kill me. He'll come and burn the place down," he said hoarsely.

He had his answer. It was a relief.

"Do you have records of the people who come here?"

He hesitated a little too long and shook his head.

Assad took out his mobile and called Weber.

A scene like this would surely encourage the head of the investigation to get a grip.

———————

No less than five men turned up, so Weber had understood the message. He still reeked of alcohol but was surprisingly attentive and collected.

"We'll take him in for questioning," he said, and nodded to his men. He looked around. "And what have you been up to here?"

Assad shrugged. "I kicked the door in until I smashed it. I'll pay for the damage. I've already promised as much to our old friend here."

Weber shook his head a couple of times, which, judging by the hand he held against his forehead afterward, wasn't a good idea.

47

Alexander

Every time his mother whimpered from behind the gaffer tape in fear for her life, Alexander lost his concentration. Important milliseconds turned to seconds, and his usual lightning-speed reaction failed him time after time. He hadn't made so many amateur mistakes since he had been a beginner at this game. The situation was close to making him crack.

"I'll kill you right here and now if you don't shut up," he said, and regretted it immediately. Hadn't he promised to wait until he had finished the game before killing her? And there were still nine wins to go before he reached 2117.

He swiveled around in the office chair and looked her straight in the eyes. It was a delight to see her fear and submission so clearly.

"Shall we agree to change the rules? If I quickly win a round, we can agree that you can live a little longer, okay? Will that make you be quiet?"

The gaffer tape over her mouth bubbled a little. Didn't she understand what he had just said? She continued rocking back and forth in her seat as if she was about to wet herself.

Alexander swore to himself. What did he care if she pissed herself?

And then she did something he hadn't seen her do since the first time his father gave him a serious thrashing. She was crying, and the snot was oozing from her nostrils while her muffled cries grew louder.

This unsavory sight made Alexander recall a memory he had long since repressed. He recalled how she had pled and cried back then, trying to protect him. He remembered how she had thrown herself in between them and grabbed at his father's shirt to stop him. But he also remembered that it was the last time she had taken her son's side in a conflict, and that since that day she had resigned herself to her husband's mood swings.

In spite of everything, there had been a time where she had shown emotion, and now she was doing it again. She was scared, she was alone, and she definitely felt regret. It wasn't much, but it was something. Alexander reconsidered. His mother knew that she would die, and yet she was still worried about wetting herself. It almost made her human. Somehow it was touching.

"Do you promise to give me peace to play if I let you go to the bathroom?"

She nodded violently.

"Don't lock the door or I'll kick it in. Do you understand what I'm saying?"

She nodded again.

He hung the sword on his shoulder, rolled her in the office chair to the bathroom door, and removed the gaffer tape from her hands and feet but kept it over her mouth.

He took a step back and pointed at the sword to make sure she understood that fighting back would be futile.

"Go on, get it over with," he said, "and don't try anything!"

She nodded and disappeared into the bathroom. There was a whizzing sound from behind the door and then it went quiet, so there was obviously more than just a piss to take care of.

Alexander waited patiently until he noticed the lock indicator silently turning from green to red.

"Hey!" he shouted. "I told you not to lock the door. Now you're in for it."

He kicked the door a couple of times while there was a loud sound of ominous clattering on the other side. When the door finally gave in and banged against the bathroom wall, she was standing in front of the leaded window without gaffer tape over her mouth and with the heavy toilet seat raised above her head.

The instant she smashed the seat against the window, she began screaming for help with all her might.

She stopped when Alexander hammered the leather-bound handle of the sword against the back of her neck and she passed out and collapsed.

Should I kill her now? he thought as he dragged her back to the bedroom.

He was contemplating his next move when, through the smashed bathroom window, he heard someone shouting to ask if everything was okay. It was the first time in a long time that the outside world was a reality for Alexander. Had his mother actually succeeded in putting a stop to his plans?

He glanced down at her and decided that she wasn't going to come to any time soon.

Then he put down the sword, walked to the hallway, and opened the door to the world outside.

The air outside was biting cold. Back when he had holed himself up, it had been just the beginning of late summer, and now winter was on its way. The branches on the trees were bare, and all the greenery in front of the house had withered. Even the grass had lost its color, and there in the middle of the brown lawn lay the toilet seat, and only a few meters from there, on the pavement, he spotted their shriveled busybody of a neighbor from across the street staring at the obscene item on the grass while her scruffy dog pulled at its leash.

The relationship between Alexander and her had always been tepid, but he now tried to turn on the charm.

"Whoops! I obviously overreacted a little bit there," he said, and picked up the seat. "I'm just so upset that I wasn't accepted into the course I applied for."

She frowned. "I see, but why was your mother screaming for help?"

He tried to look surprised. "My mother? No, she's not home. It was me screaming. I don't know why I shouted for help. I was just so upset."

"That's not true, Alexander," she said, and walked up toward the open door. "I said hello to your mother when she arrived home, and I know for a fact that she hasn't gone anywhere since then."

Alexander was sweating. Did this bitch really keep an eye on everything that happened on their street? Didn't she have anything better to do?

She stood up straight with her hands on her hips. "I need to talk to her and make sure she's okay. And if you don't let me, I'll call the police. You can count on that."

"She isn't home so just call her. We don't have anything to hide."

She stopped midstep, but it was clear that this wasn't the end of the matter.

"Well then, let me assure you that you'll be having a visit from the police."

Alexander leaned backward in despair. She was bringing it on herself. "Well, come in and have a look, then," he said, and stepped to the side so she could go first.

When she reached the doorstep, she looked at him with an expression of mistrust. "Keep this door open. Do you understand, Alexander?"

He nodded, and when she was inside the hallway, he raised the toilet seat and rammed it so hard against the back of her neck that she didn't even manage to make the slightest sound before falling to the floor and letting go of the leash.

The dog reacted instinctively and rushed to the side, and when Alexander tried to grab the leash, the animal went crazy. It leapt toward the open door and the safety of outside, and then it just stood there in the middle of the garden path with its tail between its legs, staring at him with an expression of fear while he attempted to recall it with kind words.

He tried to remember the dog's name. What was the name he always heard that bitch calling the dog? And while he was coaxing the dog and trying to figure out how to make a creature like this feel safe, the dog turned around and ran off with the leash trailing after it.

He followed it until it disappeared between a pair of villas farther down on the other side of the street. If it had any sense, it would come back at some point looking for its owner.

And then he could try his hand at killing an animal.

Inside the house, he busied himself tying up the women. The frail woman from across the street grunted a little but was otherwise out when he put the gaffer tape around her head and mouth and tied her to one of the legs of the bed with her arms behind her back. His mother, on the other hand, was coming to, so it was high time he had her back up on the office chair and tied securely like before.

"Someone from my work will call," she moaned when she realized where she was.

Alexander didn't reply and, in spite of her protests, secured the tape around her mouth extra tight. If anyone was suspicious about the smashed window and rang the doorbell, he couldn't risk a sound coming from his bedroom.

"There," he said ten minutes later. "Now you two can enjoy each other's company while you have the chance. And, Mom, I hope you used the time to go to the bathroom when you were out there, because it was the last time you'll be going."

He sat in front of his computer. He had acted very resolutely in the last half hour, just like his warriors in the game normally did. It was as if he had merged with them.

"And another thing, Mom," he said when he pressed ENTER. "I've called your work. I told them that your sister is very ill and that you're worried sick about her, so you've gone to Horsens to look after her. I hope you think that's all right! They said they'll look forward to you coming back." He laughed momentarily. "And I answered that so would I."

Then the old woman came to. Given how thin and frail she was, it was strange that she recovered so quickly. *Some people are tougher than others,* he thought with a sense of respect.

She looked around the room in confusion. When she caught sight of his mother and the deadly sword lying on the floor just in front of her, it was easy to tell that despite the present company, she felt very alone in the world.

Alexander smiled, because she had good reason to feel that way. In all the time they had lived on the street, he didn't recall her having a single visitor.

She definitely wouldn't be missed.

A few hours went by. His luck hadn't turned completely. He had met fierce resistance in the last few rounds that he hadn't been able to defeat. He had otherwise been just about to reach his goal, so the setback would be sure to cost him the entire night or more.

He stood up and stretched while he imagined the following day. After he had killed the two women, he would hang the sword on his shoulder and go into the hallway and put on one of his father's longest coats. When he had locked the door behind him, he could begin. He had decided not to wear clothes that would bring unwanted attention, even though he had dreamed of conquering the city as an avenger in his black ninja costume. He would have looked formidable in that attire and with a bloody sword in his hand, but people would have just fled in all directions. No, a commotion was the last thing he needed. When he killed someone, he would hide the sword under the coat and calmly move on to the next narrow street or alley and continue his crusade.

Alexander turned his attention to the dead woman on the wall.

"Before I go, I'll write a note stating that I'm doing this for your sake," he said. "That way I'll be sure that the world will never, ever forget you." He smiled to himself. "And I don't think they'll forget me either."

He could see his mother trying to turn the chair around so she could give him pleading looks, but so long as the gaffer tape kept the chair tied securely to the table, she could struggle as much as she liked. Alexander sat, turned the volume down on the speakers, and put his headphones on. In the next few hours, he had to concentrate and give it his all. And yet, despite his resolve, he was killed at the beginning of every round over the next ten minutes.

Alexander threw the headphones at the wall. For some strange reason, it had never worked as well for him when he was wearing them, so why had he thought it would be any different just now? Was there something he hadn't sworn by? Was this his punishment for not concentrating during his mother's escape attempt, or was it just the nature of the game? Should he forget how good he was and just coast on his intuition, which had been his main strength in all manner of other games? He smiled. When it came to it, this setback was all about his lack of patience now that he was so close to his goal. If he could just bring himself down a gear and stop his heart from racing, everything would work out for him.

Alexander looked at the woman lying on the floor. She had always perceived him as a little shit, he knew she had, but now he would show her what he was made of.

Then he took his mobile, changed the SIM card, and made a call.

He looked at his watch. It wasn't even five o'clock yet, so there had to still be someone in the department, but this time it took a while before someone answered.

"Rose Knudsen," said the female voice, to his great disappointment. "Is it you again, Toshiro? How far along are you?" she asked.

"Close," he said. "Very close!" Then he pressed SPEAKERPHONE and nodded to the woman on the floor so she could listen in.

"Okay," said the policewoman, unimpressed. "Then I have something I'd like to say to you. Are you interested?"

"How can I know yet?" he answered. But he was.

"You sound different. Are you on speakerphone?"

"Yes, I have a couple of guests listening in."

"Guests?" Just as he had hoped, she sounded suitably surprised.

"Yes! Now there are two women waiting for the scaffold. My mother and a bitch from our street."

"That doesn't sound good. What happened?"

"She disturbed me."

"Disturbed you? Did she come to visit your parents?"

"No, she was just being a nuisance."

"What has she done to you, Toshiro? You're not thinking of hurting her, are you?"

"That's my business."

His eyes met the bitch's. It was sublime watching her slowly fall apart.

"And stop getting on my nerves," he continued. "Get on with it. What was it that I might be interested in? Not your pathetic questions, that's for sure."

"You're not very talkative when I ask you something, Toshiro. That's a shame. But I want to tell you something that you obviously don't know."

"There's a lot I don't know and don't want to know."

She laughed. He hadn't expected that.

"Have you read any more about the woman hanging on your wall? Do you know that her name's Lely Kababi?"

He didn't answer. Of course he knew that. It had been everywhere in the media over the last few days, but he didn't give a shit what her name was. A name was nothing, just a label given by parents to some-one when they weren't old enough to decide for themselves.

"We're heavily involved in that case here at HQ. You ought to know that by now. But do you?"

"Involved! Yes, *I've* made sure of that."

This time the derision in her laughter was a little too obvious, and he didn't like it.

"I want to talk to dumb dick. You're really getting on my nerves."

"Listen up, Toshiro, he's looking after a boy named Ludwig. Life goes on, you know. So, let me just get to it. The fact is, no, you can't take the honor for our engagement with this case. We've always been heavily involved in this case because Lely Kababi was a foster mother to one of our best men here in Department Q. You've no doubt read about him somewhere; his name is Assad. Well, some of the newspapers are using his original name, Zaid. And Assad is working on this case, and it's a good deal more personal for him than it is for you. What do you have to say to that?"

"You're full of shit, that's what I have to say."

"I didn't know you could talk so dirty, Toshiro. Where did you learn that?"

"Do you have to learn it somewhere special? I'm just saying that you're making it all up."

"I wish I was. But the man who murdered Lely has kidnapped Assad's wife and daughters. You must have read about it."

"Then you must've planted the story. I don't give a shit either way. And all that stuff about Assad, or Zaid, is a bit far-fetched, don't you think? You're just trying to let me know that you've gone from A to Z with me. Just FYI, I prefer the former."

"I don't understand. Do you mean you prefer A to Z? Are you being symbolic again, Toshiro Logan? I didn't think that the beginning of what you're up to was your favorite position, rather your loathsome finale. So how should I take it?"

"A doesn't have anything to do with the beginning. I'm just saying that A is more me than Z. Is there more to your bullshit story? Because otherwise I'll get back to my final wins, and there's nothing you can do about it."

This time, he was the one laughing.

"Just a moment, Toshiro. Right now, Assad is in Berlin, which is also where Lely Kababi's murderer is. He's putting his life on the line to avenge Lely and the unbelievable evil his family have been subjected to. You ought to respect that, Toshiro."

Respect? What did she know about that?

He looked at his watch. Was she trying to drag the time out?

"I can hear something in the background. What is it, Toshiro?"

He shook his head. The women weren't making a noise; they were too exhausted.

"Is it a dog? Do you have a dog, Toshiro?"

He turned toward the hallway. She was right. The dog was outside again, yapping on the street. Why hadn't he heard it?

"Do I have a dog? I hate dogs, so your hearing must be bad. There's no dog here."

"Is it coming from the street? Do you have a window open, Toshiro?"

Alexander looked down at the bitch. What the hell should he do with her dog? He would never be able to get hold of it.

"Do you live somewhere with a yard, Toshiro? Is it that sort of neighborhood? Do you live on a street with villas? A fancy house where no one takes any notice if your father and mother don't show their faces outside? Should we drive around all the areas with villas and ask if anyone knows a boy like you? Should we drive around and put up posters of you everywhere? Is that what you want? On telephone poles and in supermarkets. Is that what we should do? We can easily make a start right here and now."

Now he was beginning to sweat. The second hand was ticking too quickly. Even though he was sure they couldn't trace him, this call had already been too long.

"This was the last time you'll be hearing from me," he said. "Say hi to dumb dick and tell him he never stood a chance against me. Good-bye!"

Then he hung up and looked down at the woman on the floor.

"They can't find me, and that's just too bad for you two. Have you learned that it doesn't pay to go snooping in other people's business? 'Curiosity killed the cat,' as they say."

48

Assad

"**What have you done** to him?"

The boxer they had escorted back with them looked like he had been crying. Assad had seen grown men break down many times before, but never a man like this ex-boxer from Berlin's Boxing Academy who must have been used to taking more than his fair share of knocks. What did he have to be so scared of?

It was a slightly worn-out but surprisingly alert and sober Weber who retorted.

"If you're referring to his cuts and bruises, you've only got yourself to thank, Assad. We haven't touched him."

"But he looks like you've sentenced him to death and that the sentence will be carried out any second now."

Weber loosened his turtleneck. Why did he look as if he had hit the mark?

"Hmm. You're not wrong that he's scared for his life. We had to promise to keep him in custody here at the station until all this has blown over."

"What's he told you?"

"That Hamid's surname might not be Alwan. It could just be a name he boxed under, but he isn't sure. But he does know where he used to hang out and drink tea back in his boxing days. The café still exists, so we know what's next on our agenda. He also knows that if Hamid finds out he ratted to the police, both he and his boxing club will be history. He's seen what Hamid is capable of before, and he knows he has a huge network."

Assad had never doubted it. "So, you agree with me now that we've found the right Hamid?"

Weber and everyone standing nearby nodded.

Assad let out his breath. Finally!

"What did he have to say when you told him that we're certain that it's the same Hamid who recruited Mustafa in Frankfurt?"

"He says that Hamid often turned up at the club unannounced, and that he almost always hung around after the matches talking confidentially with the young boxers. He's also heard rumors that a couple of the young guys who took part in the competitions subsequently went to Syria. So he can see how it might all add up."

"Why didn't he report all this a long time ago if he thought something illegal was going on at his club?"

"For the same reason that he required a heavy hand before opening up."

"Give me the name of the café, Weber."

"I can't do that. You can't go off on your own with this, Assad. There's too much at stake. This isn't just about your family; we have to think about the lives and safety of a lot of people."

Assad tried not to feel offended. What good would it do him just now anyway?

"If I hadn't acted last night, we wouldn't be any farther forward. You were lying pissed in your bed, so give me the name!"

Did *Weber* look hurt now? Not as far as Assad could tell.

"No, we'll all go together. Our SWAT team will move in and then we'll apprehend those running the café. It's the only way. If you go in alone, you won't only be risking your life but also ruining the last chance we might have of closing in on the group."

"A SWAT team? That's a really bad idea, Weber. If you do that, everyone will clam up. We won't have any luck that way, none at all. The clock is ticking."

The café was situated on the other side of the street and slightly sheltered by some tall buildings.

It was still early, so there wasn't much traffic to hide behind. Assad wasn't happy about the situation.

"You're too close, Weber. They can see the cars. Black Audis like these stink of trouble in this neighborhood."

Weber grunted. "We need to be able to see what's going on inside. Simple as that. Otherwise we go in with you. You've got five minutes and then we're coming in."

Assad shook his head and got out. This discussion had already lasted too long.

"And I think you should leave that here! You won't be needing it." He pointed at Assad's lower back, where the gun was concealed.

Assad ignored him and crossed the street.

From the outside, the café wasn't anything special. A combination of a sports café and hookah club with grimy windows and an entrance that hadn't been swept for some time. They advertised alcohol-free drinks, a seventy-inch TV screen showing Bundesliga and Spanish La Liga matches, and hookahs from five to eight euros depending on the time of day.

The interior of the bar matched the exterior, with the small difference that a series of shelves directly below the ceiling and along the walls were filled with diplomas, silver trophies, and posters for a multitude of sports that all focused on getting the better of your opponent: boxing, judo, tae kwon do, jiujitsu, MMA, and so on.

The small clientele were all Arabs, so it would definitely have been a mistake to send in a team of ethnic Germans on a job like this. He nodded to the three men lounging with a hookah. The atmosphere was almost tame, which suited Assad very well indeed.

The man behind the velvet-covered substitute for a bar didn't take any notice of him; after all, Assad was like the rest of the patrons: very obviously one of their own.

"*As-salamu alaikum,*" he began, and continued in Arabic. "Are you the owner?"

He nodded as Assad caught sight of the trade license on the wall.

"So, you're Ayub? Then you're the one I need to speak to. I'm looking for Hamid. Can you help me?"

Assad knew that the man could easily say no to the last sentence, but sometimes a naive approach was best. Just not here.

He shook his head. "Hamid? We get a lot of people called Hamid in here."

"I'm talking about Hamid Alwan, our boxing champion. I don't see him up on the wall, but I assume that's an oversight."

The owner stopped polishing his cheap drinking glasses. "Hamid Alwan?! What business have you got with him?"

Assad leaned in over the bar. "I need to get in contact with him pronto or he'll be in big trouble."

"Trouble? What sort of trouble?"

Assad frowned and stressed his words. "Big trouble. The sort you don't want to know about, got it?"

All three smokers behind him raised their heads. He had spoken too loudly.

"I'll let him know when I see him," answered the café owner.

"Give me his number and I'll tell him myself."

Now the café owner's movements became quicker. The glass was placed with the others and the tea towel thrown over his shoulder. Then he walked around to the other side of the bar and looked imploringly at the others in the café.

"Take this guy out the back, and even if it means you have to knock him about, don't let him go until he says why he's here. I don't like the look of him."

Assad turned to face them. "Be my guest if you three want the café to be razed from the face of the earth." Assad turned toward the owner while the three bodyguards slowly stood up. "If you knew who had sent me, you would sink to your knees. Even Hamid Alwan is just a grain of sand in the desert."

It didn't seem to work.

"Get on with it," commanded the owner, unimpressed.

However, it did work when Assad pulled out his gun and pointed it at him. All the men froze.

Assad looked at his watch vibrating on his arm. It was a text from Weber. *You've got exactly forty-five seconds and no more,* it read. Was the man an idiot?

"Stand completely still or I'll take you out one by one," he commanded.

He turned again to face the owner. "We don't have long, so now you'll have to make a decision, Ayub. Tell me where to find Hamid, because his life is in danger. Do you understand what I'm saying?"

He nodded. Obviously not totally convinced but maybe getting there.

Assad lifted his jacket and put the gun back inside his waistband.

"Now I'm showing you my goodwill. Your turn."

He nodded, but right at that moment, shadows flickered past the front of the café, and before Assad knew what was happening, the door was kicked in and Weber's troops stormed in.

It hadn't been twenty seconds since Weber sent his text, so what were they playing at? Their force was large and superior, so the three men were immediately neutralized and placed in handcuffs and then Weber walked toward Assad, seemingly unaffected by his glaring eyes.

"Lucky, we stopped by," he said, taking out a pair of handcuffs. "Arms behind your back," he said to the owner, and then turned to Assad. "You too."

"I'll give you ninety seconds from now," he whispered when he clicked the cuffs on his wrists. "One and a half minutes, got it?"

Assad understood and hoped Weber would keep his word this time. Apart from the fact they had taken his gun from him, they were actually playing the game.

Weber and his team pushed the café owner and Assad down into a couple of chairs and turned their backs on them. Assad was already wriggling the handcuff key out from under his watch.

"You'll stay here and we'll be keeping a close eye on you," said one of Weber's men to Assad and the owner. Then they dragged the body-guards outside and over to the cars.

Assad struggled for a moment with the handcuffs. "I'll be free in a few seconds, so brace yourself; we need to get out of here."

The owner shook his head. "I'm not going anywhere. What can they do to me? I haven't done anything."

"If you stay, you won't live to see the sunrise tomorrow. These are the people I need to warn Hamid about. Use your head, man! Tell me if there's a back door and if you've got any wheels."

He hesitated for a few seconds but then nodded and turned so Assad could free him.

They rushed out to a large complex of interconnected backyards, and twenty seconds later they were sitting on Ayub's motorbike and speed-ing away from the main road, where three innocent men were now on their way to the station to be taken into custody until this was over with. Assad tapped his inside pocket, where he had put his phone. Had Weber already noticed that his GPS signal was heading southeast?

After driving for fifteen minutes, Ayub stopped on a quiet road with terraced housing and low-rise apartment blocks.

"You can get off now," he said.

Assad did as he said and looked around. "Is it in there?" he asked, pointing at the house in front of them.

He just managed to notice the clicking sound as Ayub put the mo-torbike into gear. He instinctively jumped forward when the man was about to press down on the throttle. Assad didn't manage to bring the motorbike down but did get a grip on the bar at the back of the seat against which he had just been leaning.

The motorbike swayed and Assad's foot was flung toward the curb, but Ayub was skilled enough to balance the motorbike and sped off through the neighborhood with one of Assad's legs dragging along the road as he tried to pull himself up onto the seat. Ayub lashed out a couple of times with his right hand and managed to hit Assad on the side of his head, and when he tried for a third time, Assad let go of the bar and grabbed his free arm. The result was predictable and far from healthy. The unexpected tug caused Ayub to pull on the left handlebar with all his strength, and the motorbike wrenched and fell down to the left with Ayub underneath it. Assad immediately let go of his grip and suddenly found himself on the road watching as the driverless motorbike crashed against the curb on the other side of the street, only coming to a halt fifty meters farther up.

"Are you crazy? What the hell are you playing at?" shouted Assad as he hobbled over to the injured man.

Ayub's face was lying flat against the paving stones halfway up on the pavement. Apart from bloody abrasions, it appeared that his upper body was unscathed from the crash, but his left leg didn't appear to have fared so well.

"Don't you think I saw through you?" murmured Ayub.

Assad leaned in over him. "Hamid is planning an act of terrorism, and they're on to him. We have to warn him. Do you hear me? Tell me how to find him so you can save his life."

His face twitched. "I can't feel my leg," he said without any energy in his voice.

"I'll call an ambulance, but first tell me where to find him."

He looked at Assad but was unable to focus. "Hamid is my brother," he said. And then he died.

Assad held his breath; this was terrible. And when people began rushing out from the houses, asking what had happened, he couldn't do anything but close his eyes and say a little prayer for this dead man and his own family, whose fate now seemed increasingly inevitable.

Then he laid his hand on the man's cheek. "Poor, misguided fool," he said, and waited a few minutes before Weber's troops finally located him.

49

Carl

A nurse came flouncing down the corridor.

"Just a moment!" she said, and took him to one side before he opened the door to Mona's room.

"Carl Mørck, I need a word before you go in. Just to be on the safe side, we're keeping Mona in for another day or two, so promise me that you haven't come to pressure her, because she's been through a lot in the last few days, physically and mentally. And even though it seems like the baby is safe, Mona's condition isn't stable yet, just so you know. Any sort of agitation, sadness, frustration—in fact any exaggerated emotions—could trigger an inexpedient development, and Mona has been very worried about you and a case that you're working on in your department."

Carl nodded. He said he would do anything in his power to make sure the pregnancy proceeded as it should. He was just happy that both Mona and the baby had weathered the storm.

Mona smiled and held his hands as if they were her only anchor. It wasn't difficult to see the crisis she had been through without him. Her skin looked more delicate, her lips had become pale, but the strength inside her that had fought for the baby was shining in her eyes.

He embraced her carefully and placed his hand on her stomach.

"Thank you" was all he could muster.

They sat for a moment in silence holding hands. Words were so insignificant now. Why had it taken so many years before they finally found each other? Right now, it seemed meaningless.

"Thank you too," she said, clenching his hand.

"Did the nurse try to scare you?" She didn't wait for his answer. "Forget her, Carl. She's just trying to protect me, but she doesn't know me. We need to talk about everything, Carl. Otherwise, I won't be able to rest."

He nodded.

"Is there enough time? Can you stop what's about to happen in Berlin? Will Assad and his family come out of this alive? Tell me straight."

"Honestly?"

"Yes, for God's sake, give me the honest truth."

"It's all such a mess, Mona. We've had to hold back the last few days because there's been almost no progress whatsoever, and it's been driving us close to the edge. I'm worried that the odds are looking really bad for Assad's family and our chances of preventing what we're so afraid is going to happen."

"A terror attack in Berlin?"

"Yes."

"You need to go back and help Assad, Carl, or you'll never be able to forgive yourself. I'll be fine; I promise. But you need to promise you won't put your life at risk. If anything happens to you, I'll . . ." She held her stomach.

She didn't need to say any more.

"I promise," he said. "But just now, I'm here with you, and I'm staying put."

"But, Carl, you also have another case, and because of Rose, I've become very involved in it. You need to help me and Rose and Gordon. Do you understand? Now two women's lives depend on you all doing what you can to stop this crazy boy. In ten minutes, you're going to HQ and doing what you're best at, okay, Carl?"

He tilted his head. What a fantastic woman.

"What do you know, Mona? Is there anything new in the case?"

"The boy has informed Rose that he will kill both women before he heads into town on a killing spree, and we believe him. And Rose thinks he's really close to reaching the goal in his game when he'll do all this."

"You mean today?"

"Very soon at any rate. Maybe today, maybe tomorrow. I know that Marcus Jacobsen is following the case closely and has worked hard to get PET involved."

"How do you mean?"

"If you head down there, I know from Rose that there's a meeting in your department in an hour and a half."

Carl grunted. A meeting at eleven o'clock! A *morning* meeting! The straitlaced boys from PET had never been his cup of tea.

"You should also know that Hardy and Morten have been to Switzerland for the second time while you were in Berlin. I think you should contact them when you get a minute to yourself."

Gordon and Rose were staring at him like a couple of puppies hoping for scraps from the master's table. He wished they wouldn't.

Carl closed his eyes and listened intently to the audio recording. Every intonation and choice of word in the last recording of the boy they had dubbed Kurt-Brian Logan could be significant.

When it was finished, he opened his eyes and looked at them. It was clear that they were all thinking the same thing: If they didn't find him very quickly, the result would be terrifyingly bloody. Carl could just imagine the fallout: The tabloids would go crazy; TV 2 News would go into overdrive as usual with the news dominating their broadcasting for a long time; more serious dailies would hang Department Q out to dry with no consideration for the eleven years they had worked to make it the best investigative unit in Denmark. There was a lot at stake if this insane boy succeeded with his project.

"Okay, you couldn't have handled things much better, even though we don't have much to go on at the moment. However, there are two things in this recording that I think could be significant. And that's the barking dog and the fact the boy is crazy about the letter A."

Rose nodded.

"Has PET heard the recording?"

"Yes, I've given them all our material," said Gordon. "Marcus has asked them to correlate all the data, and they're coming down here to fill us in."

The beanpole looked as if this case had caused him to lose weight—if that was possible.

He looked imploringly at Carl. "If PET don't come with any crucial new information, we'll have to ask Marcus to go public with the sketch of the boy and the story. All the TV channels will clear their programming when they get wind of what it's about. You need to help us convince him, Carl."

But Carl agreed with the chief of homicide. It would create general panic and also invite huge criticism that they hadn't gone public days ago. Carl knew that Marcus had had bad experiences with this sort of thing. Only a few hours after they went public, they would be inundated with tip-offs that would lead them down blind alleys and delay them, especially if the sketch wasn't accurate enough. The information that the boy's parents hadn't been to work for a few days might possibly help, but it would still result in an enormous amount of material that they would have to consider and analyze. There simply wasn't enough manpower in the Danish police force these days to deal with a case like this in such a short time, nor were there local police stations anymore with officers who had years of experience of the local area and its residents. He and Marcus Jacobsen knew all too well the consequences of the failed police reforms introduced by politicians.

"You didn't get a chance to ask him more about this A, Rose?"

Did the question embarrass her?

"I know I should have asked him if he was talking about the letter A. I was just so hell-bent on getting him on our side that I didn't think about it, Carl. My plan was to get him to feel solidarity for Assad in his hunt for Lely Kababi's murderer so we could create a bond."

"It obviously didn't work, which says a lot about him. The boy is immensely self-centered, self-righteous, and completely messed up in the head. People with psychopathic tendencies are hard to get through to, Rose."

"Yes, I know!"

"He's given us a good tip before, and we shouldn't forget that. There was that odd statement about outliving himself by one year, and you worked out what he meant by that. It was a good piece of detective work. He hasn't once protested that you guessed his age as twenty-two, so I think you hit the bull's-eye there. I actually think his overconfidence has gotten the better of him again, which is why he wanted to give us another tip. He's a hundred percent convinced we won't catch him in time; I'm certain of it."

Rose nodded to indicate that she was following his line of thought. "So, the letter A is his tip?"

"Exactly. We're calling him Kurt-Brian Logan, but we still don't know his real name. I think his tip is about his name and that it starts with A."

Carl was very familiar with the man from PET who accompanied Marcus when he arrived, but the very young guy with pimples who came tripping behind them was unknown to him. Almost a cross of something between a manga figure and someone who had just left school. What the hell was he doing here?

"Carl, I have to confess that despite the circumstances, I'm glad you're here."

He introduced his guests. "Of course, you know Superintendent Jeppe Isaksen from PET, who has taken our needs into serious consideration and pulled out all the stops to support our investigation of the young killer."

Carl nodded politely.

"But let me introduce a new face to you, PET's new IT boy wonder, Jens Carlsen. He's processed and correlated all the data Gordon handed over to PET." He turned to the guy. "Maybe you can tell us yourself what you've concluded, Jens."

He started clearing his throat so fiercely that his Adam's apple appeared to be flying up and down his throat. And contrary to expectations, he spoke in a voice almost one octave below the average. "Yes, let me start by saying that we've been working closely with our linguist. Of course, it could turn out to be a dead end, but we had to have some basic data to build on. So, if the language analyst's theory doesn't hold, my work won't either."

"Thanks for your candor. Then we'll just have to hope that your language guy has done his work thoroughly," said Marcus.

"He has," said the head of PET. He had to say that.

"Having listened to the recordings many times, we've concluded that the boy probably lives in the northern part of Copenhagen," continued the head of PET. "We've excluded Hellerup and Charlottenlund, but the Fuglebakke neighborhood, and to some extent Emdrup, Frederiksberg, and the neighborhoods bordering on Utterslev Mose are all neighborhoods that display some characteristics of this young man's speech and vocabulary."

Carl noticed how Rose and Gordon caught each other's eye. This was obviously also their starting point.

Now the young man took over. "We owe a great deal of thanks to the boarding school in Bagsværd because they so resolutely took the time to provide us with a list of all the men who were pupils at the school who are aged between forty and seventy today. Unless there's an abnormally small or large age difference between the young killer and his father, we assume that this is the age range where we can expect that a man could have a son aged twenty-two."

"Of course, we could run with the theory that it's a young or old stepfather, but we've chosen to ignore that possibility," said the head of PET as if he had been personally involved, which Carl doubted very much.

The bass voice took over again. "I've assumed that the father and killer have the same registered address, and I've correlated the list from the boarding school of men aged between forty and seventy with those who live in the Copenhagen neighborhoods I mentioned before."

Gordon and Rose leaned forward a little in their seats. Hopefully, the figure was very low.

"I've concluded that in these neighborhoods, there are thirty-three households with a former pupil from the boarding school in the relevant age group. If we do a cross-check with the whole of greater Copenhagen, that number increases more than threefold, which would be impossible to go out and check in the time available."

Carl didn't think it sounded too good. Whether it was twenty-one households in a much more specific area or seventy-five in the whole of greater Copenhagen, the numbers sounded equally insurmountable to deal with in the hours available, because if the boy was sly enough, and he certainly was, he wouldn't just open the door when they rang the bell. And in many of the households, people simply wouldn't be home. They would need to obtain a multitude of search warrants to enter the properties where there was no answer. And even if someone did open the door, they would have exactly the same problem if they were refused entry to the house.

"To further refine this figure, I've conducted another cross-check based on the presumed age of the killer."

Department Q was all ears. Clever guy, this pimply kid.

"If we assume that he's approximately twenty-two and agree on a year of birth between 1995 and 1997, and that he's living at home and registered at the same address as his father, we're down to eighteen houses in the chosen neighborhoods and forty in the wider Copenhagen area."

Then he opened his folder and pulled out some papers.

"Here are the addresses I've narrowed it down to."

Rose and Gordon gawked.

50

Assad

Assad followed them all the way. First, to Ayub's house, where they bluntly delivered the news of his death to his wife, causing her to immediately start hyperventilating. She only managed to regain some sense of calm after they had ransacked the house and found the address for her brother-in-law Hamid. They left a couple of men behind to keep Ayub's wife under observation while a second group surrounded Hamid's house and one by one were directed into the small, well-kept garden that went around the perimeter.

They coordinated the attack so that the garden door and front door were forced open simultaneously, seconds later finding Hamid's wife and children sitting under a table as quiet as mice. It was almost as if they had been in this situation before.

Assad photographed her distorted face and the children's terrified expressions when they forced her to call her husband and say that Ayub's wife had called to say that Ayub was dead and that they were scared for their lives. Couldn't Hamid come home and get them out of there straightaway?

Thank God, Hamid wasn't prepared for what awaited him; however, he was heavily armed when, only a few hundred meters from the house, he saw that the front door had been smashed in.

His reaction was prompt. And while shooting at random, he threw himself into a bush and tried to escape down through the back gardens. When he realized that he was surrounded, he tilted his neck back and pressed his gun up against his chin. Just as he was about to pull the trigger, he was shot in the leg. And seconds after he fell down, they were on top of him and the fight was over almost before it had begun.

Assad had stood in the background praying that they wouldn't kill Hamid.

When they dragged him into the van and drove him back for questioning, he was still bleeding heavily.

Assad remained at the scene for a moment thinking about what would happen now before he then followed in the next car. The actual questioning of Hamid wasn't something in which he wanted to take part. That form of confrontation, which he had experienced physically himself, wasn't something he wanted to experience again.

Despite Assad's unwillingness and reluctance, they brought him to the station just after midnight, because even though they had come down hard on Hamid all day, he hadn't breathed a word. Now Weber's team would work through the night, but, before they wore him down completely, they wanted to see if Assad could get anything out of him.

Assad declined. When it came to a man like Hamid, who only a few hours previously had shown the will to commit suicide for the cause, even the most brutal torture wouldn't loosen his tongue.

However, Weber insisted, because no matter how slim the chance was that Assad would make any headway, he owed it to himself and his family to try. Yes, even a man like Hamid had his weak points; he even had a cold, Weber said.

"Did he have it when you brought him in?"

"Yes. So we probably have an explanation for the tissues we found. Just make sure you don't catch it."

Assad nodded and walked into the room.

Inside the ice-cold, barren room, it struck Assad that the pressure on Hamid hadn't only been of a psychological nature, because the room was flooded with water on the floor, and wet towels in a bucket bore witness to the fact that the treaties of the Geneva Conventions weren't afforded equal significance everywhere in the world when the prevention of terrorism was at stake.

Hamid's eyes were heavy due to his cold and now also half-closed with exhaustion; his clothes were drenched, which definitely didn't help with his cold; and his teeth were chattering due to the freezing temperature of the room. And yet he looked at the door with a defiance that made Assad lose hope.

When Hamid realized that it was Assad who had entered the room, he couldn't stop himself from laughing. He pointed at him and said in a rasping, coughing voice that he found it unbelievable that a short-ass like him could have been the object of Ghaalib's anger and desire for revenge all these years.

Then he stood up and tugged at his handcuffs, which were attached to the table with a chain.

"Come closer, you traitor," he shouted. "Let my teeth grab your throat and do you a favor."

And then he spat in Assad's face.

Assad wiped the saliva away as Hamid smiled derisively. He obviously thought he had made his position clear, but, a second later, the smile was wiped from his smug face as Assad slapped him hard across the face and spat on him.

"So, you finally get to meet me and see that I'm alive and kicking," said Assad, and pushed him back in his chair. "Now I'm going to ask you a couple of questions, which I hope you'll answer."

He placed a picture of his wife on the table in front of him.

"This is Marwa, and you know where she is."

Then he took out his mobile and found the picture of Hamid's shocked wife calling her husband.

"And this is your wife, and I know where she is."

He repeated this with a photo of his elder daughter.

"And this is Nella, and you know where she is, just like I know where your children are. Do you get my drift, Hamid? This is an eye for an eye and a tooth for a tooth. The choice is yours!"

Hamid opened his eyes wide and looked at Assad with a coldness that signaled death.

Assad pressed his mobile in Hamid's face. "Take a good look at your beautiful wife and your wonderful, innocent children. Tell me how to find Ghaalib and I'll spare your family. Or do you also want to be their executioner?"

Hamid was about to spit again but thought better of it.

"You can do whatever you like," he said. "I'll meet my family in paradise. When in the course of the divine eternity that will be doesn't matter to me."

Meet them in paradise? Where did he get his faith?

"Hamid, listen to me! Ghaalib has offended my wife and children. He has brought shame on his faith and on himself. And those who help him with these atrocities shouldn't hope to end anywhere other than hell."

Hamid sat back in his seat and smiled. "You miserable infidel dog. You ought to know that hell is only a temporary state. Allah doesn't answer a limited number of sins with unlimited punishment. We will all meet in paradise. Even you and I." And then he tilted his head back and laughed even louder than before.

Now Assad saw the line in the sand between them all too clearly before he decided to cross it regardless and smash his fist in that laughing face. And every time his punches landed, he saw his wife and children in that long-gone moment when they had waved good-bye to him. Maybe forever.

"You'll need to throw some more water on him," he said when he stepped out of the room. "Otherwise he won't wake up."

Weber looked seriously at him. "Did you hit him?"

What did he mean? Of course he had hit him.

"Is that so much worse than your waterboarding tactics? I thought torture was banned in your civilized Germany."

"Waterboarding? There's no waterboarding going on here. If you're referring to the water on the floor, we washed the blood away after the doctor stopped the bleeding from his leg."

Assad looked surprised. "So, what pressure have you exerted on him?"

"We offered him a collaboration with the authorities. Immunity and money. That he could work for us and live a safe life. Of course, it was naive, but we had to try."

"Yes, very naive."

"Then we threatened his family's well-being. But he just laughed at that. He said that they would all meet each other in paradise regardless of what we did."

51

Ghaalib

It had now been over an hour since Ghaalib had sent Beena over to Hamid's house, and he was feeling uneasy. It was the first time that Hamid hadn't shown up on time, and absolutely the first time that they couldn't get hold of him. If something had happened to him, it could compromise their entire mission.

He sat at the table in front of the map of Berlin and went through everything once more. They had moved their operation from Frankfurt to Berlin, and now it looked like they might have to change their plans again if Hamid didn't show up. Not insurmountable, but all the same . . .

The unease in the flat was growing. If Beena didn't return in ten minutes, he risked several of the less-experienced warriors' panicking. He had to convince them that no matter what happened, they were a completely operational and powerful team who would succeed with their mission. And if Hamid was no longer with them, he would take over Hamid's role himself and be the one to detonate the explosives.

The first thing he had to do was make sure that the Captain was okay and in position in his hotel suite and ready to act at any moment.

It had been Hamid's role as a local and fluent German speaker to maintain contact with Dieter Baumann. However, the Captain's years in the Middle East had made him fluent in Arabic, so the starting point for communication between him and Ghaalib was there.

Ghaalib called him at the hotel.

"You've become a famous man here in Germany, Dieter. It's given us just the sort of attention we hoped for. But how have you avoided unwanted attention?"

"I booked in under a different name and have used room service ever since. I actually haven't left the suite since I checked in. That was also before the newspapers splashed me all over the front pages. And Hamid arranged a suitable disguise. Why isn't he the one contacting me?"

"He isn't with us just now. I'm calling to confirm that the attack will take place tomorrow at precisely two o'clock in the afternoon. Are you ready?"

He coughed slightly. "I am. And I hope the visibility will also be tolerable tomorrow. The fog that hit Berlin last week is damn well on its way back as far as I can tell online. I can open the side window just enough to enable me to twist the barrel in all directions. And the good thing is that it'll be hard to see me because the windows are very dark and the gap is small. The hotel is another one of Hamid's great choices."

He coughed again. He didn't have much lung capacity left.

"Where is Hamid?" he asked.

"We don't actually know. But don't worry, Hamid's a rock."

"I know."

"How's your health?"

"I'm still alive." He coughed while laughing. "At least enough so that I can decide myself when I don't want to live anymore."

"Take your tablets, Dieter, and look after yourself. *As-salamu alaikum*."

"*Wa alaikum as-salam*."

Ghaalib heard noise coming from the hallway and then Beena walked in, *alhamdulillah*, praise be to God, but she looked shaken.

"Sorry it took so long, Ghaalib. It's a long way to his house."

He nodded.

"It isn't looking good down there. I spoke with a kiosk owner in the neighborhood who told me that uniformed men had broken into Hamid's house and that his wife and children are still in there. Gunshots were heard farther up the street, and some of his customers had seen Hamid being shot in the thigh and carried off by some strong, armed men in black cars. They had also seen an Arab standing at a distance in the middle of the road watching the shoot-out and Hamid being taken down, and, when it was all over, he also drove off with some of the other men."

"Did you get a description of the man?"

She nodded, still visibly shaken. "Yes, more or less."

"Zaid al-Asadi?"

"I think so, yes."

Ghaalib tilted his head back because he was struggling to breathe. He really wanted to execute Zaid's wife here and now, but where was the final, ultimate revenge in that?

"I want you all to come in here," he said to the group when he had thought things through.

He looked at them calmly so they could see that he had control of the situation.

"It would appear that Hamid is out of the game. Beena has told me that he was apprehended at his home."

There were a couple of people in the group who looked like they might panic.

"Yes, it's a major setback, but remain calm. Hamid is one of the toughest men I've ever met. He's been apprehended before, and they've never managed to get a word out of him. I can assure you that they won't succeed this time either. They will let him go soon enough because they can't have anything on him. If anyone can cover their tracks, he can."

"But we won't have him with us to execute our plans. What will we do?"

"There will be consequences, of course, but there is also a solution. I will take his place."

That went down well.

"And the distraction tactic? When will that happen?"

"Approximately one thirty tomorrow afternoon."

52

Joan

He was invisible to them. They didn't pay him the least attention. They didn't talk to him, and they didn't hear the small sounds he made when his nose was bunging up and he couldn't really breathe. He just sat there in the wheelchair in the middle of the room and heard everything, saw everything, and slowly learned what was going to happen. No one in the room did anything to hide anything from Joan, and why should they? He wasn't going anywhere, and he was also the one who would document everything for them. He was the one who would describe the events when it was all over with.

The preparations, the lead-up, the execution, and the result.

And hour by hour, it was becoming increasingly clear to him that when everything was over tomorrow afternoon, Joan Aiguader would no longer be the man he once was.

The three women were now left to themselves in the room next door, and as they hadn't given them any food all day, they no longer had the energy to make the slightest sound, which was the idea. It was their plan that later that day they should all be slouching powerlessly in their wheelchairs as if they were paraplegic. No sound, no movement, just carriers for the terrifying destructive bombs whose functionality Osman was now checking.

And while everyone went over their respective roles and positions for the following day's mission, Ghaalib was sitting alone in a corner, looking morose. Whether he was overcome with anger or desperation was hard to ascertain, but it was clear that he was missing his right-hand man and that it was worrying him because Hamid was the key person for both the first maneuver and the entire mission itself.

Ghaalib tried to hide his state of mind, of course, so that the group didn't begin to doubt that the mission would be a success. It wasn't until late that night, when he found out precisely where Hamid had been taken, that he decided on how to proceed with the mission and regained his usual balance.

He spent a few minutes typing on his phone, then scanned the statement and sent it.

He placed the phone in Osman's hand and gave him a message. Osman was apparently his new right-hand man.

Then he made a brief announcement that everything was back on track. "And then we'll have Zaid. We'll have him," he said in English to Joan, and flashed him a broad smile.

He sent Osman on his way and sat on the chair next to Joan.

"Zaid, Zaid, Zaid, Zaid," he mumbled to himself like a mantra with his eyes screwed shut, nodding to himself as if the fight was already in full swing inside him.

"I'll get you tomorrow. You will suffer more than ever. I'll make sure of that. You can count on it. The time has come," he continued before returning to his mantra. "Zaid, Zaid, Zaid."

It was the first time Joan saw the flame of insanity in his eyes. Joan counted the hours all through the night.

They had tested his GoPro camera, checked the Uzis and their magazines, examined the explosive vests, and taken it in turns in front of everyone else to go through their positions and roles. Nothing was left to chance.

Ghaalib brought everyone together. "In a couple of hours, we'll say our prayers as a group in our own clothes, and afterward, we'll don our disguises. The men among you need to be precise with the order you put things on. The bulletproof vest needs to sit tightly on top of your shirt so it looks elegant when you put your jackets on. Don't secure your beards until you're fully dressed; get Beena and Jasmin to help you. When you've done that, put on your hats with the curls. Check yourselves in the mirror and help each other if something doesn't look right. And right at the end, put on your glasses. They're not as strong as they should be because we Arabs are thankfully not as degenerate and don't share the same health problems as them."

This was cause for general amusement. Not many Orthodox Jewish men of a certain age could escape their genes and increasing nearsightedness; everyone knew that.

They had spoken a lot about what time they would put their mission into action. The first part was fixed; it had to be at precisely one thirty in the afternoon, after Ghaalib sent a series of messages to Zaid al-Asadi that he would make sure he received. Concerning the main act, they had looked into when there would be the most visitors in the square and tower, and it seemed that two o'clock in the afternoon was the best time, so they would stick to that.

As far as Joan knew, it was now just after four in the morning. Several of the group had gone to their rooms to get a few hours' rest before they unleashed their plans. The three unfortunate women in the next room and a terrible number of innocent people would be dead in ten hours.

A little less than thirty-six thousand seconds from now, he calculated.

Ticktock, ticktock.

53

Carl

It was eight in the morning, and in the last hour and a half, the police had painstakingly made their way through the address list, but the boy still eluded them.

They had made the right decision starting their rounds so early. At more than half of their house visits, the family hadn't left for work yet and answered all their questions willingly. They covered up the real reason for their visit, referring to it as a survey on public feelings of safety, whatever that meant, and no one questioned them about it. In Denmark today, it was possible to cover up just about anything with that sort of generic drivel.

"What about the ones who weren't at home?" asked a pale Gordon back at Department Q. "Are we visiting them several times or waiting until they get home from work?"

"It depends," answered Rose. "But as you know, it's a question of resources."

Gordon's feet were tapping on the floor as he mumbled that he definitely hadn't anticipated that this case with the boy would go so far.

"Why didn't I manage to get him to reveal his identity? What the hell's wrong with me? Am I any good at this job at all?" He looked over at Carl. "I'm a lawyer, Carl. I don't have the nerves for this."

Carl smiled and patted him on the shoulder. "Chin up, Gordon. You know what they say: When you're up to your neck in shit, don't hang your head."

Rose was quick to take up the reins. "You just got out of bed too quickly, Gordon. Your comb is still in your hair."

She watched as he patted his head.

He fell for the same joke every time, and they always ended up in hysterics.

"Okay," said Gordon. "I get the picture. We'll just keep our fingers crossed, and, in the meantime, we'll call every shop in the world that sells samurai swords."

Carl nodded. It was a good plan when there was nothing else to do but wait.

Then his mobile rang. It was Assad. Carl looked at the clock; it was very early to be calling.

"I almost don't dare to ask, but are you coming, Carl? Something is happening today. We're sure about it now."

Carl waved a hand in the air for the others to calm down. This sounded serious.

"What's happened?"

"Just before four this morning, an e-mail arrived in the station in-box. Let me just read it out to you."

IMPORTANT MESSAGE FOR ZAID AL-ASADI!
    Further instructions will be sent to the same address later today. Expect the inescapable, and be ready to say good-bye to your loved ones and your life.

                                    Ghaalib

Assad's voice was composed, but the same couldn't be said for Carl.

"Do you have any leads whatsoever to go on, Assad? What about the Hamid guy?"

"Trust me, they've given him the sort of treatment they don't want to come to light. He said nothing."

Carl swore.

"Yes, you put the words from your mouth in mine, Carl," Assad said quietly.

Carl didn't have the heart to tell him it was the other way around.

"Yes," he said instead, "it makes you want to kill that Hamid, but what good would that do?"

"Weber's team are going through my list as we speak, and they have some things of their own that they want to check. But the long and short of it is that I have to wait. Again."

"What about the ornithologists and the pigeons?"

"Well, more or less every square in the city with pigeons is now being watched."

"That's a lot of manpower, I imagine. The city is huge."

"I don't think there's a single man who they could spare from guard duty who was allowed to sleep in today."

"What about the sender of the e-mail?"

"It came from a cell phone that was found an hour ago in a trash can on Potsdamer Platz, near a large bank."

"The phone was on?"

"Yes. They definitely wanted us to find it."

"Data?"

"No, it was empty apart from the e-mail."

"Was the phone old or new?"

"It wasn't new, so we won't be able to trace where it was purchased. There are experts working to see if they can recover any deleted data, of course."

"What about Hamid's wife?"

"She's been taken into custody and they've put the pressure on, but she knows absolutely nothing. She's young and naive; she didn't even know that Hamid was born in Germany."

"And his brother's wife?"

"She doesn't know anything either. Trust me, we've tried everything."

"You said the phone was found in Potsdamer Platz? Any thoughts about that?"

"The place where it was found in the square is covered. It's apparently called the Sony Center. So pigeons would have to fly low there, but we're also taking everything else in the area into account. Potsdamer Platz itself is very busy, and there's actually a spy museum, so it could be a symbolic target. Berlin's largest shopping center is also close by. But there are so many possibilities, and it's just one place out of very many."

Carl took the note Rose handed to him.

"You'll keep me updated, right, Assad? Rose has just handed me a note telling me that there's a flight leaving Kastrup airport at five past twelve. So I'll be there an hour after that."

"Let's just hope it won't be too late, Carl."

"I assume you're wearing your watch?"

"Of course."

"Then I'll know roughly where you are, and I'll keep texting you while I'm on my way."

After they hung up, he turned toward the other two. "Did you catch the gist of that?"

They nodded.

Rose spoke bluntly. "Fear of flying or not, Carl, in a couple of hours, at five past twelve, you're flying. You haven't got a choice. And there's nothing to do here except wait."

The telephone rang while Rose was printing out Carl's boarding pass, and Gordon jumped up to see the number on the display.

UNKNOWN NUMBER.

Then he pressed the RECORD button and put it on speakerphone.

"Well, Toshiro, you called anyway. Rose told me we'd heard the last of you." Gordon sounded cocky, but he was far from it. Carl had seldom seen someone sweat so profusely.

"I didn't get a chance to say good-bye to you, dumb dick. Apparently, you thought it was more important to look after someone called Ludwig. Is that right?"

"Yes, sorry about that, Toshiro. It won't happen again."

"Good. That bitch gets on my nerves."

Gordon took a deep but silent breath. "Are you close to reaching your goal?"

Rose and Carl looked hopefully at each other. That was the last thing they wanted.

"It didn't go so well last night, but I've had a breakthrough this morning. So I'll definitely be finished tonight. I just thought you should know. And thanks for listening to me."

"Hey, Toshiro, what happened with the dog?" he attempted. But he had already hung up.

"Did you manage to speak with Hardy, Carl?" asked Rose when she returned with a strong cup of coffee for Gordon, who was sulking in the corner. Marcus Jacobsen hadn't been impressed with his effort for once.

Carl pointed a finger in the air; he'd obviously forgotten.

He took out his mobile, and while waiting for the man to get assistance to answer the call, Gordon began shaking all over.

"It's hard for both of us, Gordon, but you simply need to keep it together," Rose said in an effort to comfort him as she pulled his head into her plentiful bosom. And by the time Hardy answered, Gordon had almost dozed off.

"Hi, Hardy, it's Carl. Sorry I haven't been in touch the last few days, but . . ."

"I understand, Carl. Rose has filled me in, so I know what you're dealing with. Don't worry."

"I need to leave for Kastrup airport in a minute and catch a flight to be with Assad in Berlin. I just wanted to say that I'm sorry your trip to Switzerland wasn't successful. What are you going to do now, Hardy?"

Did he sigh?

"Yes, it didn't go quite according to plan, but we'll work it out. Unfortunately, it's a question of money; isn't it always? We're still short of almost half a million kroner before the final surgery can go ahead. But they've examined me, and I've been approved as a suitable candidate. It'll all work out."

"Half a million?" Carl couldn't believe it was so much. Even if he murdered his parents, his share of the inheritance wouldn't cover half that. "I wish there was something I could do to help, Hardy."

He thanked him. That wasn't necessary.

Carl felt a sinking feeling in his stomach again. There were so many things he wanted to say and so much he felt he needed to apologize for. He, Hardy, and Anker had been caught off guard that day many years ago. Anker had died, Hardy had become an invalid, but what about him? He'd gotten off scot-free. Maybe the wrong people had suffered.

"You've got so much on your plate just now, Carl, so don't worry about me." Hardy cleared his throat a couple of times. It didn't sound very good. "However, there is something you need to take care of when you get back."

Was he suggesting that Mona had taken a turn for the worse? If that was the case, why didn't he know about it? She had been doing well and was stable when he spoke to her only an hour ago. It couldn't be Mona.

"It's our old case haunting us, Carl. The nail-gun killings."

Carl breathed a sigh of relief. "That? Well, you can deal with that."

"I don't think so. It's you they want to talk to. Apparently, something has come to light that they'd like your opinion on. I don't know what."

Carl shook his head. Strange. The case was twelve years old, and nothing much had changed since then. So why now, and who were "they" exactly?

"Are they detectives from Slagelse?"

"Yes and no. It's the Dutch who have a new lead, as far as I know. But forget that for now and help Assad as best you can. It's so awful what's going on down there."

Carl nodded. He didn't have the slightest intention of giving that old case a second thought. Why should he?

"Just one question," said Hardy. "Do you know what the people who analyzed Gordon's recordings concluded?"

"About what?"

"About the background noises. The barking dog and so on."

"Nothing, I'm afraid. We're working on thin air here." Afterward, he called Mona and told her about Assad's call.

And the last thing he did before boarding the plane was to text Assad to tell him he was on his way and that the departure time was on schedule.

54

Assad

Assad waited in the barren room. No sounds to cause a distraction and no smells that could cause discomfort—or the opposite. It was completely sterile, like an operating room where everything unnecessary had been removed and the rest disinfected.

He had been waiting for hours. He had kicked the wastepaper basket hundreds of times, paced a thousand steps back and forth, and sat down and stood up again countless times. Just waiting and waiting for someone to come and tell him that Ghaalib's next message had arrived.

The last thing he had heard from outside was that he shouldn't worry because more than a thousand police personnel and soldiers were stationed and ready to act in all imaginable and unimaginable places: government buildings and embassies, media companies and TV stations, important rail and bus transport hubs, monuments and squares with pigeons, synagogues and Jewish memorials and graveyards, and even at the memorial for the homosexual victims of the Second World War.

A SWAT team charged with coordinating the surveillance operations was based in a room ten meters from him and was working flat out, yet Assad was still going crazy. What else could he be when Ghaalib was always one step ahead? "The one who goes first in a game of checkers should always win," his father always used to say, and those words were eating away at his soul because Assad was only one piece out of many, and when the first move was made, the game would be out of his hands. Ghaalib had already had many opportunities to kill him. The sniper in Frankfurt, for example. His shot to the side of Mustafa's head had proved how easy it would have been. But that was not what Ghaalib wanted. He didn't just want to take Assad's life; he didn't just want him to suffer; he wanted to *see* him suffer, and that was the path he was currently leading him down. The idea was that he should see his loved ones die before he did. And regardless of how many competent men there were on the streets just now, Ghaalib would succeed if Assad didn't stop him. But how? It seemed impossible.

He heard the steps from the corridor before the knocking at the door, and then a small delegation headed by Weber invaded the room, pumping more adrenaline into Assad's nervous system.

"We've received another message from Ghaalib," said Weber. "He's instructing you to get ready to take the S-Bahn to Halensee Station, and without an escort of any sort. You'll be watched during the journey and at the destination itself, he says. At precisely one thirty, you should go up the stairs from the platforms and wait on Kurfürstendamm for further instructions. If the police or intelligence service follow you or keep you under surveillance, your wife will be shot."

Assad reached out for the note. There was nothing in the content or form that could shock him anymore. So, from now on, he would just play the game and wait for his chance.

"How did you receive it this time?"

"We received a text from a phone that we thought was dead. It's the one we gave Joan Aiguader, and this time it only took a few minutes to trace it."

"Where was it?"

"Next to the Brandenburg Gate, of course. It was in the handlebar basket of one of the public bikes. Next time it might be Alexanderplatz or the Reichstag building, and we're fairly sure that the people delivering them are just random people being paid for it. People think they're taking part in a prank. The problem, however, is that we don't know what or who to keep an eye on."

There was an hour and forty-five minutes until the next message. And while he waited, Ghaalib was orchestrating everything. It was unbearable.

He pictured Marwa and Nella. They could have been happy with him, and they could have been happy without him, but now they had to pay the price for him and his choices. As meaningful as it had been for him to survive back when he escaped from the prison, it was now equally insignificant.

Assad's watch vibrated. It was a message from Carl that he was about to take off and that the flight was on schedule.

The end of Kurfürstendamm where Halensee S-Bahn station was situated wasn't the part of Kurfürstendamm associated with its otherwise pompous name. High-rise apartment buildings constructed from plastered concrete, the Bauhaus DIY shop as the biggest attraction in the area, rain-soaked tarmac, and, far in the distance, poking through the damp fog that had gathered over the city during the last few hours, the faint outline of something reminiscent of the Eiffel Tower.

The time was precisely 13:25, and people were rushing around with their umbrellas as if this were any other normal day. But this wasn't just any other day. People would die, and families would be crushed for all eternity.

Probably also his.

Assad tapped the back of his coat to check that his gun was where it should be.

Then, a few minutes early, the watch on his arm and the mobile in his back pocket vibrated. Assad took a deep breath so that he was 100 percent prepared when he received his instructions.

Thankfully, it was Carl who was calling. Assad tilted his head back and let out a sigh of relief.

"We're a little bit delayed because of some idiot and also due to the fog, so I only just got off the plane a moment ago. Where are you?

I can see on my watch that you're near an S-Bahn station. Halensee, right?"

"Yes. I'm waiting for my next instructions. Are you on your way?"

"Yes, I'm on my way out of the terminal building. Can you wait for me where you are?"

"Maybe; I'll try."

Everything in this world is about trying to achieve a sense of security, and regardless of how surreal it might have felt in the current situation, Assad was able to breathe easier after Carl's call.

However, it only lasted a few seconds before Assad's mobile rang again.

"It's Weber. You need to go immediately because you only have five minutes or your wife will be killed. Go left down Schwarzbacher Strasse next to Bauhaus. Not long after, you'll see a small green park on your right-hand side. That's where you'll find the pigeon that we've been searching for all this time. The message says that if you look carefully around you when you're there, everything will be clear. That's all. Be careful, Assad, and keep it together. You can't see us, but we're nearby. Stay on the line until you're there. Now go as fast as you can."

He arrived out of breath at the small green park in under three minutes. It appeared from behind an eight-story concrete box and was very modest, practically the size of a stamp, and squeezed in between two busy approach roads.

Assad immediately understood what he saw. On a triangular, winter-worn piece of grass, there was a low concrete base on which stood a metal sculpture in the form of a birdlike creature. It was approximately three meters high, headless and with outstretched wings pointing in opposite directions. It almost seemed bashfully frozen in a pose that could symbolize that its wings had been clipped, but also that it could take flight at any moment.

And under the long stem on which it stood, meant to illustrate the bird's outstretched legs, there was a small inscription:

MELLI-BEESE-ANLAGE. ERSTE DEUTSCHE FLIEGERIN
1886–1925

He put his mobile up to his ear. "Are you still there, Weber?"

"Yes, and we've identified your object now. It's a sculpture. The statue is called *Die Taube,* 'The Pigeon,' and I've got a picture of it now on the Internet. It's the low-flying one, Assad." He swore out loud to himself. It could have been found so easily—with or without ornithologists. "What do you see?" Weber asked.

"One wing points to a pedestrian bridge at the end of the park. I'm going to run up it."

He heard them talking in the background as he stood in the middle of the bridge, which had a mass of cars underneath it on a six-lane road and led to a very normal-looking residential area.

"Nothing here, Weber," he shouted, and ran back.

He looked again at the sculpture and the other wing, which pointed at ninety degrees in the opposite direction directly at the high-rise building.

Then he heard an unmistakably Middle Eastern–inspired ringtone and turned to look at the sharp metal edges where the wings met. The cell phone lying there wasn't big, one of the old-fashioned flip phones, and was difficult to see from the ground. Assad grabbed the bird's legs with the hand holding his own phone, stood up on the concrete base, and stretched as far as he could so he could reach the phone.

"Yes," he said when he was back on the grass and had opened it.

"Zaid al-Asadi," answered the voice on the other end, and it made Assad's blood freeze.

"Yes," he said again.

"It's time. Let one of the wings locate the goal and be there in a few minutes. Then you'll have a chance to see the whole thing go off."

Then the caller hung up.

Assad's hands were shaking as he tried to control his breathing and voice.

"Did you hear that?" he panted into his own mobile.

There was a scratching sound from the other end, but Weber said nothing.

"Oh God," someone shouted down the phone while others shouted that they had to leave right now.

"So? What should I do, Weber?"

"The wing points toward a known target. We already have people there but not many," said Weber finally. "It points directly at Funk-turm, the old radio tower by the trade halls. There are thousands of people in the trade hall area just now. We're on our way."

Assad gasped. It was the tower he had seen the outline of through the fog. And as far as he could tell, it was far away.

This time he was back at the S-Bahn station in two minutes and sailed down the stairs like an unmanned white-water-rafting boat.

He saw the yellow-and-red train approaching the station and jumped on when he realized that it was heading north on the circle line.

"Does this train go to the trade halls?" he shouted. People looked at him, a little frightened, and nodded.

"Where's the nearest station? Should I stay on this line?"

"You need to change in a moment at Westkreuz, and then you need to take a train heading for Spandau and get off at Messe Süd station straight after. It's very close to the trade halls."

He barely managed to say thanks before they arrived at the station and he jumped off.

"The train toward Spandau?" he shouted frantically on the platform, and managed to raise a couple of fingers in the air and point.

When he sat down on the train and caught his breath before the next station, his fellow passengers were looking at him as if he were a drug addict with serious withdrawal symptoms: sweating and unable to sit still in his seat. And that's exactly how he felt. It was as if life would end in a moment.

And maybe it would.

ENTRANCE HALL B, FAST LANE, was written on a sign on the other side of the street when he raced out of the station by the Messe trade halls. And far behind it, a metal construction was poking through the fog and indicating that if he didn't run for all he was worth, he would arrive too late. It couldn't possibly have been the right S-Bahn station to get off at.

He rounded the buildings at a furious speed and reached a parking lot, where a burly security guard refused to let him take a shortcut across the lot and informed him that it wasn't a shortcut anyway.

With his heart in his throat, Assad glanced at a map hanging in front of the entrance to the parking lot and realized that he would have to go past numerous halls before he reached the east entrance opposite the tower.

From a distance, he could already see armed men in riot gear heading up the spiral stairs that twisted around the interior of the construction, connecting the radio tower's restaurant platform with the slightly smaller platform right at the top. Was it from there that Dieter Baumann would kill people, and was it there in the open square behind the buildings that Marwa and Nella would shortly be killed while he helplessly watched?

From the road that ran along the trade hall area, sirens were going off in both directions. There was still no sound of gunshots in the area, so Ghaalib must have been holding back. Maybe he was just waiting for Assad to arrive.

Assad was in doubt. Maybe he shouldn't try to get there. Maybe this hell wouldn't be unleashed without him.

His doubts brought tears to his eyes as he ran the remainder of the way. Farther ahead near hall twelve, he could see groups of armed men shoving one another to get through the main entrance and assist their colleagues who were already inside.

He pulled out his gun from the back of his trousers and prepared himself. He just hoped Weber's men would already be there and let him slip past. If they didn't, he would—

"Assad," someone shouted as he passed a light blue Volkswagen van. He only just managed to think that they had been waiting for him and felt a strange sense of relief in the moment when he was knocked down. He watched through blurry eyes as his debilitated legs were dragged along toward the van.

55

Joan

Joan hadn't been given any breakfast and hadn't even had his diaper changed. He was given his injection and then left humiliated and soiled in his wheelchair while people checked things and frightening metallic sounds and orders being shouted in all directions filled the rooms.

The first group had been ready for a long time. Before ten o'clock, when they were due to leave, they were already standing fully dressed in their disguises in the meeting room, where Ghaalib gave them their final instructions and hugged each one in turn.

Joan had been shocked to see how authentically Jasmin and the three men were disguised. She was wearing a head scarf, a shawl, and a modest dress, while the men were wearing hats with curls hanging down in front of their ears, beards of varying lengths and slightly red in color, steel-frame glasses, and dazzlingly white shirts, which, like the bulletproof vests and black suits, were almost completely covered by long black coats.

The plan was for them to take the bus to the S-Bahn station on Landsberger Allee, where their guide, Linda Schwarz from Charlotten-burg Tours, would pick them up for the tour.

"Is Jasmin actually allowed to travel in the same bus as the men?" one of them asked, and several of them agreed that it would be wrong. But Beena intervened. If she sat right at the back with the wheelchair users, even the most Orthodox Jews in Berlin wouldn't bat an eyelid.

When the group had left, the mood in the apartment changed. Given that they wouldn't be coming back, the others began thinking about what lay ahead, and it made the waiting longer and fueled their nerves.

Ghaalib was speaking on his cell phone and wasn't with the rest of the group most of the time, and so the others began to talk about what could go wrong.

It was only when the disability bus arrived to collect them that they calmed down, and that was perhaps the most frightening thing of all.

Joan closed his eyes and felt more alone than at any other time in his life. Even when he had been about to throw himself in the waves and end his life, he had been more in harmony with his surroundings. But now, forced to be the devil's witness, he implored his god for the first time since he was a boy and made the sign of the cross in his head. *In the name of the Father, and of the Son, and of the Holy Spirit. Amen,* he prayed a couple of times, followed by three Hail Marys—*Hail Mary, Mother of God, pray for us sinners now and at the hour of our death. Amen*—and ended with making another couple of imaginary signs of the cross on his chest.

When they had driven for fifteen minutes, Ghaalib announced that they had reached the zoo and that they should prepare themselves. Joan looked away from the facades that had rushed past them in one gray neighborhood after another, and instead looked straight ahead at the tunnel under a railway bridge that they would be passing through in a moment. On the pavement by the wall, there was a long line of homeless people sleeping on dirty mattresses. Plastic bags and rubbish were littered everywhere, but Joan envied them. He would have given his right arm to trade places with them. Sleep and nothing to fear but the cold of night and where their next meal would come from.

What a luxury, living hand to mouth. Just to have a life.

And there on the other side of the tunnel, the entrance to the zoo came into view with its wrought-iron railings and granite lions. He had just managed to imagine the terrible massacre of happy children and parents when their disability bus turned right and passed a bus terminal before stopping in front of a large glass building, which he guessed was the S-Bahn terminal. Was this where they were getting off? Why else would they have stopped?

The women in the wheelchairs in front of him were breathing heavily. If only he could say something to them and comfort them with a little tenderness and compassion.

Then an old, light blue Volkswagen van stopped alongside them with its curtains shut at the back side window. Joan's parents had always wanted a van like this so they could drive to the countryside and maybe even to France one day with the children. Just another thing that never materialized to brighten their lives. Actually, nothing they or his sister or he had dreamed of back then had ever come true.

Then the curtain was drawn a little in the Volkswagen van and Ghaalib rushed over to the window just behind the driver.

From behind the curtain, an Arab with curly hair appeared. He stared directly at the three women in the wheelchairs. Within a split second, his face contorted into the most agonized expression Joan had ever seen. And in the same moment, the oldest of the women, who was sitting by the window, stopped breathing. The Arab's moist eyes clung to her, and the woman whined in small huffs. And when the Volkswagen drove off, she was unable to stop.

Ghaalib's body was shaking. When he turned toward the women, his face had completely dissolved into a sickeningly blissful expression, as if the sight could have given him an orgasm. The three men at the front of the bus also looked back, and like Ghaalib they seemed satisfied, as if the plan was already falling into place. Then Fadi nodded to Beena. She straightened her shawl and readied herself. But for what?

Joan's breathing grew heavier, like the woman's in front of him.

The next second, they drove past a large McDonald's, where people were standing in line without giving the world around them a second thought.

But the world is just here outside, he screamed mentally. *Help us!*

They pulled over at the open part of a large square that appeared only a hundred meters after they had taken a left turn. He didn't recognize the ruinous tall church tower standing majestically in the middle of the square, but hundreds of people appeared awestruck as they walked around both it and the modern building next to it.

So, this was where it was going to happen.

Ghaalib, wearing his Jewish attire, was the first person to exit the bus. He strode over to the far end of the square. Then the others took out the wheelchairs and left them for a moment on the edge of the square before the disability bus disappeared again. Joan watched it drive off. They wouldn't be needing it anymore.

Fadi nodded to the other men, who first glanced over toward the sky-high facade of a luxury hotel and then over to the far end of the square, where some sort of structure was surrounded by a cluster of futuristic, circular-shaped stairs that led down to an underground area. It was somewhere behind it that Ghaalib had disappeared.

The young guy, Afif, who had been pushing Ronia, the youngest of the women in the wheelchairs, was directed over to Joan's wheelchair and shown with a pointed finger where he should push him. The young Afif was happy and seemed to be far from aware of what was going to happen. When he placed the GoPro camera on Joan's head, he chuckled with pride.

Moments later, the second group came walking up from the zoo with the guide in front holding an umbrella in the air.

Afif cheered when he saw them and patted Joan on the head as if he were a little puppy being told where to look.

They appeared very plausible strolling along in their authentic Jewish clothes. Even the smiles they generously flashed at everyone they passed seemed genuine.

Apart from Afif's exclamation, the two groups kept their distance from each other save a few nods here and there, as was to be expected from two groups with the same cultural background.

Then the first group congregated around Ronia's wheelchair, followed by the second group, in a closed circle.

Joan knew what they were doing. In a few seconds they would all be equipped with their Uzis, which would then be concealed under long coats and women's shawls. It was just a matter of time now.

The guide, who had been standing smiling in the background, stepped forward and presented herself to Beena. She smiled warmly and nodded when Beena pointed to Nella's wheelchair. Shortly after, the guide walked over to the three women in wheelchairs and stroked each of them on the cheek. It was the kiss of Judas coming to life. But the guide wasn't Judas; she was an innocent victim who was possibly trying to secure her small office more clients. She continued talking with Beena while following her, Fadi, Osman, and the three women around the church tower and toward the ramp that led inside the tower. Meanwhile, the others spread out across the square in their respective strategic positions.

56

Ghaalib

When Ghaalib reached the far end of the square, he entered a restaurant situated there. At the counter just inside the door, he was given a plastic card instructing him to pay the amount on the card when he had eaten and was ready to leave the establishment. As soon as he ordered his food on the first floor, the chef would make sure the bill was added to his specific card.

Ghaalib nodded. The guy would have to be very lucky not to pay for the next fifteen minutes with his life given how close he was standing to the windows.

There was a lot of activity on the first floor of the restaurant. People were queuing at the counters, where a row of chefs looked at the hungry customers' orders and created risottos, pizzas, pasta dishes, and other Italian specialties. Very orderly and effective. And very loud.

BERLIN BLEIBT DOCH BERLIN was written on the wall behind the chefs. *Berlin remains Berlin.*

Ghaalib smiled. That truth would soon be put to the test.

He turned to face the large windows, which afforded a view of the whole square, and found a free seat by the window closest to the bar. He nodded to the bartender, ordered a soda with his plastic card, and watched the scene on both sides of the renowned Kaiser Wilhelm Memorial Church.

This target was a totally brilliant idea of Hamid's.

Even though most of Berlin had been left in ruins at the end of the

Second World War, the lower sixty meters of this tower remained standing. Berliners referred to their monument as "the hollow tooth," which for all eternity would symbolize the fall and resurrection of the German people.

For all eternity. Ghaalib savored the expression and smiled. When the bombs had exploded and the tower was no longer standing, the mission would be complete, and those in the group who survived would all be on their way toward the next target. Ghaalib scanned the square. At the far right stood the luxury hotel where Dieter Baumann was ready to counter any form of resistance that might come from the direction of Budapester Strasse, thereby covering Jasmin's group. He could see all four of them standing in their brilliant disguises in their respective positions and glancing around so that they weren't taken off guard by an influx of guards or police.

The left side of the square was bordered by Tauentzienstrasse and Kurfürstendamm, and everything seemed under control there. Beena's group with Fadi and Osman was slowly making its way toward the ramp that led up into the tower.

He couldn't see Afif with Joan because the angle was too sharp down toward the corner by Nürnberger Strasse; besides, they were probably already standing underneath the canopy in front of the Fossil watch shop as planned. No matter what, he couldn't allow anything to happen to Afif because he was the only person in the world whom Ghaalib loved and who loved him back.

He did, however, have a clear view of the light blue Volkswagen, which, as planned, was now parked outside the round building housing the Levi's store, straight across from the ramp that led to the church tower entrance.

They had forced Zaid to wait in the car because it would soon be the hour of reckoning and Ghaalib's big moment. Zaid would have a clear view of his wife and two daughters being pushed to the abyss. In only a matter of minutes, he would learn what revenge really was. That it *was* happening now and that the third woman really was his younger daughter, who he couldn't yet know was still alive. And he would count the seconds that passed from when they left Ronia's wheelchair halfway up the ramp until everything was over. Ronia, who would die with the first targeted explosion in her backrest. Then the shots from Osman and the group on the other side that would rid the square of all life. Then the shots inside the church tower as Fadi and Beena would race out from there while shooting all around them. And then, finally, the apocalyptic bomb in the bottom of Ronia's wheelchair that would cause the tower ruin to collapse, helped along by the explosive vests worn by Marwa and Nella, which would be detonated in the heart of the ruin.

Zaid should have killed me when he had the chance, thought Ghaalib. *Killed me and spared me the humiliation of all the years where women have looked at my disfigured face with disgust, and the dismembering that left me unable to take the women myself, leaving me no choice but to force my men to do it instead. It will all be avenged now.*

He made a call and saw the driver of the Volkswagen farther down the square raise the phone to his ear.

"I can see you clearly down there. You kept to the timetable. I'm proud of you; *jazakallah khair,* may Allah reward you for your goodness."

The brothers in the Volkswagen were another pair of Hamid's recruits from the boxing club. Radicalized, confident, and able-bodied guys who from time to time had given Hamid a hand in return for praise and payment without asking questions. When all this was over, they would suffer the same fate as Zaid. He would take care of it personally. There could be no loose ends in Berlin.

"Have you got him under control?" he asked, and took out his binoculars from his jacket pocket.

"Yes, he can't budge an inch," laughed the man at the other end of the phone. "When is it happening? We almost can't wait."

"I'll come down to you shortly. But push him a little closer to the window. I want to see him too. Tell him to look up over the atrocious structure in the middle of the square. I'm sitting here waving to him."

57

Assad

It took a moment before Assad understood what had happened at the trade hall area when he was knocked down. A young, bearded Arab with a multicolored bandanna on his head was sitting in front of him, laughing with satisfaction and holding a roll of gaffer tape in his hand. He had good reason to be satisfied, because Assad's arms and legs were taped so effectively that he couldn't move without falling off the bench.

"Welcome to the club," he said, and put tape around Assad's head and mouth. "You're going to be our guest for the next half hour, so stay calm or you'll feel my fist." To illustrate his point, he thrust a hairy fist toward him and waved it in his face.

Assad was shaken. In a split second, predator had become prey. Why hadn't he anticipated Ghaalib's offensive? It had been bound to come.

He stayed still for a moment and worked on composing himself. What good did it do him to have his adrenaline pumping ten to the dozen when he couldn't put it to good use? Just now, he had to concentrate on using his brain. It was his only weapon in the current circumstances.

He looked around the interior of the van. It was a typical camper in the style designed by DIY enthusiasts in the seventies: curtains for the side and back windows, a couple of benches with thin foam-rubber mattresses, a folding table between the benches in beige Formica, a small sink, a portable stove, and a direct view to the driver, who was currently racing through the streets.

"We got you," said the bandanna guy. "And all your friends are running around like headless chickens in the trade hall area. I wonder what they'll find."

Both he and the driver busted out laughing, but, for Assad, it was a relief. It meant they hadn't begun yet, and that might mean that Marwa and Nella . . .

"My apologies," said the bandanna guy, and pulled Assad's taped arms up to a snap hook above the window and wound gaffer tape around it. "Now you're sitting how we want you. In ten minutes, we'll pull back the curtains a bit so you can see out. I'm sure you'll see something you weren't expecting."

Assad noticed the vibrations from the watch on his wrist. He twisted his taped arms a little and could just make out Carl's message.

I'm leaving the trade hall area now. Where are you?

Your GPS says you're heading . . .

Then he couldn't read any more.

Assad looked over the driver's shoulder and tried to work out the direction in which they were heading. He could see weak reflections from a pale sun in the open windows along the road, which meant they were heading north. Then they turned right and passed the opera on their left-hand side and came to a large roundabout where they again turned right. It seemed like a detour, but it presumably had an aim.

Then they stopped.

"Are you ready?" asked the bandanna guy, who without hesitation pulled back the curtain a little. And through the dirty windows, Assad looked directly into a pair of eyes he hadn't seen in sixteen years. Eternally beautiful and in this moment the most shocked and agonized in the world. She managed to part her lips but couldn't form them into words. It was as if the world had stopped. It was Marwa.

"I'm closing them now. You've seen enough," said the bandanna guy, and held his hand like a claw in front of Assad's face. And through those spread, dirty fingers, Assad said good-bye to his life before catching sight, in the final second, of a figure behind his beloved wife who he didn't think was Nella.

He regurgitated a couple of times from behind the tape and was about to choke. His lower body twisted in vain. And when he realized that the Volkswagen was setting off again, he lost the desire to breathe.

"Wake up now," shouted the bandanna guy while hitting him across the cheek. "You can't die on us. Ghaalib would be furious. Put your foot down, damn it!" The last command was directed to the guy driving the Volkswagen, who had already overtaken the first three cars hazardously.

Assad regurgitated again and felt the liquid oozing down his chin. It was more bearable now because the bandanna guy had pulled the gaffer tape around his mouth up toward his nose so that he could breathe.

Then his watch vibrated again.

Do you know roughly where . . .

"Look over there," said the bandanna guy, opening the curtain. "It's just on the other side of the road that it will all happen. Any minute now! And you've got a front-row seat to a world event." Then he grabbed the gaffer tape under Assad's nose and roughly pulled it down over his mouth. But it wasn't quite as tight as before.

There was a muted ringtone sound from the front seats, and the driver fumbled on the seat next to him and answered the phone.

He sat there nodding for what felt like an eternity while the crazy guy next to Assad produced a video camera and prepared to start filming.

The driver turned to his buddy and silently formed the word *Ghaalib* with an exaggerated facial expression, which brought back Assad's nausea and made him start sweating profusely.

Assad closed his eyes and said a prayer. *May this devil on earth feel his punishment right now. May he suffer a heart attack and drown in his own blood. May he suffer the worst torments before he draws his last breath. And may all his evil deeds plague him in his final moments.*

Assad pushed the gaffer tape in front of his mouth with his tongue so the saliva flowed. He was sweating so much now that his entire body was covered in a layer of moisture.

What is it that's going to happen? he wondered, but didn't dare look for answers. He clenched his hands. *Will I be able to look?* he thought, and felt sick to his core. Then he noticed that the moisture was gathering under the tape on his wrists and hands. It was too much to hope that the adhesive would begin to lose its grip, but the idea made him clench his hands even tighter. His special forces training had taught him many good ways to free himself from plastic strips, but it was much more difficult when it came to gaffer tape. If you tugged at it too much, the tape twisted like the handles on a plastic bag that was too heavy and began to tighten and cut. The only thing that worked was patience, treating the gaffer tape as living tissue and sensing how it reacted and worked.

Assad carefully turned his wrists on their axis under the tape again and again, and then he felt his watch vibrating once more. Now he had to twist the tape even more so he could read the message on his watch, and this time it was short.

Am at the zoo now. You're close, right?

Carl was only a few hundred meters away! It was crazy.

Damn it, Carl, thought Assad. *When will you get it that I can't answer?*

The bandanna guy raised his eyebrows and lowered the camera for a moment while he observed his buddy's concentrated face as he talked with Ghaalib.

"Yes, he can't budge an inch," said the driver, and started laughing.

He looked at his buddy and smiled.

"When is it happening?" he asked Ghaalib. "We almost can't wait."

The bandanna guy gave him the thumbs-up. It was very disturbing.

Then the guy put the mobile down on the passenger seat. His face resembled that of a child who was about to open the biggest present of the year.

"Ghaalib says you need to push him toward the window."

Then he shouted to Assad as if he were hard of hearing and couldn't hear anything from a distance of two meters. "Look over at the ugly, round building in the middle of the square and up toward the restaurant. Ghaalib wants to wave to you. He's sitting up there on the second floor."

And while the bandanna guy pulled the curtain back even more, Assad began to feel that the gaffer tape was loosening a little and that his thumb was slowly inching toward the snap hook spring.

The bandanna guy pointed up toward the restaurant, and Assad screwed his eyes shut. Of course that coward Ghaalib was at a safe distance while he let everyone go to their deaths.

Yes, now he could see a small figure up at the window swaying from side to side. It was presumably him.

"Ghaalib has the remote control," said the driver. "And when everything is over, he'll come down to us."

Ghaalib has the remote control, he'd said. But even though it was terrible, Assad felt nothing but scorn for this update. *The driver obviously doesn't know how slim the chances are that we'll survive when the bombs go off,* thought Assad while continuing to subtly twist his hands.

Now the camera was placed close to the window so that Assad could still see out from underneath it. It was obviously an awkward position for the bandanna guy.

"Can't you take the camera?" he asked his buddy. And while he stretched in over the front seat to pass over the camera, Assad struggled to press the spring his life depended on.

Then there was a loud banging on the passenger door of the Volkswagen.

The two criminals looked at each other, mouthing warnings silently with their lips. Then the driver smiled toward the door on the passenger side while the bandanna guy closed the short curtain between the front seats and the back.

"You can't park here," said a gruff voice on the other side of the curtain when the door was opened.

"Yeah, sorry, it's only for a few minutes while I'm waiting for someone."

"That's all very well, but you're parked illegally," said the voice. "Didn't you see the road markings?"

"Yeah, but the woman we're waiting for is very weak on her feet." He pointed ahead. "It's one of the people in a wheelchair you can see on the square. She's just popping into the church her mother has told her so much about for two minutes. Then we'll pick her up and be on our way. Isn't that okay? I'll make sure I move if I'm in anyone's way."

"You're in my way and you're also breaking traffic regulations. Do you understand? You'll just have to drive around the block until she's finished."

The driver's voice still sounded as if he couldn't have cared less. "Because otherwise you'll give me a ticket, right?" he said, sounding a little too cocky now.

"Listen, pal. I can do that anyway. But if you don't move on, I'll walk the ten steps down the street and fetch the policemen drinking coffee around the corner. I imagine you have a criminal record that they'd be glad to give a once-over."

Assad heard the parking attendant laugh. It was one of the rare times it felt tempting to pat a generalizing racist like him on the shoulder.

The bandanna guy's jaws muscles were grinding when he reached for the gun lying behind one of the pillows on the bench. It was Assad's own gun as far as he could tell.

"My record is clean if you must know, you pig," said the driver, and started the van. Then he drove a few meters around the corner and pulled in to the side.

The bandanna guy laughed when he saw Assad glancing at his gun.

"Yes," he said. "FYI, we've also been looking after your phone. We've been kind enough to turn it off to save the battery."

"I'll just check with Ghaalib about what he wants us to do," said the driver, and called him.

"Okay, Ghaalib, you saw everything. I couldn't do anything else but drive around the corner. But what now?" asked the driver. "He said there are policemen in one of—" He nodded a couple of times. "Okay. I'll drive right around the block and park at the same place as before. Let me know if the parking attendant is still there."

Afterward, he leaned back and opened the curtain a little.

"Ghaalib will ask the others to wait until we're back," he said to his buddy. "He'll tell one of the others from the other side of the church to keep an eye on the side street over here so he can hit the officers when they hear the shots and come out. If the parking attendant comes back again, Ghaalib says I should shoot him. And then he'll set the whole thing off. Give me the guy's gun."

The bandanna guy gave him the thumbs-up, passed him Assad's gun through the gap in the curtains, and then turned to Assad and began tugging at his tape to see if everything was as it should be.

Assad sucked the tape into his mouth and bit it while stretching his hands so the tape was tight.

The last thing didn't fool him.

"*Zum Teufel, du Sohn einer blutpissenden Hafenhure,*" he shouted. He had obviously adopted some German high culture.

He pulled at the gaffer tape around Assad's wrists and fumbled for the tape that was lying on the bench.

This time he wound it so tightly around his wrists that Assad was hopelessly tied up. He tilted his head back and squeezed his eyes shut. Now there was really nothing he could do.

Assad wanted to cry but couldn't. Everything in him shut down, even his breathing.

I need air, he thought, and began pushing at the gaffer tape with his tongue again. This time it only took a moment before he felt the air seeping in at the sides of his mouth, which made it easier to fill his lungs.

Then his watch vibrated from under the tape.

Was Carl confused that his GPS was now showing that he was moving again? And would he start following the signal?

Oh, no, Carl, don't do that, he thought. *I'll be back in a moment.*

Then the Volkswagen started up and headed off into the traffic again.

58

Carl

When Carl was finally standing in front of the airport terminal in Berlin, he hailed a taxi straightaway.

"I need to go to an S-Bahn station called Halensee. There's a guy waiting for me there. Do you know it?"

The taxi driver nodded.

The plane hadn't landed in time, so he was in a hurry. An idiot had taken the liberty of boarding with such a bad hangover that he threw up in the aisle and smacked one of the stewards when he tried to help. He was like a bull in a china shop right up until the police arrived to take him away, and that was the first fifteen minutes gone. And then there was the fog, which didn't seem very bad now. In total, a twenty-minute delay.

Unfortunately, it now seemed like it had cost precious minutes, because as they approached the S-Bahn station, the GPS dot on his phone showed that Assad was now on the move and was to the north of them.

"Just follow my directions and drive," said Carl while he followed the small dot on the GPS map.

To begin with, the taxi driver was very patient, but after Carl changed the destination several times, he grew more and more nervous.

"You've got money, right?" he asked tentatively, and seemed doubtful until Carl pulled out a one-hundred-euro note and placed it next to the gearshift.

"I'm looking for a friend here in the city, and I think he'll be moving around for a while yet," answered Carl. "I need to reach him as soon as possible."

It was visible from the way the taxi driver was staring straight ahead at the traffic that he was wondering if there was something illegal going on.

"I'm a policeman from Denmark," said Carl, and showed the man his ID. The taxi driver glanced at it but didn't seem totally convinced. *Such a shitty ID card!* thought Carl again.

"He's to our north just now on something called Bismarckstrasse. Do you know it?"

The taxi driver rolled his eyes. "If I didn't, I'd as well be looking for another job," he said. Actually, the road did look very wide and long on the map.

Carl called Assad again but it went straight to voice mail. Then he asked the driver to put his foot down and was rebutted with the reply that if he did, they would be stopped by the police and then he could multiply his hundred-euro note many times over. They certainly wouldn't get there any quicker if the police got involved.

Carl called Assad again in vain and had a disquieting feeling that something might be very wrong. Then he found Herbert Weber's number and called him.

A few seconds later a tired voice answered.

"Yes, Carl Mørck, we're a bit busy just now. Where are you? In Copenhagen?"

"No, I'm heading toward the center down Bismarckstrasse. Do you know where Assad is heading? He was just going in the direction of Hardenbergstrasse."

It went silent at the other end. "I don't understand," Weber finally answered. "My colleagues from the Berlin police have told me where the street is, and it's quite a distance from here. Assad is supposed to be on his way here to the trade halls where we're waiting for him. I've called him, but he hasn't answered. I really hope it's because his mobile is turned off or has run out of battery. But I'm obviously worried now."

"The trade halls?"

"Yes, but it was a false alarm. So, you know roughly where he is?"

"Yes, Assad and I have synchronized our smartwatches so we can locate each other."

There was talking and shouting at the other end.

"We don't get it," said Weber. "Assad doesn't have a vehicle."

What was going on? No phone, no vehicle, no contact with the intelligence services alongside which he was working.

Carl braced himself. Given that there hadn't been any sign of life since Carl had called Assad from the airport, there was good reason to be very worried. Damn it!

"You'll have to guide us, Mørck. We're leaving now," shouted Weber, making sure everyone around him got the message.

Two minutes later, Assad's dot stopped moving. As far as he could tell, it was very close to the zoo. It didn't last long, but long enough for Carl to wonder what was going on. When the dot began moving again, it was only for a minute or less and then it stopped on the map again.

Do you know roughly where you are, Assad? he wrote in a text. But still no answer.

When they turned into the square in front of the zoo, the driver became seriously uncomfortable.

"I don't know what your game is, but I don't like this one bit. There are too many cops on the street just now."

He pulled over to the side and stopped the car. "I need to ask you to get out now. I'm done."

Carl was about to protest but then noticed the same thing as the driver. In every direction—along the zoo railings, in the parking lot, and farther down next to a large glass building—groups of ten to twelve policemen were gathering. Several of them were receiving instructions from their group leader, who was pointing down the street. Were they so sure that it was going to happen here?

"Let's just call it a hundred euros if you get out now," said the driver, and then he drove off. It was probably wise.

Am at the zoo now. You're close, right? he wrote in a text, still without an answer. But maybe Assad could read it. Maybe it gave him hope that they would find him and make it in time.

Carl looked at his watch and began running down the street past the heavily armed officers.

The dot had stopped on the next street, so he could be there in seconds. But then an arm was thrown out in front of him, stopping him in his tracks, and it was no joke. Three officers in riot gear lunged toward him, and a mass of arms were flung around him, holding him tight. He obviously shouldn't have been running here.

"Where do you think you're going?" one of them shouted.

Carl was spluttering with rage. "What the hell are you doing?" He screamed at them, first in Danish and then in something reminiscent of English. "Let me go! This is a matter of life and death!"

They shook their heads and looked at him as if he were a serial killer.

"Call Herbert Weber now and you'll find out what a big mistake you're making."

They said they really had no idea who Herbert Weber was, and if he resisted any more, they would arrest him. Pragmatic as he could sometimes be, he stretched out his arms and let them search him. He looked at them angrily when they finally found his ID card and stared at it as if it were a discount coupon for a foot massage.

"Read what it says, for God's sake. I'm a detective inspector from Copenhagen, and we're working together on this. Right now, one of my colleagues is in serious trouble, and if I don't get to him in the next few seconds, you can wave good-bye to any chance of promotion *ever!*"

But in spite of his outburst and threats, they didn't let him go. Carl looked with fear at the GPS because it was moving again.

He sent a text immediately. *Are you on the move again? Why aren't you answering?* But Carl knew deep down that Assad couldn't answer. He could just as well have written, *I'm with you, mate,* but he wasn't, and it was all down to these bloody riot robots.

"A moment," he said, and asked for his phone, which one of the idiots was staring at as if it might fly off at any minute.

He called Weber. "Where are you?"

"We're close. We've ordered all our men to head to the area near you. Where are you now?"

"Would you kindly tell the officer here at the zoo who's restraining me that he should sod off back to the provincial backwater he came from and leave me alone!"

He handed the phone to the officer. They mumbled to each other and then the imbecile pulled back as if he had never been there. No apology. Not even the slightest hint that maybe they ought to get their act together and help him. Idiot!

Carl started to run. "Assad just got away from me," he shouted into the mobile, "but I'm running in the direction of where he was just before."

"Where was that?" asked Weber.

"On the street next to a square. Right next to a church."

"What church?"

"Kaiser Wilhelm Memorial Church, it says on a street sign here."

He heard a moan at the other end.

"That's what we all feared. Be careful, Carl Mørck. We'll be there in a moment. I'll send my people near the zoo to come and secure the square."

"No, wait. I'll be there shortly. I can see the church now. Just now the square isn't very busy from this side; about forty, fifty people, I think. They seem to be building or repairing something because there's scaffolding around a second tower just next to the church tower ruin, and there's boarding around the actual church tower."

"Can you see anything suspicious?"

"No. Just a bunch of different tourists who look alike, and some Orthodox Jews in traditional dress."

"Orthodox Jews? Are they grouped together?"

"No, they're spread out like . . ."

He saw it now. "They're spread out exactly the way they would be if they wanted to cover the whole square."

"Go around the back, Carl. There's a large round building right next to the tower ruin. It's the new church. Take the passage between the two buildings. Are you armed?"

Carl swore. "No, my service gun is back in my drawer at HQ in Copenhagen."

He took out his keys from his coat pocket, and there were a lot of keys on the bunch: keys to the house in Allerød, keys to his office at HQ, keys to Mona's flat, and keys to his work car. He grasped the bunch in his right hand and let the ends of the keys stick out between the fingers of his fist. It was a convenient weapon that matched even the best brass knuckles.

Carl looked to the side toward the lavish arched entrance of the tower as he walked past a wheelchair ramp that also led up to the entrance from the other side.

Carl broke out in a cold sweat. A ramp for wheelchairs! The terrorists had thought of everything.

After the passage between the two buildings, he came to a broad and busy street. KURFÜRSTENDAMM was written on a street sign on the other side of the street where a light blue Volkswagen van was parking on yellow lines at the curb. Even though it was illegal, they didn't seem to care. They obviously *wanted* to park there. It was a realization that aroused Carl's suspicion.

Then the side window curtain was drawn slightly. The gap was small, but it brought out another cold sweat in Carl, because he caught a glimpse of Assad with gaffer tape over his mouth. After a few seconds, he tried to signal something to Carl but was distracted because in the same moment a parking attendant approached the Volkswagen van and disappeared behind it. A door was flung open and a male voice began reprimanding the attendant loudly. Then there was a gunshot.

Everyone in the square looked over, and in the commotion, Carl crossed the street and threw himself down behind the Volkswagen van. He looked carefully around the corner of the van and saw that the parking attendant was lying facedown with the upper part of his body in the van and blood dripping from his limp arm.

This is it, everything screamed inside him. Without hesitation, he jumped forward toward the parking attendant's body and threw himself on top of it.

The driver was still sitting at the wheel with the gun in his hand. His face had the expression of someone who had shot something living for the first time. He would definitely shoot again, but when Carl lunged over the parking attendant's lifeless body and in the same movement swung his right hand so hard against the driver's cheek that his keys went right through it, the man's body was thrown backward as he roared in agony. Carl let go of his keys and grabbed the barrel of the gun in the same second as the man fired off another shot. The windshield shattered into a thousand pieces and spread panic on the street in front of the van.

The more than one hundred kilos behind Carl's punch to the man's cheek had had its effect, and half-unconscious, the driver dropped the gun. In a single movement, Carl grabbed it and pulled the trigger, and before he managed to see how seriously the driver had been shot, the curtain was pulled to one side and a man with a multicolored bandanna thrust a fist over the back of the front seat.

Then Carl pulled the trigger for the second time, and the man fell backward toward a flimsy camping table with surprise written all over his face.

59

Assad

While the Volkswagen drove around the square, Assad struggled to get more air in under the gaffer tape. When they were back where they had started, the driver swerved the van for a second time onto the yellow lines at the curb.

Assad's eyes met Carl's in the same moment that the bandanna guy pulled back the curtain on the side window. Carl had come around the church tower on the other side of the road and seemed both relieved and sad when he caught sight of his friend. As if, like Assad, he knew that it was already too late. That the world would explode around them any second now.

Get out of here! You'll die if you stay, Assad tried to say with his eyes, but it was lost on Carl.

Assad struggled to push the gaffer tape completely off his mouth so he could shout and warn him. And then there was a loud knock on the passenger door.

The bandanna guy immediately closed the curtain to the front seats, so all he had to go on was the sounds. The passenger door was flung open, and just a second later a shot was fired. It went quiet, but only momentarily, before there was another commotion that shook the entire van. There was a roar from the front seats and then another shot.

Right up until the bandanna guy pulled back the curtain to the front seats, Assad was sure that it was the parking attendant from earlier who was fighting, but when the idiot with the bandanna fell backward onto the Formica table with the second shot, he knew that everything wasn't lost.

The following minute was completely chaotic.

Out of nowhere, there was a sound of gunfire from all directions. The situation had escalated.

Carl pulled at the gaffer tape around Assad's mouth and removed it.

"They're coming now, Carl. I can see them," shouted Assad while Carl coaxed his hands off the snap hook and freed them. It was a shocking sight, because as salvos resounded around them and people were wailing and screaming, a pair of wheelchairs were being pushed through the cross fire toward the ramp.

"Aim at the ones pushing the wheelchairs, Carl," he shouted as he freed his feet. "Run!"

Carl pointed warningly at the bandanna guy—and not a second too soon. Despite the wound to his chest, he had grabbed the broken Formica tabletop and in the next second would have stuck it in Assad's throat if Assad hadn't managed to free his legs and heel-kick the guy's head just as he raised the Formica top in midair, causing his head to twist toward his shoulder at an angle that looked more than life-threatening.

The gunshots sounded very close.

Assad pulled himself out of the side door and knelt down behind the Volkswagen to find his bearings.

Carl nodded to him and Assad carefully stood up. Behind Nella's wheelchair, a woman was lying dead on the ground with her head turned to the side. But the relief was short-lived, because there was the wheelchair with Marwa, and the man pushing it had an automatic weapon in his hand that he was firing in all directions. There were many who had not made it to safety and now lay lifeless on the pavement right in front of a clothing shop window. It was awful.

Carl and Assad turned toward the side street, where the firing was being answered. It was probably the policemen with whom the parking attendant had threatened the idiot in the van, and Carl took advantage of the situation again to get behind the back of the van.

He fired a couple of times at the man pushing Marwa, which was answered with a volley of projectiles that ripped apart the corner of the van and penetrated the side with hollow, metallic sounds.

Assad swore and pressed himself against the ground when another salvo perforated the sardine tin's thin sides and smashed all the windows.

There was another shot from Carl and then he rolled backward toward the pavement. He lay motionless for a moment, and then pushed the gun over toward Assad.

"I think I got him," he shouted over the noise while pressing his hand against his hip.

"Are you okay, Carl?" Assad shouted back while picking up the gun.

He nodded but didn't really look like he meant it.

Now the shooting was intense on both sides of the church tower. Assad knew only too well the sound of salvos from automatic weapons that became constant and brought death and mutilation with them.

He walked over to the battered corner of the car and leaned tentatively forward.

Marwa's wheelchair was lying on its side, and she was motionless, just like the man next to her.

Then she coughed a couple of times. Thank God, she was alive.

Assad looked at the gun. Had nine or ten shots been fired off? If so, there were at least three left.

Now he stepped out from his cover. Farther back, there was a guy pointing an automatic weapon at a young woman in a third wheelchair. He stood motionless like a pillar of salt, ready to meet his destiny. It was clear that he had accepted the situation and that he was waiting for an order or, worse, for the bomb to detonate.

Assad looked up at the restaurant where he knew that Ghaalib was watching everything, but he couldn't see him.

Why was he waiting to press the remote control? Was Ghaalib unable to see him? Was he waiting for that magical moment when Assad would see the unimaginable happen? Was he waiting for the two guys

in the van to tell him it was time? If that was the case, he would be
waiting a long time.

Assad stepped back toward Carl. He had to round the Volkswagen
and keep close to the wall because as soon as Ghaalib caught sight of
him, he would detonate the bombs. No doubt about it.

"It's nothing," said Carl, staring at the bloody stain on his trousers.
"It's a flesh wound, I think. I just got a shock."

Assad crawled in through the side door of the van and searched for
his phone. On the front seat, the driver lay awkwardly with the back of
his neck against the door, breathing heavily. There was no doubting
that his time was up, judging by the way the window behind him had
been shattered by gunfire. He didn't need to look at the bandanna guy.
He was already dead. He was certain. He fumbled for his phone under
the cushion and found it, but it was totally smashed.

Meanwhile, Carl was still outside and had managed to get hold of
Weber.

"Here," he shouted, and passed the phone in to Assad.

"Where are you two?" shouted Weber.

"We're on the far side by Kurfürstendamm. Get over here quickly!
I'm worried one or several bombs are going to go off any moment now."

"I'm sorry," answered Weber. "We've got our hands full with the
people at the front. They've holed themselves up in the entrance to the
Europa Center—the weird-looking building at the far end of the square.
And we're in the cross fire from the sniper shooting from the hotel, and
he's a good shot. It must be Dieter Baumann."

"Send someone up there to neutralize him, damn it," shouted Assad.
"And get someone to find Ghaalib. He's sitting in an Italian restaurant
at the back of the square, wearing the same Jewish getup as the others.
He's got the remote control to detonate the bombs."

"What's he waiting for?" screamed Weber.

"Me."

Assad turned to hand the phone back to Carl, but he wasn't there.

"What are you doing, Carl?" he shouted when he saw Carl pulling
the parking attendant's body onto the pavement.

"I'm making room for myself."

Then he crawled up on his knees and began pulling at the driver's legs. A moment later, the driver's seat was free.

Assad understood straightaway what he had in mind.

"Let's hope it starts," shouted Carl when he turned the key in the ignition.

It did.

"You've only got a millisecond to shoot him, Assad," he said, putting the van in gear while nodding over at the third wheelchair. "There are two shots left in the magazine, just so you know."

Assad knelt on a cushion among the shards of glass. He had tried shooting from a moving vehicle before, but this was something else!

He took a deep breath. He needed a clean shot at the man because if he missed, he would kill the poor woman. One of the mantras he had learned in Afghanistan came to mind: *Only shots to the head can neutralize the enemy.*

He held his breath and aimed while Carl drove steadily forward. In two seconds, they would be in line with the woman in the wheelchair. Assad closed one eye. The distance was only ten meters. If the van stayed on course and managed to avoid driving over anything that would shake the vehicle, this would be over quickly.

And then he noticed the birthmark on the young woman's cheek. He froze.

Assad gasped for air. He couldn't do anything else. "Shoot, Assad," shouted Carl with a stifled voice.

But Assad was unable to move. He didn't dare shoot now. It was his younger daughter, Ronia, that the man was holding an automatic weapon to. She was just sitting there in front of him. How was that possible? There was no doubt in his mind that it was her.

"I can't! Oh God, it's Ronia in the wheelchair. She's alive, Carl."

Now the van had stopped and was right next to them, but the man next to the wheelchair didn't react.

"He nodded to me," whispered Carl. "He must be in shock if he still thinks their people are sitting in this van and have come to pick him up. This is your chance."

Assad dived down so he didn't give himself away. Then he aimed again, held his breath, and fired. It didn't feel at all good. Just like a regular execution.

And as the man fell shaking to the ground with a bullet hole in his hat, shots were fired at them from the other side.

"It's the police!" shouted Carl. "They think—" Then he grabbed his arm. It was clear that they had hit him. Nonetheless, he put his foot down as hard as he could.

Assad fell down when the van took a sharp turn into the square, and salvos were hammering the back of the van. He could feel the body of the dead bandanna guy knocking against him.

The van only came to a stop when it crashed into the Europa Center monument, at which point the two surviving terrorists who were still shooting from their positions halfway down the steps pulled back and disappeared into one of the center's lower levels.

"Are you okay, Carl?" shouted Assad. "Where've you been hit?"

He was moaning and bleeding profusely.

Assad grabbed Carl's mobile and called Weber.

"Carl's been hit. We need help. We've neutralized three of Ghaalib's people on this side, but your guys are shooting at us from the side street. Stop them!"

Moments later, it was totally quiet on the square.

Assad crawled over to Carl, who was wedged tightly behind the steering column and the demolished front. He was conscious and apparently unharmed by the crash, but there was a nasty gunshot wound on his forearm.

"Will you be okay?" asked Assad as he slid out of the passenger door, but Carl didn't answer. The last thing Assad heard before raising his arms in the air and walking slowly toward the anti-terror squad running toward him was Carl's slowly beginning to laugh.

"Get out of here," shouted one of the anti-terror squad as they ran directly over to the door on the driver's side. They had obviously listened to what Weber had said.

Now Assad was standing directly under the windows of the restaurant.

Don't let Ghaalib be up there or have seen me, he prayed.

He looked over at the three women in front of the church tower. All three of them were tied to their wheelchairs and immobile. Marwa's wheelchair was lying on its side on the pavement, and the other two were sitting in their wheelchairs with their heads hanging as if they were in comas.

"Listen," he said to the anti-terror squad. "If I run over there, the ringleader will detonate the bombs the women are wearing or sitting on. He's just waiting to catch sight of me. So you'll need to go over there and get the women away from the tower."

They looked at him as if he were an idiot. Did he want them to approach potential suicide bombers?

He called Weber again. No answer.

Assad looked up, took a deep breath, and took the opportunity to take cover under the canopy on the facade. He had just reached the window of a Fossil watch shop when he saw a fourth wheelchair to his right.

Assad stood still for a moment before he realized who the man in the wheelchair was. But who was the young guy standing crying behind it?

Now it was Weber who called him. "What's your status? We can't see you. Where are you?" he asked.

"I'm standing on the corner under the Italian restaurant just in front of the Fossil watch shop. I can see a fourth wheelchair, and I'm fairly certain it's Joan Aiguader sitting in it. There's an Arabic boy crying behind him. What should I do?"

"Stay where you are. There could be a bomb in his wheelchair. Maybe that's why the boy is crying."

"You need to get the bomb disposal team down to the women, Weber. See what you can do. What's the status at the front of the square? I can see bodies on the ground."

"Yes, there are many, many people on the ground just now. We don't have any overview of the situation yet, and we can't get near them because of the sniper up at the hotel. But we think that between you and Carl and our guys, we've brought down all the terrorists except the two who disappeared inside the shopping center."

"You're forgetting Ghaalib and the boy standing over here."

"We think Ghaalib has joined the two in the shopping center. Remember they have bulletproof vests on if you try to shoot them."

Assad shook his head. As if he hadn't assumed that. And why on earth would Ghaalib corner himself with the others? Up until this point, his entire mission had failed, and Assad and his family were still alive. No, Ghaalib was ready and waiting somewhere close by.

He looked over to the wheelchair. It looked like Joan was trying to make contact with him, but he wasn't saying anything. Just like Marwa, Nella, and Ronia, he appeared to be paralyzed. Did he want him to come closer or get away from there?

Assad took a step forward and nodded to him. *Was it okay that I did that?* he tried to express with his eyes.

Joan pursed his lips. Was that a yes or a no? "Is there a bomb in your wheelchair?" shouted Assad. He moved his eyes from side to side.

"If that means no, show me what you do when I ask you: Is your name Joan?"

His eyes moved up and down. So, a yes, and no bomb. He took another step closer.

"Is the boy dangerous?" he asked.

His eyes moved again from side to side.

"Is Ghaalib close by?"

His eyes didn't move. So he didn't know.

"Is the boy normal? He seems very distant."

His eyes moved from side to side.

"Is he on drugs?"

Another no.

"Is he armed?"

"*No,*" he said with his eyes.

"Hello, buddy," he said to the boy in Arabic. "My name is Assad. What's yours?"

The boy was looking down at the ground, scared like a cornered animal. Then Assad took another step closer, which the boy obviously didn't like. He covered his side closest to Assad by raising his shoulder and pulling his arm into his stomach.

"I won't hurt you," said Assad as gently as possible.

The boy looked at Assad with fear in his eyes. Assad understood his reaction given the last few terrifying minutes.

Assad shouted over to the anti-terror squad that they should come over to him.

Joan made some inarticulate sounds, so Assad now went right up to him and put his head by his mouth.

It took him a long time to muster the energy to get the words out. "His name is Afif," he said faintly.

Assad nodded.

"He's important," he then said.

"To Ghaalib?"

"Yes."

Assad turned his head toward the officers. "These two need to stay here. They're both important in their own way."

The men looked at the boy skeptically.

"And you're sure he isn't wearing an explosive vest?"

Assad looked at Joan, who moved his eyes up and down.

"Yes, I am," he answered.

Then he put his head next to Joan Aiguader's mouth again.

"What have they given you?" he asked.

"Injection," he replied with difficulty.

"Will it wear off?" he asked.

"Yes."

"That's my wife and my two daughters over there. Marwa, Nella, and Ronia. Do they have explosives on them?"

"Marwa and Nella explosive vests. Ronia, the bomb."

"And Ghaalib has the remote control?"

Tears were running from Joan's eyes, and his yes was so feeble that he had to repeat it.

Assad felt a stab to his heart. His soul was in turmoil, but he had to press on and keep his wits about him. Otherwise everything would end.

From the moment Assad saw the bomb disposal experts driving their vehicles up toward the square from Nürnberger Strasse, he knew that he had an infinitesimally short amount of time to find Ghaalib and disarm him. It sounded so simple. Disarm him! But where was he? Was he a coward who had just run off to save his own skin? Assad shook his head. Why would he just run off when he had all these plans?

Now a sound of gunfire came from the center. He heard screaming and saw a mass of people running out from the street-level entrance just a few meters from there.

He got hold of Weber. "They're shooting in there. Is your team in position?"

"Yes, we've sent in ten men from the anti-terror squad."

Assad grabbed a woman running directly toward him.

"What's happening?" he said with a firm voice. "I need to know!"

She was breathless and beside herself. "There's two of them. A man and a woman. They're standing at the top of the landing next to the fitness center and shooting directly at people down in the center square," she said with a trembling voice.

Assad let go of her.

"Did you hear what she said, Weber?"

"Yes, I heard it. But it's only a matter of seconds before we've got them. Same goes for Dieter Baumann. He's barricaded himself in, but we've worked out where now."

Assad turned to face the glass window and the entrance to the Italian restaurant behind him. Hopefully, they would be able to tell him inside whether the man with the Jewish curls was still upstairs or when he had left the building and in which direction.

Through the glass front, he could see that a lot of people were standing inside, which was understandable. They had probably all sought refuge in there during the first wave of attacks.

Before Assad entered the restaurant, he nodded to the man standing behind the counter just inside the door. He seemed distressed at seeing Assad approaching. He just stood there staring at him as if Assad were one of the attackers.

Assad could see it from his point of view. An unshaven brown man with a gun in his hand and scratches all over him. Was he one of them?

So, Assad put his hands in the air to show that he had nothing to fear. And then he entered.

"Stay calm, I'm one of the good guys," he said: "I'm looking for a man who came in here a while ago dressed like an Orthodox Jew, just like the people who were shooting. Full beard, hat, and curls. Do you know where he is?"

Why is he standing there shaking? thought Assad a second too late. The blow to the back of his head was so hard and exact that it made him fall to his knees in front of the counter. In the next second, he was kicked in the ribs, which caused him to momentarily lose his balance and his grip on the gun. Several people in the restaurant started screaming, and Assad tried to roll onto his side to get up. It was only when the next kick hit him that he really understood the extent of what had happened.

"Don't bother looking. The gun is under my foot, Zaid," said a voice in Arabic above him.

This is the end, thought Assad, and looked ahead. Stupidity and a momentary lapse of concentration, and life was over.

"Get up," said Ghaalib. "Get up, you dog. Finally, I have you. You've always been good at hiding, Zaid, but you don't have to do that anymore."

Assad turned around slowly, and there he was. No beard, hat, or curls. His old self. The most heartless man on earth with Assad's gun in the back of his trousers, an Uzi in one hand, and a small, terrifying remote control in the other.

"I have some friends here who would like to come with us. You know what to do, and if you don't, I'll kill you." He pointed at them with his weapon.

There were three men and three women. The woman in front had very blond hair and was wearing a uniform with a logo that read CHAR-LOTTENBURG TOURS. Her face had an expression of disbelief. She had presumably just been on a tour with a group of tourists and had run in here to seek refuge when everything began. The others were not wearing coats or jackets, so probably normal guests who didn't have luck on their side today. They all appeared very shocked and scared. With good reason.

"Perhaps you don't know the Romans' best weapon, but it was their defense," lectured Ghaalib. "Their attack was the phalanx, and in defense they formed an effective shield formation. They called it testudo, and now you have become my testudo."

He asked the man at the counter to open the door and ordered Assad to go first. If any of them started moving too quickly, he would shoot them, especially Assad.

"But don't think you can get away simply with death, Zaid. I'll find a point on your body that will stop you without killing you."

Assad noticed how the hostages were pushing him forward. Had Ghaalib already instructed them?

Ghaalib told the testudo to stop when he was standing by the counter. "Here, my friend," he said to the man standing behind it. "You need your plastic card back. I have a small debt to the establishment, but I'm sure you'll cancel it for me."

And then they were standing outside.

"Call the person in charge, Zaid, and tell him he's got two minutes to get all his soldiers and police out of here," commanded Ghaalib. "And I mean *totally* gone from the area. Otherwise, I'll detonate the bombs."

Assad took his mobile and briefly relayed the message. Weber sounded shocked.

"If we abandon the area, you won't get out of this alive, Assad."

"I won't anyway. Just do as he says. You've got two minutes."

Assad looked around. The plainclothes officers, police personnel, and anti-terror squad put their hands up to one ear as they received the message and moved slowly and calmly backward.

Ghaalib was watching as he stood in the middle of the cluster of hostages. "Good boy, Zaid. We'll bring this to an end in a proper manner." Then he turned to face the corner where Joan's wheelchair was positioned.

"Afif!" he shouted. "Just stay where you are until I come back." He said it with a warmth in his voice that made Assad feel nauseous. If it hadn't been for the three women who were so close now, he would have refused to walk any farther.

"I want you to look your family in the eyes before you reach the end of your journey, Zaid. I want you to look deep into their souls so you understand what you've subjected them to. And I want them to see you and hear you so they know how guilty you feel. It will give them the peace of mind to recognize what a relief death will be for you all."

They approached very slowly. Assad's abdomen was burning with pain. The three dead bodies by the wheelchairs were lying in their own blood. It was a frightful sight. The guy Assad had shot was lying in a grotesque position with a very small hole in the side of his head, and his hat with the attached curls was lying at arm's length near him. Poor Marwa, Nella, and Ronia. Their lives had become nothing but misery and horror. Marwa would have been better off with another man. If only she had never met him.

Ronia was sitting motionless in the wheelchair when the testudo stopped next to her. Her expression was lifeless, but she was beautiful in spite of that. Her birthmark was still shaped like a dagger.

"Ronia," he said softly in Arabic. "I am Zaid, your father. I've come so that we can go to Jannah together today. Me, your mother, and your sister are with you." But Ronia didn't react. She had long ago withdrawn to a place where they could not reach her.

They pushed him away from her without any warning. He didn't even manage to touch her. The little girl whom he had lost when she was only five years old and had never gotten to know.

Farther ahead lay the body of the man who had shot Carl in the hip, lying facedown with his false beard ripped off. If Carl hadn't hit him, they would already be dead. In reality, it might have been the best thing that could have happened.

"May I pick her up?" implored Assad when he saw his beloved lying by his feet in the toppled wheelchair.

"Of course!" said their tormentor in a merciful tone.

Assad put one hand under her shoulder and one behind the wheelchair armrest on the ground. She groaned when he pulled her and the wheelchair upright. Then he knelt in front of her and gently took her cheeks in his hands. It was plain to see that the years had been hard on her, but, in spite of all her misfortune, her eyes were still gentle and vulnerable. She was also heavily medicated, but when she fixed her gaze on Assad's pleading eyes and his gentle smile, he noticed a momentary light in her eyes that revealed recognition and relief.

"My love," he said. "We will all meet shortly. Don't be scared. Eternal life awaits us. I love you and always have loved you. Sleep well, my darling." On Ghaalib's command, they pulled him up, but the last glimpse between them gave him strength.

He recognized the dead woman behind Nella's wheelchair immediately. Weber had said her name was Beena when he showed them pictures of her. Now her beautiful hair was sticking to her own blood, and her previously sensual lips were forever frozen in a face full of hate. What a pitiful fate she had chosen for herself.

Nella appeared more ready than the others. It almost made him sad. Was she really going to be tormented with a consciousness of what was about to happen?

"Dear Nella," he said.

His voice caused her to half raise her head toward the group. It was clear that she didn't know why they were there. Her searching and sensitive gaze made the tour guide sob out loud, at which Ghaalib hit her so hard that she fell down unconscious close to the body next to the wheelchair.

"Gather around me," Ghaalib ordered the remaining hostages, who were all completely white with terror at what was becoming clearer and clearer.

"Nella," said Assad again. "I'm your father, Zaid. I've missed you so unbelievably much all this time. You, Ronia, and your mother were the lights of my life. When I was lost, that light led me back to life. Do you understand what I'm saying, Nella?"

She blinked a little faster. And then they pulled him away from her.

"Back to the starting point," Ghaalib ordered the hostages. "Now you've seen them, Zaid al-Asadi. I almost regret that I let you." He laughed.

Assad looked around. He could escape. With a dive roll or two and a zigzag leap toward the entrance to the Europa Center, he might be able to make it. But did he want to?

He took a deep breath. The question was whether he wanted to live if his family were shortly going to be sacrificed. The blast from the explosions would knock him to the ground and stop his heart from beating, he was sure of it. And if not? He had lived with the nightmare of their fate for so many years, but would he be able to go on living with the echo of that blast, which would be forever etched in his mind?

He wouldn't.

Ghaalib stopped the group ten meters in front of the restaurant. He probably thought that they would be safe here from both the explosion and the glass raining from the restaurant windows when the blast wave caused them to shatter into a thousand pieces.

"I've waited for this moment for a third of my life," he said, stepping backward away from the group. Assad turned to face him. He didn't want to see his family when Ghaalib pressed the remote.

Now Ghaalib was standing with the remote in his other hand and the Uzi ready under his arm. He took out a cell phone and pressed a single button.

"I have a little surprise for you, Zaid. A sophisticated execution, and I'm referring to yours. Not like the time you evaded the noose. No, you will be shot, but not by me. I'll quietly withdraw."

Ghaalib smiled and walked backward toward the Fossil watch shop and the place where Joan and the boy were waiting.

When his call was answered, an insane expression spread across his face.

"Yes, Captain," he said with his eyes wide open. "Are you in position? We're ready down here. I can see your window up at the hotel. Nice view, isn't it? You've done well, Dieter Baumann; I've been eagerly following your precision shooting from up in the restaurant. When I've detonated the bombs in ten seconds, shoot this man here. Understood?"

He changed his pitch and spoke to Assad while still holding the phone to his ear. "Turn to face your family, Zaid," he commanded. "Or I'll shoot all your friends standing behind you!"

But Assad didn't turn around. Ghaalib would shoot them anyway; they all knew it.

"On your head be it," he said, and lifted the remote control above his head. "Are you ready, Baumann?" he said into the phone.

Then his expression changed. He frowned and looked directly up toward the top of the hotel building. And in the final second before he was hit by a single shot to the forehead, he obviously knew that it had all been in vain.

The group behind Assad scattered like the wind in a commotion of deafening screams. Assad looked up again at the hotel building and waited for the second shot that would hit him. But nothing happened except the boy next to the wheelchair's screaming and running over toward Ghaalib's body.

Is he going to grab the Uzi and shoot me? thought Assad.

He lunged forward but the boy got there first. However, instead of grabbing the weapon, he threw himself on the body and wailed.

"Daddy, Daddy, Daddy," he cried.

Assad picked up the Uzi and the remote control, carefully pushed off the plastic cover on the back of the remote, and removed the two small batteries, which with a total voltage of just three volts could have shaken the world.

His mobile rang. "Weber, what happened?"

The portly man sounded shaken and yet very relieved.

"We forced entry into Dieter Baumann's hotel suite five minutes ago. The situation was very clear. There were cartridge cases lying around him, but also tablets. He was lying with the rifle sticking out of the window and the telescopic sight pointing straight at the right-hand side of the square where you ended up standing. He had a phone in his hand that we took from him when it rang and then handcuffed him. You can thank your lucky stars we had Magnus Kretzmer with us up here. I don't think the anti-terror corps has ever had a finer rifleman. When we had Baumann's phone, we listened to Ghaalib's speech and Kretzmer didn't dare wait any longer. 'It's *you* who is going to die, you bastard!' he shouted down the phone, and then he shot Ghaalib."

There was a short pause. Both Weber and Assad were deeply moved.

"Have you noticed that the shooting in the center has stopped?" Weber then asked.

Assad turned around. He was right. For the first time in twenty minutes, apart from the screams of agony from the injured and the sirens from the approaching ambulances, everything was peaceful around him.

"That's good," he said. "I only noticed it just now."

Life on the street started to stir again. The riot police and military came rushing over toward Ghaalib's body and the boy who was trying to cling to it. It was heartbreaking to see the young guy being wrenched free and dragged away. He hadn't done anything.

Now Assad heard the sound of boots from the other side and the bomb squad came rushing in with all their equipment and armored suits.

When Assad saw these people coming to the rescue of Marwa, Nella, and Ronia, he couldn't contain his emotions anymore. All the tension and terror that had been pumping his body with adrenaline and mobilizing both his defense mechanisms and his aggressiveness simultaneously were released in that moment with such a force that he fell to his knees. The dead, the living, those left behind, like the boy who had now lost his father, regardless of how horrible he was. All that together and the consciousness of how close he had been to losing his loved ones caused Assad to cry like he had never cried before.

And now the bomb disposal experts were risking their lives so he could have his family back. It was an indescribable relief.

Assad stretched his palms toward the sky and prayed a short prayer. He gave thanks for life and the outcome of the day and promised that from now on, he would be the person his parents had raised him to be. For himself and for all those around him.

When the bomb disposal experts were finished with their work, he would accompany his three loved ones to the hospital and ensure that they received the care and attention that their miserable state demanded.

Then he turned toward Joan Aiguader, who was sitting silently in his wheelchair.

"I'm sorry, I lost myself in my thoughts for a moment, Joan."

Joan tried to nod. Wouldn't he understand better than anyone?

Assad placed a hand on his shoulder and gave it a squeeze.

Then Joan said something a little louder than before. Perhaps his sedation was wearing off.

Assad bent down and asked him to repeat it.

"What was her name?"

"What was whose name, Joan?"

"Victim twenty-one seventeen."

The gaze of this man who had been through so much became intense. The question was still hanging in his open mouth. Then he closed his eyes for a moment and took a deep breath.

"She also meant a lot to you, didn't she, Joan?"

"With time, yes."

"Her name was Lely."

"Lely . . ."

Assad nodded. He wanted to hug him more than anything just now.

"If there's anything that I can do for you, Joan, please tell me. I owe you so much."

He thought for a moment, as if after all these awful events, nothing could give him back the life he'd had before.

"Anything," said Assad.

Joan looked at Assad with a serene expression.

"Yes," he said. "Take the camera off my head and put it in my lap."

And while Assad took it off, Joan kept an eye on the video camera as if it were the greatest treasure in the world.

"Is that all?" asked Assad.

Joan made some deep guttural sounds reminiscent of laughter.

"Call my boss, Montse Vigo, and tell her that she can go screw herself."

He appeared to be smiling. But it was hard to tell with his twisted mouth.

Assad waited patiently while the bomb disposal experts carefully and painstakingly removed the explosive vests from Marwa and Nella and lifted Ronia out of her wheelchair. The courageous men were still on their knees deactivating the bomb in the backrest and in the box under the seat when a new wheelchair was brought over for Ronia.

He followed them as if in a trance over to the ambulances while holding Marwa's hand. She was now able to turn her head slightly toward him as the effects of the sedation were, thankfully, wearing off.

Marwa was still very closed off, which Assad understood. He was like a stranger to her. Everything in her world had been based elsewhere over the years, far away from him. But Assad would fight to bring life back to them. Fight for them to once again breathe freely in a life together with him in Denmark.

"Where is he?" asked Marwa out of thin air.

"Do you mean Ghaalib? He's dead, Marwa. You don't have to fear him anymore."

"No, not him. Afif! Where is he?"

"Ghaalib's son? He was taken away by the intelligence service, I think."

"Then find him. He isn't Ghaalib's son. He's yours!"

60

Rose

The time was 19:55 in the evening, and the Internet and global TV media were exploding with coverage of the events at Kaiser Wilhelm Memorial Church in Berlin.

Never before had a terror cell's movements been followed so closely and for so long by the press. The persistent and tenacious investigation by the German intelligence service was praised to the skies by the world media for being uncompromising and timely, and the operation was dubbed as iconic as the rescue of the flight hostages by the Israel Defense Forces in Operation Entebbe.

The German media, however, was not so unreservedly praising in its coverage. Several people had been killed in the days leading up to the attack, including two policemen in Frankfurt. The operation itself now counted thirteen dead and over thirty wounded, two of whom were in critical condition. Of course, it was a redeeming fact that all nine terrorists had been killed and that a final catastrophe had been averted, but their persistent probing into whether the head of the operation, Herbert Weber, had diverged from normal procedure was unavoidable. Both Weber's superiors in LfV and a representative for the top intelligence service agency in the country had their hands full trying to answer prying questions in the media spotlight. If the ringleader behind the attack hadn't made it a personal vendetta, things could have been a lot worse, according to the journalists, to which the answer came that the opposite was actually the case. If there hadn't been a personal score to settle, the preparations would probably never have been discovered and they therefore owed a debt of gratitude to the two Danish policemen.

The coverage was accompanied by a myriad of clips. Kaiser Wilhelm Memorial Church in a retrospective photo series before and after the Second World War, and coverage from earlier terror plots with terrible consequences such as the massacre on a morning train in Madrid and the similarly coordinated attack in London. And there was quite a lot of fuss about the Dieter Baumann case, the antihero from Freiburg as he was dubbed, who had now passed away. Cancer in both lungs and the pancreas had done him in, not a shot as some media outlets otherwise claimed. And panel discussions about what one ought to have done in this hostage drama were all the rage.

One of the most viewed clips on the Internet was down to a TV crew from a local Berlin station. They had settled into the Mercedes building on Kurfürstendamm as soon as the shooting had started, and blurry, intense close-up photos of Assad accompanying his family to the ambulances had made Rose and Gordon cheer and cry in equal measure. Finally, something good had happened. It was impossible to describe how relieved they were to see Assad and his family safe, because on the home front, the situation over the last few days had developed into a nightmare.

Every attempt to find the deadly, dangerous boy had been in vain. Gordon had been glued to the telephone, and everyone had hoped that the boy would call him and call off his project. The police had visited not only the most likely addresses but more than two hundred addresses in greater Copenhagen, and the media were beginning to get wind that something was going on.

What was behind all these police visits?

In the chief constable's office, a meeting was called with all manner of VIPs, including the minister for justice; the heads of PET and RSIOC Ø, one of two new centers with a focus on terrorism; the police commissioner; and poor Marcus Jacobsen, who had to take the heat for not immediately bringing together all the relevant authorities.

Those present at the meeting concluded that Marcus Jacobsen and

Carl Mørck were personally responsible for their failure to inform the relevant people, agencies, and media in reasonable time.

Marcus informed Rose and Gordon of the situation when he came down to find out whether they had anything new to report in the case.

He was very pragmatic about the whole thing. "It'll be management's responsibility when the press is informed," he said. "We'll be busy and they'll get all the honor. But trust me, it won't help one bit. They have no idea about the floodgates they're opening; we're going to drown in tips from the public."

And he was right, though the press, particularly the national news broadcasters, seemed confused when they were informed. Wasn't Carl Mørck one of the people who had prevented the huge catastrophe in Berlin? Hadn't he just been treated for his wounds at Charité hospital in Berlin and wasn't he now on his way home by charter flight? He was a hero, they said. So how could he also be the opposite at the same time?

The coverage on all the Danish TV channels switched constantly between the police sketch of the boy and the terror plot in Berlin. The efforts of Hafez el-Assad and Carl Mørck were praised, followed by information on the disturbed boy's parents who hadn't shown up for work, and the boy's enthusiasm for shooting games and samurai paraphernalia. Everything was scrutinized and discussed. Were intelligence agencies around the world facing insurmountable challenges in the future? And wasn't it high time to ban prepaid telephone cards and violent video games?

In no time at all, the telephones in all the police stations across the country were red-hot. In just twenty minutes, they had received over two thousand tips from near and far, and there was no sign of the influx's slowing down. Even someone from the Faroe Islands had called to say that they knew an idiot in Tórshavn who would definitely do something like this.

The entire country was in a strange state of panic. If they didn't have any idea where the boy was calling from, he could be anywhere.

If they'd had nothing to go on before, they had really hit rock bottom now.

One thing was certain: While the PET wonder boy's algorithms might have been very accurate, when journalists pressed the linguist, he had to admit that the boy's language use could be influenced by anywhere other than a house in Copenhagen. For example, his family could have moved away from Copenhagen, as one smart journalist pointed out. She was originally from Jutland and you could still detect that in her voice. So, what about the opposite? Couldn't someone born and raised in Copenhagen still speak with a Copenhagen dialect even if they now lived in Frederikshavn?

It was simply flawed detective work according to the most outspoken critics.

Rose stared at Gordon's telephone.

"Call us, you bloody moron," she said.

Gordon nodded. Wasn't the boy following anything that was happening? If he was, he would know that the whole country was keeping a careful watch on all the houses where young men lived. Even in Stalinist Russia, the willingness to inform on each other had never been as high as it was just now in little Denmark.

"But, Rose, if he knows what's going on, he won't come out," said Gordon. "And besides, the streets are almost deserted. So, what would be the point of coming out?"

She grunted a little. "Yes, but the opposite could also be true. Given that he's been desperate for attention, he's very close to beating the terror attack in Berlin."

She tried to get an overview of the situation. "He might also wait a couple of days and strike once the media storm has died down a bit."

Gordon looked at her. He was as white as a sheet.

And then the chief of homicide called.

"Can you pop up here, Rose? We need to coordinate some things before Carl gets here so we're on the same page with our responses to any criticism we might face. I'm sitting with the chief constable and some of our colleagues."

"Is Carl coming?"

"Yes, he's on his way. He's willing to give interviews about the case."

"That's a terrible idea, if you ask me. He's wounded, don't forget, Marcus," she said.

Gordon threw a hand in the air. Now his telephone was ringing.

Rose slammed the receiver down. The chief of homicide and the police constable would just have to wait.

Gordon turned on the speakerphone and recorder.

"Hello, Toshiro," he said, and instantly started sweating profusely.

"Hi! I'll be finished with my game in less than an hour, I reckon. I thought I ought to let you know."

"Okay," said Gordon, and looked at Rose. "Can Rose listen in?"

"I imagine she already is." He laughed. "My mother has fallen asleep, but I think I'll wake her up before cutting off her head. What do you have to say to that?"

"Well, I think that's a pity," answered Rose. "You're never yourself when you've just been woken up. I think you should let her sleep as long as she can. That way she'll be fresher when she wakes up. Fresher and more present. Isn't that what you want?"

He laughed. "You're a naughty girl, Rose. I think you're the smartest of the two of you. Sorry, dumb dick, I don't mean to offend you."

Rose looked at him. The white ghost suddenly looked like a volcano that had lain dormant for too long. Offended? That was an understatement!

Rose waved at him disarmingly. This was not the time for Gordon to explode. But he did.

"Listen here, you sick, infantile, laughable, disturbed half-wit psychopath. The whole country has heard about you. Happy now?" he raged. "You're on the television, you egocentric, self-righteous, primitive little shit. You can go on the streets as much as you like, but there won't be a soul out tonight. Only that dog that's barking like crazy in the background. What the hell have you done to it?"

It went quiet at the other end when Gordon's first lava eruption momentarily subsided.

"What TV channel?" the boy asked.

"All of them, you imbecile. Take a break in your game and go into

another room where there's some sort of connection to the world outside, and see for yourself what they're saying about you. It isn't anything positive, I can tell you that much. And nothing whatsoever about
victim twenty-one seventeen. But they have a lot to say about two of
our colleagues who managed to kill the man who murdered the old
woman. What do you say to that? Just go in and watch, then call me
again when you've seen it and tell me what it feels like to be a TV star
for a night."

Then he slammed the receiver down. Rose was shocked. Not because
he had risen to the occasion but because she had finally seen the light.

"Did you hear that? The dog is still barking! It's over twenty-four
hours now since we first noticed it. People must be going insane listening to that racket."

Gordon took a deep breath. He looked like he had run the hundred
meters and stopped ten centimeters before the finish line.

"We have to go up to the chief of homicide," he shouted, and
stood up.

61

Rose

They ran all the way up the stairs in the rotunda and were panting like two punctured bellows when they stormed into the chief of homicide's office.

"Don't say a word, just listen to what we have to say," shouted Rose.

Marcus Jacobsen raised his eyebrows, as did the others present in the office.

"Who's been doing the house-to-house inquiries?" asked Rose.

"You'd be better off asking who hasn't. We've had almost all the patrol cars, people from RSIOC Ø, the anti-terror squad, and everyone we could spare from HQ on the case. Pick a name and they've been doing it!"

"And what have they been looking for?"

"The boy, of course!"

"Sod the boy. They need to look for a dog barking outside a house. There are lots of dogs that bark but not for bloody well going on a day and a half."

The chief of homicide sat up in his seat. "Are you saying the dog is still barking?"

"Yes! We've just had him on the telephone, and we heard it in the background. It's still there, Marcus, and the boy could start his insane plans at any time. Less than an hour he reckoned, and that's already five minutes ago."

The chief constable nodded to the others, who all, with the exception of the chief of homicide, stood up and left the room.

Rose was beside herself. Could they have realized this and made a head start yesterday if they had been a bit more alert?

"Let's hope we get there in time," said the chief constable.

There were a couple of short rounds of applause from the offices out front and then a man came in through the door with his right arm in a sling and a surprised expression on his face.

"People are running about like lunatics," said Carl. "What's going on?"

The chief of homicide, the chief constable, Gordon, and Rose stood up. That's just what you did when a hero entered the room.

"Sit down, for goodness' sake. I'm not the queen. But thanks!"

He looked at Rose, who contrary to her nature looked immensely moved and relieved.

There he was. Still alive.

"I was just in the basement, and it's in a right state."

"Why aren't you with Mona?" asked Rose.

"She's doing fine and back home now. She insisted that I come in to hear what's happening in this case with the crazy guy."

Rose stood up again. Apart from having his arm in a sling and looking like shit, he was here and acting like his usual old self, thank God. She carefully wrapped her arms around him and rested her head on his chest out of sheer emotion; however, she couldn't help but notice that he raised his good arm and pulled back a little.

"Er, thank you, Rose, but I can stand without support," he said.

She nodded in recognition.

"And what about Assad?" she asked. "Is he also fine standing without support?"

Carl shook his head a little. "He's standing, yes. Actually, I've never seen him so determined. But there's a lot for him and his family to sort out before things will be good again. Berlin municipality have offered them a place to stay to recuperate for a while, and I think a longer leave of absence will be needed. But I should send you all his best. The last thing he said was that we should get our tongues out of our throats and catch the boy."

"What did he say?" asked the chief constable. She was the only one who wasn't laughing.

"Well, there was definitely something wrong with the way he expressed himself, but you don't know Assad as well as we do." Carl turned to Rose. "What's the current situation with the case?"

It only took twenty seconds to bring him up to speed.

"Then we've really got to get our act together, and fast," said Carl. "There must be fifty dogs in Copenhagen alone that drive people crazy with their incessant barking and that have probably been doing it since they were puppies."

"So, what do we do?" asked Gordon.

"Come on, Gordon. Use your head. Where are people quickest to react these days? Get on Facebook or Twitter, or whatever they're called, and be quick about it."

"Social media!" Rose thought for a moment. "I'm sure that Facebook is too slow and I doubt enough people use Twitter, but it's worth a try."

She grabbed her mobile and paused to think again. "What the hell should I search for?"

"Try 'hashtag stray dog,'" suggested Gordon.

"No, that won't work. We certainly don't care about stray dogs in Vejle."

"So, try 'hashtag stray dog cph.'"

Rose pointed a finger in the air and typed. "Stray dog cph," she whispered to herself. A few minutes passed while they all sat staring at her phone with their eyes peeled.

Then she suddenly shouted, giving everyone a shock.

"Bloody hell, here it is! There are two places with dogs barking just now. One in Valby and one in Dragør."

"Where? Where?" burst out Carl. "Ask where!"

She typed again, and the answer came promptly. She pointed at her phone.

"Here it is!"

They all stood up, and Marcus walked over to the safe in the corner
and opened it.

"Here, take it, Carl. I'll find another one." He handed him his service
gun. "You drive to Dragør, and I'll take Valby."

They heard the dog barking from far off, and it sounded both hoarse
and hysterical, so Gordon knew what direction to drive in.

The area where it was running around bewildered and scared was
one of the more fashionable in this highly sought-after part of town.
Large and small well-kept and undoubtedly expensive houses, which
only a few decades ago would have been described as picturesque, were
now ostentatiously lit up and welcoming. It wasn't the first place you
would connect to the awful events of the last two weeks.

"Haven't there been house-to-house inquiries out here today?"
asked Carl.

"Yes." Rose nodded. "They started on Amager this morning. It's
very strange that they didn't find anything."

Carl nodded and listened to the dog barking. One second it sounded
really close, then a little farther away again. It was really desperate.

"Just take the streets one by one, Gordon. Keep your eyes peeled."

After a few minutes of going back and forth, Carl leaned forward
toward the windshield, concentrating on something ahead. He pointed
at something dark on the lawn of a house a little farther up that was
only dimly lit by the streetlamps. "Stop here, Gordon. There's something on the grass over there. It looks strange. What is it?"

They pulled up in front of a villa a few houses away from the one
they were interested in, which was unquestionably one of the most well
built and trendy in the area.

"Is it glass? Can you check, Rose?" said Carl.

She strode over the withered lawn and bent down to inspect what
was there and seemingly got a shock, judging by the way she jumped
back. Then she composed herself and tentatively took a few steps closer
to the house while scrutinizing it.

She turned to face them, put her index finger to her lips, and gestured to them to get out of the car and join her.

"Shattered pieces of a leaded window," she whispered. "And it used to be there." She pointed at the hole that the smashed window had left in the window frame.

Now the dog came darting from behind them, barking uncontrollably. It jumped from side to side, around in circles, down to the road, and back again. Rose tried to grab its lead so she could try to calm it down, but not even a hundred dogcatchers would have been able to catch it when it was acting up this way. Then it ran off again.

"He's in there; I'm sure of it," whispered Rose, and nodded when Carl pulled out his gun.

"Take it, Gordon," he said. "I can't release the safety catch with one hand."

The beanpole looked lost holding it in his hand.

"What should we do?" Rose whispered. She carefully grabbed the door handle, but the door was locked.

"Give the gun to Rose," said Carl when the fool fumbled to try to release the safety catch. Had he never held a gun before?

"We can't call him because he uses prepaid cards. But we could check if there are other telephones at this address," Rose tentatively suggested.

"What good would that do?" asked Carl. He was scratching his neck. It had been a long, hard day for him. "Call Marcus and tell him that we've found the place. Tell him to send someone down here with a battering ram or something so we can break the door down."

"A battering ram?" Rose couldn't picture it.

"Yes, or an excavator, whatever."

"It'll take too long, Carl. But we still have this." She pointed at their car.

Carl frowned. He didn't seem particularly keen.

Which one of them should do it? Not Carl with his bad arm and hip. And right now, Gordon looked so nervous that it was doubtful he would even manage to hit the house.

"Give me the keys, Gordon," she said, stretching out her hand.

Gordon hesitated and looked at Carl. Surely, he wouldn't agree to this. Then she would be the one covered in bruises.

Then she released the gun and handed it to Gordon.

"You just need to pull the trigger, but please wait until you're totally sure what you're aiming at," she said, and walked toward the car.

The airbag had better bloody well work, she thought as she fastened the seat belt.

She turned the car ninety degrees across the road and prayed that the stupid dog wouldn't get in her way once she came racing.

Carl and Gordon moved to the side at a safe distance. She would have to ram precisely, otherwise it would be steel against wall, and none of them wanted that.

For a moment, she reminded herself why she hadn't graduated from the police academy. *"You're a terrible driver under stress,"* her instructor had told her. *"In an emergency response, you'd be like a bomb in traffic,"* another instructor had said.

And now, here she was, fumbling to put the car in first gear and pressing her foot down on the accelerator.

It was farther up to the house than she had thought. Far enough to give her time to realize the craziness of the situation, far enough to know that she might be seriously hurt, far enough to . . .

The crash was followed by an unexpected hailstorm of small shards of glass, the crack from the airbag, and white dust whirling around in the light from the headlights, while sounds of metal crushing together and the wooden front door splintering signaled that she should back up so the others could get in.

Rose felt as if her lungs had been deflated and all her ribs had broken off her breastbone. The pain was agonizing, and where was the reverse in this car?

Then Carl was standing by the car door and pulling at it. "You're doing the right thing with the gearshift, but you need to restart, Rose. The engine has cut off."

She restarted it, and despite the terrible sound it made, the car slowly edged backward. And then Carl and Gordon were inside.

She struggled in vain with the front door, which was hanging like wreckage from its hinges. Then she freed herself from the seat belt and crawled onto the back seat and began pulling at one of the doors while shouts were coming from inside the house.

When Rose entered the house, panting and out of breath, it was strangely quiet inside. Had they arrived too late? Was it now that she should prepare herself to see the decapitated heads of two women lying on the floor?

I don't think I can, she thought.

Then she heard Carl's voice. It sounded authoritative and clear, and it was coming from a room adjoining the corridor.

"Take it easy, Toshiro," he said.

She stood in the doorway and looked into the room with half-closed eyes to shield herself from the sight she feared would greet her.

There was a rancid smell emanating from the room, and in the middle of the floor a boy was standing with a sword raised above his head. He looked nothing like the police sketch apart from his blond hair and samurai man bun.

It was only now that she saw what was really happening as she caught sight of a woman tied to an office chair with her neck bared just in front of the boy.

He was standing in front of the computer desk in exactly the same position as a samurai would stand before attacking; his body was twisted with one leg forward and the other an extension of his arm lifting the sword.

Carl was standing in the corner, but Gordon was close to the boy and pointing the gun at his head with trembling hands. It looked like everyone was frozen in their positions.

There was a woman shaking on the floor, and a large dark stain under her body was growing because she was already prepared for her execution with her blouse pulled down over her shoulders so her neck was completely bare.

The boy was beginning to sweat. It was all too clear that things hadn't developed as they should have and that his mind was racing. Should he attack? Would he manage to kill before he was killed? Were there any other options?

The only person who appeared totally calm was the woman Rose assumed to be his mother. She was sitting with her back to the others and breathing calmly, as if she had already come to terms with everything, regardless of what happened.

It was Gordon who broke the ice. Whether it was due to his nerves or his usual clumsiness, he pulled the trigger. The bullet landed with a bang in the wall above the computer and made a large hole in the newspaper clipping with a picture of victim 2117.

The boy looked at it, visibly shaken. "Nooooo!" he shouted, and in frustration lifted the sword and was about to bring it down on Gordon, who was still rattled.

The only person who could react was his mother. With a quick jerk of her body, she toppled herself, along with both the office chair and table she was tied to, into her son, causing him to tumble toward the wall in the corner.

He was clearly caught off guard and looked as if he couldn't comprehend what had happened in the last few seconds. But before anyone could manage to react, he stretched the sword handle in front of himself, pulled up his T-shirt, and placed the point against his stomach, ready to slash it open.

"I'll commit seppuku, and there's nothing you can do about it!" he screamed in a high-pitched voice. His hands were shaking, and a little drop of blood dripped from under the sharp point of the sword. He definitely meant it.

Gordon raised the gun again. Taking into account his previous miss, it didn't seem very likely that he would shoot, and even less so that he could hit the boy somewhere that would stop him. But Gordon had his own agenda.

"You ignorant little shit. That isn't seppuku. It's called harakiri. You should know that."

The boy frowned and seemed stupefied when he heard Gordon's voice.

"Dumb dick?" he exclaimed, and looked at Gordon. Then he turned his attention to Rose and looked her up and down. "I imagined something different," he said. "You're as fat as a sumo wrestler."

After too many days of tension and mental unbalance, it was a step too far for Gordon, who now moved closer to the boy, waving the gun in front of him. "Shut it, you little shit. Go on, get it over with. You don't dare!" he said fiercely.

A slightly dangerous tactic for a policeman to encourage another person to commit suicide, thought Rose, but with a slight smile on her lips. It was touching that he was so mad. You could always count on Gordon to defend you.

"As far as I'm concerned, you can start cutting," said Gordon coldly. "It'll save me the bother of having to testify at your trial."

His tactics were making Carl and Rose a little uneasy.

"I don't understand. How did you find me?" the boy asked in a feeble voice. There was saliva sticking to the corners of his mouth. He finally realized that he couldn't win his game.

"That's none of your business, just keep wondering," replied Gordon. Then he walked toward the women and placed the gun in front of the computer screen, where the display was flashing a suggestion to continue on to the next level—number 2118.

With an outstretched arm, he grabbed the ruined picture of the dead woman and scrunched it up right in front of the boy.

"Right, we don't want to see that anymore," he said, picking up the mother's office chair and the table she had been tied to and pulling the gaffer tape off the women.

The old woman cried with relief, but the boy's mother stood up with difficulty and approached her son with a completely cold expression.

"*Perseverando,* my boy," she said frostily. "Perseverance. Don't stop in the middle of something. Isn't that what I've taught you? Just press hard and get it over with."

She expressed no empathy or understanding for her son, who was sitting trapped in a corner like an animal. The last few days had had an understandable effect on their relationship.

But the boy looked at her defiantly. She wouldn't decide when his final act on this earth would be. So he waited while thin trickles of blood collected in the top of his trouser lining.

Rose didn't understand. Why had the PET wonder boy's algorithm not worked? Here was the boy with the cultivated accent. He was the right age. Dragør had been on the address list this morning. So why hadn't the police called at this house?

"Did you say 'Perseverando'? Your husband went to the boarding school in Bagsværd, didn't he?" she asked the mother.

She turned to Rose with a puzzled look.

"My husband?" she said. "My husband left secondary school when he was fifteen; that was as much education as he could cope with. But why did you ask that? Because I used the school motto?"

"Yes."

"Then let me tell you, young lady, that Bagsværd is a boarding school for boys and girls. I went to the school."

Gordon and Rose stared at her. This was perhaps one of the most embarrassing moments in their careers.

Carl, on the other hand, burst out with uncontrollable laughter. Despite his arm's being in a sling and his body's generally aching all over, he slid down to the floor in hysterics.

He lay there for a moment like a crazy man and tried to catch his breath. Had the day's events made him lose his mind?

He suddenly stretched his entire body as much as he could and then with a violent twist and with every muscle tensed, he used all his strength to smash his foot directly against the blade, cutting the guy's stomach and resulting in the sword's landing with its tip firmly lodged in a shelf.

Carl stood up calmly but with difficulty, and without the slightest sign of a smile on his lips, he looked at the boy, whose arrogance had now turned to complete confusion and desperation.

"Call an ambulance, Gordon," he said while the boy looked

incredulously down at the deep wound and the blood that was dyeing everything under him red.

"What's the boy's name?" he asked the mother.

"Alexander," she answered without deigning to even glance at her son.

"Alexander! Of course, it began with A," said Carl, struggling to recover his authority as a detective inspector. But then his eyes caught sight of his smartwatch and he began smiling. His next sentence hung in the air. He waited.

Rose didn't understand why. What was he waiting for, and why were his lips moving as if he were counting down?

"*Now!*" said Carl, and turned to face the bleeding boy.

"Alexander," he said dryly. "The time is now exactly twenty-one seventeen and you are under arrest."

ACKNOWLEDGMENTS

Thanks to my wife and soul mate, Hanne, for her fantastic and loving support and not least for her excellent comments. A huge thanks to Henning Kure for pointing me in the right direction with reading, suggestions, and insightful observations. Thank you to Elisabeth Ahlefeldt-Laurvig for research, multitasking, and resourcefulness. Thanks also to Elsebeth Wæhrens, Eddie Kiran, Hanne Petersen, Micha Schmalstieg, Kes Adler-Olsen, Jesper Helbo, Sigrid Engeler, Pernille Engelbert Weil, Kor de Vries, and Karlo Andersen for their intelligent initial proofreading and suggestions. Thank you to my new and fantastic editor, Lene Wissing, at Politikens Forlag for the speed with which she familiarized herself with this universe with open eyes and professionalism. Thanks to Lene Juul and Charlotte Weiss at Politikens Forlag for their unfailing faith, hope, and patience. Thanks to Helle Skov Wacher for her PR work with the novel. Thanks to Lene Børresen for always keeping track of the things that mustn't go wrong. A big thank-you to the rest of the team at Politikens Forlag for their invaluable work and for ensuring that things run smoothly. Thank you to Police Commissioner Leif Christensen for police-related corrections. Thank you to Kjeld S. Skjærbæk for the times you made the everyday so special. Thanks to Rudi Urban Rasmussen and Sofie Voller for keeping the world turning. Thanks to Daniel Struer for his damn fine IT work. Thanks to Benny Thøgersen and Lina Pillora for their inventiveness. Thanks to Olaf Slott-Petersen for providing new and even better writing conditions in Barcelona. Thanks to Detective and Investigator Tom Christensen for important police-related information. Thanks to Michael Behrend Hansen for the introduction to Falah Alsufi, to whom I offer my thanks for permission to use his fantastic poem. Thanks to Bernd-Alexander Stiegler for his videos and photos from the photo museum in Munich, and thanks to Petra Büscher for supporting him. Thanks to Jesper Deis, who quite literally lit up our daily lives. Thanks to Hanne, Olaf Slott-Petersen, the eye clinic in Barcelona Centro de Oftalmología, and especially my own ophthalmologist, Per Haamann, and the Rigshospitalet department of ophthalmology in Glostrup for saving the sight in my left eye. Last but not least, thank you to Anne Christine Andersen for our wonderful fifteen-year collaboration.

JUSSI ADLER-OLSEN is Denmark's number one crime writer and a *New York Times* bestselling author. His books routinely top the bestseller lists in Europe and have sold more than twenty-four million copies around the world. His many prestigious worldwide crime-writing awards include the Barry Award and the Glass Key award, also won by Henning Mankell, Jo Nesbø, Stieg Larsson, and Peter Høeg.